APOLLO

Bosnian Chronicle | Ivo Andrić

Now in November | Josephine Johnson

The Lost Europeans | Emanuel Litvinoff

The Authentic Death of Hendry Jones | Charles Neider

My Son, My Son | Howard Spring

The Man Who Loved Children | Christina Stead

Delta Wedding | Eudora Welty

The Day of Judgment

Salvatore Satta

Translated from the Italian by Patrick Creagh

◬

APOLLO

Apollo Librarian | Michael Schmidt || Series Editor | Neil Belton
Text Design | Lindsay Nash || Artwork | Jessie Price

www.apollo-classics.com | www.headofzeus.com

First published in Italy as *Il giorno del giudizio* by Adelphi Edizioni,
1979.

This paperback edition published in the United Kingdom in 2016
by Apollo, an imprint of Head of Zeus Ltd.

1 3 5 7 9 10 8 6 4 2

A CIP catalogue record for this book is available
from the British Library.

ISBN (PB) 9781784975708
    (E) 9781784975715

Typeset by Adrian McLaughlin
Printed and bound in Denmark by Nørhaven

Head of Zeus Ltd
Clerkenwell House
45–47 Clerkenwell Green
London EC1R OHT

The Day of Judgment

The Marvellous Word: An Introduction

Visitors to Nuoro can follow a Salvatore Satta Itinerary, linking locations in this book. The Caffè Tettamanzi on Corso Garibaldi is still open. Beneath its painted ceiling and mottled mirrors, old men pore over newspapers; a television screen mutters on the wall; backpackers gurn for selfies. Communing with the writer and his phantoms is not easy. Better to take a minor road away from the town and halt in the open, during 'the season when the sun brings nothing but fire and death'. The burnt ochre landscape of Sardinia's interior begins to whisper in dolorous voices – the voices of Satta's unique novel.

When *The Day of Judgment* was published in 1979, four years after its author's death, it was acclaimed as a masterpiece. Some 60,000 copies were sold within a few months. Vying in their praise, some critics likened the book to *The Leopard*, another unexpected novel from Italy's periphery. Translations quickly multiplied (there were nineteen at last count); conferences were held; Susan Sontag – vigilant for excellence – saluted this 'improbable gift, for which one cannot be too thankful: a great European novel.'

Salvatore Satta (b. 1902) might have reacted to the applause with a mordant smile and then made his excuses. As a young man, he yearned for literary success. He wrote a novel about his spell in a sanatorium, being treated for tuberculosis, and entered the manuscript for a prestigious prize in 1928. When he failed to win, Satta renounced fiction and dedicated himself to the legal studies which he had started when he left his native Sardinia for mainland Italy in 1920. He became an extremely distinguished jurist, one of Italy's foremost experts on procedural law, a prolific author of standard works on civil procedure and bankruptcy and an esteemed teacher at several universities.

By the end of the nineteen-sixties, Satta was approaching retirement, living quietly on the outskirts of Rome with his wife, who had her own career as a scholar; their children were grown; his brothers (he was the youngest of seven) were all dead. Amid the isolation of old age and the strong premonition of mortality, Satta was swept back to the lost world of his childhood. In the summer of 1970, he began to write a novel about his family and his birthplace in Sardinia. He told a friend that it was 'a crazy endeavour', a 'book of memories', a 'secret book'. The upwelling of 'infinite' material seemed to 'submerge' him.

As the months passed, he found that the 'terrible shades' in his novel had become 'necessary to my existence', more real than the living people around him. And he knew the worth of what he was writing. 'Everything I've been trying to describe was a living world. If I succeed in recapturing that life, as itself, simply as what it was when it was alive, I'll make a masterpiece; but I lack the strength in every sense.' That last clause was characteristic. Despite his achievements and domestic fulfilment, Satta was convinced beyond reason that aspiration was inscribed with defeat. Conservative in outlook, he possessed – or was possessed by – a reactionary imagination, grounded in a Catholic faith which was never secure against despair. Humankind was sinful; people continually, compulsively violate the (Christian) values which should be sacrosanct; change meant decay; failure was the norm. Satta's widow Laura said that he had seemed to bear the griefs of the world on his back.

Many sensitive people wear some such armour. Satta's excitement while he wrote *The Day of Judgment*, conveyed in his letters, surely reflected the pleasure of finding that his lyrical voice had not been suffocated. The taproot to childhood was still alive. The sentiments in the book may often be gloomy, but the zest of the telling – the sense of imaginative recovery – counters the darkness of the tale, to haunt us ever after (in my case, at least) with its warmth, evocative power, and the fascination of its style: one that has been steeped in legal texts and is now serving a radically different purpose.

Before his death in April 1975, Satta had revised his manuscript but not completed it. The last sentence breaks off: '*In tutta questa confusione era tornato in campo Mussolini,*' (Amid all this confusion, Mussolini came back on the scene). Satta's family decided that the book as published should conclude instead with a page of reflections compiled from the last portion of the manuscript. 'To know ourselves we must live our lives to the very end', Satta enjoins. 'And even then we need someone to gather us up, to revive us, to speak about us both to ourselves and to others, as in a last judgment.'

What sort of novel, then, is *The Day of Judgment*? Of no sort at all; it is sui generis. Much is provided to the reader: a fresco of a particular place and time, with summaries of rituals and customs, almost ethnographic in their detail; a vision of a remote fastness on the edge of Europe as modernity approaches and changes it forever; a family chronicle across two or three generations; vivid portraits of townsfolk. This is all supplied with poetic concision by a narrator who, far from pronouncing in the manner of a judge, interrupts his story with anxious asides. 'My problem,' he remarks in Chapter Twelve, 'is whether there is any sort of connection between these women and the drinkers in the Caffè Tettamanzi.' He could make one up, of course, but that would violate a principle. ('In what I have written there is not an untrue word, and it has been really painful to reread it.') Satta allows himself the freedom to remember, not the liberty to invent. Even this might not have overcome his innate reticence, had he not also released his pen from fealty to anything juridical in nature. He trusted his memory to lead him, and trusted himself to receive its dictation.

The family portrayed is Satta's own, with altered names. Don Sebastiano is a notary, masterful with his clients, cold with his wife and seven sons. His life is governed by iron routine; tenderness is confined to the plants in his cherished garden. Neglected as a spouse, abandoned over time by children who leave home, Donna Vincenza is a study in unhappiness; her inarticulate suffering permeates the book. Satta relates her story with profound sympathy, sharpened by filial guilt. She becomes a tragic emblem of Sardinian womanhood in its several phases, as in this remark about her maidenhood: 'young girls in those days were made for the future, and therefore not only did they have no "past", which is only too obvious, but no present either.'

Modernity demands the articulation of what had never needed putting into words. Satta communicates the muteness of tradition and implication; he interprets the manifold silences of Nuoro and makes them expressive. If he gives voice to the voiceless, it is not done with the political aim of empowering the disempowered, but in a religious spirit of ultimate commemoration and an artistic spirit of passionate inquiry. His parents' generation was the last for which 'the simple, humble certainties of life' were a given, the last that was bound together in a 'mysterious communion'. Satta evokes the harshness and 'wondrous abundance' of life in a small society governed by immemorial custom.

We each discover that we were raised in prehistory; as childhood recedes, it becomes our painted cave, accessible to nobody else, lit by flares of adult memory which intensify over time. The advance of modernity (which Satta regarded with implacable distrust) differed in its contours from place to place. And Nuoro was small and separate enough to be a laboratory.

A word about Nuoro. Spreading over a rumpled granite plateau called the Barbagia, this ancient town reaches down toward the brown plains and up to the flanks of Mount Ortobene, matt green with holm oak and juniper. After the unification of Italy all Sardinians felt neglected, but none more so than the landlocked Nuorese. The abolition of communal grazing rights by the new authorities provoked an uprising in 1868 that brought members of parliament across the sea to investigate social and economic conditions. The ferment encouraged cultural creativity. By the end of the nineteenth century, young intellectuals were calling their town 'the Athens of Sardinia', with pride as well as irony. For it produced writers and artists of real distinction. The Nobel laureate for literature in 1926, Grazia Deledda, was born here and did not leave until her thirtieth year, when she travelled to Cagliari

– now only two hours' drive away. Among her early books was a series of essays about the ethos and customs of her birthplace. 'The character of the Nuorese is spirited and grave,' she wrote. 'Their concept of life is said to be severe and melancholy.' Nuoro was the 'most characteristic of all Sardinian towns', it was 'the heart of Sardinia', and 'the open field where emergent civilisation wages a silent struggle with outlandish Sardinian barbarity.'

Then there was Salvatore Satta's uncle Sebastiano, a poet, and no less heartfelt a conservative than his nephew, according to whom 'Sebastiano Satta saw the first car in Sardinia drive past and he immediately foresaw the death of his homeland.' The encounter is enshrined in plangent verses: '...an alien rumble and alien beasts / Pass by. O nightingales 'fore dawn, O flowers, O flocks, O sylvan scenes, / No more are we alone', and so forth. By this time, Nuoro had some 7,000 inhabitants; the total now approaches 40,000. Half a century ago, Alan Ross reported that the hills around Nuoro were 'tourist country that has not received its tourists'. Traditional costume was worn here after it had disappeared from other Sardinian towns. Alan Ross again: 'The black stocking-caps, smocks, waistcoats and gaiters of the men are shiny with use, the velvet rubbed away. And the women, too, in brocade jackets over white blouses, in embroidered skirts made out of two solid-coloured materials, the front and the back different, dress to their surroundings.' While these visible differences have passed, a faintly archaic atmosphere still lingers.

In *The Day of Judgment*, Satta depicts the town's modernisation as coinciding with his own childhood, in the first decades of the last century. The author's prehistory coincided with his community's entrance into history. The electrification of the streets, the irruption of the First World War, the arrival of democratic politics: these seismic events in Nuoro are matched by the growth and disappearance of Don Sebastiano's sons.

Although the book's tones are sombre, not everything is gloomy. The gorgeous descriptions in Chapter Five read almost like a Mediterranean *Cider with Rosie*. Such rapt evocation is a pure form of love. Besides, the note of threnody in the book never turns into lamentation; Satta shows how terrible the past was. And there are several grim jokes, perhaps Irish in flavour. 'An enormous silence filled the dingy room, and the dead man was not the most silent among them.'

Judgment was a concept that Satta had pondered for half a century. As a jurist, he once wrote that the essence of judgment, its constitutive element, is this: it must be rendered by a third party. 'No one can be a judge in his own cause, which is to say that whoever judges in his own cause does not deliver a judgment.' As the servant of a truth which stands outside and above him, the judge must participate [*partecipare*] in the trial without becoming partial [*essere parte*]. In this role lies 'the mystery of the trial'. For a man of his religious and moral temperament, every day is the day of judgment, when all our acts may be weighed in the scales of eternal justice and found wanting. In this novel, Satta the narrator is that third party who alone can render judgment, the one who gathers up his family and neighbours and speaks about them. It is not comfortable to play the part of a recording angel; as he wrote elsewhere, 'Whoever judges another knows that he judges himself first of all'. If he shies away from doing this, however, something real will be lost forever.

In an essay from the nineteen-fifties, Satta had written that Sardinians were possessed by 'the idea of immanent sin', and even more by 'the imperious sense of judgment, conceiving of life itself as a judgment, with no margin for liberty and the heedlessness of action'. This burden could crush the islanders' initiative, thickening the torpor that blanketed and blighted their lives. On the other hand, 'whoever has such a lively and troubling sense of the law and of sin (the sense of death, to put it more briefly, for nobody knows that he must die as the Sardinian knows it) has something more than faith. He has a vocation of sanctity: an absurd and anachronistic vocation, which stops us from entering the process of history and leads us, fatally, to dissolve history in utopia'. The Italian word for process, *processo*, also means trial. History is a trial; its sentence cannot be appealed. Yet there was more to judgment, in Satta's understanding, than punitive severity. He once praised it as a 'marvellous word' that expressed the unity of knowing and creating, 'knowledge as a truly creative act'.

Mark Thompson, 2016

1

At precisely nine o'clock, as he did every evening, Don Sebastiano Sanna Carboni pushed back his armchair, carefully folded the newspaper which he had read through to the very last line, tidied up the little things on his desk, and prepared to go down to the ground floor, to the modest room which served as dining room, sitting room, and study for his brood of sons, and was the only lively room in the large house, partly because it was the only one to be heated, by an old fireplace.

Don Sebastiano was a nobleman, if it is true that Charles V distributed minor titles of nobility to the Sardinian natives who had grafted the wild olive trees throughout their countryside (the higher nobility with real pretensions was almost entirely confined to Cagliari, and practically foreign to the island). But the double-barreled surname was only an outward show, the "Carboni" being nothing more than his mother's name tacked on to Sanna, which was the only real family name. This was due partly to the Spanish custom, and partly to the need to distinguish between one person and another, given the small variety of names caused by the sparsity of population. Every yokel in Sardinia has two surnames, even if in the course of time both are usually triumphed over by a nickname which with luck becomes the much-feared distinguishing mark of a dynasty of shepherds. A typical example is that of the Corrales clan. Time and necessity have eventually given some measure of legitimacy to these double-barreled names, and in fact "Sebastiano Sanna Carboni" in roman letters surrounded the coat of arms of the House of Savoy on the official brass stamp which Don Sebastiano scrupulously locked away every evening in a drawer of his desk. For Don Sebastiano was a notary, a notary in the provincial capital of Nuoro.

Who this Carboni woman was, who had left her name on a stamp, no one could have said. Don Sebastiano's mother must have died young, and nothing is more eternal in Nuoro, nothing more ephemeral, than death. When someone dies it is as if the whole town had died. From the cathedral—the Church of Santa Maria high on the hill—there falls upon the 7,051 inhabitants registered at the last census the tolling of the bell that announces that one of their number has passed away: nine strokes for men, seven for women, tolled more slowly for prominent people. No one knows whether this last is at the discretion of the bell ringer or according to the clergy's scale of charges, but a poor man who gets himself *su toccu pasau,* the slow tolling, is little less than a scandal. The next day the whole town winds along behind the coffin, with one priest in front, then three priests, then the entire chapter (for Nuoro is the see of a bishop), the first one unpaid and in a hurry, the others making two, three, four stops on the way to the graveyard—however many are asked for—and truly the wing of death descends on the little low houses and on the occasional more recent mansions. Then, when the last shovelful has brought the scene to an end, the dead man is dead with a vengeance, and even his memory vanishes. The cross remains on the grave, but that's up to it. And in fact in the graveyard, or rather, in the cemetery, dominated by a crag that looks like one of the Fates, there is neither chapel nor monument. (This is not the case today: ever since death ceased to exist, the place has been crammed with family tombs. *Sa 'e Manca,* Manca's plot, as it used to be called, I imagine after the name of the long-expropriated owner, over and beyond its costly walls and absurd colonnades, has become a continuation of the now middle-class city.) And in this way the Carboni woman dissolved into nothingness, in spite of the five sons she had brought into the world, who didn't even remember her Christian name, launched as they were into the adventure of their own lives. After all, apart from this fatiguing adventure, were they alive themselves? And the people whom destiny had hitched to their wagons—wives, children, servants, relatives—did they feel them to be living?

Don Sebastiano picked up the oil lamp, a great white globe on an iridescent stem, and started into the stairwell. The darkness was vast, and his hesitant steps caused a round eye of light to flicker swiftly here and there on the ceiling. Twenty years earlier he had built this house, on a piece of land bought from some impoverished Neapolitans whom the winds had blown as far as Nuoro, and the winds had then carried off God knows where. This undertaking had not been easy, with seven sons to launch into the future, and—it may be added—starting from scratch in a world that rejected the least mention of hope. But being a notary in a small town is an incalculable privilege, for (as they used to say) a power of attorney keeps the pot boiling. And apart from the lunatic document that is a power of attorney (three lire charge plus fifty lire fees) there were wills, there were sales of property which—since word of honor was losing its value—were beginning to be made in writing; there were the contracts which gentlemen from the Continent came to draw up, for the cutting down of the woods and the devastation of the island. Those were fabulous people, who turned all they touched into gold (though some of them ended by remaining on the island, bewitched by its demoniacal sadness). Accustomed to the profiteering notaries of the mainland, they could scarcely believe that they had found a notary who romantically described himself as the depository of the public's trust, who procured business for them and bargained over prices with the owners, and all this without demanding a penny (and indeed refusing all offers) above the fee laid down for the deed in question. No matter: what counts is not earning much, but spending little, and in fact not spending at all, if possible. And possible it was, on account of the lambs and kids which honest folk sent as gifts. On one occasion, and it was the first and last, he had allowed himself to be inveigled to the Officers' Club (for Nuoro was also the headquarters of a garrison) and had sat down at a gaming table. After half an hour, inexpert as he was, he had lost thirty lire. He waited until the hand came round to him (dignity above everything) and then he stood up, holding firm against all blandishments. Back at home, for three nights in a row, with his own hand he wrote the copies meant for the clerk, until he had made up for the thirty lire. Therefore, said malicious tongues, it was the clerk who paid. But what matter? Someone always has to pay.

If you can buy a brick for a penny, the house will build itself. Ah yes, that would be fine. But the fact is that a notary's house simply can't be like the house of a peasant in Sèuna, with its yard, its rustic patio, its log pile, its *lòriche** for the oxen, and the

---

* Contraptions for attaching the yoke to the shaft of a Sardinian cart.

kitchen at the end, with the fireplace in the middle of the room. Such houses had grown by themselves over the centuries, like bird's nests. But Don Sebastiano needs an architectural engineer, and the engineer is right there in the house across the road, perhaps the oldest middle-class dwelling in all Nuoro, clapped tight like a fortress, full of women and maniacs, with its windows constantly shuttered and doors that open only at prearranged signals. Don Gabriele Mannu, like all the Mannu clan, was a rich man living in penury. But he had been to Rome, he had studied, and he had come back as an architectural engineer to a town where no one had built a house for a century. That land of the impoverished Neapolitans, and that enterprising notary, offered his ancestral idleness—based on distrust of himself even more than of others, for he invariably answered no before finding out what someone wanted of him—both a test-bench and a challenge. So he made design after design, calculation after calculation. All very well, but he had in mind the palaces of Rome and the staircases which (he had read) men of old climbed up on horseback. And thus, instead of a house he made a staircase, an enormous space from which at every landing little holes opened off (which were the rooms, one leading into the other); and he thereby committed the growing family to hardship and irritability. It is true that people peering in across the threshold were astounded at that immense, useless atrium, and began to imagine who knows what untold riches—even if the master builder did go around saying that without his providential intervention Don Sebastiano would have had to crawl into his palace on all fours, so low had the designer planned the architrave of the front door.

For this reason the evening descent from the study to the ground floor was something of a voyage, and for this reason the round eye of light from the oil lamp flitted here and there over the vaults with the faltering of his footsteps. But at last he heard laughter and shouting and quarreling, and Don Sebastiano was able to put out the lamp, blowing across the top of the long glass chimney with the flame burning at the bottom.

Another, larger lamp was alight in the dining room, this one consisting of a bronze base sustaining a vessel very like an urn, decorated with transparent hunting scenes on a pale-blue background. Goodness knows how much a lamp like that would be worth today, but the Sannas, with their accursed instinct for dissolution, have not left even the most meager trace of their past. In Sardinia death is eternal and ephemeral not only for men, but for objects as well. This lamp was burning on a massive oval table that filled almost the entire room. The mahogany sideboard with the good china on show (at one end the bowl containing copper soldi and silver lire for housekeeping money; below, the huge rounds of bread in tall stacks replenished every fortnight) was inserted into the wall shared by the neighboring kitchen. But the light that played on the faces of the seven boys, the youngest scarcely more than ten years old, did not come from the lamp, but from the oak logs burning in the fireplace, the only source of warmth in the whole house. Donna Vincenza, wife and mother, sat apart in a corner, wrapped in black garments such as befitted her fifty years, exhausted, swollen from childbearing, her head perpetually bent upon her breast. For her it was as if each of those sons were still in her womb, and in the depths of her silence she listened to their voices as if feeling their hidden, mysterious movements within her. They were her life, not her hope. For Donna Vincenza was a woman without hope.

The entry of a father into his children's room damps their shouts and laughter down to a murmur, especially when the children are many and the father has to maintain and raise them by his own labors, rendering them present to him but unfamiliar. The evening meal had been over for some time, if indeed it had ever begun, because everyone ate what they wanted or what they could find, and whenever they saw fit; or else they formed into intimate little cliques within the family, each going its own way. At five o'clock, when there was still no one around, Donna Vincenza would heat herself a cup of milk and soak half a round of bread in it. For five years Don Sebastiano had not dined at all, and in fact it was this decision that had started the break-up of the evening meal. For some time before that he had been having dizzy spells when work was particularly fierce, and the treatment provided by Dr. Manca, the family physician, who (though intelligent) was an alcoholic like half the male population of Nuoro, had been of no avail. So one fine day, without breathing a word to anyone, he set off (believe it or not) for Sassari, 120 kilometers away. He was gone for two days, throwing everybody into despair. At last he returned, and by way of greeting announced that he was never again going to eat in the evening. Doctor's orders. Donna Vincenza's cries rose up to the heavens, but they did not remotely touch Don Sebastiano's heart. The dinners ceased and the dizzy spells ceased, and it was then that he took to spending the hour of the evening meal in the study where we found him. The void surrounding Donna Vincenza increased. So that evening, as usual, he moved toward the fireplace, and in passing stuck two icy fingers down the neck of one of his sons.

It was a familiar gesture, which made his younger boys jump, and by this time maddened the older ones. Certainly, it was meant as a joke, but deep inside he took pleasure in displaying his self-sacrifice, or at least his virtue, by reminding them of the cold he suffered while the rest were in the warm (and all thanks to him). "All you have to do is have a brazier brought up," said Donna Vincenza from her silence; and this was obvious, but for precisely that reason it should not have been said. Then Don Sebastiano joined them at the table, with his back to the fire, which gilded his bald head; and he began to talk.

He usually talked about things he had read in the paper. Not about political matters, of course. Politics in those days, for people of his station, born to work and to reap the precious and costly fruits of middle-class toil, literally did not exist. Politics was the government in office, those far-off, fabulous people called ministers, who due simply to the fact that they were ministers possessed merits such as put them above criticism. Anyway, who went in for politics in Nuoro? Those four or five lawyers who perpetually presented themselves as candidates (each with his own personal ballot paper, bearing his first and last names surmounted by a symbol for the benefit of the illiterate—Avvocato Manca had a plow, while Avvocato Corda had a four-leaf clover, which never managed to bring him luck) did not really practice politics as such. They aspired to speak in a chamber larger than the courtroom and (some hope!) to become one of those ministers. Only the priests—one perceived this vaguely, like the glitter of a distant wave—ever put forward anyone who was not a lawyer, nor among lawyers could they have found a candidate. But they never managed to get their man elected. Men such as Don Sebastiano not only did not meddle with politics, but did not even vote, because men of his class had a duty not to vote. As a notary Don Sebastiano collected the four or five hundred names of the voters, and during those days the staircase to the study was a constant procession. He himself stood the expense of the stamped paper, since for the sake of impartiality he made no one pay. Donna Vincenza pointed out that it would have been equally impartial if everyone had paid, and this also was obvious, and because it was obvious it should not have been said.

But in this abstention from politics there was something more profound, more freighted with inevitability. Don Sebastiano was Nuorese, and he would have had a family tree consisting entirely of Nuorese, had he been able to conceive of the past at all. The people who went in for politics, the candidates, were all from the villages: from Orune, from Gavoi, from Olzai, from Orotelli, and even from Ovodda—those minuscule settlements as remote from one another as are the stars, which look upon Nuoro as their local capital. They were villages of shepherds, of peasants, of people toiling away to get nowhere, but whose children had discovered the alphabet, that prodigious weapon of conquest; or at least of redemption from the arid, grudging soil. The *zii*, or uncles, as these elderly rustics were called, came to Nuoro with their massive beards, clad in their brand-new costumes as if entering a drawing room, and went to testify, or talk to a lawyer or a notary (when they were not brought to town in handcuffs) once or twice a year, dragging their children behind them. These children, got up in modern dress, feeling stupid even in their own eyes and growing more and more ashamed of their fathers (in comparison with those gentlemen who were no less at a loose end but who sat at the caffè tables as if exercising a class prerogative), saw the huge shop windows spread with sweetmeats or toys or books, or with headless dummies dressed in ready-made clothes, very likely all moth-eaten and moldy, but nonetheless symbols of something never seen or even imagined: wealth in hard cash, so different from being rich in sheep or goats. The Nuorese lawyer and the Nuorese notary, who spoke to their fathers in a Sardinian dialect more refined than their own Olzaese or Orunese or Gavoino, were men who "knew," even if the lads could not understand what they were saying; and they "knew" because they were Nuorese. They began to feel that if they wished to be *someone* they had to become Nuorese, and this notion encouraged them to study, to go to secondary school, and even to undertake the great adventure of the university, if possible with a scholarship to the Collegio delle Province—all that was left of the old Kingdom of Sardinia—or else by bartering away their father's plot of land. But even in Turin, or Sassari, or Rome, the goal was always Nuoro: the goal or the battlefield, no matter which. Finally they burst into the fortress like plebeian blood into the veins of a decaying nobleman. Intelligent, astute, despised but not despising others, they had only one advantage over the Nuorese, but this was a great one: they knew what they wanted. They could not, of course, become Nuorese, if only on account of their speech, which even after twenty or thirty years still retained traces of their native village; but the jobs swung more and more toward these newcomers. Among other things, they brought with them the quarrelsome clientele of their native villages; and then, someone who works will always get the better of someone who just dreams his day-dreams and doesn't do a stroke. Francesco Cossu Boi, known as Armchair Cossu, a penniless would-be painter whose means of livelihood was a mystery to everyone, saw fit to reply to those who offered him jobs: "We Boi have never worked." But these other smart fellows, so modest in their dealings with the Nuorese, even the poorest of them, knew the way to become Nuorese in the end. In the smooth walls of those decaying old town houses there was a breach, invisible but unfailing; and this was the women. All such houses were full of them, because it appeared that the Nuorese—the "suitable" ones—had a vocation for celibacy; and in truth, marriage becomes impossible for those who do not acknowledge the simplicity of life. So they spurned those rich, pale women who dreamed and pined in their cloistered life, and occasionally ap-peared like ghosts behind the windowpanes, or left the house to go to Mass. The newcomers knew the value of these women, quite apart from their fortunes. They did not come forward merely as dowry-hunters, but tipped the scales with their Sword of Brennus, which was their industriousness. The spinsters were only too glad to leave the title of "Donna" behind in their gloomy mansions and to live in the spruce, tasteless houses of the newcomers, which were already springing up on the outskirts of town. What could Don Serafino, Don Gabriele, or Don Pasqualino do except open the door to the applicants, if only to shut it again at once? Life was in their hands. None of them, of course, would have been able to handle a case like a Nuorese lawyer; but thank you very much, the latter took twenty years about it (one had to take twenty years be-cause lawsuits are serious matters), whereas the newcomers made three or four quick thrusts and everything was settled.

For the Nuorese, Nuoro itself was one of those grand, sad ladies, and it took an outsider to appreciate the amount of hidden power that lay there; that is, what it meant to have the administration in one's hands. Basically Don Sebastiano, and those who like him worked to build a house and a family, were unable to understand the public domain, for the simple reason that they identified it with themselves. Even the poor, and even the great mass of those who had chosen idleness as their occupation, could not feel otherwise. Of course, 7,051 persons did have common needs that someone had to provide for. But when it came down to it, what was at stake? Of the water system, with the not inconsiderable expense that it entailed (not to mention water purloined from the surrounding countryside), there was no need to speak. Could they not make do with those meager springs on the outskirts of town—Obisti, Istiritta—with their cool waters, which at twilight the serving-maids brought home in amphoras set lightly upon heads barely protected by a little pad? Even today, when there are so many aqueducts, the true Nuorese spurns the water that passes through pipes, and sends out for the time-honored water from the hillside.

And what about street lighting? Certainly, with life changing as it does, they could not go on making their way down the street with flaming firebrands whenever they went out at night (and they went out only when necessary). In fact Don Priamo, Don Sebastiano's brother, had concerned himself with this when he was mayor. That meeting remained memorable because the council wanted to limit oil lighting to moonless nights. But Don Priamo had shut everyone up by observing, "And how can we tell if the moonlit nights aren't going to be cloudy?" He still boasted about it. The drinking troughs at the three entrances to the town had always been there, and the peasants themselves, arriving with their oxen thirsty from the long climb, saw to keeping them clean and scraping off the moss and lichen. In short, all was in place, and everyone was in his place, for the common good. But the outsiders had understood, precisely because they *were* outsiders and had rescued the women from their sepulchers, that the administration of Nuoro did not lie in these trivialities, but in something quite different—the power one could lay one's hands on. Being mayor meant seeing the Nuorese, including Don Sebastiano, Don Gabriele, and Don Pasqualino, come forward hat in hand to ask for something. And, foreseeing the future, the outsiders knew that such people would have increasing need for that something from the administration. Power meant conceding this certain something; and this was all the more important because, in spite of appearances, power is shown more by giving than by taking away.

Then there was another thing the Nuorese had not realized: that the city or town, as the case might be, did not consist solely of themselves, but also of people who had come from the outside world, from the far-distant Continent: the subprefect, the garrison commander, the captain of the carabinieri, the president of the tribunal. These were employees, agreed, but because of them Nuoro was no longer or not only Sardinian; it was a fragment of Italy, in communication with Italy. And so the horizons widened. The conquest of the administration was also the road to politics—to Rome, to Rome! In short, the Nuorese found themselves administered and represented by outsiders, and all things considered, they were not sorry. It was one thing less to bother with.

Don Sebastiano did not mention politics, but he spoke about the King, who on the occasion of his birthday had entertained a hundred poor children at the Quirinal Palace, and luncheon had been served by the Queen and the princesses. Don Sebastiano was not a monarchist except insofar as there was a king, and it did not occur to him that it might be otherwise. But that the King, in whose name he drew up deeds on stamped paper (and it did not cross his mind that the stamp was a tax or a levy: it was what lent prestige to his profession), that the King should humble himself to the poor in this way profoundly moved him; as he had been moved by the story of the minister who had gone to visit his constituency, where they had prepared a huge luncheon; and when he found that they had laid a separate table for him and his entourage he would not sit down until all the tables had been put back together again. His voice would catch a little in his throat, but not from sentimentality. It was one of those things that lent value to life, which he believed in because he was alive. The same applied to the news that a doctor in Milan had injected his son with a serum against some disease or other, or that a member of the Chamber of Deputies in Turin had forced a policeman to fine him for an offense he had committed; or that by crossbreeding they had obtained a new strain of sheep that gave a hundred liters of milk per head, whereas Sardinian sheep achieved twenty liters in a good year; or again, that a ship had sunk in the Atlantic and the captain had refused to enter the lifeboat, even as the last man. Not everyone listened to these accounts, but Don Sebastiano really spoke only for his own benefit. He repeated what he had read without suspecting for a moment that it might be nonsense. Newspapers were not what they are today, commercial enterprises. They were something of an encyclopedia, a source of knowledge, the only source of knowledge in a small town, and it was impossible not to believe what they said. Otherwise, why would they have said it? (This was the case even with the *Giornale d'Italia,* let alone the *Corriere della Sera,* which never published a single photograph, but did not reach Sardinia.) In Don Sebastiano and men of his class it was as if the Age of Enlightenment had been prolonged into the late nineteenth century, manifesting itself in a serene and entirely unconscious atheism, without aversion for religion or even for the priests, though Nuoro had a swarm of them; and this attitude was nourished by a sure faith in the power of man over the forces of nature. Atheism is a static moment in life, and life then was static, like a chessboard on which one can play thousands of games, though the combinations are not infinite. The infinite was there (who knows?) in some of those youngsters, if while growing up they had ever felt it impossible to be reduced to pawns, or jacks, or even to kings. Or maybe it was there in that poor woman shorn of hope, who from out of her silence listened to Don Sebastiano's chatter with a few muttered, unheard comments.

But there was another component to Don Sebastiano and his vacuous discourses, and this was democracy, also unconscious of course, but indisputable. By this time Don Sebastiano could consider himself a rich man, or at least on the way to wealth, but he felt that his gains were legitimate because they were the fruit of his labors, accumulated according to the orderings of Providence, and if of necessity he had left behind crowds of poor people, in Nuoro and in the world at large, this had no effect on his intrinsic humanity. The poor could be and should be the rich of tomorrow. It is doubtful whether he dispensed charity, but he provided work for numerous people in his little improvement schemes, and the workmen would ask him as a favor to be godfather to their children, which he granted very willingly, thus becoming their relative and (as the custom was) addressing them as *voi* rather than using the more formal *lei*. Hence his emotion over the King, or the minister he had read about in the paper; but there was also something more serious. It was a kind of nostalgia for poverty, a concept of poverty as a spiritual experience or exercise, a glorification of manual labor as opposed to work with the pen or the mind, which could not satisfy his profound humanity because it was profit-making. His dream, as his sons grew up and went ahead with their studies, doing extremely well, would have been for them to devote themselves to some trade out of school hours. He did not say so openly, but every evening (and that evening was no exception) he would tell them how the sons of American millionaires earned a living selling newspapers. This he had learned from the paper, and his voice would take on a lecturing tone, and one of obscure reproof. It was then that Donna Vincenza emerged from her silence, lost all restraint, and became her true self. For she it was who worked in the kitchen, with the help of one poor woman who came in for the price of her food. She it was who saw her sons wasting away over books, while one in particular, Ludovico, worried her a great deal because he was growing up thin and delicate, with constant stomach trouble, and she could never stop him from studying.

"But those people," she cried, "have every comfort. They're not like us."

His dream in ruins, Don Sebastiano rose to his feet, took up his lamp, and turning toward that shapeless mass forgotten in a corner, said solemnly: "You're only in this world because there's room for you."

And off he went without even saying good night.

So that evening ended, one of many evenings of family life, in the family that Don Sebastiano and Donna Vincenza, over so many hard years of quarreling, had nonetheless created. The boys went up to their freezing bedrooms on the top floor, Ludovico helping his mother out of her chair and supporting her on her way up the stairs, which were becoming difficult for her. Sebastiano, named after his father, was responsible for securing the window giving onto the street. In thinking only of the façade, that beast of a Don Gabriele Mannu had set the window so high that they had to have two wooden steps made in order to look out. Sebastiano climbed up as best he could, and paused a moment before pulling the shutters to. Nuoro lay spread out in the deep night, racked by a bitter wind. Far off, a cart trundled over the cobblestones. Not a voice was heard. Two *carabinieri* on patrol, stiff and bored, came up the main street. It was almost frightening.

2

Nuoro was nothing but a perch for the crows, yet like all Gaul, and even more so, it was divided into three parts. The history of Nuoro did not go back further than two or three hundred years; that is, if we can give the name of history to the scraps of information collected in the archives of the bishop's palace by Canon Fele, who had a reputation for learning. Anyway, Canon Fele was not from Nuoro but from Dorgali, and this you could tell without even hearing him speak; you had only to see his long, thin face, his shrewd, washed-out eyes, his long chin beneath two bright-red, feverish-looking lips. Whenever he saw him passing by, Canon Floris would describe him, almost out loud, as a reptile. Though it now seems impossible, the real capital in those days was not Nuoro but Galtellì, a village in Baronia beside the river Cedrino, not very far from the sea. Some trace of this is left in the name of the diocese, which is not "Nuoro" but "Galtellì and Nuoro," Galtellì coming first. In fact, it seems that it was a certain Bishop Roich (evidently Spanish or half-Spanish) who had the bishop's seat transferred thirty kilometers farther inland, to the site where Nuoro was destined to arise.

In wintertime Baronia was a garden. And if from time to time the river went mad and overflowed its banks, flooding the fields and isolating the absurd little villages which—heaven knows how or why—had come into being on the vast plain, when it withdrew and composed itself into a gentle stream, remaining here and there in blue pools that looked like patches of sky, it left among the stones, by way of compensation, a fine damp soil that in an instant became wheat or barley, or above all the broad beans or the melons with the bluish flesh that had made the name of Baronia famous throughout Sardinia. What fragrance there was among the cane brakes, and in the underbrush populated by hares and partridges, when the sun returned to revive the dead, abandoned stumps of the low-growing vines. The trouble was that paradise in Baronia lasted three months. After that the sun became spiteful, began to repent for the joy he had brought to men, and went mad in his turn. It took him a week to create a desert. And what is worse (for the heat can be borne), from the marshy patches among the oleander shrubs, bogs into which the Cedrino had dwindled away, there emerged whole armies of death-dealing mosquitoes. The peasants collapsed with scythe in hand, the doors and windows closed as if in the face of an invader, the women were reduced to skeletons, the children of the poor wandered the roads, with shriveled skins and bellies like nine-months-pregnant women. The curse had fallen on Baronia. So Monsignor Roich, who was a practical man like all outsiders, had scarcely arrived before he decided to take his miter and carry it up into the fresh air.

I believe that this story (or another like it—it doesn't matter) is the truth. Galtellì today is nothing, a mere wrinkle, a scab on the ferocious limestone of Monte Columbu. But anyone who manages to fight his way through the swarms of flies, and the clouds of dust, finds himself before a church and a church tower that have remained even though the bishop has departed; and they are in the pure Romanesque style. He will find wretched, filthy hovels, but beside them, still standing, certain crumbling, deserted houses of some substance, now with two crossed planks where the windows once were, but with carved doorways, or at least a lintel of volcanic stone, on which with a bit of effort he can decipher an ancient date. And through a rusty iron grating he can see or imagine what in better days was a patio. Not to mention the fact that in some of these old houses, or their outbuildings, he may catch a glimpse of the faint shadows of women who are or were of the Sanna or Bellisai families, and may be the true descendants of that stock, even though now impoverished and resigned. One of these women, indeed, recently had a modest reflowering, because a petty local landowner, dressed in costume, had the temerity to knock at her door, and she had the wisdom not to say no.

Nuoro, for all the pretentiousness of its big public buildings, cannot hold a candle to the church, the grand houses, or the ruins of Galtellì. So what they say must be really true. And yet a mystery remains. Two or three centuries ago Nuoro did not exist even as a group of huts. None of the old maps of Sardinia, which include the now modest names of Ollolai, Orani, or even Orzullè, records the name of Nuoro. This means that Monsignor Roich laid the first stone, just as they did at Brasília or Canberra, and peopled the new capital with his priests and his parishioners from Galtellì. If I look today at the people of Galtellì (and they are the vestiges of the people of those times); if I see those lean, wiry men with their red jackets fastened at the shoulder and buttoning down the side, and their light, almost dancing way of walking; if I listen to their soft, almost aspirated way of speaking—God forgive me if I give offense—they seem like marionettes, and if I were a musician, far from writing this book I would produce a ballet. On top of this they are good-natured and mild, and in their brief youth their women have breasts that burst forth to such an extent that they bridle them in with a pair of slender cords. The people of Nuoro are like the garrison of a sinister castle: close and taciturn, men and women alike, dressed in a severe costume that yields as little as possible to the allurement of color, with an eye always on the lookout for offense and defense, immoderate in eating and drinking, intelligent and treacherous. How can those carefree marionettes have produced these dramatis personae of a tragedy? My own explanation of the mystery is to think that it happened as it still does today, when social structures violate the laws of nature, creating provinces, regions, and other administrative devilries; that at the advent of the bishop's seat the forests of the surrounding Barbagia poured forth those uncouth men who, according to the poet, feed on meat and honey, and that they installed themselves around the prelate and his capital, with their huts and their physical strength. The fact is that in the immediate environment of Nuoro there is more than one *domus de jana* (fairy house), while near Balubirde (which the Italians have translated as Valverde, which has nothing to do with it) there is a hillside perforated with these little fairy houses, which by a splendid analogy are called *Sas Birghines* (the virgins). In the forests on those heights there might therefore have been a prehistoric settlement that had fled the terrible coastal areas before Monsignor Roich, and which the curia settled next door to in peaceful cohabitation. And from this marriage Nuoro emerged. In short, all hypotheses are possible; either that Nuoro was born yesterday or that it is more ancient than Rome, with Monsignor Roich acting only as the modest and predestined best man to history. But maybe the most correct hypothesis is that Nuoro is the bureaucratic outcome of a series of overlords who carved up Sardinia; and in fact and in truth, even until the descent of the barbarians of our own day, there were three Nuoros, the "three parts" which we mentioned above.

Nuoro is situated at the point where Monte Ortobene (more simply known as the Mountain) forms something approaching an isthmus, which becomes a plateau. On one side is the fearsome valley of Marreri, the haunt of footpads, and on the other the gentle valley of Isporòsile (if anything can be gentle in Sardinia). This extends down to the plain, and under the imposing guardianship of the mountains of Oliena stretches as far as Galtellì and the sea. Protected by the hill of Sant' Onofrio—goodness knows who he might have been, since he left no trace of himself, even as a Christian name—Nuoro begins at the little Chiesa della Solitudine on the isthmus, slopes gently downward as far as the Iron Bridge, and appears to stop there. But in fact it starts again immediately after a short rise and finally dies in earnest a little before the Quadrivio, an intersection from which the dreaded roads branch out toward the interior.

In this last stretch rises the first section of Nuoro. It is called Sèuna, and it "rises" purely in a manner of speaking, being a huddle of low houses arranged without any order; or rather with that marvelous order that emerges from disorder. All are on one floor, with one or (the richest) two rooms, with a roof of rust-colored tiles sloping toward the *cortita*, a courtyard with a floor of earth just as God made it, surrounded by a dry-stone wall such as they build to enclose *tanche*,* and an opening toward the road barred by a tree trunk. In front of this strange doorway is that masterpiece of abstract art, the Sardinian cart.

The Sardinian cart becomes a cart when the oxen are yoked to it, oxen that are now asleep, drooping on their weary legs along the roadsides or, if there is room for them, in the *cortita*. Then indeed it is more than a cart, it is a weapon of war on the incredible little lanes out in the country, which the water has been eroding for centuries, laying bare granite boulders like great steps. The Sardinian cart climbs creaking up onto those humps, sways like a ship in a storm, balances for a moment, then crashes down on the other side, only to face more stones, more massive boulders. It is specially made for this, and indeed in the course of centuries, of millennia, it has left the roadway grooved by the iron hoops of its wheels. These grooves are like the scars of its toil, the toil of the oxen that haul it, straining on their short legs; and also the toil of the drovers who goad them on, so that they seem to be pushing and pulling as well, calling the beasts to task by name (*boe porporì, boe montadì!*) in voices that resound at evening the length and breadth of the valley. The town councillors are justified in saying "Why mend the roads?" But when the oxen are unyoked, and the cart is left there for the night in front of the sleeping dwellings, it no longer looks anything like a cart. It leans at an angle on its long shaft, raises heavenward two useless arms polished by the friction of the ropes; it breaks up into absurd vertical and horizontal lines, and lets the moonlight

---

*   A *tanca* is a piece of enclosed land of any size, from a small field to a vast pasture. The nineteenth century saw progressive enclosure of land on the island, leading to brigandage, rebellion, and events such as are referred to in Chapter 13.

in through the cracks in the tailpiece. It might be an invocation and a prayer, it might be a curse or an enchantment, or it might be nothing. In fact it is nothing, absolutely nothing. On summer nights the peasant stretches out on the sun-scorched planks, with his stocking cap folded under his head, and sleeps.

Had Sèuna been the objective, Don Gabriele Mannu need not have gone to Rome to get his degree in engineering. The builder in Sèuna (the "master of walls," they call him) obtains his sense of perspective and proportion from poverty, to the extent that when someone comes home after making a fortune, and has a plushy house built for him, the result is a false note; like a woman who has given up the long skirts of the local costume and displays her shapeless legs. The Seunese are peasants to a man. They make a town within the town, and it is said that they are the original nucleus of the settlement. Nuoro, in a word, was born out of Sèuna; and I am inclined to believe it, because in Sèuna we find the oldest church in Nuoro, Le Grazie, which is scarcely more than one of those same little houses, but with a gabled front and a bell in a kind of dovecote. The priest who officiates there is himself a peasant, and lives off the four or five turnips which he grows in the kitchen garden, and (believe it or not) off a little charity, since he does not have cure of souls.

In any case, it is certain that no shepherd would ever think of living in Sèuna, where he would feel degraded and out of his element. The shepherds all gather at the opposite end of Nuoro—the other town within a town, which is called San Pietro, although the place has no church of this name. San Pietro, *Santu Predu*, is the black heart of Nuoro. Sèuna is a painter's palette transformed into a picture. With its windows picked out in white and the calm clear skies above it, it could well be a seaside village. All it needs is the sea. San Pietro has no color. The houses here are tall, giving onto narrow streets, not alleyways, and to see the sky you have to look up. Here Don Gabriele Mannu might well have left his mark, and made those huge cement entrance halls, the kitchen immediately to the right as you go in, the useless dining room, the stone staircase, the rooms that stand empty even when there is company, with the chairs lined up against the walls. In the *cortite*, and here they are genuine courtyards, instead of the cart there is the horse waiting to be mounted and the saddle resting on a peg under the archway: the very horse that announces dire homecomings in the dead of night. The fact is that the shepherds are a race apart from the peasants. The shepherd belongs to the dynamic side of life, the peasant to the static. The difference between the shepherd and the peasant is that the first runs a household on the move while the other's is fixed. If, for the one, the land where he plows and harvests grapes is the end, for the other it is only the means. If the peasant, when he has dug and pruned the vines and olives, sits down at the foot of a tree and eats his bread sprinkled with olive oil, he rests; when the shepherd sits down in the fierce heat of noon he is not resting, because his whole life is without repose. He watches the sheep resting in the noonday shade, but he knows that at a certain moment they will move off at their slow dawdle, that no one will be able to stop them, that they will lead and he must follow, aided only by the dogs, which he has trained for war. And then, even when seated, he cannot but see those immense pastures that stretch from Monte Spada to Corte, to Lardine, to Sa Serra, where there are other flocks, other shepherds like him, and his thoughts run on and run on, and the devil knows where they end up. Virgil, a servant of the sovereign, could with indifference write both the *Bucolics* and the *Georgics*, without distinguishing herdsmen and farmers. But what a shepherd has is quite different from what a peasant has. The latter, in any case, is confined to certain valleys and certain plains, divided into so many parcels of land, each one different from the next. A man has to ask permission even to cross them. The other is everywhere, and is of course divided up and registered, but law is law and fact is fact, and no law can prevent the shepherd from thinking of everything as his property as far as the eye can see. And not just the land but the flocks as well, which are only yours as long as you are able to defend them. God is on the peasant's side, not on the shepherd's.

San Pietro is an urban extension of the sheepfold, and the smell of sheep and goats is in the air. The evening is all a clatter of hoofs on the cobblestones, for the masters, muffled up in costume, come home with saddlebags full (their employees return only once every two weeks to change their clothes and lay in a stock of bread). In the shadows two hands reach out and take the saddlebags, and the door swings shut behind the master.

The houses are large, because masters and servants all live together, eat at the same table, and warm themselves at the same fire; and this makes the servants more servants and the masters more masters. Once the door has closed behind the master, it is unlikely to open again. The sound of knocking in the night bodes no good: anyone who wants the door opened has no need to knock. If in his remote hut the shepherd has a thousand eyes fixed on the unsuspecting wayfarer, in town there are a thousand eyes fixed on him, whether he be servant or master, for all are subject to the same destiny. And then, there is Justice, which it is better not to get involved with, Anyway, what is Justice? Justice is authority, the power someone wields over someone else, and authority does not discuss matters: if it condemns you, you are condemned, and that's that. But for this reason it is also justice to escape from authority if possible, exactly as it is also justice to bump off a possible witness, if necessary. (If he has already given his testimony, then he himself has become Justice). In short, whenever someone knocks by night, the door that opens is the door to the back yard and the open country. The shepherd knows he is always innocent in his own eyes, but not in those of the authorities.

San Pietro is the base— and no other base is possible—for the Corrales dynasty. There are four or five branches, descending from the founder of the family, Bainzu, whom they called Deus (God) on account of his majestic bearing in the saddle. They used to ride into their houses, just as they would into the sheepfold. The houses are high, with three or even four floors, even though life was still essentially nomadic, and took place entirely on the ground floor. As it did in Don Sebastiano's house, though the company was different. The Corrales, like the other shepherds, had walked and walked behind their sheep, and still walked behind their sheep, and like the rest they had gazed on that boundless landscape with the eyes of pirates gazing at the sea. And their gaze had turned into action, the mysterious act of theft that is at the root of all property. Theft, what we call theft on the artificial assumption that there is such a thing as "yours" and "mine," the kind of petty attitude we take toward a ring or a wallet, in Sardinia, or rather in Nuoro, or better still in San Pietro, consists of stealing a flock of a thousand sheep and making it disappear into thin air. The impoverished owner goes on foot around the entire island, sends out his minions left, right, and center, follows all the tracks he sees in the soil and at the fords: nothing, nothing, absolutely nothing. That flock does not exist, but above all, it has never existed. Obviously the Corrales do not have a magic wand, and a thousand sheep (which in the final assessment become a hundred or two hundred thousand, not to mention the cows and oxen) cannot be stolen unless they are stolen by Sardinia as a whole. But this is the magic of the Corrales: they have made thieves of all Sardinians, or at least all the Barbaricini.* Other Sardinians don't count anyway. The newspapers in Sassari and Cagliari, and even those from the Continent, cried scandal, the ruin of the island; or rather of the island's economy, which was based on sheep-raising. The authorities intervened with savage laws against rustling, making an inventory of the livestock and describing it in a "bulletin" which every shepherd had to carry with him. But what did they gain by this? A wretch who had stolen a pair of oxen from a peasant was thrown into prison for five years. I say wretch because one does not steal a peasant's oxen. No laws are needed to prevent this. On one occasion they stole the oxen from Ziu Cancarru, father of five children. Bainzu Corrales at once started a collection, and the whole of San Pietro bought the poor peasant from Sèuna another pair, even finer than the first.

In the course of time (and meanwhile the houses of the Corrales were growing floor by floor, and along with them many of the

---

* The people of Barbagia, the wild central area of Sardinia, of which Nuoro is the provincial capital.

lesser houses, and the whole of San Pietro) the sheep began to leave tracks. The unfortunate owners from Ozieri, from Pattada, even from Campidano, followed a million meanderings from one end of the island to the other, staying overnight with their *amico de posada* (for, as there were no hotels, in each village one had a house that offered hospitality, with reciprocal rights), and after going here, there, and everywhere, the tracks led to the houses of the Corrales. Those peaceful sheep farmers from the Logudoro would enter, in their black, funereal costume, their stocking caps pleated on top of their heads, their trousers as tight as bandages, and the long staff polished by time grasped in their hands like an ineffectual scepter.

"*Bonas dies, ziu Bainzu* [Good day, Uncle Bainzu]."

"*Bene bénniu* [Welcome]. What's the news from Ozieri [or Pattada, or Buddosò, or Bonorva]?" replied Ziu Bainzu.

"We're empty-handed," the other replied.

"What do you mean, empty-handed! The pastures at Ozieri are among the best in Sardinia. It's not like here, all stones! And drought, drought all year round. It's eight months since we had a drop of rain. And then in the winter, snow and ice. Even the sheep bells freeze. When I was a young man I was drafted to Ozieri. I felt like going on hands and knees and cropping the grass myself. And your livestock is all hale and hearty. Your land is worth three times what ours is." Then, lowering his voice and talking as if to himself, though with a hint of reproof: "I'd even have liked to buy something from you myself, but you don't want to sell to us Nuorese. You say we bring robbery and plunder...Ah well..." Then, after a pause: "And how is Don Bustiano? He must be getting on in years by now."

"He died this year. Didn't you know?"

"What a shame. He was a good man, God bless him. And what about Zaime, Gianuario's son?"

"It was he who told me to come to you, Ziu Bainzu."

Ziu Bainzu, of course, knew this perfectly well.

"Ah well, in that case—Mariangela, bring some coffee and biscuits. Zaime is a friend, and I am godfather to his son, who must be grown up by now."

And Mariangela, Ziu Bainzu's wife and the mother of all those children, came in with the tray and the coffeepot, which was always ready on the hob. She did not glance at the guest, deaf-mute witness that she was, because she knew how to stick to the basic rule of life, for herself and for others: What the master does is right.

"Zaime himself is one of my *amicos de posada*, and told me, 'Put your trust in him, and if he doesn't take care of things, then no one can.'"

Ziu Bainzu scratched his forehead. "I see. You've got yourself in trouble."

"No, no, not at all! But a terrible thing has happened. They've stolen my sheep. They were all I had."

"Well, not exactly all...But what am I supposed to do about it?"

"Zaime told me to come to you, because you have influence."

In a word, it was no easy matter, with all the riffraff there was around. And, worse luck, money would have to change hands, because men would have to be sent out to scout, and you don't get anything for nothing. A livestock merchant had said that he had seen a flock without a shepherd out around Mamojada.

How many head? Two or three hundred? Many more? There'd be a lot of work to put in, but Ziu Bainzu would have done a lot more than this for Zaime. Let's see. In the meantime, put down a thousand or two thousand lire and he would see what he could accomplish for the price.

A couple of days later the flock suddenly sprang out of nowhere, as if the clouds had opened and gently rained it down into the fertile *tanca* at Ozieri. And the fame of Ziu Bainzu spread the length and breadth of Sardinia.

There is the other side of the coin, and things are easier said than done. Because the *carabinieri* could not possibly turn a blind eye to Ziu Bainzu Corrales, or to his children or his employees, and a hundred times the great door of the Rotunda, the circular prison that met your eye as soon as you emerged from the station, had closed behind him…behind *them*. But it was like the door of his own house closing, and never did he feel more sure of his innocence than when they put him inside. So much so that after two or three months they were forced to fling him out, because the news of his arrest spread over the countryside like the beating of a tom-tom, and in as little as two days he was supplied with so many alibis that it seemed he must have the power of being everywhere at once. And then, and then…When the shepherd thinks of the land, the flocks, and the property of others as belonging to himself, even the lives of others become his. Killing and stealing are not all that different, except in the Penal Code. Certainly no one kills without a reason, but if the reason is there, it will not be the fragile existence of man that will stay the killer's hand.

Why did they bump off Banneddu Zucca? No one will ever know. He was a peaceful young man without any enemies, and even a bit townified, though he rode every day to Lardine to help his father with the milking. There must have been some reason. The same applied to so many others. But no one would have dared to suspect Ziu Bainzu's hand in this—or the hand of any of his children. On those long summer evenings, after eating a bit of bread and cheese, because he was thrifty, he would sit himself down at the foot of an elm that had grown at the far end of the *corte*, and read. For, though no one knows where, he had learned to read and write.

The dynasty of the Corrales was by no means an isolated phenomenon, as might have been the case with a feudal lord immured in his castle. Ziu Bainzu was the embodiment of San Pietro's will to live: the very thing that was lacking in the inhabitants of Sèuna. In his unpolished way, he could be said to resemble those lawyers from the villages who had, or thought they had, conquered Nuoro. But there remained the usual unbridgeable gulf, that Ziu Bainzu was Nuorese and the others were not.

The boundaries of San Pietro were a little vague, unlike those of Sèuna, which were marked by the Iron Bridge. I would say they ran more or less along the dotted line that starts at the old carabinieri barracks, turns toward the Piazza di San Giovanni (which is outside San Pietro), reaches the opening to the tiny alley where Maria Pisu lives—always seated in the center of the patio surrounded by the swirls of her scarlet-bordered skirts—and finally dwindles away at Montelongu, which is already in the country, within sight of the Mountain. Briefly—and this is the important point—San Pietro ends where the long, newly paved Corso begins. The Corso is the symbol of the third part of Nuoro, the Nuoro of the law courts, the town hall, the schools, the bishop's palace; the Nuoro of Don Sebastiano, of Don Gabriele, of Don Pasqualino—in a word of the "gentry," whether rich or poor.

If the boundaries of San Pietro were not geographically certain, the people of San Pietro knew them to perfection, and no one from up there would ever have dared to cross the threshold of the Corso (formerly Via Majore). One of the Corrales clan might happen to go there, if he had dealings with a lawyer, either on his own account or for one of his servants or friends. But not one of those shepherds who stank of cheese, not one of those youths who behaved like drunken hooligans at night, while waiting to grow up and become robbers, and meanwhile didn't have two pennies to rub together—not a single one of them would have mixed with the gentry in the Corso, or would have entered one of those shops where the "Cagliaritano" (whose real name no one knew) measured the cloth he sold by so many handsbreadths, or where Marianna Zedda weighed pasta or rice on her lever scale, or the *istancu* (tobacconist's) where Don Gaetano sold cigars and official stamped paper, though he was an aristocrat, as one could see from his long beard. Nor would they have sat down at the caffè where "the gentry" exercised their right to do sweet nothing, or shown their faces on the *barandilla* (veranda), against which the more staid and elderly gentlemen would lean to enjoy the cool air coming from no less than the public gardens, which most people still called *sa tanca*, the pastures; and indeed it became pastureland immediately beyond the acacia trees which some mayor from the Continent had planted in orderly rows. The gap between the three Nuoros was far greater than between the first, second, and third classes on the little train that linked Nuoro to Macomer and to the world. And even that gap was far greater then than it is today, because Don Sebastiano, for example, who was an aristocrat and by now almost a rich man, would never have traveled either in first class or in third, since second class was his natural place. It was the result of a tribal feeling, of a choice as free as whether or not to be baptized.

The Corso sloped slightly downhill from the Piazza di San Giovanni, where the market was, to the Iron Bridge. Halfway down, just before a wide curve and after the little piazza of the *barandilla*, there was a flat stretch containing the houses of some consequence, the house of the "Registry" (which Don Sebastiano had bought in order to rent it out), the house of Bertini, who was one of the Continentals who turned stones into gold and ended by being Sardinianized (except for the tall figure typical of Northerners, which they passed on to their bastard children), and the house of Tettamanzi, another Continental, of whom there remains no memory except the name of the caffè on the ground floor. It was an elegant caffè, with little rooms with red sofas around the walls—rather like the caffès in Venice, if I may make so bold as to say so. The owner of the caffè and of the whole building was now Giovanni Maria Musiu, who had perhaps inherited it through his mother, but there was nothing in the least Continental about him. He was short and fat, with dark eyes and a pointed beard, and he had nothing but an accursed will to live; that is, to play cards in the little rooms of his caffè. The whole of Nuoro, of course, gathered in this flat stretch of the Corso. Here the lawyers met their clients; the small landowners in the dazzling costumes of the villages eyed the merchants, on the lookout for good deals for their produce, oil and almonds from Baronia, wine from Oliena, cheese from Mamojada and Fonni. And this was the route followed perforce, in the morning, by all those on their way to that earthly god—the law courts—or to that equivocal god that was the vast, badly proportioned church erected by some rich bishop who on the cornice of the façade had carved the words DEIPARAE VIRGINI A NIVE SACRUM, which not even the priests succeeded in translating. Santa Maria della Neve and the law courts stood opposite each other, and to get there one had to go up a broad, well-paved thoroughfare and through the archway of the seminary, beyond which soared the great rock of one of the peaks of Monte Ortobene, like a petrified giant. On days of the Assizes, or on some major religious festival, there was a colorful procession, each person climbing up with his own secret load of sins.

Santa Maria was perhaps the original nucleus of the "historic center," as they say nowadays, meaning the part where the gentry lived. The word "gentry" does not mean "rich"; it is merely the opposite of rustic, and the difference—a great one—is embodied in the wearing of ordinary clothes, which have replaced local costume.

How many people lived in this area, what with the paved Corso, the road to the station with its two parallel strips of granite in the cobblestones, and the jumble of streets just off these, not very different from the streets of San Pietro but with very different inhabitants? I think that if we made a count it would not be more than about 1,500 to 2,000. That is not many in the abstract ocean of life; but it is a lot in the material space in which people take on a face and a name. Then they are not a thousand, but one plus one plus one, and so on, and every one of them has to live, to live on his own and at the same time live with his neighbor. This was at bottom the great problem in Nuoro. There were priests, there were lawyers, doctors, professional men and merchants; there were poor laborers, the cobbler and the builder (the "master of shoes" and the "master of the wall"); there were the idle, the penniless, the wealthy, the wise men and the madmen; and there were those who felt a commitment to life and those who did not feel it. But the problem they all had in common was that of living, of enabling their being to come to terms with the extraordinary and lugubrious fresco of a town that has no reason to exist. Of a town as of the world at large, perhaps. Therefore there was no hatred, and there was no love either. There was the struggle with others, which became a struggle with themselves. Love and hate balanced each other out, and converged in the need to preserve others in order to preserve themselves.

No one could escape this destiny (not even Don Sebastiano, although he was an honest spider spinning his web, and knew other people solely by the signatures which they put to legal documents). Divided from Nuoro by insurmountable barriers, maybe San Pietro had another life. With its patriarchal crimes San Pietro was building a bridge toward the future, while Sèuna was nothing but a cart and a yoke of oxen, and did not know it existed, or care about it.

But the infinite poverty of Sèuna had one advantage over the potentates of San Pietro. When someone died, he had inevitably to pass along the flagstoned Corso, from end to end, because the cemetery, *Sa 'e Manca,* was on the other side of town, beyond San Pietro, near the Chiesa della Solitudine. And when the dead man passed by, the gentlemen in the Caffè Tettamanzi rose to their feet and bared their heads.

3

I am writing these pages that no one will read, because I hope to
be lucid enough to destroy them before I die, in the little loggia
of the house that I have built for myself in the course of the long
years of a hardworking life. It is dawn in mid-August, an hour
of day when summer, though still at its height, gives way to the
passion of autumn. In a few hours' time all will be otherwise; but
in the meanwhile, I am living out this foretaste of a season that
more properly befits me. The house is large, and beautiful, and
comfortable: I tried to recapture the lines of the old Sardinian
houses, which I have been carrying in my heart for fifty years; but
naturally the architect understood not a thing. It doesn't matter.
The house would not have been mine in any case, because "our"
house is not the one we build for ourselves, but the house that is
passed down to us by our forefathers, the one we appear to get
for nothing, but in fact acquire by means of the labor, honest or
otherwise, as the case may be, of generation after generation.

In front of the loggia is a short stretch of garden, which I have
filled with oleanders. They are still in flower, and in the moist air
they seem to be listening to the song of the birds, which God has
made such early risers. One of them darts among the branches,
the leaves quiver, but only for an instant. I have always thought
that there is a secret relationship between plants and animals and

the wind. A bird does not alight in vain among the foliage, not for nothing does the wind sway the great leafy crests of the trees, that only we think of as immobile, classifying them under the horrible, unjust heading of "vegetable." Their motion is certainly not like ours, but it is like the motion of the sea, which it is senseless to call immobile, just as it is senseless—with apologies to Homer—to call it infertile. And then, trees have a rising motion, in a joyous conquest of the sky that to us animals (or, as the laws on livestock rustling put it, self-propelled beings) is denied.

Enough of this. Even in the *corte* of Don Sebastiano's house there was an oleander. Rather than being a single *corte*, it was a series of courtyards, obtained from a succession of little houses bought and demolished, at the end of which a narrow passage led on one side to the stable and on the other widened out into a space that was called the garden, and would indeed have been a garden if Don Sebastiano had cared for flowers. This man had created several little farms, down in Isporòsile with its robust soil traversed by a mountain stream that was always in a bad temper, and on the hill at Locoi, with its fine dry soil, beneath the *nuraghe** that in the course of centuries had come to resemble a vast bowl containing an oak tree. And these farms he had created practically with his own hands, for he knew how to prune and graft vines and olives. But he understood nothing about flowers. Admittedly, when he mounted his horse before dawn so as not to keep his clients waiting, leaving his household asleep, and set off for his fields, and saw the meadows smiling with dew, or rode

---

*   Circular, towerlike structures built of massive stones, a familiar feature of the Sardinian landscape. Reckoned to be two to three thousand years old, they are in all respects a complete mystery.

beside hedgerows snowy with blackthorn, or saw the shiny lentisc berries and the elegant asphodels among the hardy cistus and
the melancholy Saint John's wort, he would feel a slight pang, a
nostalgia, a vague remembrance. He was also sensitive to smells,
and sometimes he would break off a sprig of wild thyme, and
put it in the pocket of his fustian jacket. But odors have more in
common with fruits than colors have; they are more concrete,
easier to grasp. Once, however, on the descent into the valley of
Marreri and its rugged solitudes, he was left, as it were, enthralled
by the sight of those rivers of oleander that groove the sides of
the whole valley, and cascade toward the bed of the main stream,
which is itself an even broader river of oleanders, till all flow
down together, soft and voluptuous, toward the sea. First light
was in the sky, but it was also there in those vermilion flowers
emerging from the night. Dismounting, he tore off a branch; and
he planted it at the far end of the *corte,* beside the well; and the
branch put down roots and grew prodigiously, maybe because it
had struck water, and in a short while it stretched like a canopy
over the well. It was a marvel, with its mass of vivid red above
the dead things that accumulated in that lost corner, above the
few vegetables cultivated in the kitchen garden (since greenstuff
never flourishes in towns), and the children loved to climb onto
its whitish boughs, which were as sturdy as tree trunks. The trouble was that the oleander is a poisonous plant, or at least so they
thought in Nuoro, and so thought Donna Vincenza, who as the
years went by began to hate that single tree which her husband
had planted in his *corte,* evidently to spite her. Every day, while her
husband was busy sorting out the troubles and wrangles of his
vociferous clients, she would take a pot of lye and pour it over the

plant, in the vain hope of burning its roots and killing it. It was a senseless thing to do, purely symbolic; but what could this fifty-year-old woman do that was not a symbol? Before very long her legs would be completely crippled by arthritis, and she would be unable even to reach the vegetable garden; she would be confined to a chair in the first *corte*, with her hands clasped over her breast as if in prayer. But she did not pray.

Donna Vincenza was not entirely Sardinian. Like Don Sebastiano she had been born in the Kingdom of Sardinia, but the idea of that kingdom being Sardinian was simply a joke, while in Turin there was no Sardinian to be seen. On the other hand, a few Piedmontese came to Sardinia, either to trade or to command, and among them, from the very frontiers of France (two steps in that direction and destiny would have been completely different), there came a certain Monsù Vugliè, of whom absolutely nothing is known. Rumor has it, as a sort of echo, that he was an architect, but who knows what architect meant in those days, seeing that we are not sure even now. The old people still remember a tall man, evidently the commonplace notion of a Continental, who rather impressed them—and this is a commonplace too. It was also remembered that he had been carried off in his prime by a stroke. That is all that was known of a life which must have been an intense one, since in a few years he acquired two houses and an orchard that was practically a garden, just outside Nuoro. Until yesterday it was still called after him. Now they have built a local government office on the site. During those years he met a girl who wore costume, but was of good family, and who became Signora Nicolosa, the mother of Donna Vincenza. The latter's golden hair revealed some trace of her father, which she then passed on to her eldest son, but nothing more, at least in a physical sense; and in fact though she could understand Italian she couldn't speak it, like so many people in the smaller villages even today. Ten years her senior, the young Don Sebastiano fell for this lass, who in her girlish costume was like a flower. How could Signora Nicolosa, alone with so many children and so little luck, have said no to a qualified notary, full of promise and a nobleman to boot? So it was that Monsù Vugliè's daughter laid aside the costume and became Donna Vincenza, as glad to be married as was consonant with modesty. Don Sebastiano was a just man, and married on the principle of equal shares between partners. In this way, every acquisition he made would be the property of both of them.

It is hard to say how great a part love played in this marriage. In fact we know nothing of the sort of love that leads to marriage, or even if love has anything to do with marriage. I am inclined to believe that the marriages arranged by parents for children who saw each other for the first time at the altar were perfectly within the bounds of logic, even if naturally we cannot accept this today, just as we cannot accept so many other things. It is not that love is a frivolous thing, far from it: for love is marriage, and on this is based its indissolubility. However this may be, Don Sebastiano called his wife Vincenza, but Donna Vincenza called her husband by his surname. "Tell Sanna that," or "I'll tell Sanna that," she would reply to those who came to her about something involving the family. In this way the family was founded, practically on paper, because there was no property on either side, or precious little, and what is a family without property? In the Civil Code, which Don Sebastiano kept on his table, the family was considered as distinct from property, but in real life the family that has nothing is an abstraction, a mere pompous way of talking, rather like an individual without property, whom professional jurists refer to as a "subject of law." There was once someone (this comes back to me from the days when I myself studied law) who said that each and every man possesses a patrimony. Good stuff! He had never clapped eyes on Fileddu, the village idiot of Nuoro, who followed the gentry around like a dog, and like a dog lost his head if they left him on his own, until his starving mother came and dragged him home to her hovel, protecting him exactly as a bitch protects her pups. We will come across him again in the course of this story. And anyway, aren't the really grand families called "houses"? It is true that the essence of the Gospels lies in having made every man a "subject of law," but in the other world, not in this one. Don Sebastiano owned no property, but he knew he had it in the pen which scratched across the stamped official paper, and that the family would come into being by means of that stripling girl with whom he had gone to live in the shadow of Santa Maria.

Donna Vincenza was too young to carry off the aristocratic title so suddenly bestowed on her. Her neighbors called her by it at once, because it was hers by right, but also because they were proud of her and happy at her good luck. And she was too young to have the thoughts that we mentioned above, thoughts which Don Sebastiano nourished without knowing it. Signora Nicolosa had brought her up in the only way a woman can, if she has lost her husband too soon, and if she feels, or once felt, that she must do her duty by him. But even without this, young girls in those days were made for the future, and therefore not only did they have to have no "past," which is only too obvious, but no present either. There were no problems. Problems, of whatever kind, arise when the simple, humble certainties of life begin to fail, the certainties one carries from birth; and no one needs a priest to help him recognize them. Donna Vincenza vaguely realized that she was destined to take a husband, but her imagination did not go beyond that. Hers was the state of mind of a madonna who knows that the angel is bound to come, who understands his words at once, and who welcomes them with serenity, as in the myth, or the fact, as may be. Many, many years later she said that when she was expecting her first baby she thought they were going to cut open her belly to get it out; but she said it with rancor, she said it against Don Sebastiano, to get back at him for the havoc he had made of her life. These, however, are sorrows still to come. At that time Donna Vincenza was happy, because she had been blessed with a simple soul, and everything had a value for her. She had finished the first years of school, had learned to read and write as well as was necessary (and in fact one needs so little), and her life revolved around the people and the things she saw; all the more so because that Piedmontese who had died early, whom she herself had never known, had bequeathed to the family a stamp of modest refinement which attracted the neighboring women and made them obsequious.

The women seldom left the house, so every time they did it was a fabulous adventure. Donna Vincenza's adventure was her outing to the Vugliè garden at Istiritta. There would be no point in mentioning it, except that she still thought back to that garden, seated in her chair in the first *corte* at the back of the house, all but motionless by this time. There was a great big red gate that creaked on its hinges, and was hard to open because of the clumps of mallow and wild cardoons invading the threshold (though mallow has an edible little lump in the middle and cardoons, under the spikes, have a soft green layer that tastes a bit like artichoke). And then, at the top of a short path, one could see the crest of a palm tree, which was a rare thing, because Nuoro is high up, almost in the mountains. The peasant's house smelled of bread and cheese, that is, of his daily fare, and it was a wholesome country smell, like the smell of the spade, the mattock, the saddlebag hanging on the wall, and even of the cat asleep in front of the dead fire. They were all living things, belonging to a life that was new every time for her. She would chat with the peasant who had known her from birth and therefore addressed her familiarly as *tu*, while in the presence of Signora Nicolosa he took off his cap. And the garden itself, the garden with its lettuce and celery and tomatoes and cucumbers... A kitchen garden is a peasant's masterpiece of orchestration, for he creates it day by day, following his instinct, opening up the long channels flowing with water, which he skillfully controls. There is a long ditch down one side of the garden, running with water from the well, which he deviates into smaller cross-channels with a shovelful of earth, one for each channel. It is an ancient method, perhaps man's first attempt at making an aqueduct. But the peasant does not know that it is ancient, because time for him has neither past nor future: this is simply the way it has always been done. Slightly less ancient, perhaps, was the ingenious contraption Monsù Vugliè had installed above the well, with a lot of square tin cans that went down empty and came up full, leaking because the rust had corroded them. The machinery turned at the ambling pace of a blindfolded horse which needed no encouragement from voice or goad. They had only to harness it up and it started off.

Donna Vincenza ran, she practically flew, in this world just beyond which there was nothing; or if there was something it didn't matter. She was happy, and this was only right. When it comes down to it, what does a woman need, if we want to be honest at a time like this, when it is so hard to be honest? Nothing but love, and the ability to love. All the rest will be added unto it, as it said in that little book she sometimes used to open at Mass. The trouble is that loving is a difficult thing, and it is easier to be a great woman scientist or writer, such as indeed there have been. Because love is not willpower, or study, or what we call genius—it is intelligence, the only true measure of a woman, and of a man too. Donna Vincenza was highly intelligent, even though she scarcely knew how to read and write, and for this reason she overflowed with love, without knowing it. She loved the humble furniture in her house, the embroidery on the pillow-cases, which she used to work on with her mother all day long (because Signora Nicolosa did this work on commission, as the meager income from the property left her by Monsù Vugliè was far from sufficient). She loved the *cortita* of the house, with figs and tomatoes laid out on boards to dry amid the eager buzzing of bees and wasps. And above all, she loved the garden, where she still went to pick flowers and fruit, even though her swollen legs bore her up less and less well. And she had loved Don Sebastiano, the man who had come to ask for her hand and was destined to take her to live in another house.

Perhaps their quarrels had really begun with the sale of this garden. It is all but impossible to know why two married people quarrel, and why the source of life changes so soon into a source of hatred...Come to think of it, maybe just because it *is* the source of life…but let that pass. The fact is that at a certain time, when some of the children were already quite big, Don Sebastiano forced Donna Vincenza to sell that garden, along with the few other things she had inherited from Monsù Vugliè. Donna Vincenza, a grown woman by this time, resisted tooth and nail. She yelled, she wept, and went so far as to insult her husband, to throw all the pride and arrogance of the Sannas in his face. But Don Sebastiano didn't even listen to her, as indeed he never did, and the garden passed into other hands for a song. Why did he do it? God alone knows, but my explanation is this: from the scratching of his pen, Don Sebastiano was beginning to earn himself houses and fields; in the terms of his time and place, he was becoming a rich man. His wife's few possessions now began to upset him. It seemed to him that he might begin to suspect that his wealth came at least in part from there and not from his own hard work, and that above all he would be the first to suspect this. It was an insane thing to do, if we bear in mind that Don Sebastiano had deliberately married, as we said, on the principle of property-sharing. That is, all acquisitions made during the marriage by one partner or the other would be held in common (though one partner, his wife, was a silent partner, to say the least). What interested Don Sebastiano was not property or the enjoyment of it, but the actual acquisition of it, the building of a fortune. For this reason he did not allow Donna Vincenza to stick her nose into the administration of things, except for selling off the superfluous goods that accumulated in the house. Indeed, and worse still, she only had to express an opinion or offer some advice for it to be turned down, and the more reasonable it was, the more this was bound to happen. And maybe, since sons are also part of one's fortune, this was why he made her bear him a son almost every year, without thinking that each child shortened her life, and little by little reduced her to a mere encumbrance.

But it could be that I am wrong about this, because Donna Vincenza was the mother of her children even before they were conceived. Equally, the reason might be the deeper and more general one: that in Sardinia women do not exist. I will explain myself. In Sardinia there is no jealousy, there are no crimes of "honor," as they are called: there is simply nothing. Unlike in the rest of southern Italy, and in many other countries as well, a woman does not follow her husband on foot while he straddles the ass on the way down to their little farm. She rides on the cart with him, and when they are on the steep road back, and the oxen are lowing with the strain, the wife stays on the cart, and it is the husband who gets down and toils even harder than the oxen. In the house she is in charge of the household goods, she gives orders to the maids and even the manservants, she keeps the keys and sells off produce for petty cash (for every house is like a shop, equipped with all the weights and measures, the scales and the bushel measures for wheat). But she never appears when there are guests, not even if they are *amicos de posada*. The reason is, as I said, that women do not exist. For the Sardinian—and I speak of the Sardinian of those days of course, before he became the mere tenant of his island, as he is now—a woman, a wife, was the object of a tacit cult, exposed to the ups and downs of life, a slave to life's demands, and therefore also to the needs of her husband and family; but all this in a rarefied way, quite separate from the realm of the male, the government of the miniature "state" of the family. Into this government she could not and should not enter, any more than a queen can enter into the government of the king. It is conceivable that in this set-up there lurked an inferiority complex on the part of the husband, but the fact is, this is simply the way things were. Once again, in a word, what the master does is right. If one therefore wants to think of the wife as a slave, then the queen is a slave as well. Anyway, the difference between queen and slave is no more than a hairsbreadth.

Don Sebastiano was no exception to the rule. At the times of the most obstinate disagreements, there was no danger that he would help himself first at table. For according to tradition the main dish was given to him for carving and distribution, and the first mouthful was Donna Vincenza's. He would have left the table if she (as she was sometimes tempted to) had refused it, though this did not prevent him from shrugging his shoulders or, when she opened her mouth, silencing her with those terrible words that we have already heard: "You're only in this world because there's room for you." The fact is that Don Sebastiano, for all his culture and perspicacity, had not understood one thing, probably because he was incapable of understanding it. This was that Donna Vincenza was half Piedmontese, and though as we have seen she was Sardinianized to the point of not knowing any other language, that blood, or the admixture of that blood, worked on her willpower and prevented her from not existing. And—what was worse for Don Sebastiano—it was at work in her intelligence, which was superior to that of the ancient, worn-out race of the Sannas and the Sardinians in general. She therefore saw things more clearly, kept her feet on the ground, felt that destiny was in her hands as well, and gave such shrewd and reasonable advice that Don Sebastiano flew into a rage as soon as he heard it, and always did the clean contrary of what she said. The only advantage Don Sebastiano had over Donna Vincenza was power. Shared property or no shared property: these are mere legal figments. Power was the money Don Sebastiano earned in his profession (and with his ability, and the trust he inspired, this was becoming more and more considerable). Without that money Donna Vincenza's intelligence counted for nothing. Even the petty cash was passed to him by ancient custom, so that she had to go to him to beg for small change to cover the most trifling household needs. Not that he begrudged her anything. Had she asked, he would have given her even a thousand lire, almost without bothering to find out why. But beg she must, because the government was in his hands.

It was a small thing, let's admit it. What does it cost one to ask a husband for a few pennies for the housekeeping, which amounted to a little meat, and not even every day at that, since everything else came in from the country or in gifts from clients? But those few pennies were the terrible price she was made to pay, just to admit her own nonexistence, and she would never have stooped to this. He could claim anything but this. Indeed she gave him everything, for not only did she run the house shrewdly and thriftily, but she took loving care of him when he happened to fall ill, and made him broth or milk puddings while he was convalescing. In the early years she had begged him to give her some housekeeping money, but he had answered with a shrug, and said there was no need, that everything was hers in any case. As time went by this clash of wills took on far more serious aspects, as we shall see, for they are a large part of our story. In the meantime Donna Vincenza got by as best she could. At night, when her husband was asleep (for being an early riser he went early to bed), with steps that were light enough, though already slow, she entered his room, leading her youngest son by the hand. There she rummaged in his waistcoat pockets, where in those days men used to keep their silver coins—their small change, in fact.

She was not stealing: it was *her* money, with which life began again each morning. Then she vanished into the silent house. Don Sebastiano did not notice, or pretended not to notice, because she was always careful to leave something. Anyway, with so much to do, Don Sebastiano would not have counted the copper soldi, or even the silver lire.

4

After an interval of some days (for writing is not my trade, and then I have so many small things to do, now that I have been *admis à la retraite,* as the French so kindly put it), I have reread what I jotted down without thinking too deeply, and realized how difficult, if not downright impossible, it is to write a history. In what I have written there is not an untrue word, and it has been really painful to reread it. Yet the true story of Don Sebastiano and Donna Vincenza is not, or not wholly, to be sought in these gloomy pictures. The fact is that between Don Sebastiano and Donna Vincenza, as with every person, obscure or celebrated, there was life itself, and life is never reduced to a portrait or a photograph. Not even movies reproduce life, because even though they move they are nothing but one photograph after another. Now, the lives of Don Sebastiano and Donna Vincenza were not simply their own. They were also the big house in which they lived together, they were the children who inhabited it and the people who went there for a thousand reasons; they were the whole of Nuoro, to which the two of them belonged and which belonged to them, as in some mysterious communion. Perhaps only music in all its abstractness could represent this communion of angels or devils, as the case may be, and perhaps the only true history is the day of judgment, which is not called "universal" for nothing.

The truth is that the family had attained its fulfillment with the birth and growth of seven children, all of them boys. There had been two girls as well: the first (and their firstborn) was so long ago that she was a vague memory, but the other had died recently, and that memory would never, ever fade from Donna Vincenza's mind. She had a vague feeling that among all those males she would come to miss that girl's support. Her daughter would have adored her, would have talked to her, and would not even have married, or at least not until she herself was dead. Instead, the child had gone off just like that, at three years old, without a word, and Donna Vincenza was left with the modest frocks of a little girl of good family, the straw hat with a bow, the little white shoes. She had arranged all those senseless, useless things in the bottom drawer of the cupboard in her room, and she kept them there like little relics. Don Sebastiano had discovered them, and had said nothing. However, he had complained about it to other people, as an eccentricity, something he absolutely failed to understand.

It is a solemn, almost religious moment, when according to the laws of nature the formative cycle of a family comes to an end; or, to put it bluntly, when the wife ceases to bear children. I am speaking, you understand, of the ideal family, of which Don Sebastiano and Donna Vincenza's was a model. That in practice things go differently, and a thousand terrible things occur, as we read in the papers or in novels or see at the cinema, does not concern me. Let everyone do as he sees fit. At the birth of that son who could only be the last, to such an extent that they gave him his father's name and called him Sebastiano, Donna Vincenza and Don Sebastiano took to separate beds. He stayed in the room next door to his office (as we have said, Don Gabriele made the rooms leading one into the other), while she emigrated to the third floor, with two extra flights of stairs to negotiate, and took the room directly above Don Sebastiano's, the only difference being that the one next door, giving onto the staircase, was not an office but a bedroom for two of her sons.

They slept in pairs, according to the elective affinities that form in large communities (and a family of seven sons is already a large community). Sleeping next door to Donna Vincenza at the time I am thinking of were the two youngest, Sebastiano and Peppino, who had four years between them (the girl who died had been born in the middle). Another four slept on the same floor, in the rooms opposite; Pasquale and Ludovico in the first room and Michele and Gaetano in the room off it. The other boy, the eldest, slept alone on the floor below, in the room opposite Don Sebastiano's. He was called Giovanni, like his Piedmontese grandfather (or so they say), and he slept alone partly because the numbers were uneven. Very well, but between him and the youngest there was sixteen years' difference; he was almost a grown man and had some grown-up characteristics that seemed very strange to the others. For example, he was finicky about how his shirts were ironed, and about the untidiness of the house, and he went so far as to criticize his father's country shabbiness. There may have been something behind this that the others did not understand, and that produced in them a mixture of awe and anger. Anyway, that distribution of rooms, that crib-like image we have given of the house, was purely formal.

In fact, in the house which was beginning to belong to the children, even if Don Sebastiano continued to hold the reins just as he held the reins of his horse, everything belonged to everyone and no one. Each one of them, with the possible exception of Giovanni, might try at times to lock himself away, but two seconds later the door was off its hinges. War and peace traded places every minute in that way of living. But these are things that happen in every family. What is important, however, is that the house, slowly and unnoticed, began to wear a new face, the one it was destined to keep for a long time, and the one that would be remembered. It was still the ungainly house built by Don Gabriele, but in the imagination and the actions of the children it was changing. Don Sebastiano had a single ambition: to keep his sons studying. Seven sons, seven university degrees. And for each of them he built a future, as he had built one for himself, in that town of Nuoro, where there was room for everyone. His sons measured up miraculously to his dream, because they were intelligent and worked hard. Don Sebastiano, bent over his pen, kept watch over his dream without intervening, because there was no need to. They all got up early on freezing winter mornings, had a wash outside in the first courtyard, sometimes having to break the ice in the tub, and then ran to school. Donna Vincenza got up even earlier than they did, and heated the milk with the help of the maid, who had been there for countless years, forever in fact, and who took care of the house as if it were her own. And in effect it was, for she was already well on in years and where would she have gone had she not been there? But apart from this, both maidservants and manservants had a feeling of possession toward the houses and places in which they lived, and in any case, people's lives were infinitely closer to one another than they are today. What did Donna Vincenza possess more than Peppedda (this was the maid's name), except for the bunch of keys hanging at her side? Keys that she didn't know what to do with anyway. And as for Don Sebastiano's country servants (Ziu Poddanzu, for example), what did he have that they didn't? Ziu Poddanzu had no idea of what it might be. He lived permanently out at Locoi, and was more of a father to the boys than Don Sebastiano himself, so much so that the youngest ones thought that he was the owner. There was the money, of course, the produce that went to Don Sebastiano while the others only gathered it for him. But what is the meaning of money when everyone suffers the selfsame heat in summer (because it does not even occur to one to take a holiday) and in winter the same cold; when no one travels or buys expensive things, or even eats meat every day? There was the "caste," that's it: that mysterious membership of a caste that one can see in the face and hands, and that one cannot purchase with money, or even with the passing of generations. The country people, who had become the masters of Nuoro because of their vitality, had also become gentry, but they had not infiltrated the caste. The servants saw and felt this dimly, accepting it as a thing that was both right and good. And maybe it was.

The boys had brought books into the house. Let us not speak of Donna Vincenza; but even Don Sebastiano, who was an educated man, had never read a book. His book was the newspaper, and occasionally the *Medicina delle passioni,* which was fashionable at the time and had come into his possession by some unknown means. He would read a few of its yellowed pages from time to time, because it was full of snippets of information that amazed and moved him, which he then poured forth at table to the boys, who would wink at one another. (One example is the story of a big dog, who when attacked by a little whelp had simply lifted its leg and pissed on it.) It was one of those well-meaning books written by learned persons to educate a society they firmly believed to be unshakable, books inspired by a sincere spirit of enlightenment, by an almost religious urge to help people to live, as one who *knows* is honor-bound to help those who do not know. The priests looked askance at them, because they had not been approved by the Church; and they may have been right, for when it comes down to it they were the unconscious heralds of all that bogus knowledge that now swamps the booksellers' windows (which in those days didn't even exist) and arouses the instincts, rather than educating them. But the irony of it is that the books of today do get approved by the sacristy, and as likely as not are written by the priests themselves. Perhaps the trouble today is that everyone can read and write. In any case, Don Sebastiano had never read a real book, for the simple reason that he had never felt the need. Books for him were schoolbooks, to be studied, not read, and he himself had studied them in his time, and with what profit was plain to see.

Whether for his sons or from his sons, Don Sebastiano asked nothing but this: that they should study and more or less repeat his own life, building their own for themselves as he had built his. The trouble was that, like everyone else, he did not know what his life was, or which of the myriad seeds within him, which of course he was unaware of, would begin to germinate in each of his sons. There was, for example, that tenderness and sympathy that he, who was so coarse and almost violent in his active life, felt toward people and things, toward life in general, to the point (as we have seen) of bringing tears to his eyes. Was this not the real Don Sebastiano, or at any rate, might this component not prevail in his offspring? We shall see. In the meantime, his sons were bringing home this novelty, which was books. And each one brought them in his own way.

It was, in fact, the two youngest, Sebastiano and Peppino, who had founded that enormous library of about a hundred books that occupied two shelves of a bookcase set into the wall of a tiny room of about three square meters—the result of Don Gabriele's absurd design and apparently destined for no purpose. The others, already getting quite big, had commitments at school; and some would soon be starting the great exodus toward Sassari, the fabulous city 120 kilometers away (the equivalent of 12,000 kilometers today). For in Nuoro school stopped at fourteen. Of the older boys only Ludovico collected books, but he did it by himself, according to ideas and choices that astonished the two young ones and filled them with awe and respect. Ludovico was already in the senior school, and unlike the others he was delicate in health. This acted as a slight screen between him and life, an unconscious shelter behind which his already complex personality was at work. He was just a young fellow, of course, but he was also, without knowing it, an inveterate invalid, and his illness, partly real and partly imaginary (but intensely worrying to Donna Vincenza), bred in him a scrupulous introspection and gave him a studied judiciousness that created around him an aura of great things to come. He took part in family life, of course, and made himself well loved, for after all, that age has its needs…But at the same time he did not entrust himself to the simplicity of things, which seemed to him, as in fact it is, brutal; but, even though in embryo, he planned his existence, for without a plan it would have had no meaning for him. One might think that he was inclined to take himself very seriously, which was true. But maybe this was merely the result of the seriousness with which he regarded life in general, which he never managed to feel at home with, perhaps because he did not want to, even unconsciously. He was like someone obliged to run a race, who stops to measure the miles before he runs them—and not just the miles but the feet and the inches. When he was still little more than a child, this led him to make judgments, and to give advice, and enabled him to gain ground on his brothers, even the older ones. Don Sebastiano paid no attention to the dangers that might arise from this in the future, and indeed was incapable of imagining them. The important thing was that his delicate son was doing better at school than the others. Naturally enough, because the development of a thesis was right up his alley, since a thesis is a kind of programming, precisely that of a racetrack on which he could measure his steps before taking them.

Now, the books which Ludovico brought home, and kept rigorously separate from those of the others, were not really books so much as the objects of a cult, like everything else. He had a sort of abstract intuition that human knowledge was potentially infinite, that beyond the narrow streets of San Pietro or the low houses of Sèuna there lay the universe, and that this universe lay open before him. This was an extraordinary thing for a boy, at that time and in that place. However, knowledge could not be acquired by groping around with one's hands as blind men do, nor did it proceed from modest, familiar things and then extend outward, like the ripples in a pond. One had to grasp it in its entirety, practically all at once, which could obviously not be done except by methodically arranging all the means to that end, which is to say the books in which knowledge is contained. One had to start with books of grammar, in particular Italian grammar, because that was his own language; then collect dictionaries, and there were so many of them, unfortunately very expensive; then the glossaries of names, instigators of ideas, which were much in use at that time; then Latin grammar, and then Greek; then anthologies, that is, the books read by others, because one had to learn from those who already knew; then a few samples of absolutely incomprehensible things, such as philosophy; then…In a word, his was a genuine encyclopedic calling, which would be fulfilled on the day he was able to read all the books he had collected. Meanwhile, the pages remained uncut, waiting for that day. Sebastiano and Peppino opened them secretly, when Ludovico was at school, and they were dazzled by the words they glimpsed there, and proud that all that wisdom would one day enter the mind of one of their brothers, and in fact had already entered it, simply because he had collected those books.

For those two, the books had crept into the house on the sly, as if the books were seeking them out, rather than the other way around. Perhaps it was love, or perhaps it was a game, if indeed it is possible to tell the two apart. One day Peppino came back with something he could scarcely keep a grip on, his hands trembled so. He was a boy who looked as if he was going to be tall, with a long, slightly irregular face lit up by youthful hope, and by nature he sought out his younger brother, whom he thought of as more lively than himself, even though he was scarcely out of the cradle. On his way back from school he had stopped in front of the tobacconist and newsagent's kiosk (opened by a Sicilian who had turned up from God knows where) at the point at which the

Corso widens out, right on the border of San Pietro. His name was Tortorici, and the children drove him to distraction by calling him Tortorella (turtledove). He conducted the town band, or to put it more exactly he conducted the rehearsals, because with those blockheaded Nuorese, who insisted on seeing sharps and flats where there were none, he had not yet been able to give a public concert. Tortorici saw the world from the little window of his kiosk, and so it was that he noticed a small boy gazing at a little book which had arrived at some unknown date and which he had displayed outside that very morning, along with a handful of schoolbooks. Not even he knew what it might be. It was the *Lives*, by a certain Plutarch, in the Sonzogno Series of cheap classics, which along with the Universal Library and the Popular Library, left its stamp on past generations. "Plutarch" in itself meant nothing; it was a name like any other. It meant nothing to Tortorici, it meant nothing to Peppino, except that it was a different way of meaning nothing. To Tortorici it was unsold stock, while for Peppino it was a mystery. He gazed and gazed at that book with the light-blue cover, without daring to touch it. "Translation from the Greek by Girolamo Pompei," he read. Viewed on the same level, Plutarch and Pompei, along with Sonzogno, and along with Milan where the book had been printed, revealed a world so vast and different that it might well have been infinite. From his little window Tortorici saw no one but the few yokels who bought half a Tuscan cigar or the occasional gentleman who bought a newspaper; and he was not happy with his lot. For this reason he was sometimes given to sudden impulses, which in a sense were protests against life; and that morning he had an incredible one, for when he saw the boy entranced by that old book, he thrust out his bearded face and shouted in his Sardinianized Sicilian: "If you like it, take it!" And this in spite of the fact that he didn't much care for boys, because they made fun of him. But it could be that he had recognized the son of Don Sebastiano, toward whom he had some obligations (and who didn't?). Peppino had grabbed the book as in a trance and run for it, fled down the Corso, climbed the three stories all a-tremble, and now the heads of the two boys, leaning one against the other, were bent over the pages covered with print too dense for them to read. The house was filled with a deep silence.

The Sonzogno Classics had blue covers and cost one lira each; the Universal Library had yellowish covers with a picture of an angel blowing a trumpet, and in a hundred pages at the price of thirty centesimi offered a staggering list of ancient and modern writers already denizens of the Hall of Fame; the Popular Library had black-and-white covers, and its small volumes of not more than fifty pages each contained everything there is to know. They were ten centesimi worth of history, mathematics, philosophy, literature, and everything that might come under the heading— so elastic and so fascinating—of knowledge. Even today there are collections such as these, which are well produced, wide-ranging, and less expensive in view of their size, though I myself would not venture to say in what respects they differ from the Sonzogno Classics, which have vanished into thin air. (However, in an antiquarian bookseller's catalogue yesterday I found a Sonzogno Polybius, an Appian, and a Diogenes at appalling prices: they must all be there in Don Sebastiano's old house.) There is nothing I detest so much as the past; but I must say that today's editions smack of commerce and supermarkets. Perhaps it is the usual trouble: everyone can read these days. Or perhaps…perhaps so that a book may become a book, and be transformed into a dream, perhaps one needs the carpenter, the "master of wood," such as there was then in Nuoro and in all the villages; and in Nuoro he was called Zerominu (Gerolamo), though this may have been a nickname, and at two o'clock in the afternoon on summer days he would lay down his saw and his plane and start playing the cornet; and the sound flowed into the scalding alleyways, crept into the houses, and the whole of life hung on those notes. Even the dogs, stretched out like corpses in what little shade the houses gave, would twitch their tails. In the stuffy room Peppino and Sebastiano would read to the accompaniment of that voice, and they read for the same reason that Zerominu played the cornet, that is, for no reason at all; for people had a little chink through which the mystery entered. Also a mystery were the pink pages they had discovered at the end of the volume, which contained the complete list of the Sonzogno Classics and revealed the wondrous abundance that was life. Was there here perhaps a pinch of that feeling that brought tears to Don Sebastiano's eyes? I think not. In any case, Don Sebastiano was a little worried by these books piling up in the tiny room, which seemed to him to be too many; and he was even more concerned about the youthful industry they had created around the books themselves. For they had learned to make covers for the books with newspaper (taking a sheet, making two oblique cuts to fit the spine, folding in the little flap thus formed, making two further cuts at the corners of the cover, and then folding in the edges on either side); and—an even more marvelous thing—they had learned to bind them. They had built a small sewing bench (where on earth had they seen such a thing?) and for the most part they bound to-gether the booklets of the Popular Library, which were too thin to stand upright on the shelf, in batches of six or seven according to subject. Don Sebastiano thought of all this as a game, and he did not care for games. No such thing as a toy had ever entered his house, except for one or two for the girls who had died; and these had died with them. Luckily he almost never went up to the floor above, and he was becoming less and less aware of what was going on around him.

An absent father in the house is a terrible presence. But on the day of judgment I don't think I could blame Don Sebastiano, or at least I would not blame him altogether. All those things writ-ten about fathers and sons, all those dramas, are just literature as far as I am concerned, and all that famous theorizing is stone-cold fatherhood and nothing more. Don Sebastiano had seven sons, and seven sons are to a father more than to a king are all his people. And his dream of them all achieving university degrees, which incredibly enough seemed possible, because his sons were intelligent, began to come true with the terrible diaspora of the eldest ones. As I think I have said, to go on with their studies they had to face the adventure of the distant city, of Sassari or even Cagliari. For Don Sebastiano this meant sending a hundred lire a month to each son, and for the notary of Nuoro this was a big strain on his resources. It seemed to him that his wealth was now measured by a new yardstick. That a fifteen-year-old boy should he catapulted out of the house and out of the town into a distant city, a real city, where he had neither friends nor contacts, except perhaps for some important notary whom it would not do to disturb; and that arriving there after a day's journey he should have to busy himself finding lodging with some old spinster, and live on a shoestring; that in the course of this impact with the world he might suffer: these were not things that worried Don Sebastiano or even entered his head. Really, this was nothing more than a stage in the great game of his life, a game he was playing without even being aware of it. The grief was all suffered by Donna Vincenza, who saw her sons leaving her bosom, who got up before dawn to prepare provisions for the journey (the things each of them liked, or she thought they liked), and who knew that this was not a beginning but an ending. At Christmas and Easter (the long journey and the expense did not make it possible to come home during the year) she would be sending them those good sweetmeats of sugar and almonds, the *culurjones* of marzipan enveloped in a disc of bread and fried, which she herself made with the help of Peppedda and a few female dependents of the household, who lent a hand in a spirit of devoted and sorrowing friendship. But she felt that when they came home for the long holidays they would no longer be her children.

Donna Vincenza looked with love on the books that her boys collected with love, and that she would never read. Sebastiano, who still used to bounce onto her lap, sometimes wanted to read her a page or two, but first she asked him if they were "true things." This ingenuous question had a profundity of its own, because it was the unconscious rejection of the imagination. In this there was a point of contact with Don Sebastiano, because he also lived on the truth and only the truth, and indeed his whole job was simply to record the truth. But in fact, imagination crept into that austere house by way of the books, and silently it went to work, touching both people and things with its magic wand.

5

B ut if the "little door," as they called the double door that gave almost onto the Corso, was never opened except in answer to the sound of one of the brass knockers (and whoever was knocking could only be one of Don Sebastiano's clients), the "great door" behind the house was always open to the vast breath of the countryside, because it gave onto the *corte*, and through it came the fruits of all that the notary had sown with such skill; and their variety announced the variation of the seasons. And so the house had two faces, one sad and the other joyful, and the inhabitants seemed to have two faces also, even Don Sebastiano, who was prouder of those triumphant arrivals than of his pen, even though it was his pen that earned them for him.

Everything was brought to the house and everything was prepared there, and for this reason around the courtyard there was a series of outbuildings, each named after the particular gift of the soil stored in it: the oil house, the granary, the fruit store; and in addition there was the bake-house, which was like an altar, or an Etruscan tomb, with sieves, riddles, and baskets (*sas canisteddas*) both large and small, woven from palm leaves and hanging on the walls. Women came in from the neighborhood to bake the bread, because it was a big job. They had to knead the dough and roll it out into large round sheets, hand these one by one to the woman sitting at the mouth of the oven, with the corners of her kerchief tied on top of her head, and her face glowing red in the shadows. She laid the sheet of dough on a smooth, flat shovel of the kind made by shepherds in Tonara when they were marooned by snow in winter, which they came down to Nuoro to sell in the spring-time, riding their skinny nags. She then thrust the shovel into the oven, and if it was properly made the dough would swell into an enormous balloon, which was then passed to another woman seated cross-legged at a low bench. She sliced it around the edges with a knife, making a pair of steaming hot discs that gradually hardened, became crisp, and went to build those tall stacks that were later stored away in the sideboard. God only knows from the depths of how many centuries this bread has come down to us. Maybe the Jews brought it when they were driven out of Africa in the ancient of days. The making of it had all the solem-nity of a ritual, partly because the work went on until morning, and the small hours brought a hush with them. The boys would slip in through the narrow doorway, become flushed from the heat, intoxicated by the smell of the bread and glowing mastic wood, entranced by the flickering of the flames over the smoky walls; but they were also a little intimidated by those industrious women who were, after all, servants. The women were glad to see the master's children, and hey presto! in a matter of seconds they prepared a round, ring-shaped loaf, which they quickly im-mersed in water, where it hissed like red-hot iron, and then came out as polished and shiny as a mirror; and in fact they called it "glazed." It was a joyful moment for them and for the boys, who felt that they had all been brought together by that ineffable thing called life, which has no masters.

But I really must restrain these waves of memories rolling in one upon the other in absurd disorder, as if the whole of existence had taken place in a single instant. The most eagerly awaited arrival at the great door was that of the grapes, during the crystal-clear October days. The approach of the carts, lined for the occasion with canvas mats, was mysteriously felt in the house from the very moment they entered the town. Led by swarms of small children, the carts climbed the almost-country road through the "gardens" (those rows of acacias planted by the mayor from the Continent), then struck thunder out of the cobblestones, interrupted only for the width of the Corso, which they had to cross. It was the triumphal moment in their long journey, because the pharmacist, the shopkeepers, and the gentlemen at the caffè all followed with their eyes the slow pace of the oxen, and made a count of the number of carts, and in their heads translated the grapes into liters of wine. That is, they totted up Don Sebastiano's profits. But more than this, what may have been unconsciously at work in those sedentary gentlemen undermined by arteriosclerosis was the message that came to them from the countryside, which was no less distant and unknown for being close by and around them on all sides. The peasant, standing upright on the tailboard of the cart and wholly taken up with his work, goaded the oxen on up the last incline, and that was the moment when the great gates opened wide, in austere expectancy.

On account of the antediluvian construction of the place it was not easy to get in, partly because just inside the threshold the courtyard was nothing but a steep, narrow slope down toward the main house, where it widened out barely enough for them to turn the cart and start work. The peasant went ahead of the oxen, deafening them with his yells and curses. "You're blind! Can't you see where to put your feet?" And maybe the great eyes of oxen truly are blind. Manservants and maidservants alike followed this difficult maneuver with bated breath; then, when at last the turn had been accomplished and the oxen were unyoked and sank in exhaustion, with the cords of the harness still hanging from their backs, everyone besieged the cart and began to unload, as in a well-disciplined ship.

This was the urban sequel to the grape harvest then going on in the vineyard in the valley or on the hilltop. The question of whether to tread the grapes in the country or bring them into town for treading had been talked over at length between Don Sebastiano and Ziu Poddanzu, his trusty alter ego, and the decision was made in favor of the town by a wretched ox that slipped on a rock and spilled a river of grape-must all over the road. From that year on, the right wing of the house had been converted into a wine cellar, with long oaken beams laid down to support the vats and barrels; and the mysterious life of wine began to be a part of the life of the family.

Don Sebastiano, like every other man of his time, knew nothing of the State, because he himself *was* the State. Whatever he did, he did at his own risk, and he did not expect anyone else to pay the bill in whole or in part. So it was with his own money, and not that of the benefits now assured one by the State, that he bought a mechanical grape presser which, to the great astonishment of everyone, put an end to the age-old practice of treading with the feet; just as later, on the threshing floor, he replaced the oxen and the winnowing fan with a brand-new machine. (He did not know that in this way he was working toward his own destruction, in the same way that he was destroying himself by not wanting to recognize his title of nobility, even though it had been earned, as we have said, by the toil of his distant ancestors. And maybe this responsibility for his own actions—upon which, incidentally, all eyes were fixed—was what gave him such a severe expression, and why his world was so withdrawn and isolated.) On top of one of the vats they placed the rollers, which were rotated one against the other by turning a handle, making a din that reached even the most distant rooms. And of course the ones who turned the handle, until they got tired, were the boys.

The making of wine (vinification, as Don Sebastiano called it, using a fancy word that he had learned from catalogues of agricultural machinery) turned the house into something like an enormous cradle. Wine is not like wheat, that heaped up in its barn is like a golden dune, and needs only to be defended from the devilish weevil; nor is it like oil, that, emerging from the night-working millstones and the presses, sleeps quietly in great oil jars old as time. Crushed by the rollers, the bunches pile up at the bottom of the vat, with their stalks and their innocent juice, rise slowly toward the rim, and there they lie, pouring out their perfume, which is still the perfume of flowers or of fruit. But in that many-colored mass there is a hidden god, for not many hours will pass before a liquid purple fringe will appear all around the edge, and then the mass will heave up as if taking a giant breath, and will lose its innocence, and a low gurgling sound will betray the fire that is devouring it. An earthy odor, like the one the soil breathes forth after the first rains, will rise from its very bowels, and during those days this will be the odor of the house, of the courtyard, of all the neighboring streets;

and maybe it will reach the sky. Everything happens at night, because both life and death are daughters of night, and the boys will be asleep. But Don Sebastiano will not sleep, and neither will Ziu Poddanzu, who will have taken up residence in the house; for they know that in this mysterious birth every hour is vital. And it will be Ziu Poddanzu who at a certain point (and only he knows it) will catch Don Sebastiano's eye, and this means that the moment has come.

Warm and murky, the new wine gushes from the vat, as from a deep wound, as soon as the expert hand of Ziu Poddanzu removes the cork bung that holds that sea in check. The barrels sleeping on their trestles receive the liquid, which will fill them to the brim, while the many-colored mass loses its vividness, falls gradually toward the bottom, and is reduced to nothing. But the barrels are not inert things; they are not like oil jars. When they receive the must, they know they are harboring a living thing, a thing that will feel imprisoned and will press outward against the staves, trying to break them, seeking an outlet at the bunghole, like lava in a volcano. For this reason the barrels are bound with great iron hoops, and for this reason also, now that all is over, Ziu Poddanzu performs one last rite. Into the big hole at the top he inserts some weird tin contraptions which are immersed at one end in the liquid and at the other in a basin full of water. The whole volcano is reduced to a breath that passes out through a narrow tube and is dissolved in the water. The water breaks out into a hundred little bubbles which rhythmically swell and burst, with a sound like a sob or a song. The cellar, the barrels, the wine, can now be left to themselves. But during the night, when Don Sebastiano is asleep, the youngest boys creep down half-dressed, go into the dark cellar and stay there for hours, listening to that song which they may well carry with them all their lives.

The wine will be born when the last bubble has burst and Ziu Poddanzu has taken away the basins, which will be used another year, and sealed up the bungholes. The broken-in colt will lie in silence there, waiting to take his revenge on the brains and arteries and livers of the men of Nuoro, who will form long, solemn queues in the taverns that sell Don Sebastiano's wine, unless they come to fetch it directly from the cellar, bearing bottles great and small, because it is the best wine in Nuoro.

But the grape harvest is not over, for when he built the house Don Sebastiano put up a pergola along the various windings of the courtyard, all the way to that accursed oleander in the little kitchen garden, and from this pergola there hung great stalactites of bunches, waiting to be plucked. Pergola grapes (the fact is proverbial) are a very different matter from vineyard grapes. They have the frigid beauty of alabaster, and neither taste nor fragrance. The very wasps disdain them, because they have never seen the sun. Yet Don Sebastiano cared for the pergola very lovingly, pruning it as only he knew how, thinning out the long, long shoots that rested on canes; for if those grapes did not produce wine, they nonetheless had another important function; and this was that when the harvest was over they were useful for "sharing around," as they used to say; in other words, to show them off to one's friends. If the truth be told, Don Sebastiano had no friends—no one in Nuoro had friends—but it was the custom that anyone who possessed things was obliged to give, if only to show that he possessed them, and it might even be that there was in this an echo of a very remote agricultural or pastoral community. Surrounded by the boys, Don Sebastiano in person clambered up a stepladder, terrifying Donna Vincenza, and cut off the bunches, laying them gently in the baskets which the boys jostled one another to hold up to him with outstretched arms, the littlest ones climbing up the legs of the others as best they could.

The end of the wine harvest restored the house to its solitude. The odor of must hung about the stairs and the entrance hall for a long time to come, but it was as if everyone returned to his place with the onset of winter, which in Nuoro comes early and is often bitter. The house now seemed to rest on that recent harvest, as if it had risen another rung on the ladder to wealth; but no one felt rich. Apart from everything else, Don Sebastiano would not have allowed anyone to feel rich, even himself. The cemetery was rich. This was the feeling that every Sardinian bore in the bottom of his heart, and it was the answer Don Sebastiano gave whenever anyone, even as a compliment, pointed out that he was a rich man. This institution of poverty bound the father to the children and the children to one another, and determined their existence. For poverty creates around itself an aura of poetry, but it erects a barrier against the world, which is rich by nature. The Sannas in fact, the old Sannas, were afraid of living. They were not like those mercenaries who came to Nuoro from the impoverished villages to make themselves masters of it with official documents, or like the predators of San Pietro, who little by little were making their thievery legal.

Perhaps this was why Don Sebastiano had never allowed his sons to get involved, as he was, with agriculture. It could also be that subconsciously he was covetous of his skill, but in the depths of his soul he distrusted property and had no love of the land as such, which he thought of as a transient thing, for all its pathetic fences. It is called "immovable property," but he had seen it pass from hand to hand through his notarial deeds, when it did not pass by the grimmer route of the wake and the wax candles. This man of ancient mold, who had put every penny that came from his pen into houses and fields, and if need be would have defended his own with tooth and nail, had some strange foresights: he was afraid lest any of his sons develop a feeling for being a landowner, to the detriment of work, of earning his own bread and butter. He knew that all he had done, and was proud of having done, would die with him, even though unknowingly he did not want this. This state of mind, which may have had an ancestral background of nomadism, was reflected in the house, which for all its respectability remained as bare as a mud hut, populated only by the lives he had put in it, more to suffer it than to enjoy.

But the countryside, discounted as wealth, entered into his children as poetry, which is also a kind of riches, and more dangerous. On summer afternoons Don Sebastiano would mount his horse and ride down to his beloved Isporòsile, the great undertaking of his life, the land he had wrenched from the fury of a stream that fell unrestrained from the Mountain towering above. There was an unspoken war between him and this stream, which in summertime showed its bleaching bones among the brambles, but in winter revealed its true demonic face, tearing boulders from the mountainside and hurling them against the walls that Don Sebastiano had built to protect his garden, rebuilding them thicker and thicker.

With immense labor he had managed to cheat that stream of the little water that survived underground in the season when the sun brings nothing but fire and death. Through a long channel he had led it first into a cistern where one went to drink out of a cork cup (though the water was very heavy), and then into a pond that supplied the terraced vegetable gardens falling almost perpendicularly until they reached an ancient pomegranate tree, which marked the end of the property. No one picked the fruits that broke open on that tree like laughing mouths. Don Sebastiano had better things to do than care about that note of poetry in the midst of his good vegetables. Every day there was a new one ripe, for the leathery sharecropping peasant devoured by malaria knew only how to water the soil with his sweat. He too was in this world only because there was room for him.

Toward evening, when the shadow of the Mountain spread across the landscape, the ritual of departure took place. Into each pouch of the saddlebag the farmhand put a wicker basket full of grapes or figs, apples or pears, and, overflowing on top of that, lettuce or fennel or celery, the trophies of that interminable battle. Then, back in the saddle, Don Sebastiano would retrace his way up the road, the road of his life. His horse, well trained and thinking of its manger, forded the little torrent upstream, and then, in the sunset, from every gateway along the road came other horses and other farmers, and they all rode along with Don Sebastiano, and in their quiet exchanges of conversation each one appeared to be accounting to God for his day's work. They formed a small procession, riding shoulder to shoulder as far as the drinking trough at the entrance to Nuoro, and then breaking up into a thousand rivulets, without a good-night, each one making for home, the horses finding their way without a touch on the reins, while their hoofs struck sparks in the darkness.

The boys often used to go down to Isporòsile on foot, because the valley grapes were tastier and the figs dripped honey; and then there was the pond, which took the place of the fabled sea, unattainable because it was over twenty kilometers away and Don Sebastiano was unable to imagine any respite in life, for himself or anyone else. But their favorite spot was Locoi, the hilltop vineyard that Don Sebastiano had left in the care of Ziu Poddanzu, because it was already a going concern. It formed a huge rectangle, almost a perfect square of vines amid the sterile allotments of his neighbors, and was overlooked by a *nuraghe* in which in the course of two thousand years an oak tree had grown. Don Sebastiano had planted the vineyard with his own hands, meaning that he "owned" the hands of the hundred laborers who dug the deep foundations of the protecting wall, under the command of Ziu Poddanzu. (However, in those days there was not one man to command and many to obey, for each man knew his own place and kept to it.) His was their sweat, his was their resignation. In the midst of that desert, in the course of a few years, an oasis of green had been created, the first sign of life for anyone arriving at Nuoro from Orune or Bitti; an oasis that put an end to the nightmare of solitude. The wine from Locoi was clear and light, and went down one's throat like a cooling stream. The whole of Nuoro waited for it, because it was more thirst-quenching than any other wine. The only man who scarcely tasted it was Don Sebastiano himself. The year of the phylloxera* was a year of mourning, of perpetual mourning,

---

* Phylloxera is a disease, originating in America, which killed all the vines in Europe during the second half of the nineteenth century. All vines are now grafted onto American stock, because some of these proved immune to the disease.

because, as everyone said, with the American vinestocks the wine was never the same again.

Locoi was only a rifle-shot outside the town, approached by a broad road that wound up many curves, from which one could see the Mountain and the dark valley of Marreri below, with Montalbo in the background, outlined against a sky that already made one dream of the sea. Don Sebastiano would ride up that road, clad like a shepherd in his sheepskin jacket, nothing more than a fact of nature. But the boy's went on foot, and in that heady air, in that sweet yet awe-inspiring place, in that infinite silence, unwittingly they felt the touch of poetry. Dreams raced at a gallop over those barren uplands, and caught hold of the boys, and snatched them away from Don Sebastiano. A terrible thing for those forced to live in the real world, which does not allow for the dimension of poetry. The youngest of the boys would one day realize this, when he had left the town, and the landscape, and Locoi, and felt himself still bound to them, among people who had never seen those things, and therefore were unable to understand him. But anyway, after the last curve the road flowed happily out onto the plateau, beneath the brightest of skies, and the vineyard was already in view, with its green or its gold, according to the season, or in the winter with its nullity, for in the winter a vineyard is reduced to nothing at all.

You entered the vineyard through one of those massive gates constructed, like the carts, of oak timbers running crosswise and diagonally, and bearing the antediluvian name of *jacas*. The vineyard was protected by high dry-stone walls, largely overrun with brambles, which in the midst of that desolate landscape gave it the appearance of a fortress. But inside, as soon as you were past the *jaca*, it had all the warmth of an earthly paradise. The vineyard stretched out like a great open book, and because a robust wine was demanded from the soil, the plants were kept low, with no more support than a slender cane to which the shoots were tied, and in rows so wide apart that it seemed a waste of space. A large red house, a really impressive structure, rose in the middle, surrounded by an ample clearing, and here Don Sebastiano had had his moment of inspiration, for along with the first vine he had planted a pine tree, and this pine had grown like a giant, giving shade (alas) even to a few of the vines, which wasted away and died. But they could not cut the pine down, for it had become almost a coat of arms. The boys used to clamber like cats up the rough trunk and relax in the breeze, which was always there in the topmost branches, even when the vineyard around it was dead-still and scorching in the sun. Anyway, if the pine tree was the one and only pine tree, and lived its life in solitude, the impassive witness of men and events, the vineyard also had other trees: the figs, with their skeletal branches, which gave forth fruit, either yellow or black, twice a year. They spread along the overgrown paths on the edge of the vineyard, but Don Sebastiano did not take them seriously. In his austerity he could not conceive of a fig as it emerges from night all pearled with dew, or what it becomes as the day goes on, when the sun begins to enter the flesh of it and dwells there until dark begins to fall. This is the real, true fig. The bees know this as they buzz around the drop of honey that oozes, as though from a superabundance of life, from that mysterious little hole; the blackbirds know it as they choose the figs one by one; the boys knew it, when they were out of school, for they would often dare the blaze of noon to fill their mouths with those drops of fire, without peeling them.

In the clearing shaded by the pine, as I have said, stood the red house, which really was nothing more than a vat room (in the days when the wine was still made out in the country), a kitchen with the fireplace in the middle, a stall for two oxen, and—this was something prodigious—a perfectly useless room, intended for the proprietor to rest in, and that needless to say was full of equipment and of figs laid out to dry. But it retained something of the destiny imagined for it (maybe because it had whitewashed walls), for Ziu Poddanzu never went into that room, or if he was forced to do so he was always careful to relock the door.

Ziu Poddanzu was not his real name, of course; that is, the name that would be painstakingly hunted for in the records when he died. But it would be as Ziu Poddanzu, and as no other, that he would meet his maker. He lived at Locoi, even though he owned one of the little houses in Sèuna: his wife and daughters lived there, and worked as servants for Donna Vincenza. When Don Sebastiano had first set eyes on the waste ground that was destined to become the vineyard, perhaps he had found him already there within it, and had built walls and plowed and planted all around him. He was not a servant and he was not a foreman. He was a rustic Don Sebastiano, he was Locoi, and he was everything that the notary had brought into being. I do not think that there were even any money dealings between him and Don Sebastiano. They were born together, had grown up together, and were growing old together. They did not call each other by the familiar tu, because this would first and foremost have displeased Ziu Poddanzu, but Don Sebastiano was godfather to his daughters, and therefore from *bostè* (the polite form in Sardinian) they passed to *voi*, which was the happy medium. Between them there was neither command nor obedience, but a single common will, in the sense that what Don Sebastiano wanted had to be filtered through what Ziu Poddanzu wanted, or it was worse than useless. When Locoi was all Don Sebastiano had, and he went there every day astride his pony, Ziu Poddanzu would wait for him at the gate and help him to dismount. Then, side by side, they would walk up the rows of vines, while Ziu Poddanzu, who knew each single plant, would point out the day's developments, for each day there was something new. On one occasion he had found an early-ripening vine all dry and shriveled, and in showing it to Don Sebastiano he had explained that it had been touched by "the tip of a rainbow." Don Sebastiano listened, without smiling.

As evening came on, weary and beaded with sweat they would sit in the clearing amid the pungent aromas of wild thyme and cistus. The "rustic" Don Sebastiano, with his kindly face and his noble beard, which was beginning to whiten, would light half a Tuscan cigar, which his employer never failed to bring him; though even more he liked to chew the leaves with the few teeth he had left. Don Sebastiano did not smoke; instead, he drank a glass of water from the well, which was always very cold and clear. And their lives, past, present, and future, flowed out in their ancient tongue, which in their children already betrayed the contamination of time.

Now Don Sebastiano had migrated toward other dreams, toward the warm lands in the valley, and Ziu Poddanzu, even if he guided his footsteps from afar, was left alone at Locoi. Donna Vincenza had a liking for Poddanzu, as she called him, and gave him a warm welcome and a glass of wine on the rare occasions when he came to the house with cap in hand. But in her heart she had a small grudge against him, because (as she would say) he breathed all that fresh air. In the absence of Don Sebastiano the boys had been left as masters of the vineyard and the clearing, and their mythical Ziu Poddanzu received them as young masters, but made them realize the limits of their proprietorship. For example, he did not allow them to pick single grapes from the bunches, leaving them disfigured, and would have preferred them to ask him for the grapes, firstly so that when he saw the vines cut he would not suspect some thief or some stranger, and secondly because in that uniform jungle of vine leaves he knew where to find the muscatel plants, and other grapes not used for wine. The boys accepted everything, because the old man had been there so much longer than they had, and they had been brought up to think of themselves as poor. And then, and then…It was not true that Ziu Poddanzu had spent all his life at Locoi, like a clod of earth. In his youth, before Italy was Italy, they had made him do military service and sent him to distant worlds, to places called Narni, Amelia, and Camerino, which were goodness knows where. But it was the world itself that filtered through those names of his into their enchanted imaginations. Now that I come to think of it, and I have looked at the map, to get to those places Ziu Poddanzu must have passed through Rome, but he can't have realized it, because the boys never heard him mention it. Narni, Amelia, and Camerino, on the other hand, had filled his life, and he would talk about them when evening came to the clearing, and the sun marked the end of another day. He remembered the terrible cold in those places.

While out on a day pass on one occasion he had seen some strange, enormous birds in the trees, like balls of wool. "What the devil are they?" he had been asked by another soldier, also a Sardinian. "We don't have them in our parts." And they were only sparrows, sparrows just like ours, all puffed out against the cold!

But this was Ziu Poddanzu's frivolous life, just as the pine tree, the clearing, the vines, the chats, were the frivolous, or at least the superficial, life of the vineyard. In that rectangle of land, above that rectangle of land, beneath that rectangle of land scarcely bigger than a handkerchief, mysterious things happened, perhaps the invisible things we read about in the Creed; or at least tokens of them. In the perfectly limpid sky, when everything was calm, a cloud of starlings suddenly appeared out of nowhere, hovered for an instant, then vanished back into nowhere. The mongrel dog, which Ziu Poddanzu talked to as if it were human, once near the hedge found a hare with young, and the dog, instead of behaving like a dog, began to lick the young hares, which wriggled with delight. A grass snake had crossed the clearing and dragged its slow length all the way to Ziu Poddanzu's feet, and stayed there staring at him, with its shiny little head, darting its tongue out in rapid signals. From the depths of their hiding places the crickets communicated with the stars. And one afternoon in August (to this I can myself bear witness), while all around was silent, with not a leaf moving, and the sun-chariot high above the vineyard, Ziu Poddanzu and the boys were in the stall spreading straw for the two oxen which were grazing in a paddock some way off, when they saw their heads appear through the half-door, like two enormous, sad beggars. Ziu Poddanzu was staggered.

Quickly, quickly! He let the animals in, barred the doors and windows, and began to wait. Half an hour later the devil lashed at the landscape, uprooted twenty or thirty trees, and carried sheep and dogs hunting for shelter up into the air. Ziu Poddanzu then reopened the doors, and everything was as before.

This was the hidden life of Locoi, the pagan mystery of nature that accompanies the Christian mystery: the oxen, the asses, the sheep, the kings led by a star gathered around the cradle of a child fated to die. In Don Sebastiano's house they made no Christmas crib, as no one paid attention to these follies, and in fact they were not great believers, even if Don Sebastiano was never missing on the last day of the year at the *Te Deum* in the cathedral, and Donna Vincenza, in her blackest moments of solitude, would tell her beads and utter distrait prayers. But without knowing it the boys found the crib in that vineyard, and that rectangle of earth, with its people, its buildings, its myth, opened their hearts to mystery. If Don Sebastiano had been able to imagine such a thing, maybe he would not have planted the vineyard.

6

The ring which Donna Vincenza, in spite of her troubles and fits of rage against Don Sebastiano, still wore on her finger bore the date May 5 1883 engraved on the inside. This was the date of the birth of the new family (called the Sanna-Vugliè, according to custom), and Donna Vincenza had brought to this family little or nothing apart from herself: the memory, faded by time, of a father who was an outsider and practically a foreigner, and a Sardinian mother, Signora Nicolosa, clad in the costume of eternal mourning for a husband who had died more than twenty years earlier. (God alone knows, of course, what she brought in terms of the world of the invisible.) After a while, with the growth of his fortune, Don Sebastiano had taken his mother-in-law into the house, and there she had lived long years, conscious of being an outsider, and therefore an impassive witness of her son-in-law's cruelty toward her daughter during the birth and growth of her grandchildren. In any case, if Don Sebastiano had been the sort of man to allow his wishes to be questioned, she would have taken his side.

Late one May evening, when the house was swathed in silence, Peppedda the maid took the hand of the youngest of the boys, Sebastiano, who was not yet six years old, and led him furtively up the stairs to the top floor. In one of those small inner rooms there was something large laid out on a bed, with four big candles around it. The darkening sky entered through the wide-open window, and magnified the scene. The maid knelt down and told the child to do likewise; he did not know what had happened, because he knew nothing of death. He would think of it many years later, and it could even have been a far-off dream. As usual, there remained no trace of Signora Nicolosa, not even the memory. Or rather, there remained a large portrait of her, painted who knows when or by whom, but this was immediately buried in an old cupboard and no one set eyes on it again.

Don Sebastiano, on the other hand, carried with him the gloomy presence of the family to which he belonged, those Sanna Carboni from which he had sprung, who had their progenitor in Don Ludovico, the first of that name, and the husband of the Carboni woman who also had vanished into nothingness. Don Ludovico was still alive, and was destined to live—or to survive—until the age of ninety-four, when he went quietly to sleep on a bench in the garden of his house at Santa Maria. His youngest grandchildren, Peppino and Sebastiano, in their pristine innocence, used to go to visit him from time to time. His house was on one floor, and on one side it rested directly on a great boulder, which is the cheapest way of laying foundations. I think it dated back to the times of Monsignor Roich, because the front was covered with moss, and in short it was little more than a hovel. But at a corner near the faded red door there was still the ring to which the judge of the Royal Assizes used to tie his horse when he came up from Cagliari—a sign that this was the most important house in town. When he recognized the timid knocking of the boys, Don Ludovico would open the door from his armchair by pulling at a bit of cord, and they would clamber up the sacred stair that led directly into the main room. The floorboards at a slight slope, the doors that swung shut by themselves, time measured by the bells of the church that loomed above, the dominion of shadows in which moved a large white blotch, which was Grandfather's beard... Tall and bony, with his hat on even in the house, he did not say much to the boys, but he went with firm steps to the chest of drawers, pulled open a drawer full of those reddish, slightly wrinkled berries which I think are the fruit of the jujube tree, and stuffed his grandsons' pockets with them. Don Ludovico was a landowner on a small scale and had an estate called Sa 'e Masu, between Nuoro and Orgòsolo. There, at the top of the hill, he had planted this wonderful tree, the only one in the district, and everyone remarked on it. The berries are fruits only in a manner of speaking, and in fact are nothing but skin and pips, rather like those of the arbutus, which at least are wild. But the old man and the children communicated by means of those berries, and the tree was a coat of arms like the pine at Locoi. When Don Ludovico died, and Don Sebastiano came into the property, he decided that this was a useless tree; and he had it cut down.

I think I already mentioned that Don Ludovico had fathered quite a number of sons, and it is here that the mystery begins. For these sons were all alive and all getting on in age, and though when he married Don Sebastiano seemed to have said, "Enough of all that," though they were ignored in his family and not a word was said about them, one could not erase them from the face of the earth, and in fact this silence made their presence more felt than ever. The boys did a lot of whispering among themselves, feeling that there was a shady something in their father's clear, unblemished life, but they got nowhere, and each of them had to carry it as a secret to the grave. It was useless to ask Donna Vincenza, who knew less than they did about "those Sannas," as she called them.

The one known fact was this: Don Ludovico's eldest son, Zio Matteo, when he was twenty years old, when others are scarcely more than children, had left the house one morning, and when he got as far as Montelongu, where the road falls away toward Orosei and the sea, had turned back toward Nuoro, made the sign of the cross in the air, and said, "Goodbye, Nuoro, you'll never see me again." From that moment on, he had become a ghost. It was not that he had had a spirit of adventure and had begun roving around the world. They said he had joined the carabinieri, and in the course of time had been sent to Samughèo, an obscure village near (I think) Oristano, and there he had stayed, taken a wife, and had children. It was certain that he lived there, but the point is that after the day of his departure seventy-five years were destined to pass (for he lived to be ninety-five), and for seventy-five years he kept his word. His father, his mother, his brothers, and his nephews died off, but he never showed his face. Toward the end of his life—so many things had happened, including the two great wars and the Russian Revolution, which had its repercussions even in Sardinia—one of Don Sebastiano's older sons, Gaetano, who was also getting on in years, happened by chance to be at Samughèo (the miracle of the motorcar) and was curious to meet his phantom uncle. He saw approaching him an old man with an enormous beard, frighteningly like his grandfather, who appeared glad to welcome this first comer among the new generation of Sannas. Zio Priamo, Don Sebastiano's brother, had recently died, and Gaetano was unwary enough as to mention him with respect. A spark came into the old man's eyes, already slightly dimmed by cataract. "Gaetà," he said, "you've come here to pull my leg. Priamo is in hell, and there he is waiting to be joined by his wife Franceschina."

This hatred locked up in a heart for seventy years could find no expression but in silence; that is, in the most terrible way of fuelling it, because it renders it futile. But it hovered around the house, goaded the imagination of the boys, and cast a shadow of mystery over the house of Sanna, and therefore over their father. In all families, if one goes back far enough, one finds someone who is a blot on the escutcheon. But the dead are dead, and death confers a kind of respectability even on the worst scoundrels. The old Sannas were all alive, and they were all solid folk; as far as was known not a soul had anything to say against them. If there was something wrong it was in their own hearts, for in that tiny town they lived in isolation, as far from one another as are the stars. And then, what wrong could have been committed against someone at the age of twenty to make him reject a society, a father, a mother, a home, and in the last resort himself? The mystery thickened. Unless at twenty years old—an age at which the new Sannas were little more than children, dominated by that instinct for poverty for which their father set the example—the old generation were already vigilant enemies, aware that the model for brotherhood is Cain and Abel, and already counting the stones which one day would divide them. Everything is possible, though later on there must have been other things to put even more tangles into that nest of vipers—and over these also hung a funereal pall of silence.

There was, just for a start, the enigma of Zio Goffredo. The boys knew him because they saw him in the street from time to time. Never had he crossed the threshold of their house, either because he didn't want to or because he had been turned away. He was a tall, strongly built man, and his face had a stupefied expression, quite untypical of the old Sannas. Behind him he had an obscure history of financial difficulties, that had completely estranged the family from him, and all the more so because he had earlier had a period of great prosperity. It seems that he had devoted himself to the accursed products of the Sardinian soil. But nothing was known for sure. Don Sebastiano and Don Priamo (the other brother, Don Domenico, counted for nothing—he was one of those innumerable provincial lawyers who live off procedure) simply ignored him. Don Goffredo in his prime had also fathered a number of children, who were intelligent and hard-working, and side by side with Don Sebastiano's sons they would have formed another branch of the Sannas—the poor relations, of course, but one never knows what life holds in store... One by one these children died of consumption and their uncles did not even notice. Don Sebastiano's boys accepted all this naturally, because they were embedded in history and could not but be at one with their history. But in the evening (especially the two youngest, who slept in the same room), they would talk for a long time, in low voices, and the sense of the enigma of life entered into them. Or else, which is the same thing, the incomprehensible sense of evil.

To complicate matters, there was also Don Priamo, whom we have already met as the mayor of Nuoro, in the famous affair of the street lighting which certain witless councillors had wished to limit to moonless nights, and the very one whom Don Matteo had for his part consigned to hell. Zio Priamo was the only one who had kept up relations with Don Sebastiano, if one can call them relations. Of all the brothers, he was the only one who had been faithful to tradition. He was born in the little house in Santa Maria, ennobled by the presence of Don Ludovico, and in the house at Santa Maria he was destined to die. He had seen the other brothers leave home one by one, and had paid no heed. He stayed on with his father, and one being a widower and the other a bachelor, they supported each other, not with love but by combining their two solitudes. He looked after his father's interests, of course, for they were also his own interests, and nearly every day he rode down to the little farms with strange names, that had come into the family who knows how, who knows from whom. But he was not like Don Sebastiano, who created his cultivated land and made a business of it. He merely looked after "his own" like a proper landowner, and therefore he was infinitely more down-to-earth than Don Sebastiano. On the whole he succeeded in doing nothing without being idle, and this had gained him that reputation for wisdom which had taken him for a while to the town hall. When, many years later, he found he had a hernia, he stopped going into the country; but this did not alter his life—he continued to do nothing, only he did it with more commitment than before.

He was tall and thin and always dressed in black (if indeed it was not the same suit, worn for thirty years), and when his beard became long and flowing he was well on the way to being a repetition of his father. In the dark rooms the two old men (for Don Priamo also was already well on in years) rarely met, and even then only to talk business. The son respectfully addressed his father as *lei*, but this did not prevent him from imposing his will when need be. Thus, when the insignificant lawyer Don Domenico conceived the notion of marrying a certain woman (a senseless thing, rather than a *mésalliance*), Don Ludovico was annoyed, and said to Don Priamo, "I've got to tell him he mustn't do it." "You won't tell him anything," replied Don Priamo. "Isn't he old enough to know his own mind?" And that was that. There was in this an unconscious philosophy, or more simply, a rule of life: Everyone has to make his own mistakes. A very just and terrible rule, which took it for granted that communication was impossible.

Then it was his turn. He had already reached fifty and the idea of marriage had never entered his head. Womankind had no place in the strict commitment of life. The women whom he saw around him were farmers' wives, or grape harvesters, or olive pickers, and as such he viewed them. In town he had no connections of any kind. On his rare outings, the only house he visited was that of Canon Murtas, an old priest who had come from Olzai (one of the villages that center on Nuoro), and who lived in a little house near the Corso with his decrepit mother and a niece of mature years named Franceschina. Franceschina was unmarried, but not what one would call a spinster. A spinster is a woman rejected by love, and love had had no more dealings with her than it had had with Don Priamo. She had simply stayed as she was, in the same way as so many others had got married: that is, secure in her uncle the priest, the old granny, and herself. Above all in herself, because within her tranquil horizons, and perhaps merely because there was a priest in the house, she felt the eternity of her journey through this life, and of every such journey, and the eternity of the little things one does, preparing lunch or dinner, knitting, or conversing on the sofa in the sitting room, with the Madonna and saints under their glass bells. And those who are eternal do not marry. Almost every day for at least twenty years Don Priamo entered that eternity. He came down at dusk from Santa Maria and went and sat on that sofa, immersing himself in those silent colloquies. He was the only acquaintance she had, and he was always welcome, because he was of good family and, when asked for it, would give good advice. Both he and Canon Murtas took snuff, and they exchanged pinches of it from mother-of-pearl snuff boxes.

Now (and this was told twenty years later by Don Priamo himself to his youngest nephew, one winter evening by the fireside), during one of the countless days spent in the house at Santa Maria, Don Priamo happened to look at his father, who had fallen asleep while eating, and he realized that Don Ludovico was an old man. He was already over eighty. One thing then seemed to him abundantly clear: that his father might die. And if his father died he would be left completely alone, at the mercy of a maid, and he himself so advanced in years. That solitude frightened him. Whereupon he picked up his hat (which had retained the shape it had when it came from the hatter's, with a small dent on one side) and crossed the threshold of the canon's house. It was a day exactly like any other. The canon was not yet home, and Franceschina was waiting for him, seated on the sofa. On that occasion Don Priamo did not sit down, but turning toward her he said, "I am here to ask if you wish to come to my house, to be mistress of it." Then, without giving her time to recover: "I add one thing. Don't answer at once. And if you say no, don't think I'll take it badly. We will remain friends as before." And he went off home, without so much as a goodbye.

Franceschina must have said yes, because now there were three of them in the house at Santa Maria. Nothing was changed, either within her or without; only that she now said "Priamo" to the man whom she had looked up to for twenty years, and who had made her into Donna Franceschina, a title somewhat at variance with the country dialect that she had never managed to replace with the austere parlance of Nuoro. No marriage was ever happier, for all Franceschina did was extend her own confidence to her conjugal relationship. No children came, but this did not matter. Neither of them felt the need to perpetuate themselves, because neither had a sense of his own incompleteness. As for the property, there was plenty of time to think about it, and even that was merely part of their existence, about which they were quietly confident. The change that had come into Don Priamo's life was that in the evening, when he was due to return on horseback from the country, Franceschina would stand at the white-framed window no bigger than a loophole, and wait for her husband. Don Priamo would see her from afar off, and the shadow of a smile would light up his dark, almond-shaped eyes. The Nuorese had noticed all this, and used to leave their homes to witness the scene.

Don Priamo's smile was not ridiculous. It was the symbol of the infinite that entered into that finite conjugal communion, made up of little daily tasks, of modest accomplishments, so perfect that it had no need even of God. The bells of the church looming above rang out the passing hours in vain: in the house of Priamo and Franceschina time did not pass at all. The only novelty was that, in marrying Franceschina, Don Priamo had discovered space, because he had been obliged for the first time to venture outside Nuoro, to Olzai, to meet his wife's relatives. It was twenty kilometers on horseback, an undertaking never to be repeated. Franceschina had a few little bits of property in her village, but he was to administer them scrupulously without having to budge. The tenants themselves would come at the proper time, with money for the rent; and in their saddlebags they carried cheeses that smelled of mint and myrtle. If occasion arose, they too would ask Don Priamo for good advice.

And this same Don Priamo had been consigned by his brother Matteo to hell, in the expectation that Franceschina would join him.

7

I have been, in secret, to visit the Nuoro cemetery. I arrived early in the morning, wishing to see no one and not to be seen. I got out at Montelongu, the point where Nuoro in my day began and ended, on the edge of San Pietro, and I started off along the little streets of my long-lost childhood. In spite of the efforts of recent administrations, the traces of them still remain in the low houses, with a few dusty relics of pergolas, a few neglected courtyards. They have given names to the streets. These are written in blue on white ceramic plaques with a thin blue line around the edge, and are the names of forgotten splendors—Canon Fele must have had a hand in this business. I am sure that Don Priamo would have disapproved of them. "What do you need plaques for," he would have told the council in memorable words, "when everyone knows where they have to go?" And he would have been right, for in fact most of them, now chipped and cracked, have been used as targets by boys who have made them illegible. The rivulet of sky above the streets is slashed across by the electric wires, forever in a tangle.

Electric light came to Nuoro incredibly early on. Someone back from the Continent talked about these cities that suddenly came alight, of lamps that went on of their own accord: not one here, another there, but all at once, as if from San Pietro to Sèuna.

But this was just talk. Maestro Ferdinando, who was called "maestro" because he was a builder, but who had taken on the task of lighting the oil lamps every evening, went on with his task. He was a tall, thin man, and wore local costume, in spite of the fact that because of his trade he was somewhat townified. The streetlights were like iron urns, with long brackets embedded in the corners of the houses, and they had a massive elegance all their own. When the first star appeared, Maestro Ferdinando picked up the tall, tall ladder that in the daytime lay on its side against the red wall of his house, and started on his rounds with it over his shoulder. The children ran along with him, all wrapped up in that solemn public ceremony; and not just the barefoot children of the poor, but also those of the rich, with their shoes hobnailed to preserve the soles. Maestro Ferdinando, without looking around, hoisted the ladder and leaned it against the lamp bracket, opened the little glass door, struck a wooden match on the iron, then let it fall. This was what the children were waiting for, because they hurled themselves with shouts upon the useless prey, of which all of them had a collection. The one who amassed more than anyone else, because he was the nimblest, was Don Sebastiano's youngest, who took them to Donna Vincenza and asked her to keep them safe for him.

Donna Vincenza kept her son's burned-out matches in the big sideboard set into the wall—the keys of which were in the bunch attached to her belt—along with the small change left her by Don Sebastiano. In her ignorance she knew what Don Sebastiano, for all his studies, could not have understood: that is, that behind those dead things there was immense life, an endless world of love, far more than behind any toy, if such a thing as a toy could be conceived of in Don Sebastiano's house. There was the idea of an earth, the earth that for us is dry and miserly, abounding in wondrous gifts. There was the fantasy of what is ours for nothing, of what moved the Creator to His creation, and the joy of feeling that one shares in this creation and this gift. The sense of what is useful or otherwise is foreign to God and to children: it is the diabolic element in life, and it may be that Don Sebastiano felt this, with his response to those who told him he was rich—that only the cemetery is rich. But this was not an awareness of grace, but rather a kind of curse. Grace had remained in the spirit of Donna Vincenza, because Don Sebastiano, intent on what was useful or useless, had locked her up in her childhood memories; and perhaps for her, too, these spent matchsticks symbolically fell from heaven, albeit only the heaven of a rusty street lamp.

But the fact is that the days were numbered for the oil lamps and Maestro Ferdinando, for the matchsticks and the dreams. Don Priamo and Donna Franceschina still had supper by the restless flame of a tallow candle, and copper lanterns still filled the servants' rooms with light and shadow. But Pasqualino knew what he was doing when he intrigued with the Continent to blow out all those prehistoric flames with one mighty puff. Handsome, tall, and possessed of immense riches (he owned whole mountainsides of pasture in every village round about), Don Pasqualino Piga had a vocation for industry, almost alone among the Nuorese, who did not even know what industry was. On the outskirts of Sèuna he had set up a steam mill, with a baker's shop attached to it, and it filled the whole neighborhood with its pulsations, like the beating of an enormous heart. The millstones worked day and night, and in a fine mist of flour groped the shadows of Don

Pasqualino's sons, who toiled away like workmen, or even harder than workmen, with that frenzied dedication that always comes over the gentry when they discover work. To maintain tradition, the women stayed at home (old Donna Rina, Don Pasqualino's mother, who was like a kind of banner; suffice it to say that a Nuoro shepherd who had been taken off to Rome, and had new experiences, came back saying, "They're not like Donna Rina, those whores on the Continent!"—his wife, Donna Angelica, and his three splendid daughters, one more lovely than the last), surrounded by a nimbus of riches new and old. The sacks of grain piled up in the immense warehouse, as was only right and proper. The only trouble was that up until yesterday the wheat in Nuoro had been milled by grindstones like those owned by Zia Isporzedda, a tributary of Donna Vincenza, turned by a donkey perpetually circling in a tiny windowless den. The women used to bring the bushels of wheat, balanced on their heads, in brimful baskets bordered with red, and this was not only a chore like any other, but also an act of charity. Don Pasqualino's mill had at a single blow halted all the donkeys and snuffed out the charity. And now he was preparing to blow out all the little flames in Nuoro, to abolish the ritual of lamplighting in the houses of rich and poor alike, and to change people's faces by showing them in a different light. It was his destiny. It was destiny itself. The streets of the town, all of them still cobbled except for the long Corso, became cluttered with wires, which looked purely ornamental. Who knows where from, but Don Pasqualino had succeeded in importing a weird sort of ladder, composed of several ladders fitting one inside the other, and he hoisted it up to unbelievable heights. Maestro Ferdinando, incredulous, continued to do the rounds with his humble equipment; but the children no longer followed him.

The electric light arrived one freezing October evening. Nuoro was covered over as with a spiderweb; the wires ran the length of all the streets and alleys, and the owners of houses which had no iron bar with little porcelain cups attached to the wall felt diminished, because the sense of the novel and the unknown was stronger than the sense of property. But in the Corso, in the former Via Majore, Don Pasqualino's sons had strung the wires crosswise, and every thirty meters, in the middle of the roadway, light bulbs hung in enameled iron shades. The whole town had left home in good time to witness the event, full of mistrust and even hoping for the worst. The women of good family peeked out through the windows, and everyone kept his thoughts to himself. Only Signor Gallus, who was the gymnastics instructor, and was from some other town, said what he thought out loud to a group of listeners, "I'd just like to see these candles burn upside down!"

And all of a sudden, as in an aurora borealis, the candles did light up, and light flooded every street, all the way from San Pietro to Sèuna, a river of light between the houses, which remained immersed in darkness. An enormous shout arose all over the town, which in some mysterious way felt that it had entered history. Then, chilled through and with eyes weary from staring, people gradually drifted back to their houses or their hovels. The light stayed on to no purpose. The north wind had risen, and the bulbs hanging in their shades in the Corso began to sway sadly, light and shadow, shadow and light, making the night-time nervous. This had not happened with the oil lamps.

These stayed fixed to the walls, fixed and dead, and they posed a great problem that no one had thought of. What should be done with them? They had cost about twenty lire each, as Don Priamo still remembered. The electric lighting was, as they say nowadays, an irreversible fact, meaning that the old lamps would never come back into their own. Then something occurred that I think has never been recorded in any newspaper in the world. Nuoro, in its nimbus of light, looked like a great ship in the darkness of the ocean. The nearby villages continued in their black of night. The nearest of all, just on the other side of the valley, was Oliena, as the maps say, though its real and more poetic name is Uliana, with the accent on the i.* It is a marvelous village, at the foot of the most beautiful mountain that God ever made, and it produces a wine into which all the aromas of our countryside have crept: myrtle, arbutus, cistus, lentisc. The mountain is calcareous, and is therefore starred all over with white dots, which are the lime kilns. They say that every Olienese owns "a bit of vineyard and a bit of kiln," and therefore they are all both rich and poor; and they are happy, the only happy Sardinians, in their gaudy costumes. Every Sunday they do a round-dance in the odd-shaped piazza outside the church. They even dance when they walk, especially the women when they return from Nuoro, with bare feet and their shoes hung around their necks, almost floating over the white road grooved by the rains. The Nuorese are a little contemptuous of them, or think of them merely as grown-up children. Now from the piazza of Oliena, Nuoro looks like an immense fortress, with the apse of the church perched high above the valley, the red mill, and the tall houses of San Pietro. Only a corner of Nuoro, because (as I think I have said) most of it slopes down on the other

---

*   The people of Oliena still put the accent on the i.

side. But that October evening all the Olienese, men, women and children, had gathered together, looking upward, because word had got around. And that luminous magic suddenly appeared in the immense void, and Oliena also gave forth a shout of joy. What concern it was of theirs, except as a miracle, which is a miracle for everyone, is not clear. But it did concern them—very much so. No one knows exactly who first had the idea, but the fact is that the dead street lamps of Nuoro took the road to Oliena. They were sold along with the lamplighter's ladder to Nuoro's poor neighbors, and the mayor in a brand-new costume and the town secretary came from Oliena to draw up the deed. The Nuorese secretly rubbed their hands with glee, and in the evening went to Sant'Onofrio to see Oliena light up, one lamp after another, so that one could count them. And who knows whether the children didn't run after the lamplighter there as well, picking up the spent matchsticks.

But here I am on my way to the cemetery, and my thoughts go wandering off in this fashion. I have come here between ferry boats to see if I can put a little order into my life, join the two halves together, re-establish that dialogue without which these pages can go no further, and here I am meandering among the electricity wires, a prey to empty memories. I am walking in the middle of the road, without turning my head; but I can hear that doors are opening as I pass, and curious, distrustful eyes are scrutinizing the stranger venturing through the outskirts at this early hour. Soft whispers reach me, and I realize that no one recognizes me. What would happen if I stopped and turned to that middle-aged woman with the pot belly, who is eyeing me keenly, and said, "You are the granddaughter or great-granddaughter of Peppedda 'e Maria Iubanna"? Or, if I said to the one, who has just appeared with a folded kerchief on her head and a ladle in her hand: "You are the granddaughter or great-granddaughter of Luisa 'e Maria Zoseppa"—using the matronymic which is the mark of the ancient race we have in common. As in a photographic print as it develops, remote faces reappear in those around me: people vanished from the earth and from memory, people dissolved into nothingness, but who on the contrary are repeated without knowing it down the generations, in an eternity of the species; of which we are uncertain whether it be the triumph of life or the triumph of death. I feel I am already inside the cemetery I am heading for; a cemetery of living beings, of course. But is it not the living I have come to seek in *Sa 'e Manca*, in the graveyard dominated by the crag that looks like one of the Fates? And here I am, already in the square in front of the Rosario, the church on the edge of town where the dead used to pause as if to draw breath, before the fatal five hundred meters, between meadows and low walls, that led them to be dead with a vengeance. The surroundings of the Rosario were part of San Pietro, no doubt about it, but the church's particular mission gave it a metaphysical stamp, which San Pietro was careful not to acquire. Strictly speaking, the officiant was Father Delussu, the blacksmith's brother, who limped along with his heavy body full of blood and wine; but in fact it was the whole quarter that received the dead man. At the hour fixed for the burial, the bells of Santa Maria sent forth those great, rocking notes that made people stop in the street and ask, "Who's dead?" Unless it was a well-known person, of course. These continued for a quarter of an hour, and then that austere bell suddenly broke into a kind of gallop, pouring down the steep slope. This was the moment at which the priest in his black cowl, a sacristan before him with the processional cross and another beside him with the censer, emerged from the cathedral (for everything started from there) to fetch the dead man. There might be three priests, also in black cowls, if the family wanted them and paid them, and this was always a hurried scene that put heaven and earth into a sulk. But there might even be the entire chapter, with the canons in a double line and the ermine and the red-braided birettas. Then everything proceeded with gainful slowness, amid hymns of death and glory for which the detested dean signaled the start and beat out the time. A burst of color, a spectacle which the family offered (and was bound to offer if it was rich) to the common people, who emerged from house after house as the coffin passed, and followed along behind it. The procession of canons wended its way along the Corso and between the rows of little low houses, and in the solemnity of the singing one could tell that they were listening to their own voices, and not one, for sure, thought of putting himself in the place of the poor fellow in the coffin, But these are things of small importance. The fact is that as soon as the bell started galloping, the women poured out of the houses near the church, roused Father Delussu, forced him to hand over the keys, threw open the russet-colored door, and dragged an old table out of the sacristy, setting it up in the middle of the rough-cast nave. One of them gave a quick sweep around, raising a cloud of dust; another cleaned the saints frozen in their niches, or straightened the garland of stars around the blue-and-white Madonna, or laid out the utensils for the benediction or the lighting of the candles. Then they all crowded to the doorway in eager expectation, for they were hostesses to the newcomer, and kept a close lookout for his arrival. When they saw him coming, borne on the devout shoulders of the confraternity, they called Father Delussu and ushered the dead man to him; and he received him, had the coffin put on the table, and there recited the prayers in a low voice, as if he were having a chat with the corpse.

Now they have restored the façade of the Rosario with little cement blocks, and it is clear that they no longer take the dead there, either because they have no need for rest or because no one dies any more, which seems more likely. But that also is of small importance. When it really comes down to it, the characteristic of our time is to have made things unimportant. I leave the piazza and the new streets that I do not recognize, I leave the last houses facing with indifference onto the cemetery (for the very first time I think I understand the hidden meaning of the *pomerium*), and I have arrived at the place which is the object of my journey, or the reason for it.

> *Fanciulla, attorno al tuo bianco recinto*
> *Prono è un bifolco sulla stiva, ed ara.*
> *La lodoletta con sua voce chiara*
> *L'accompagna dai cieli di giacinto.*

> Maiden, round the white wall of your graveyard
> The farmer strains over the shaft, and plows.
> With his clear voice, the lark
> Accompanies him from skies of hyacinth.*

---

* These lines of verse come, slightly misremembered, from *L'allodola* (The Lark), a poem by Satta's relative, Sebastiano Satta (1867–1914).

Why do these old lines come welling up in my memory? It is as if the first dawn of the world were rising again before my eyes. These costly walls, that have replaced and swallowed up the old cemetery and made it too large for the living and the dead alike, now vanish (and whatever would Don Priamo say, if he were to wake in there?): the plowman has grasped his plow again, and the labor of life that furrows the soil is matched inside the enclosure by the labors of Milieddu, the sexton of all the Nuorese; which is also a labor of life. And the skylark soars for all of us into the skies, and sings. It is a moment of poetry, such as occurs from time to time, and my secret anxiety gives way to a mood of inward joy. I approach the gate, which they have substituted for the rust-eaten door, and I get ready to search for Milieddu, without thinking that he would be at least a hundred years old by now. He had a long, reddish beard, and red also was his face, grooved by the wind and the sun. He might have been that very plowman, who had left his plow for a moment, and in truth he was nothing but a peasant, even if freed from the risks and storms. He was a kindhearted man, and seemed to ask forgiveness of each dead man for having to bury him, though the fact is that he did bury them, and without caring whether they were rich or poor, if they were Fileddu or Don Sebastiano. This earned him neither love nor hatred, but made him in a sense the master of them all. It was as if everyone had a second self, himself and Milieddu: and in conversation, when someone was asked if he was really sure of what he was saying, the answer was: "A man's sure only of Milieddu's shovel." In Nuoro death had a name.

I cross the threshold. Inside are two strapping young fellows in black uniforms, seated idly, like bodyguards. (Who knows how Milieddu managed to bury himself?) They eye me with complete indifference. The cemetery has spread to the very foot of the Mountain, reminding me of those displays of plaster or terra-cotta statuettes one comes across on the outskirts of towns. I make my way along prim avenues full of names that mean nothing to me. I am about to succumb to the terrible anguish of nothingness, as when crossing a square or wandering through a deserted house; and at last, at the end of an avenue of dusty cypresses, I see a cement church resembling the Rosario. I realize at once that they have built it on the site of the crumbling little chapel in which the bishops of Nuoro lay quietly in a row, waiting for the inevitable resurrection. This is the place. There are the two marble angels, one bent mournfully above the other, eternally lamenting the proud dead of the Mannu family. Here is the tombstone of Boelle Zicheri, the pharmacist, who left everything to the hospital out of hatred for his relatives, and that of Don Gaetano Pilleri, who unceasingly pursued his loathing for the priests; here are the first graves of the families of shepherds, with their nicknames that became surnames and the haughty portraits in costume, framed in little enameled ovals; here is the broken pillar commemorating a young man, with the inscription—"You weep, and I sleep far off in the graveyard"—that used to trouble my nights; here is the modest iron railing that encloses Maestro Manca, preventing him from turning back into Pedduzza (the Pebble) and going back to the low dive where he slid under the table, dead while imbibing his last glass of wine…Within a radius of a hundred meters from here I could trace the limits of the old, damp walls. I would only have to follow everything that is black with age, chipped, forgotten—everything that has died for the second time. And beyond these poor tombs there is still a short stretch of ground, short and infinite, with the remains of a few slanting crosses, and others overturned, as if they had exhausted their function. I wonder whether there is more hope in all those tombs where the dead lie alone, or in this bit of earth beneath which the bones of infinite generations are heaped up and mingled together, being themselves turned to earth. In this infinitely remote corner of the world, unthought of by anyone but me, I feel that the peace of the dead does not exist, that the dead are released from every problem except for one only, that of having been alive at all. In Etruscan tombs the oxen now chew the cud, and the largest have been turned into sheepfolds. On the stone beds lie pans and wicker baskets, the humble implements of the shepherd's life. No one remembers that they are tombs, not even the indolent tourist who climbs the path cut into the rock, and ventures into the dark depths where his voice resounds. Yet they are still there, after two thousand, three thousand years; for life cannot conquer death, nor can death conquer life. The resurrection of the flesh begins the very day one dies. It is not a hope, it is not a promise, it is not a condemnation. Pietro Catte, who in the *tanca* of Biscollai hanged himself from a tree on Christmas night, believed he could die. And now he too is here (because the priests made him out to be a madman and buried him in consecrated ground), along with Don Pasqualino and Fileddu, Don Sebastiano and Ziu Poddanzu, Canon Fele and Maestro Ferdinando, the peasants of Sèuna and the shepherds of San Pietro, the priests, the thieves, the saints, the idlers from the Corso...All in an inextricable tangle beneath my feet.

As in one of those absurd processions in Dante's *Paradiso,* but without either choruses or candelabra, the men of my people file by in an endless parade. They all appeal to me, they all want to place the burden of their lives in my hands, the story, which is no story, of their having been. Words of supplication or anger whisper with the wind through the thyme bushes. An iron wreath dangles from a broken cross. And maybe while I think of their lives, because I am writing their lives, they think of me as some ridiculous god, who has summoned them together for the day of judgment, to free them forever from their memory.

8

Every morning at half past eight (except for Thursdays and Sundays, which were holidays at that time) Maestro Mossa would leave his little house on the edge of San Pietro, near the station. He emerged by stepping over the base of a large, useless carriage-door, through an opening made in one of the sides of the door and scarcely larger than a hole for a cat; then it swung to after him. What he left behind him, what kept his home life going, was not a question that occurred to the four little local boys who were waiting anxiously for him in the still-leaden light of winter mornings. He was their teacher, and they followed him all the way down to school. Maestro Mossa went frisking down the alleyways, bouncing over the rough cobblestones. Out of each doorway came a schoolboy, who joined the others, so that before long the whole student body was behind him, as if attracted by a magic flute; and as his step was still long and agile, their walk broke into a run, faster and faster, and stopped at the door of the Monastery.

The school was, in fact, the Franciscan monastery that at some long-forgotten time had been suppressed and confiscated, along with all Church property, on account of some law or other imposed from abroad. The name had remained (like that of the huge tract of land adjoining it, which they still called the "monks' *tanca*"); and to be at the Monastery, or to go to the Monastery, was the same as saying to be at school, to go to school. In fact nothing had changed, either inside or out, because people were content with little; or rather, the very concept of "little" did not exist. Even the bell was still there in its bell-cote perched on the top of the yellow-painted wall, as in all the little country churches in Sardinia, which have no bell towers, and Ziu Longu, the caretaker, used to pull the rope at nine o'clock on the dot, just as the sacristan did in the time of the monks. The selfsame sound announced the beginning of the sacred office and of the lay office, as if nothing had happened; and in point of fact nothing had happened. It was not like the other Church property, which had ended up for a song in the hands of the least scrupulous or least superstitious private citizens, who were nearly all from San Pietro. Of anything else to do with the monks there was not the least trace, except for a few mastic bushes pushing up here and there in the playground.

Inside, there remained the huge entrance hall paved with slate crumbling from the damp, and leading off it were two large rooms with vaulted ceilings. The one on the left must have been the monastery chapel, because through the keyhole one could catch a glimpse of some empty niches, and in one of them there was even a saint with raised hand, who persisted in giving his blessing in the midst of filth. Mysteriously enough, the door was always locked, but it may have been that the roof was collapsing on that side. Just as it might have been a kind of sacristy or refectory or meeting place, while on the contrary the chapel had been the right-hand room, which was the schoolroom where Maestro Mossa taught, because to get to his desk, which was nothing but a simple table, you went up four steps, obviously the steps to an altar. The master, who was deeply religious, never climbed those steps, but sat right in front of the children as if he were one of them. Anyway, prayers were still said in that room, because before starting lessons every morning the master made the children stand up, and they all made the sign of the cross and said the Lord's Prayer.

A short flight of steps led down from the entrance hall to what must have been the monastery proper. It was a sort of quadrangle, with a yard too small to be a cloister, and two long corridors on opposite sides leading to the classrooms, which in fact were nothing but the monks' cells. In those cells, lit more by loopholes than by windows, and so high up that the monks could see God but not the world, an incredible number of boys were jammed in, as if some fresh miracle had multiplied the space. The cells in the opposite corridor, on an upper floor, were used by the so-called normal school, alias the training college in which young men studied to become teachers in accordance with the new rules, which aimed at producing educated teachers, not pathetic wretches like Maestro Mossa.

The schools were organized in such a way that one master taught the children from the first grade to the third, and another master took over for the fourth and fifth. But it worked out so that the second teacher was determined by the first, and anyone who went into the first grade with Maestro Mossa found himself in the fourth with Maestro Fadda; whoever started with Maestro Manca, known as Pedduzza, went to Maestro Piras, and so on. This is not without its importance, because education had not then made the progress that we see today. It was not even a science, which is to say that each master created an educational system of his own, if indeed he did not carry it with him from the day he was born. Anyway, the same was true of the boys, who were receptive only to what they wanted or what they were born to; and the result was that a human relationship was established between master and pupil, a thing justly condemned by modern doctrines, which within the metaphysics of the state or of society could not, for example, allow Maestro Mossa to begin his teaching in the name of the Father, the Son, and the Holy Ghost, or Maestro Manca to hymn the praises of the wine that since first thing in the morning had pervaded his veins, or Maestro Murru to let off steam with the boys about his wife making life difficult for him on account of his modest resources. They all knew, not least because they hid around nearby corners, that when he left home to go to the Monastery, after the first squabbles of the morning, he would turn around and shout from the doorstep, as if delivering the Parthian shot: "Money grubber!"

But in any case, the same applied to the boys, for each one of them, rich or poor, brought into class his own particular world, which had made him what he was, and teaching was the experience of two individuals face to face, of two lives revealing themselves reciprocally in the interstices of mathematics, Italian, and history. The school that resulted from this was the most multicolored imaginable. Maestro Mossa was short, like most Sardinians, but this was disguised by the thinness of his body, which was still lean and wiry in spite of his fifty years. He had a white beard and mustache, which grew at their own sweet will, though they were clean and combed, around a gentle mouth into which neither smoke nor wine had ever entered, and from which only kind words had issued forth. He was not from Nuoro, but from a tiny village in the district of Logudoro, whose manner of speech he had retained, which made him slightly ridiculous at school; and he came of peasant stock. When he became a teacher he had naturally given up the local costume of his forefathers, but he had kept his faith in God, which he based on the very simple argument that one day he had been born and one day he must die; and on close scrutiny this is at bottom the only unexceptionable proof of the existence of God. Unless an objection might be raised by the brass tacks of living: but this was too difficult a matter for him, or it implied a judgment, both of himself and of others, such as he could not make. It was the same faith and the same reasoning that guided him in his work as a teacher, preventing him from realizing that his wage was miserable, because it is life that has to adapt itself to the wage and not the wage to life. In any case, on big feast days the parents of the well-to-do boys did not fail to let him have a bit of pork or a quarter of lamb, which cheered his family up—for he was married to a good woman and had fathered two children.

In the classroom that had been the church (or the refectory or the monks' meeting place, it doesn't matter) the generations of Nuoro passed before the little master, and many of today's children were the sons of yesterday's. His own sons had grown up too, but the miracle that had delivered him from the land was not repeated, for they were not very intelligent, and he had to find them work, which was no easy matter. It worried his wife, and was an affliction to his life, because a father ought to think of his own children before those of others, This is what that poor woman told him when he left the house in the morning and began his descent toward the Monastery with his swelling retinue of schoolboys. Was she right? Was she wrong? But there were the eighty lire a month in wages, and this put her clearly in the wrong, even though (to avoid argument, a thing he feared like sin) he didn't have the courage to tell her this outright. From time to time he was tempted to ask for help for his sons from one of his old students who had become a prominent lawyer, but he had an obscure feeling that this would have made his miserable life more miserable still. When it came down to it, why couldn't they straighten themselves out? The birds of the air get by, while we don't, he said to himself, recalling his ancestral links with the soil, while he lengthened his stride and forced the boys to run to keep pace with him.

Once they were at school, praying together kept master and pupils united for an instant, as in a chorus, and the word of God filtered through the door into the entrance hall full of other schoolboys making an uproar as they waited for their own teacher. It took a good quarter of an hour before everyone was in his place, and there fell that mysterious silence that occurs in school corridors when all are intent on their work. This was the time of day when Ziu Longu, the caretaker, also set to work, which meant keeping his eyes open in case some boy spent too long in the lavatory, or getting mad at the idlers whom the master had sent out of the classroom. That day Maestro Mossa had begun to talk about the kings of Rome, who were seven in number, and had got as far as Tarquin the Proud. It was an old story, one that he had been telling over and over for twenty years, but it was always new because there were always new children listening, while on the other hand he knew, and was obliged to know, not a word more than he said. The boys' eyes sparkled, especially those in the front rows, because these were the boys of the elite, since the selection of men occurs automatically as early as elementary school, and Tarquin's pride became for them a moral fact.

Then Maestro Mossa said: "Pietro Catte, tell me who the last king of Rome was." Pietro Catte, who had the fleshy lips of a Mauretanian and a bovine eye that roved around of its own accord, rose from one of the back benches and said, "The Quirinal…" Naturally enough there was a great burst of laughter from the front benches, but Maestro Mossa did not know how to laugh. He seized the boy by the back of the neck, turned him around, and gave him a good thrashing; then, having regained control of the Sardinian language, he ordered him back to the fields from which he had come, and meanwhile to get out of the room—and be quick about it. Pietro Catte, who was used to such things, left the room willingly and fell into the arms of Ziu Longu, who had been listening at the keyhole. "Shame on you," he said, "to confuse the kings of Rome with the hills, and not to know who Tarquin the Proud was." For he also was halfway to being a teacher, having learned to read and write; and then, everyone knew about Tarquin the Proud. The fact was that Pietro Catte (a child only in a manner of speaking, because the pupils in the back benches were ten or even twelve years old) lived in a small house near his own, with an old aunt who had no one in the world but him, and she used to give presents to Ziu Longu to propitiate him, as if destiny lay in his hands.

Maestro Mossa's whip was nothing more than the flat calibrated ruler which the school supplied, along with ink and an inkpot—and they were all it did supply. This man, whose hair was already flecked with white, was the mildest person imaginable.

And how could he have been other than mild, with that frail body rescued from the plow, and that mind which had undergone, and one might say daily underwent, the adventure of the alphabet? For a time, when he had begun to teach, he had believed that with him a new era would open for his family; but now, as he looked at his sons, who repeated the old generations, and in addition had grown lazy in the city, he realized that his experience had been a parenthesis, and would soon come to an end. But he did not grumble about it. There were all those lads who waited for him every morning outside the house, and it was clear that he had studied for them, that God might put them in his hands; and it seemed as if they knew it. He returned their childlike love with his own love, which was that of a schoolmaster, and part of the job. He knew each and every one of them better than they knew themselves. He knew which of them would go back to the land, and which of them in a few years would know more than he did; and among the latter was Don Sebastiano's youngest son, who hung on his lips, and already talked to him about Plutarch, forcing him to pretend he had read him, so as not to lose face. But in one respect all these boys were equal, and that was in the Original Sin on which his teaching was based. This was the reason for the ruler: it punished Adam and Eve, who still existed. The master was extremely skillful at discovering traces of the first evil; he sniffed it even on the breath that came from those innocent small bodies, and he rose up like a terrible, pedagogical God when he made a fool of someone in front of the class and yelled at him, "Watch your step!" accompanying the yell with a blow from his ruler.

And so Maestro Mossa went on his way, without realizing that the world also went on its way. And in the next-door classroom

Maestro Manca realized it even less than he did, but for different reasons. The fact is that he did not go straight to the Monastery, bowling along over the cobblestones when he left the house in the morning, but made a tour of the *milesos*, which is what they called certain little shops where the merchants from Milis, a village in the Campidano district, came during the season to display luminous piles of oranges and little bottles of their Vernaccia wine. So when he crossed the threshold of the school he already had four or five glasses of Vernaccia in him. He was a small man, with blue-green eyes, a pointed beard, and a head crowned with a top hat, as the fashion then was. His perfectly round belly atop his skinny little legs had—I seem to remember having said this already—earned him the nickname of Pedduzza, the Pebble, by which he was known throughout his life. On entering the classroom he adopted the stratagem of exuberance, which he sorely needed, for he was a trifle overawed by the boys, who looked at him with some curiosity and did not understand—especially to begin with—why the Rubicon tended to come out as the Buricon. The master had a skinful, as the saying goes, and as the day went by it caught up with him, and the lesson ran the risk of turning into a circus. But not to the extent that the master, in a sudden reawakening of conscience, did not utter a shriek and, before the eyes of the dumbstruck children, bring Julius Caesar and Augustus back into the limelight.

Maestro Manca had this drinking problem, which was not entirely his, since he shared it with his whole family. But he was the first to take it to heart, to the extent of asking himself in his lucid intervals where that blemish had come from, and attributing it to his mother, who (he said) had a passion for Fernet when she was pregnant. But he was a kind man, and also extraordinarily gifted: he played the guitar, wrote poems that were gay and bitter at the same time, and was incredibly good at mimicry, which implies the ability to see the essence of people in their acts and gestures. These were all things that set him apart from the rest of the Nuorese drunkards, who were legion. And on top of this he was cultured, which meant that he had gone right through school; but what he had learned of Homer, Dante, and others had sunk in and become part of his nature, so that he had his classical quotation or nickname for everyone; and this too was a kind of mimicry. His misfortune, he was wont to say, was that of having married a Continental. And maybe this was true, though perhaps he ought not to have said so to the boys who, according to the academic rote, came his way.

Maestro Mossa would never have done it, but Maestro Mossa would never have done a lot of other things. In the little room in the Monastery where Maestro Manca taught, there was a fireplace, which the last of the monks had left burnt out; and in the hard Nuoro winters one shuddered with cold. So Maestro Manca had thought up a perfectly simple solution: he made a bargain with the boys, that in the morning each of them was to bring a piece of wood hidden under the loden coat which they used to wear in those days. But they should tell no one, not even their parents. Involved in this secret task, the boys arrived, walking stiffly, and in this way the first rite of the school day was lighting the fire. The master did not do it himself, since his legs and belly did not permit him to bend down, but in the back rows sat the sons of shepherds, destined to remain shepherds themselves, and they knew all about such things. Thus, while Maestro Mossa was dying of cold, and accepting death, Pedduzza was happily snoring in the chair which he had transported from his useless desk to the corner of the fireplace, while the boys took turns fanning the flames. It therefore occasionally happened to him, as in a twilight, to see his wife riding astride a bottle of Vernaccia, but he immediately roused himself, grabbed the boy nearest the fire by the collar, scolded him for his way of life, his parents, and his grandparents, and kicked him out of the door. He turned purple in front of the silenced student body, and began to talk about geography.

The boys were accustomed to these outbursts of rage, and had even organized themselves so that they all took turns at being the victim. They realized that their master, long since exposed to the jests of the ignorant gentlemen of the Caffè Tettamanzi, who nonetheless sought him out and encouraged him to drink because he amused them, found in them a refuge, and thought of them as the only friends he had. One morning they saw him arrive with a large bundle under his arm. They all crowded around him, and out came a guitar. He sat down as usual beside the fire, and very softly, because of the headmaster, who was none other than Maestro Fadda, the teacher of the fourth and fifth grades, whom the boys called Porsena because of his extraordinary resemblance to this Etruscan king as pictured in the history book, he plucked the strings. From them came a melancholy sound that tamed even the back-benchers; then the teacher's voice intoned a song in praise of wine, which he had composed during the night, a parody of hymns to Jesus that would have been blasphemous had it not been a lament for himself, for the misery into which he felt himself falling.

Benitu siat su frore
frutto de puru sinu

became (atrociously enough) in the parody:

Benitu siat s'acriore
*fruttu de puru binu**

while in the chorus, instead of the name of Jesus, came those of the worthless characters of the low life of Nuoro.

Maestro Fadda threw open the door at the very moment when Maestro Manca's voice was beginning to ring out. He too, like Don Priamo, was one of those men who never laugh, and he differed from Maestro Mossa only in two respects of equal importance: he taught the more advanced classes, and he didn't much believe in God. There was nothing human in his voice now; it was a bleat, the wheeze of someone who feels he is choking, while his eyes rolled as if to pop out of their sockets—Maestro Fadda, who never got flustered, never left his seat at the desk, and gave his lessons with his bowler hat on his head because he was bald.

"Very good, very good!" his expression said. "We'll see about this in the records." And he vanished. Maestro Manca had leaped to his feet in terror. He was not worried about the "records," because he knew that Maestro Fadda was kind, and when it came down to it would not ruin him, No, it was the terror of finding himself unexpectedly faced with a man who made sense, who didn't reel on his feet and didn't sing. He put down the guitar, so

---

* "Blessed be the flower / fruit of a pure womb" became "Blessed be the belch / fruit of pure wine."

near to the flames that it all but caught fire. Then the boys, and not just the sons of the rich, of Don Pasqualino and Don Sebastiano, but also the lanky fellows on the back benches who already had a few bristles on their spotty faces, ran up to the teacher, tugged at his jacket and clung to his knees, shouting and singing. They all but danced around his belly. The master wept.

Was Maestro Manca right? Or was Maestro Fadda? If we were to put it in educational terms, I would be tempted to say that under the influence of his addiction Maestro Manca was a forerunner of the education of today, which puts the teacher in the place of the pupils and the pupils in the place of the teacher, only that it does so in complicated terms. Perhaps it is more correct to say that education has dethroned Maestro Fadda without putting any Maestro Manca in his place, because Maestro Manca was a phenomenon of nature, and nature is not made of theories. In any case, there were many more people at Maestro Manca's funeral than at Maestro Fadda's (and I saw them both); and this also counts for something. When he returned to his classroom, this same Maestro Fadda appeared calm behind his beard, which was reddish, partly because it really was so and partly because he took snuff, for which he was avid. But from the way he took out his snuff box, and the wide sweep he made with his hand to take a pinch, the boys understood that he was inwardly upset, or at least pensive. He resembled Maestro Mossa in knowing exactly where his duty lay, only there was more dignity in his behavior, and even a kind of haughtiness, because he taught the advanced classes and had married a woman with a bit of property. The boys liked him, because they were older, and felt his studied speech was a sort of introduction to life, while the first three school years had been a

joke. The ages of the three of them—Mossa, Manca, and Fadda—
totaled at least a hundred and sixty years, which at that time was
an enormous amount. And for at least a hundred of these they had
been plowing ahead in the gloomy classrooms in the Monastery,
without realizing that the world was also plowing ahead.

They became aware of this, or at least had a vague inkling of
it, on the day that a new master appeared in the old home of the
monks. He was young, but not very young, because he came from
the village schools, where he had taught for a number of years.
He was Sardinian, but with a non-Sardinian name, which was
Marinotti. He was short, and ugly to boot, and he aroused some
suspicion, particularly on account of two things: he was immediately assigned to the advanced classes, and he at once teamed
up with the most discredited of the teachers, Ricciotti Bellisai.
The latter claimed to be a nobleman, and even a relative of Don
Sebastiano, and it is possible that he was. What is sure is that his
father, Don Missente, had been very rich: the house at Loreneddu,
rented out to the carabinieri, was once his; Isporòsile, the sunny,
fertile holding between the Mountain and Nuoro, was his; so were
a lot of *tanche* in the Serra and orange groves around Orosei, and
heaven knows what else. And if Don Missente had continued to
spend his life stroking the long side whiskers that distinguished
him from his peers, all would have gone well. The trouble is that
money has the tendency to multiply in the heads of those who
have it, especially if they have not earned it penny by penny like
Don Sebastiano, and Don Missente amused himself by going
to the Caffè Tettamanzi and lighting a long Virginia cigar (the
only kind a person of his sort could smoke) with a hundred-lire
note—at the rate going then. One night, for fun, he played cards

for Isporòsile (which today in fact belongs to Giovanni Maria Musiu, the owner of the caffè). At least, this is what they said. What is certain is that shortly afterward Loreneddu passed into the hands of Don Sebastiano, who did not really want it, faithful to his principle that one ought not to profit from the misfortunes of others; and similarly all the rest was frittered away. When Don Missente had nothing at all, he at last seemed content, and went on stroking his whiskers without any longer going near the caffè, where no one noticed his absence. He was left, to use a French word, with this *rejeton* Don Ricciotti, who maintained himself, his father, and his family with his teacher's diploma. But just as his father was sunny and smiling, he was gloomy and glum, with drooping bluish cheeks; and he did not deign to notice the Mossas, Mancas, and Faddas of this world. He thought of himself as still owning the properties his father had dissipated, and if the law was not on his side, then he was dead set against the law, or against those who profited from the law to deny him what was his. Nor did he hesitate to say as much at school, where he also taught the sons of the usurpers, though they understood none of it. For this reason, when Maestro Marinotti came on the scene, expounding certain new ideas, talking about identity of thought and action, of education as the very act in which the personality is made, of the synthesis of pupil and teacher, and other complicated matters, Don Ricciotti at once saw the newcomer as an ally. The three old teachers held more than one secret meeting. "What is the meaning of this kind of talk?" asked Maestro Fadda, who because he taught the fourth and fifth grades imagined himself to be closer to knowledge than the others. "Could we have got everything wrong?" asked Maestro Mossa humbly. "It seems to me that's what we've always done," replied Maestro Manca, as his understanding unclouded for an instant. Maestro Fadda wanted to scold him for his drunken binges, as being to blame for everything, all the more so because, as far as he could make out, according to the new theories, the headmaster was quite separate from the teachers, and he would lose this small sign of distinction between himself and his colleagues. In reality, all three of them had an obscure foreboding of their own decline. Don Ricciotti, on the other hand, knew that behind incomprehensible words there always lurks a will to power, and he needed this man, not those three mummies who played at being children with the children. He therefore immediately supported the new master's aims, began to talk in the same manner, and thought he should be appointed headmaster. He even went so far as to disregard his own corpulence and adopt a swaggering gait, as if the school had become his property.

Maybe those incomprehensible words were what might enable him to force Don Sebastiano to give him back the house at Loreneddu.

The new master was of course a decent man, and if he had suspected that Don Ricciotti was out to exploit his philosophy for shady purposes, he would have avoided him like the plague. His greatest ambition was one day to become a school inspector, a job instituted recently, when the schools passed from the jurisdiction of the communes to that of the state; this would give him authority over the old schoolteachers in the area. At any rate, he behaved affably, and they seemed reassured. Maestro Manca reached such a point that one evening, when he had drunk more than usual, he included him among the saints in one of the hymns of praise which he improvised while accompanying himself on the guitar, and which soon became the common property of all the drunkards, who made the heavens ring with it in late-night choruses in the abandoned streets. The new master accepted the joke for a number of reasons: first, because he was Sardinian, and knew how to keep his mouth shut; then, because a joke, if it is not malicious, always bestows a degree of useful popularity; and finally because he had guessed that, beneath the bad habit that was destroying him, Maestro Manca was more intelligent than himself. And the habit made him harmless.

The first sign that something was changing, or had changed in the world, came one morning when Maestro Mossa, bowling over the cobblestones with the swarm of boys in his wake, noticed that his steps were not accompanied and almost measured out by the little Monastery bell. He thought that lazybones Ziu Longu must have overslept, although he took pride in opening up the school on time, with the huge key which he took home with him every evening; but all the same his heart missed a beat. It seemed to him that a vast silence was spreading throughout the town, and that everyone ought to just stop, as in mechanical puppet shows, depicting the various trades, when the spring runs down. At the Monastery he found Ziu Longu wide awake, his face as black as thunder and the veins in his neck fit to burst.

"What about the bell?" asked Maestro Mossa.

"He said that from now on it won't be rung." There was no need to ask who "he" was.

In the entrance hall he found Maestro Fadda and Maestro Manca talking in low voices. "We must appeal," said Maestro

Fadda. "The headmaster can supervise the running of the school, but not change things."

"Who do we appeal to?" replied Maestro Manca, who was already planning one of his poetic vendettas. Maestro Mossa was on the point of saying that he would come down every morning and ring the bell himself, when Don Ricciotti passed nearby without even glancing at them, and they realized there was nothing to be done. The bell was dead forever.

It was no small matter. The Monastery bell had nothing in common with the bells of Santa Maria. These, with their various accents, were a voice of command, whether they called the Nuorese—frankly, not great churchgoers—to their Sunday obligations, or packed off the dead to the cemetery, or announced that Christ had risen or that the bishop had crossed the threshold of the palace on his way to Pontifical Mass. The Monastery bell made no demands. It had a *voice—ding, ding, ding—*sent forth by Ziu Longu's long tugs at the rope, as formerly by those of some sleepy monk or lay brother; if indeed, after so many years, it did not ring all by itself. But this voice climbed up the long road past the gardens, met with boys who were coming skipping down to the Monastery, made its way into the Corso and the hidden streets, and hovered in the limpid air of Nuoro. It was one of the two voices of Nuoro. The other was the drumroll of Ziu Dionisi, the town crier; and this was the evening voice, as the bell was the morning voice. *Duradum-duradum-duradum*: Ziu Dionisi appeared at about sunset, when the streets and the houses were rousing themselves from their sunstroke, with a drum hanging on his belly by a worn strap, to announce that the wine of Oliena was now available at Mucubirde's cellar at twenty centimes a liter, or that a stranger had "come down" to the house of Peppedda e' Maria Jubanna to buy fox skins, or that there was a new program at the Olympia Cinema. Sometimes there were so many announcements that Ziu Dionisi reached into his pocket and pulled out a text written in Sardinian, and each announcement was preceded by a drumroll that kept the women, who had run to their doors, glued there with their hearts in their mouths, because it seemed as if Ziu Dionisi had gone to sleep over his drum.

These were the two voices of Nuoro, and now one of them had been silenced forever. The other would soon follow, because Ziu Dionisi was old, and it would not be easy to find him a successor. And so Nuoro would be left dumb, like any city, like any town, and the Nuorese would no longer recognize themselves in these little things that were unimportant, but were the sign of that mysterious communion that grows up among men who live beneath the same sky. From then on, to know if it was time, everyone would look at his watch, as after all is only natural.

The old teachers had all this bitterness in the bottom of their hearts, even if they were unable to translate it into words. But in Maestro Mossa there was another feeling, one which he would not have dared to show his colleagues, for they would have ended by quarreling among themselves. He was, as we have said, very religious, and that still bell was not the voice of Nuoro: it was the voice of God that had fallen silent. This was not a fixation, nor was it the superstition of a bigot. Maestro Mossa was not a bigot: he had let the Lord walk with him all his life, and in his modest labors he had walked with the Lord; and the prayer he recited with the boys before lessons was a kind of agreement which he made with Him every day. It was all very well for him to pray himself, but the point was to get the boys to pray, so that they were at least for a moment delivered from evil. Everything had always gone smoothly. But for some time now he had noticed that certain youths would hang about outside the ex-church or ex-refectory that was his classroom, first singly and then in larger and larger groups, at first silent but later noisier and noisier, making fun of his prayers. They were the young men from the teachers' college, the schoolmasters who would take his place, the ones from the floor above. He had taken a long time to understand, because he had no idea what was going on in the world while he was teaching the children of Nuoro to make the sign of the cross. But then they had begun to whistle and catcall and make noises even more obscene, and his boys had got frightened. Why, why? This had been his custom all his life. But all his life, also, he had heard the voice of that bell, guiding him to the Monastery. Now the bell rope hung sadly above Ziu Longu's bench, like the rope after a hanging.

9

That Bishop Roich who, in flight from the scorching sun and the mosquitoes, had moved the episcopal seat to the high ground and the site on which Nuoro was to rise (assuming Canon Fele's fairy tales to be true) had unintentionally stamped the appearance of a holy city on the little town. The Church of Santa Maria, with its Latin inscription which not even the priests could understand, dominated it from the brow of the hill, a bell tower to the right and a bell tower to the left, like an immense snail. Nor were the bells just any two bells, because they had names (one was Lionzedda, the other Lollobedda) and they told different tales, according to the service, or even according to the mood of the bell-ringer, which, it was said, people claimed to recognize. Chischeddu (which was his name, meaning Franceschino) must have quarreled with the vicar, they thought at San Pietro and Sèuna when the tolling for a funeral was too hurried or a note rang false. Chischeddu was one of those wrecks who for some unknown reason drift into churches, and are allowed by God or the vicar to take part in the life of the spirit as vergers or sacristans, or to take the collection, or—if they have a decent ear, as was the case with Chischeddu—as bell-ringers.

Rejected by what is finite, they are attracted by the infinite, an empty church, a priest in skirts, two arms opened in broad gestures of benediction; and this they serve from the outside, in the little things and the little people needed even by the infinite. Halted on the threshold, they live the mystery more fully than their masters, and you should have seen Pozeddu, the sacristan of the Grazie, when after the collection he emptied the bag with the long handle onto the sacristy table. The small coins scattered like mad things over the worm-eaten wood, flashing in the meager light that made its way through the dusty windowpanes; and from time to time a silver lira would tumble out among them, and Pozeddu would swear he knew who had given it, although he did not satisfy the curiosity of the celebrant. Those little coins were the tangible signs of God, the service which he rendered to Him every day, but especially on Sundays, at the "rich people's Mass." In any case, although he was on the edge of things, he had more faith than the priest, and while he unfailingly helped him on with his surplice, it was as if he were putting it on himself. Even after years he had not ceased to be unctuously respectful, because between the priest and himself there was the barrier of the impossible; but he had drawn nearer to the priest, was the recipient of his outbursts and his confidences, and measured his yawns. Nor was there a Mass or church service that he would not have been able to celebrate, and in perfect Latin, although he could neither read nor write. If he had had less self-respect he would have accepted the priest's invitation to play cards on occasional summer evenings, while they waited in the cool of the deserted church for the sun at last to make up its mind to go away.

But let us leave Pozeddu, who is not relevant at the moment, because we are in the Church of Santa Maria with Chischeddu, whose bells regulated the life and death of the town, from the silver *ave* of the morning to the resonant *ave* of the evening, which made the peasants doff their caps as they came home on their carts, and the middle-class children stop their play in the piazzetta. Even Don Sebastiano rose from the bench in the Piga pharmacy (which had nothing to do with Don Pasqualino's family) and went up the short cobbled stretch that led him home, where the study, the newspaper, and the oil lamp awaited him. Life, at a certain point, must stop, at least for the middle classes. But the great outpouring of the bells, in which Chischeddu sounded not a note wrong, even if the vicar had given him what-for a few minutes earlier, was not that of Holy Saturday, at exactly ten o'clock in the morning, when Jesus rose from the dead (and everyone stood and waited, gazing upward) but the peal that announced that the bishop had left his palace with his suite of canons in ermine, for the celebration of Pontifical Mass. Santa Maria awaited him with its immense doors flung wide, and the dean on one side, ready to give the note to the chorus of seminarists, was a splash of violet in the dark interior of the church. In his embroidered shoes, and with his long train held by two young deacons, the bishop went up the gentle, oak-shaded slope that divided (or united) the cathedral and the palace, and upon that psalm-intoning cortege there fell the gigantic chimes of Chischeddu's bells, which came no longer from the bell towers but from the blue sky, from all the blue skies of the island, that arched themselves above the fleeting scene.

It is likely that at the time of Monsignor Roich the church and the forecourt and the bishop's palace formed a single unit. There was no other reason for the granite walls surrounding the tree-lined slope outside the church as in an embrace, and open only onto the vast steps leading to the recently made cobbled roadway that borders the bishop's palace. It is true that the tall, severe, disproportionate cathedral has nothing in common with the dwelling of the bishops, that earthly dwelling reminiscent on a larger scale of the peasant houses of Sèuna. Rather than actually seeing it, one senses it through the palm trees rising above the red-tinted wall. Come to think of it, it might well be the summer residence of a minor provincial landowner, with its shady patio, and indeed a place of pleasure, had it not been for those gaunt black priests who came and went when on duty. The bishops would arrive, would take up their abode, and then be carried off by death like the popes in Rome; and each of them was like a little pope in that town of 7,051 inhabitants, which had at least forty canons and priests, two convents of nuns (the rich nuns and the poor nuns, as they were called), and a seminary that was the first glimmer of hope for peasants from the villages, who even then were longing to move to the towns. And all this in the midst of a population that was pagan by instinct, as in fact the canons and priests were half-pagan, not acknowledging each other and acknowledging the bishop only because he was an outsider.

But it had not always been this way. Like Rome, even Nuoro had known its golden pontificates, shall we say its Julius II or its Leo X. A dark Middle Ages endured for two centuries after the phantasmagorical Monsignor Roich. The first real bishop of Nuoro, the one destined to leave people's minds stamped with an image of himself and his times more durable than the wordy memorial tablet dedicated to him in Santa Maria (which no one succeeds in reading because it is written in Latin), was Monsignor Dettori, who came with the cultured manners of Gallura to the wilds of Barbagia. Here I have to warn you in all honesty that what I say might be entirely a fantasy, because I learned it as a child from

Don Sebastiano's stories, if indeed I didn't dream it myself; for the figure of the first bishop is surrounded by an aura of myth. The fact is that he was a rich man, and from Gallura to the little red-painted bishop's palace he had brought his wealth along with him.

When he arrived—and it must have been in the last quarter of the nineteenth century—the Chischeddu of the time filled earth and sky with his peals of bells, and Don Priamo, who as we have said lived right in the shadow of the church, would have been deafened by it, had he not gone with all the prominent citizens to meet him at the Quadrivio, the crossroads that formed the terminus of all the roads coming from the grim interior, before they amalgamated into the single highway that, when paved, was to become the Corso. Both peasants and gentry always used to go to meet the bishop when he "took possession of the diocese," as the pompous phrase goes, but in substance he was an honored guest and nothing more. Then everyone returned to living his own life. But this time the little aborigines of Nuoro saw a tall, strongly built man getting out of the coach, blessing them from on high, caressing rich and poor alike with a celestial look, and smiling. Even the canons in their ermine and the priests in their slightly dingy surplices were surprised. And they were even more so when they saw that the bishop had not come alone, but had brought with him two humble friars with white cords around their waists. Friars or lay brothers, no one could say for sure.

Monsignor Dettori was a bishop just like all those others of whom no trace remained even in the cemetery, but he had a kingly air. This stemmed from his own personal wealth, naturally, but even in Nuoro there were a lot of rich men; it was just that solitude had made them anarchical and close-fisted. Having

THE DAY OF JUDGMENT | 133

spent his life not in the depressing parishes of the interior, wasting time on people's sins, but in the secretariat of the Archbishop
of Cagliari, he had naturally found himself on the highroad to
honors, and the honor of a bishopric was the most exalted open
to him, the one he would have aspired to as soon as he had taken
the tonsure, if the priest with a true calling did not, almost by
an act of exorcism, refuse himself any aspiration whatever. The
bishopric of Nuoro was the least in Sardinia, and therefore in
the world, but apart from the fact that the unit of measurement
in Sardinia and in the world is not the same, all bishoprics are
kingdoms for those who have a vocation for ruling. And in that
remote place, devoured by crags and bandits, Monsignor Dettori
made the bishop's dwelling into a royal palace, where he held his
picturesque court, with Pontifical Masses and banquets; these
always in the name of God, which was not a mere pretext, but
sure faith, founded on long-standing custom, and gratitude.

The two friars or lay brothers (but to simplify matters we will
call them lay brothers from now on) were basically two cooks.
They turned their hand to everything, needless to say, but above
all else they catered for the bishop's services of the mouth, as they
used to say in the days when kings were kings. That is, they were
responsible for the kitchen and the table. Monsignor Dettori was
a person of blameless habits, but he understood why, at the archbishop's school, they had taught him the boundaries between the
human and the divine. He kept his excellent table within these
boundaries; and not only that, he made them more flexible,
because good food sweetened and conciliated souls. When he
received the news that the distant pope had deigned to provide
for the diocese of Nuoro in his modest person, he knew very well

that he would be going to a desolate place where there were none but poor people, since the rich were even poorer than the poor, among people ruled by their passions, with contentious, fanatical priests who were therefore far from God. But this very contrast with his own civilized Gallura had awakened his interest. And then, if you really want to know, every Sardinian, however superior he thinks he is, even the pompous asses of Sassari and the grandiloquent grandees of Cagliari, look to Nuoro as to their second home. Therefore, when he alighted at the Quadrivio and crossed the threshold of his kingdom, and was confronted with the sea of little houses in Sèuna, which we have already described, with the carts before the doorways and the oxen garlanded in his honor, he left the procession and set off, escorted only by the two lay brothers, over the rocky country roads among the odoriferous droppings of animals. He towered head and shoulders over the wretched hovels, and had to stoop down to talk to the Seunese. But his manners were so strange, that is to say, so kindly, that to the poor people he seemed a messiah.

"Ah, I see," said Canon Mocci, who was a pious soul but always a bit tipsy. "This monument has a mania for popularity."

"Keep a civil tongue in your head," replied Canon Mura, of whom Canon Mocci said it was doubtful whether he could read and write.

The dean, who was Canon Pirri, and came from San Pietro, where he worked at tempering the thievish spirits of his rich relatives, watched the flies forming haloes around the heads of his brother clerics. But he was nearest in rank to the bishop, and this prevented him from allowing the least expression to cross his dewlapped face.

The bigwigs, with the mayor in the vanguard, felt that with this Galluran bishop something was about to change in the life of Nuoro.

And in fact, a few days later they saw a message delivered to their fortresses by one of the lay brothers. In it Monsignor Dettori invited them to luncheon the following Sunday, after the sung Mass.

The Nuorese were by nature laymen, not least on account of the Church property that many of them had bought up at the time of the abolition of the monasteries, not so long ago in those days; but above all because they knew each and everyone of the priests, and esteemed them little, though preserving their respect for extreme unction. They therefore received this strange invitation with distrust. That Sunday Don Gabriele and Don Serafino, who lived across the street from Don Sebastiano, settled down at the window to watch what he would do, and when they saw Don Sebastiano, who was by nature sensitive to flattery, setting off up the slope to the bishop's palace in his best suit, they rushed downstairs. And Don Pasqualino must have done the same thing, because a little while later he was seen hobbling up the slope on the stick he used to help his gout. The gout (the ailment of the rich) forced him to be sober, while the terrible swellings on the knuckles of his hands took away his appetite. But the bishop's invitation had intrigued him, and he was unable to resist the offer. Anyway, by midday, when the last echo of the *ite missa est,* drawn out in the celebrant's throat by at least ten meters, was well and truly dispersed in the lofty skies of Nuoro, twelve of them were standing by a table as decorative as an altar, beneath a pergola from which hung stalactites of grapes still blue with copper sulphate. It was in the open, but it could have been an annex to the long priestly rooms because the doors were flung wide. Unknown bishops looked down from the walls, and seemed to screw up their eyes in the unaccustomed light. Along the wall the huge palm trees displayed great eagerness to mature their dates, and from the orchard below (the Monsignor's Orchard, as they called it) came a pagan scent of honey, and the buzzing of bees at work in the glory of noon.

When Monsignor Dettori appeared in his long, spotless cassock and red skull cap, they were already a little exhilarated. This man, so different from them, nonetheless spoke their language, because the Archbishop of Cagliari loved to travel in the Barbagia when he could, and used to take the monsignor with him, knowing him to be loyal. He spoke with simplicity and learning at the same time, since a bishop could not allow himself to speak with simplicity alone, and he stuck to earthly matters, well knowing that especially with these ultra-shrewd provincials it would not do to name God in vain. And so it came about that before seating themselves at table they all made the sign of the cross, if only so as not to displease him. While waiting to be served, he told them that he had loved Nuoro ever since, at the seminary in Sassari, he had known a pale, melancholy lad who sang of his distant homeland in sorrowful verses, and he recited some of his poems.

> *So solu*
> *mischinu*
> *chin dolu*
> *continu.**

---

* I am alone / poor me / with incessant / sorrow.

"That was Canon Solinas," Canon Sanna almost shouted out (for a few canons had joined the notables. This one was related to Donna Vincenza on her mother's side). "I used to know him very well."

"And where is he now?" asked the bishop.

"He's dead, poor chap. He was only twenty-nine, although he was already a canon."

A brief, imperceptible silence disturbed the serenity of the occasion, as in a drawing room when someone makes a gaffe at the expense of the hostess. But luckily, at that very moment, a lay brother arrived with a huge dish, which everyone turned to look at.

"This is Brother Giossanto," said the bishop. "He has been with me for twenty years. He's not the cook, though. The cook is Brother Baingio, who traveled all around the world before coming to the curia. He has even been in America, and has cooked in the houses of kings. But now I shall never let him go again."

The dish that Brother Baingio had prepared was a chicken. But it was an odd sort of chicken, which lay like a cushion on the huge silver oval. This was placed in the middle of the table (because the luncheon of a Sardinian bishop, however refined, always retains something countrified) and Giossanto served it around, starting with his bishop. The guests then realized that the chicken was boneless, but with its skin intact. Don Pasqualino, who was the most traveled of those present, having been in Turin when it was the capital, and then in Rome, said out loud what everyone was thinking: that he had never seen a chicken prepared like that. At this there was a chorus of praise, and Brother Baingio had to be sent for to explain to those lamb-and-piglet eaters how one removes the skeleton of a chicken from its sheath.

There were six courses. Then coffee was served, the canons drinking it from the saucer, where they poured it to let it cool. When the bishop stood up he said grace, which everyone echoed. Then off they all went, and each one became himself again. But at the same time they obscurely felt that life could have a certain grandeur and sweetness, and that Monsignor Dettori combined this grandeur and this sweetness in his own person. For the very first time those Nuorese barbarians became aware that they had a bishop. And the trouble was, he was destined to become the model for all bishops.

Monsignor Dettori did not, of course, reduce his ministry to a love feast with the middle classes. He was charitable, and he exercised charity with kind words and with alms. As time went by, he even instituted a dispenser of alms, in the person of Brother Giossanto. Every Friday the beggars, so abundant in Nuoro, came up from Sèuna or down from San Pietro to the bishop's palace. From Sèuna came Poddanzu, who was an old peasant, short and rotund, and he might have seemed normal if his brain had not forgotten to grow. He had simply remained a child at seventy years of age, and as his people were dead, he was left alone in the world. He had therefore entered into the vast sea of charity and hatred that was the town, for there were those who gave him five coppers and those who just laughed at him and scared him. He lived in a hovel right on the edge of the Corso, and went to do his business behind the Workers' House, which was at the far end of the *tanca*, the gardens planted by that mayor from the Continent, but already a dungheap. On one occasion snow had fallen for three or four days, and Nuoro was almost obliterated. But Poddanzu still had his needs, and when evening came he set out for the usual spot. At that point the habitués of the Caffè Tettamanzi thought of a new game. The best shot among them, a keen hunter, took aim with a snowball and hit the bull's-eye...Yes, the bull's-eye. The terror-struck Poddanzu brushed off the mush with his cold hands and shouted aloud for justice, which meant the *carabinieri* on foot and on horseback, who were stationed in Nuoro. "Carabinieri on foot and on horseback, help me, help me, they want to kill me!" What a lark! This bit of bravura became part of the history of Nuoro, and maybe it is still remembered. At any rate, it came down to me.

From San Pietro came Zesarinu, who was not Nuorese but from Dorgali, so that the little he said, he said in the aspirated, almost Arabic, idiom of those people. If Poddanzu was short and round and dressed in local costume, Zesarinu was tall and skinny and dressed as a *cosinu,* which was the name then given to those who wore town clothes without being middle-class. In fact he was not just tall but enormous, and his arms, legs, and head were all uncoordinated. He did not live alone, because he would have been absolutely unable to survive on his own. He found shelter with two old Sardinianized Continental women, who put him in a hut at the far end of the yard, and he was of some use to them, because in the evening he shouldered a tin can containing those poor women's rubbish (no one knew exactly what *they* lived off either) and went down to the dump at Mughina—since each quarter of town had its own—to empty the rubbish. The boys knew this, and waited for him at the entrance to the gardens, and threw stones at the can, with a battering clang. Zesarinu did not retaliate, because he was afraid of children. Only once did he chase after one, making a fearful grimace. The boy was frozen with terror and peed in his pants, but Zesarinu did him no harm. Perhaps in the darkness of his mind he realized that if he struck him the whole town would blame him. On another occasion, the Chiseddos, who were shepherds from San Pietro, took him to their sheep pen and roasted him a lamb. Zesarinu had a meal once a week, and he hurled himself upon this gift of God. After a few mouthfuls he was stuffed, but they forced him to go on eating, until at a certain point Zesarinu collapsed like a corpse. The shepherds were scared, but when he recovered his senses he began to sing their praises all over Nuoro, saying: "What good people those Chiseddos are! They kept urging me to eat more, and I nearly died of it!" And this, too, went down in history.

Another one who came was Dirripezza, who lived at the end of the Corso, near the Iron Bridge, and it seemed that he came of good family, and had been (so he said) at Custoza,* but now his arms were no longer capable of work, and he sat on the paved roadway without ever asking for anything. If someone gave him a coin, he kissed it and put it in a leather bag he had hanging around his neck. With him one could even converse. Yet another was *Sa Tataja*: the word means wet-nurse, which implies that she had had children and nursed those of others; she had been three or four times to Tunis, where the working-class women escaped when they were pregnant, to "have their bastards." So she must have been quite beautiful, not as she is today, with a nose so hooked it seems keen to get into her toothless mouth. She was shaky on her pins, and leaned on a long staff shiny from use. And Baliodda would come, the one who always dressed in mourning, no one

* A village in the Veneto where the Austrians defeated an Italian army in 1866.

knew for whom. Another regular was the jest of all and sundry: Raffaele, a well-set fellow who had once been a stable boy, and at a certain point started trotting like a horse up and down the Corso. He had been doing this for years and years, and always won his races.

All these folk, and who knows how many others, made their way to the bishop's palace every Friday, which was the day Our Lord died. Brother Giossanto gave each of them a specially baked loaf and a little money as well. And they all sang the praises of Monsignore, and the fame of this rich monsignore spread far and wide. Even the priests (and I can't say more than that) looked more relaxed, and scowled at each other less. There was enough proof of miracles for a canonization. Monsignor Dettori naturally did more substantial things, such as beginning the construction of the seminary, restoring the Chiesa del Monte, which was starting to collapse on account of the devilish storms up there on the heights, welcoming the nuns whom the French had thrown out of Corsica, and lodging them at his own expense in the large house belonging to the Mastino family (the mother of whom was a Mannu). These were the sisters who, expelled by the Revolution, had brought revolution into the feudal life of Nuoro, because they had begun teaching French to the buried young ladies, thereby compelling them to emerge into the sunlight. These were the rich sisters, as they were dubbed at once, in contrast to the local sisters who lived on air, bits of embroidery, or the income from a funeral or two, and who therefore became the poor sisters.

In short, Monsignor Dettori did everything that any bishop would have done for the Church Militant, but, to an extent no one could have imagined, it was the Church Triumphant. His Pontifical Masses bore no resemblance to those of his predecessors, and not only the canons but the priests also, even those without cure of souls, and therefore without money, walked more briskly, and were regarded indirectly with a certain respect. I do not think it impossible that from time to time the good bishop gave a helping hand to some of the more contentious priests. Certainly under his rule there was not a squabble between the hierarchies, and not so much as a complaint.

Instead, every evening unless it was raining, the doors of the palace opened, and Monsignor Dettori and the whole chapter, he with a green cord on his hat and the canons with red ones, came out and set off for the broad walks of the gardens, for a two-hour constitutional beneath the shady trees. It was a custom which he had introduced, or had come about of its own accord, because he was bishop. They walked at a staid pace, in a half-moon that stretched the whole breadth of the avenue, with himself towering and masterful in the middle, laughing rather than smiling, among the children running up from all directions to kiss his ring, and beneath the severe and respectful gaze of the watchers on the veranda of the pharmacy. And he would talk to his traveling companions, who listened in silence to his tranquil words. What did he talk about? It must have been about God, but it might also have been about the vineyard, or the harvest, or the marvelous things he had seen on the Continent; or it might even have been a soundless movement of the lips, since his majestic presence needed no words. Thus, for an hour or two hours, as in a mystical glass window, up and down the public gardens which, not many years earlier, before the usurpation, had been Church land, and now for those two hours became so again, because of his presence there.

The Lord called Monsignor Dettori to Him on a certain day in a certain year. And it was certainly a mistake, for the bishop took his myth with him, and the priests of Nuoro started scowling at each other again.

The new pastor (the historical pastor, one might say) was Monsignor Canepa, who had a Continental name but was in fact from Cagliari, so that he was already off to a bad start. He had the typical look of a priest aged by his sedentary life, the face like curdled milk (the expression was Father Mele's), the cassock falling at an obtuse angle over his protuberant belly, the nasal voice, slow and apathetic. The cross did not simply precede his name (which was Luca), as is usual with the names of bishops, but his very person, whenever he went unannounced by bells up the slope to the church, or to kneel before the tombs where the diocesans who had preceded him now rested. For he was incredibly pious, and had a special cult of the Madonna, to whom every year, on the feast day at Gonare, he devoted a long homily. He would work on this for months, rising early in the morning, in a small room giving onto a dense hedge of prickly pear, and in which he had neatly arranged the theology books he had brought with him.

Monsignor Canepa had a single fault: that of not being rich. Worse: he had a dense swarm of nephews and nieces left him by a brother and a sister who had died on him. When he was prefect of the seminary in Cagliari, he had had to provide for them by giving Latin lessons. Many of them he had arranged for as best he could, but he was left with four, the youngest; and it was with them, rather than with Brother Giossanto and Brother Baingio, that he had alighted from the carriage at the Quadrivio of Nuoro. He made the mistake of being poor in comparison with Monsignor Dettori, of venerated memory; and in the eyes of the chapter and the priests, and also the whole of Nuoro from Don Pasqualino to Dirripezza, because even to receive charity from a poor man is less of an honor than to receive it from a rich one.

The episcopal revenue was perfectly wretched, the fault of those priests who at the time of the expropriation had set a modest value on the properties of the Church, thinking thereby to avoid robbery. Instead, their salaries had been fixed according to that assessment. And on that revenue, apart from the character of Monsignor Canepa, who "embroidered homilies," as Canon Floris said scornfully, there was little holding of banquets and also little to distribute in charity. And thus the bishop's palace, with its red walls and waving palm trees, once more became the Sèuna shanty that it had always been before Monsignor Dettori reconsecrated it. One thing only was retained from the happy times: the canons' evening walk, in the long half-moon with the bishop in the middle.

The truth is that it was no easy matter to be bishop in Nuoro. The holy city contained a dozen canons who comprised the chapter, and six or seven priests scattered in San Pietro and Sèuna. There was one single parish, and the parish priest was Canon Monni, who since time immemorial had been verging on ninety, with his tiny, transparent, almost albino body. He had wealthy connections in the villages, who all came together in his presbytery clinging to Santa Maria, as if on neutral ground. Old

Camilla, her eyes devastated by trachoma, served God by way of her master, and kept up contact for him with the rest of the world, bringing him all the news, which he then sifted through in the silence of his mind. For Canon Monni never left his house, no longer even for the funerals of the rich, but he kept in constant communication with the outside world.

Canon Monni in fact had a mission to perform. Although for fifty years he had not been back to his village, lost among the mountains of Barbagia, he held the threads of the destinies of all his nephews and nieces and the nephews and nieces of his nephews and nieces. As soon as they were born, they were brought to Nuoro for his blessing, and a grand long blessing it must have been, to have sent them out from their villages to shine in the "capital," to become, or attempt to become, Nuorese. How many of them he had borne in his frail hands! And now that he was old he had to face the biggest challenge of all, something he would never have meddled in, had he been able to think any task beyond his powers. The problem was this: Dr. Porcu, one of his great-nephews on his mother's side and the showpiece of the family, or at least of its educated members, was presenting himself as a candidate in the political elections. That blessed man the pope, there in Rome, had at last decided to shut an eye to the political itches of the Catholics, and Dr. Porcu, already well on in years, at once joined the race for a single-member constituency on a ticket which used the symbol of the plow for the benefit of illiterates. But it was not easy to get one's hooks into those miscreant Nuorese, even with powerful friends, and Canon Monni needed all the feelers of his housekeeper, who from the market or the water fountain brought him far more of the hidden secrets of souls than he could glean in the confessional. The whole business was shaky, very shaky...

Far more fortunate was the other doyen among the canons, Dean Pirri, who lived in a wing of the vast Corrales possessions in the heart of San Pietro, at the top of the short slope up from Santa Croce, one of the semi-rustic little churches in Nuoro, with the plain façade, and the bell-cote above, like the Grazie in Sèuna, and as the Monastery once had been. Canon Pirri was fat, and resigned to it, with drooping cheeks on a large, ill-shaven face and eyes still dark in the pallor yellowed by the years. He, also, no longer left home. His daily constitutional was from the bed to his armchair, in which he sat, with his feet on the wood for the brazier and his biretta on his head. One knew at a glance that in all his long life he had never once smiled. Every morning, from nine to ten, his nephews and great-nephews who were not at the sheepfold would pass before him, striving to guess his thoughts. For from his room, bare except for a single crucifix, he ruled the entire dynasty of the Corrales, and like Canon Monni he had a mission to fulfill. But this was not concerned with elections or trifles of that sort. The Corrales, his nephews and the sons of his nephews, were, as we have said, a band of predators, and their fierce instincts had been retained by other descendants, many of whom had taken degrees and become middle-class. Some had even abandoned the nest in San Pietro and infiltrated the Corso. For this reason he had become a priest, because men need a law, and the law is not a written sheet of paper, which is a joke, but a man who does not judge you, but shows you the limits imposed on your actions. Canon Pirri, an honest priest and a man incapable of evil, had well understood his function, and had fulfilled it with simple dignity, gaining the respect of all his relatives; partly because he was very rich in his own right.

The dean was not a man of wide reading, but between the lines of the breviary he was apt to meditate deeply, and came early to the conclusion that free will does not exist. It was not a question of philosophy: he perceived as much in every one of his people, and perhaps even in himself. Those nephews and great-nephews had no need to confess; it was enough for them to file before him, as they did every morning, for him to know what they had done during the night. But he also knew that it would have been useless, or even downright imprudent, to give advice. On the other hand, there were the fruits of their robberies; for he saw the family—or rather, the network of families that had formed, and that recognized him as their protector, because he was close to God—buying houses and *tanche* and herds, and in a word growing rich; and this too had its mysterious justification. What he personally had to do was avoid scandals. More than once he had paid off some wretch, who had come with threats, out of his own pocket. But above all it was internal relations that had to be swathed in silence, and here it really came home to him that he was a priest.

Seated with his feet resting on the wood for the brazier, undermined by the heart condition that prevented him from lying down, Canon Pirri stroked the cat with the singed fur, and thought with terror of the danger that the entire family had been exposed to during the murky business of Avvocato Orecchioni's will. That had been his masterpiece, the justification of his whole life, even if from that day on he had suffered from this dreadful breathlessness that deprived him of sleep. Avvocato Orecchioni,

Zio Mario to the nephewry of the Corrales, was a lawyer only in a manner of speaking, because in ancient times he had taken a degree in law, which had enabled him to dress like a gentleman and do nothing from morn till eve. This was not an unusual thing in Nuoro, which was full of lawyers who had never set eyes on a codex, so that it was not clear what they lived on. In this case, Avvocato Mario possessed some very fine *tanche*, which were the envy of all his relatives, and he got conspicuous rents for them. But his degree had had the singular effect of estranging him from his relatives, and practically turning him into a misanthrope. He still lived in San Pietro, in a rustic house that bore the traces of his shepherd ancestors, looked after by a maid inherited along with the house. She had once been young, and had borne an illegitimate girl, who was now a young brunette full of innocent promise, and she was the only person the lawyer would allow into the house, to give a hand to her mother. In any case, her employer appeared not even to notice her, although little by little the girl had become more familiar, and went so far as to call him "uncle." He continued to read the newspaper, seated on the granite bench under the great fig tree that shaded the whole courtyard, and continued to take his walk around sunset, along the dusty road to Orosei, bordered with prickly pear, without exchanging a word with the peasants returning on horseback from the fields, their saddlebags laden with baskets of fruit. So every day was the same as every other. But one day cannot have been the same, because the girl disappeared. No one paid attention to it, the more so because at seventeen or eighteen all the girls in Nuoro disappeared, and went to Tunis where the wages were higher, though in reality to give birth to their bastards without being shamed.

After a while, in fact, the girl returned with a baby boy, to whom she had given the name of her old employer, as the custom was. But big Mario did not want either little Mario or his mother in the house, and so it all ended. Old tales, old tales...In the meanwhile, time had passed and the lawyer's little goatee was tinged with white. The boy's mother had worn herself out, like all the women who went to the river down at Caparedda or Mughina, doing the washing and carrying it in baskets on their heads, while little Mario had become a builder, or a blacksmith, like so many others. Anyway, they had all grown old, in Nuoro, and no one remembered anything any more, partly because there was nothing to remember.

Zia Luisa, by this time the grandmother of all the Corrales, who had once been young and beautiful, sat at the corner of the carriage-gate with a kerchief pulled forward over her head and her enormous breasts overflowing from her corset. On her knees she had a flat basket, and with skilled hand was separating the wheat from the little stones that had got mixed in on the threshing floor. But her thoughts were elsewhere. Her brother-in-law Mario's *tanca* at Lardine was next door to their own *tanca* (that is, her husband's), and in fact the lands of all the Corrales were near one another, since they all sprang from the same stock. That *tanca* was a perfect wonder, even if she had never seen it. Mario was already old, as in those days one was old when past sixty. What was he going to do with it? He was as lone as a mushroom, and solitude is a bad counsellor. He would be quite capable of leaving all his belongings to the hospital—a gross betrayal. Unless perhaps...but this was impossible. There had, of course, been that gossip all those years ago about the girl who had gone off to Tunis, but it had come to nothing, and Mario was too stingy to give away his property, even after death. Maybe one ought to keep an eye on that maid he had had with him for all too many years. She was a sphinx, that one. There was no way she would open her mouth, and she did not even give a greeting when they met. Her thoughts took wing, while the basket of grain lay inert on her lap. Well, Mario was luckily still in good health, and there was time to think about it.

But on the contrary, Mario's death was right beside him, as it is with us all, and it came one evening as it was growing dark, due to an attack of pneumonia, which in those days, without penicillin, left one with little hope. The news spread at once, and at long last the various generations of Corrales were able to get into the house. The maid could not prevent them, because without her master she counted for nothing. Never were so many grieving figures seen, as there were around that useless dying man. Natale Cherchi, known as Bersagliere, since nicknames proliferated within the already vast Corrales clan, was the most heartbroken of all. The sound of the death rattle passed out through the window, poured down into the yard among the yellowed leaves of the fig tree, meandered among the little houses in the alleyway, where the shepherds sitting on their doorsteps heard it impassively. At last it stopped, and Avvocato Orecchioni left his house and his *tanche* without a master.

An enormous silence filled the dingy room, and the dead man was not the most silent among them. At last Pilime Corrales, who was one of the oldest, regained his voice enough to call the maid. She emerged from the shadows, her eyes shining with tears, but hard and malevolent. The old man seemed to avoid her gaze, feigning some inner commotion. "Your master is dead," he told her, "and we remain. He is now atoning for...We will add that you have been a faithful servant, and you will not be forgotten, whatever arrangements he has made." Then, after a long pause: "By the way, you don't happen to know if he left anything?"

The old woman froze. She felt alone and defenseless, and she had to be careful what she said. "I know," she began slowly, "that before he fell ill he went looking for a pen and an inkwell, and began to write, upstairs, on the parlor table. I don't know what he wrote, because I can't read."

Those people were too used to lies not to know that she was lying. But it was Bersagliere who saved the situation. "This is not the moment to think about tomorrow," he exclaimed, leaping to his feet. "Now we must think of paying homage to the dead man, who deserved it. Poor Zio Mario! In fact...excuse me for a moment. I must go and put on a tie, because I rushed here like a mad thing as soon as I heard he was ill." He went out, shutting the door behind him, climbed noiselessly up the wooden steps, and found himself in the parlor. On the table there were in fact some yellowed papers, but they were old account sheets. He quickly leafed through them and came across a sealed envelope marked My Will. His heart was beating hard. He opened it and read: "I leave everything to my natural son Mario, grandson of my maid." That was all, but it was enough. Slowly he folded the envelope and put it in his pocket, from which he had pulled out an old tie, placed there before leaving home. And decked out in this tie he re-entered the other room, flung himself on his knees before the dead man, and wept desperately.

Canon Pirri stirred the charcoal with a long poker. The memories assaulting him beaded his brow with sweat. For the old woman had not stayed there mourning over the corpse, but had hurried upstairs herself to look for the will. There and then she was too afraid to speak, but after the funeral she began to spread the rumor that there was a copy of the will, though unsigned, and that several people had seen the envelope on that table. Soon the whole of Nuoro rang with the story of the tie, and in Nuoro there were not only shepherds, but also the authorities, and there was that round building overlooking the town, which the Corrales knew very well, since they had spent many years of their lives inside it, and ought to have stayed there forever. The dean saw the mire rising up to his knees. For one can do anything—rob, plunder, even kill—but deny the last wishes of the dead, no. If these nephews of his had evil in their veins, he had to exorcise it.

He summoned them one by one, threatened them that he would leave all his property to the Church, and made them hand over the will. Then he sent for the old woman and said: "What are all these rumors you're spreading?"

"It's the truth," replied the maid. "I saw the will with my own eyes, and I have the unsigned copy."

"Well then, let's suppose that this is true, and that you can prove what you say. What do you hope to gain? The taxes would eat up the lot of it, let alone the legal costs." And he made an estimate of what that desperate undertaking would cost her. Then, looking her straight in the eye (and his were still the eyes of a Corrales, even if he was dressed as a priest): "Look here," he said. "You know how fond I was of Mario. He was a good soul. I'll speak to you as he would have spoken himself. Wouldn't it be better"—and here there was a long pause—"better for you to let the properties go where they have to go, and take what they are worth instead? I have made a calculation, and it comes to two hundred thousand lire, which would be paid to you at once. Two hundred thousand lire," he repeated. "With this money your grandson would be able to find a good job on the Continent and would not have to slave away in the *tanche*, which is not the sort of work for him. Think it over carefully."

The woman at once came to the conclusion that there was nothing to think over, after those prudent words. And so, without a word in writing, as in the confessional, for the first time in their lives the Corrales handed over money instead of raking it in, and the family bastard vanished from Nuoro. But the *tanche* remained in the family, and Zia Luisa felt that the one at Lardine, now all of a piece, must be the grandest *tanca* in all Nuoro, even though she had never seen it.

But Canon Monni and Canon Pirri, although the bishop went to call on them once a week and set great store by their advice, were by this time extraneous to the church, and their stalls in the choir behind the high altar were always covered with dust. The boss of the curia, destined to become dean when Canon Pirri died, was Canon Floris, a man as vigorous as Monsignor Canepa was frail; he therefore played it both ways, not turning up his nose at social life, but frequenting the pharmacy, and occasionally even sitting down at a table in the Caffè Tettamanzi. He was also the master of ceremonies at religious functions, the "director," as one might say today, because when Pontifical Mass was celebrated he moved the other canons and priests around like puppets, and the bishop himself moved at a nod from him. His baritone voice floated down the aisles, hovered motionless over the bent heads of the faithful, and then dispersed in the blue skies of Nuoro and reached God. The other canons detested him, but they felt his superiority. No one in any case would have been able to do what he did, not even Canon Fele, the scholar of the diocese, whom we already know. The dean-to-be called Fele "the reptile," because he walked in that spindly way, always rubbing his hands together, and was suspected of being the author of certain anonymous letters which the bishop had received—some, it appeared, had even reached Rome. Canon Fele had taken on the task of visiting the rich widows, and had procured a number of good bequests for the Church, which gave him quite a few points over his colleagues. The latter, in any case, preserved an attitude of neutrality toward the two rivals, satisfied with the red cord that hung from their hats and with the ermine that distinguished them from the ordinary run of priests.

The six or seven priests constituted a kind of fourth estate. Since there was only one parish, they lived virtually on charity. Some had a small field which they still cultivated, but most suffered from hunger, and if they did not drown it in wine, they sated it with hatred for the canons. Father Delussu was better off than the others because he was assigned to the Rosario, where the dead paused on their way to the cemetery. But he, as his name betrayed, was a Continental in origin, and was good-natured.

In the evening, after the meager supper, everyone in the quarter would hear the stroke of a bell. It was not a dead man who was delayed, or who had retraced his steps. It was Father Delussu telling his brother, who lived on the other side of the piazza,

that the bottle was ready on the table for them to get drunk together in silence.

The black-hearted priest, the one who lived at the far end of
Sèuna and never ate, firstly because he had nothing to eat, and
then because he was anxiously awaiting the day of judgment,
was Father Porcu. Gloomy and spectral, he spent his time sending off exposés of Canon Floris, the rubicund dean-to-be who
was the incarnation of the Church Triumphant. His complaints
suffered the fate of all complaints, and this fueled the fire of his
hatred. A ray of light seemed to creep in on the day when, following Monsignor Canepa, a Continental bishop arrived. Fame
with its fanfares preceded the advent of this pastor, and in his
hallucinations Father Porcu had no doubt that he had been sent
entirely for him. And in fact after a few days the bishop sent for
him, because the canons had told him about this contentious
priest, who should be suspended *a divinis*. He tidied up his clothes
as best he could and set out for the palace in trepidation. The
bishop, who had a kind heart, was struck by how thin the priest
was, and he addressed him in loving words, in the name of their
common Lord.

"All right," replied the priest, "but Canon Floris is a scoundrel
and you have to get rid of him."

"What are you saying, my son? How can you be so lacking in
respect toward a superior?"

"I understand," said Father Porcu, getting to his feet. "You are
a racketeer like the rest of them." The conversation had lasted
five minutes.

Father Porcu grew more and more spectral, and they say that
little by little he fell ill. One morning, when he felt close to death,

he got up, and he dressed with difficulty, and then with halting steps started off toward Santa Maria, up the endless slope, along the flagstoned Corso. Followed by stares of curiosity, step by step he reached the cathedral. He wanted to cry out a last prayer to God, there in His house. He knelt down before the high altar, and his weary voice resounded in the stillness.

"Lord, you see how old I am and ill. Take me to you. I can no longer say Mass to you, as I can't stay on my feet. Lord, take me to you. And for the good of the Church, take Canon Floris as well. Then all will be at peace."

10

D on Sebastiano had no wish to go down that evening into
the room cheered by the firelight, and would willingly have
gone to bed without saying good night to anyone. He had been
working all day, and when it was getting late a couple came in
to draw up a marriage contract. They came from a village in the
Costera, he being well over seventy while she was a young thing
of twenty. She was accompanied by her parents, who were much
younger than the groom, and their shabby clothes revealed their
modest means. Don Sebastiano had listened to the declarations
on both sides, and had begun to write. Just as usual. But his hand
was heavy, and his pen unwilling. He was anything but a senti-
mentalist, and had seen a thing or two in his time. At a certain
point he got to his feet, called the parents into the next room,
which was his bedroom, and said, "I am prepared to pay for the
stamped paper if you will not sell your daughter."

"You do your duty" was their reply. "First the white wedding,
then the widow's weeds."

And he had done his duty, as he always did. Like the time that
poor fellow had died on him when he had just taken down his last
wishes in favor of a penniless woman who had lived with him all
her life. He had died before he had finished reading over the document, and Don Sebastiano had not felt equal to making a small

false statement, even though it would have saved the woman from penury. He was not a cruel man: it is life that is cruel, and the law expresses all the cruelty of life.

Bent over the newspaper, Don Sebastiano, perhaps for the first time since he had sat at that desk, reviewed the events of his life. Along the walls, in cupboards with glass doors, stretched the hundred or more morocco-bound volumes of documents, each with its registry number printed in black on the spine. It was his library, the only books he possessed, and he had written them all himself, day after day. He thought back to the early ones, the enormous efforts undergone when, as the only notary in the whole district, he had to do tens of kilometers on horseback, ford-ing rivers, with his official stamped paper in tin tubes, which he still preserved. A pity that these volumes were dependent on his own existence, for when he died they would come and take them away, because notarial deeds end up in the public archives, just as their authors end up in the cemetery.

Don Sebastiano was not a man to live in the past, or to waste his time in useless sentiment. The fact was, that day there had been the umpteenth quarrel with Donna Vincenza, brought about by one of those bits of advice of hers which hurt her hus-band in proportion to how judicious they were. Don Sebastiano had thought he could cut things short with the usual terrible phrase: "You're only in this world because there's room for you," but this time his sons had rebelled and sprung to their mother's defense. So he had got to his feet and left, slamming the door behind him.

It was the first time he had found himself exposed to the judg-ment of his children. Or maybe it would be more correct to say that it was the first time he had really encountered them, after devoting his entire existence to them. But what did they expect from him? What did they know about life, about that invisible web which one blunders into like a fly and then does nothing but struggle to escape the spider scuttling out from its ambush in the center? What did their mother know about it, after twenty years of not leaving the house? And why did they need to defend her, when he himself had always defended and protected her? That day she had broached the old topic of the pastureland at Orotelli, which was up for sale and which she wanted her husband to buy, while he, on the contrary, was negotiating in favor of a third party. It was one of the bees in her bonnet that afflicted her life. What did she know about that land, which she had never seen and never would see? The soil was poor and stony, and it was even dangerous to compete against the local people. This was what he thought. Could she not be content with the vineyards he had created with his own hands, and with this house, which for Nuoro was a palace?

The truth that Don Sebastiano did not want to admit was that the family to which he had given the whole of himself had always been alien to him. Anyone who works as he had worked has the right to be loved, but has no time to love in return. This was the root of it all. He had demanded only one thing of his family: that they should not disturb him in his work, and that each should therefore do his duty, as he had done. From this sprang that preference for outsiders which Donna Vincenza had reproved him for, his tendency to put his children in the wrong in their childish squabbles, and his susceptibility to the charms of others, especially those cunning rogues from San Pietro who were beginning to become urbanized, and therefore used to flock around him, convivial and fawning. Donna Vincenza seemed to loathe everyone who came near him, and who wrapped him round their little finger. She had even got to the point of turning them out of the house when they came to call, putting him in the position of having to apologize and make his wife out to be mad. And now, over this matter of the Orotelli pastures, it seemed that it was Giovanni Maria's turn. He was the son of that Matteo, the eldest brother among the old Sannas, who (as I have related) left Nuoro and his family with curses at twenty years old, and at ninety expressed the certainty that his brother Priamo, who had died earlier, was already in hell and waiting for his wife. No one had ever had word of him again. But one day thirty years later, there turned up in Nuoro a sturdily built young man with a broad face, untypical of Nuoro, and not even speaking the Nuorese dialect correctly. He introduced himself to Don Sebastiano, calling him "uncle." He was Matteo's son, and wanted to settle in Nuoro and start in business. Had his father sent him there to wreak his revenge? Everything is possible. At any rate, he asked for help from his all-powerful uncle, and the latter gave him so much that in a short time he became really rich in the almond trade, and his wealth turned to fat, for he weighed little less than four hundred pounds. He was cheerful, expansive, and liked a good time, and he occupied Don Sebastiano's house as if it were his own, smothering the boys with toys and tidbits. Donna Vincenza had dubbed him Milord, and the name had spread all over town. Then, suddenly, hatred and fury. She realized that he had become a rival to herself and her children, and that Don Sebastiano, bewitched by his blandishments, was negotiating the pastures for him. At that point she set the whole family against him, so that he was forced to leave, and not to set foot in the house any more.

The usual story. And the house that might have been happy, since nothing was lacking, because of this woman's stubbornness was the most unhappy of all. Don Sebastiano felt himself to be innocent. In the oncoming night he heard confused, excited voices from the caffè in the Corso. It was the Nuorese finishing off their idle day, in idleness. If he listened carefully he could recognize the guffaws and the sneering laughter of every one of them. No doubt they had put Maestro Manca in the midst of the company and were buying him drinks; or Fileddu, that troglodyte who had the mania (though perhaps it was necessity) of attaching himself to the gentry, and who therefore had become the laughing-stock of Nuoro. At that hour they must have been a bit high already, perhaps on his very own wine, which the caffè proprietor had bought from him. Never had he been tempted to set foot in that gentlemanly pothouse, nor had he ever wished to rub shoulders with such people. His brief relaxation was at the nearby pharmacy in the hour before dusk; but that was like never leaving home, because as he chatted with Don Pasqualino or Don Serafino, he would keep an eye on the "little door," and see who went in and out. He did not notice a sad figure leaning on the windowsill of the dining room, immersed in her black garments, peering shortsightedly at the passers-by on the cobbles of Via Asproni. This was the recreation that Donna Vincenza allowed herself every evening. Or rather, it was her way of taking part in life.

The exit of the head of the household from the dining room had left the nestful of fledglings, and Donna Vincenza herself, as if in the dark. However violent, and however unjust, the father has on his side some arcane legitimacy that throws all hearts into confusion. The two youngest, who were clinging to their mother, were crying. Each of the others went on silently with his homework, without a word to his brothers. Donna Vincenza slowly told a string of rosary beads that she had been given on her wedding day, but her eyes, staring into the void, did not see God. It was doubtful in any case, with all her toils and troubles, if she had ever seen Him.

While Don Sebastiano on the floor above was searching for his innocence among the red volumes of deeds that were the fabric of his life, Donna Vincenza, as in a last confession, was looking back at herself in each of the many years she had spent with this man; and every year, every day, was an indictment that she would face him with in due time. She had married him when she was twenty and he was ten years older. He had taken her from the house at *Sa bena* where she lived with her mother, and she was so naïve that when she became pregnant she thought that they would have to cut her belly open to get the baby out. This memory, so far in the past, and even ridiculous after all the children she had borne, gave her a feeling of elation. It seemed to her that she had wasted an enormous gift, and that that supreme innocence, even today, gave her an edge over him. What had happened after that? Her gaze rested on the unlovely shapes of a woman already old at forty, on her enormous body, on her knees swollen with arthritis: all that was left was her face, her brow both high and unfurrowed. But she had not always been like this, for she had once been beautiful, with the fair hair of a Continental, with slender limbs, with the great *joie de vivre* that was part of her nature.

When she became a Sanna, she had had to lay aside local costume, and this had been the beginning of her misfortunes. For it is not a simple matter of changing one's mode of dress. It is a whole world which one accepts, with its laws and its people, with its pretensions and its prejudices, even in a little town like Nuoro. Moving from *Sa bena* to Santa Maria, which was no more than eight hundred meters, or perhaps a kilometer, she had passed from one world into another. And in that world she needed his help, because she was poor, and alone, and scared of everything. She remembered the first time she had gone to church with her mother, who still wore costume. She got the impression that everyone was looking at her, that the cheap dark dress with the white dots had all eyes fixed upon it. She had told Sanna (this is what she called the man she had married, according to the custom of the time) that she needed another dress, and he, between one deed and the next, had replied, "The money's there. Go and buy it." It was the first slap in the face she had ever received. How can an inexperienced girl take the money and just go and do it without some help from her man, even if only to cross the threshold on the way out?

After her first pregnancy she told him, "The veins in this leg hurt me."

"Then call the doctor. The money's there," was the reply.

The usual story. It was true that he worked all day long, that he never allowed himself the least pleasure, that if he picked some fruit at Isporòsile or Locoi he did not dare to eat it, because he had to take it home to the family. But one simply couldn't leave a woman on her own like this, on the edge of an abyss; for that was what the doorstep meant to her, in the house where little by little she was walling herself up. For this is exactly what happened, that when she was still young and full of life she no longer set foot outside, and immersed herself in a desperate solitude, which only the endless task of looking after her children, and the house that after all she was mistress of, enabled her to bear. But the worst of it was that her immobility began to undermine her health. Her legs swelled up and she became deformed; and so her natural shyness was aggravated by the embarrassment of being seen in the outside world, which is composed of nimble people who can walk. He, he could have rescued her. And he wanted to do so, and gave her money to go and take a cure. But where, and how, and with whom, if she found it impossible even to cross the threshold?

The flame was slowly dying in the fireplace. The approaching night dispersed the phantoms that the onrush of rage had dredged up from the bottom of her heart, where they lay hidden. Maybe the time for hating would come, but in a family with so many sons who have to build a future for themselves, who have to survive, such soliloquies could not last long. And in fact the two youngest, Sebastiano and Peppino, who had run to her in tears when tempers flared up, had gone to sleep with their heads on her lap. She must put them to bed. Gently she woke them up and, taking each by the hand, started up those grandiose, useless stairs that were the pride and joy of Ingegner Mannu, alias Don Gabriele. It was a trial for her poor legs, and every so often she had to pause. On the second floor, passing the study, she saw a light filtering under the door. She was dumbfounded. Sanna, who went to bed with the hens because he got up before dawn, was still awake.

11

D on Ricciotti spent his life at the Caffè Tettamanzi, the very
place where his father had gambled away his whole fortune. But he neither ate nor drank, and still less did he allow these
pseudo-gents to get him drunk, like that imbecile Maestro Manca.
He spent his time there, when school was out, because the house
he had been left with was unbearable to him, denuded as it was
of everything; and the sight of his spectral wife, and his children
playing among rubbish (for such appeared to him the niggardly
furnishings and scanty decorations), made his life intolerable.
But also, his suffering was of the kind that required witnesses,
and above all people whom he could involve in the hatred bottled
up in his heart for so many years. He brooded over calling on Don
Sebastiano and asking him to give back Loreneddu—in return, of
course, for the sum paid by him at the auction twenty years ago.
Some reaction was inevitable. In the meanwhile there he sat, on
the cast-iron chair from which his enormous rump overflowed,
looking daggers at the people crowding the tables, as if spoiling
for a fight. But no one paid him any attention.

And who could be expected to do so when all the customers
were crowding around Maestro Manca, with Boelle Zicheri and
Paolo Bartolino goading him on to amuse them with one of his
improvised ballads, tempting him with the mirage of a glass of

wine that he could no longer do without? If Don Ricciotti had approached Boelle Zicheri and Paolo Bartolino with the notion of retrieving Loreneddu, that is, of simply putting the clock back, they would have laughed in his face, and so would all the others who paid court to them. And they would have been right, unless the world turned upside down.

Boelle (which is short for Raffaele) and Paolo Bartolino were the outstanding characters in the life of the caffè, because they were well off and, as their names showed, of Continental origin. Boelle was a pharmacist, but this means little, for so was Signor Piga, who owned the pharmacy frequented by Don Sebastiano and the other bourgeois bigwigs, and who was fit for nothing except grumbling about the doctors, who sent him illegible prescriptions. In Boelle's pharmacy stood a glass-fronted cabinet with POISONS written on it in huge letters, and word went around that he kept his thousand-lire notes in it.

Paolo Bartolino we already know. He was that two-meter-tall Piedmontese, or half-Piedmontese, of whom a few old men used to say that they had seen him as a child chiseling the grooves in the granite flagstones of the Corso, along with his father. But if this was the case, he had left it far behind, for he had scarcely set eyes on the stinting soil of Sardinia but he had entered the contracting business and built himself a Venetian-style house right next to the caffè. It towered above all its neighbors; but most of all, it was not gloomy (like Don Sebastiano's house almost opposite), because it had red shutters and a few flowers on the balcony.

As bachelors, both these men had pasts shrouded in a veil of myth woven by the fantasies of the faithful husbands of Nuoro, and perhaps even more by the disappointed hopes of the womenfolk. It was said, though in hushed tones, that when the men who wrecked the woods came over from Tuscany, when Nuoro was scarcely more than a den, these two used to give banquets in their houses and were served by Giggia with not a stitch on. Giggia was the lovely creature, now reduced to penury and halfway to madness, who almost without knowing what she was doing worked as a prostitute in San Pietro. There was also a rumor that they had caught syphilis, which was then more of a sin than a disease. I think this was true. But now their stage was the caffè, where they flaunted their mature years, as well as their superiority over those swarms of Nuorese who had no life to live, and who became ever more numerous as the town grew larger. These abandoned the drinking dens which their fathers continued to frequent, because inwardly they felt they were becoming gentlemen, going up a rung on the social ladder and entering a world which they thought was more respectable, while in fact it was only less arduous and more fatuous. There was no doubt that those dead-ended old cellars, or pothouses, or however one wants to describe them, with the casks up on trestles, the waxen-faced man opening and closing the spigot behind the bar, chalking the number of swilled-down glasses on the staves of the barrel, and toting up the damage when the binge was over—and with the washed-out flag above the doorway—were very like catacombs, and getting drunk in them was a silent, solitary business. Those bearded fathers came and went in long lines like ants, with the blue faces of candidates for cirrhosis of the liver, which among the sneers of the survivors reaped a couple of them each year. Late at night the last glimmer of reason, or perhaps just instinct, led them back home, weaving along the alleyways like blind men. Their Sardinian wives heard their steps and hiccups in the distance, and opened the door for them like nurses, because the drinking habit is a calamity, and calamities must be accepted.

That evening Maestro Manca was the butt of the company. Since we first met him he had gone a long way—downhill, of course. Half a glass of wine was enough to make him drunk, and his hands were beginning to shake. In moments of euphoria he would play the braggart with himself. "Will I kill this vice?" he would shout in the middle of the caffè. "No, the vice will kill me!" But in fact he had a terrible fear of dying, and because the vein in his temple had swollen up, he had got it into his head that it was going to burst, and that death would come that way, all of a sudden. Therefore he went around pressing the vein with his fingers, while everyone laughed madly. "Maestro, how goes it with the vein?" they would ask. He would fly into a rage and shout, "Go shove it up your ass!" And the laughter redoubled. In ruins as he was, he still retained his gift for comedy, or what seemed comic to others, and therefore they sought him out, and he was surrounded by the fine gentlemen of the caffè, who egged him on to improvise his ballads.

Sa fide la professo
chind'una timinzana
de' cussu e zia Tatana
*Faragone…**

It was a hymn both sacred and profane, in praise of life, and at the same time in praise of death. Boelle, Bartolino, and their whole

---

* I profess my faith in a demijohn of that [i.e., wine] of Zia Tatana [Sebastiana] Faragone, etc., she being the owner of one of the hillside vineyards below Locoi.

court laughed fit to bust. He knew he ought not to sing, and had an unconscious yearning for a more serious life, but at bottom he was afraid of all those people who made the next wineglass sparkle, as if tempting a child. Every so often he would recognize the face of one of his ex-pupils in the crowd, and then he would stop suddenly and reprimand him, including his father and grandfather in the most atrocious insults. "So this is what I gave you an education for, you son of a whore, you jailhouse jackass! Just for you to end up at the bar and poke fun at your teacher!" But these were storms in a teacup, and no one took them seriously. In any case, that thoughtless laughter was better than Don Ricciotti's sulk, as he sat endlessly in his corner, watching the scene with loathing, and planning his revenge.

Don Sebastiano, like Don Pasqualino and Don Serafino, had never and would never set foot in the Caffè Tettamanzi, but this simply meant that they were behind the times, thinking of nothing but penny-pinching. Like all growing cities, Nuoro daily spawned forth more and more people who had nothing to do, or rather, could not possibly have anything to do. The shepherd community continued to live its murky life in San Pietro, and the peasant community of Sèuna remained immobile in its aquamarine light. But these new people belonged neither to the one nor to the other, and the infallible sign of this was that the local costume was beginning to disappear. "*Insignoriccati,*" or "money-gentrified," as they called those who had turned their backs on their own origins, they were attracted to the caffè because there they could stand shoulder to shoulder with Boelle and Bartolino, with all those lawyers who had never opened a law book, with whom Nuoro was crammed; and the caffè helped them to disguise their own poverty. No one, in any case, asked anyone else about their business.

Among the novices who had drifted in was Pietro Catte, whom we met as a boy in Maestro Messa's class; the one, you remember, who confused the seven hills with the Etruscan kings. Now, of course, he was a grown man, corpulent, with eyes more bovine than ever. His misfortune was that he had ever learned to read and write, because he had been given a job as conductor on the first bus to be seen in Nuoro, and he had got caught taking the money without giving the tickets. Well, they gave him the sack, and now, still living on that aunt of his, he had found the only position he was suited to occupy; that is, the caffè table. He was boisterous and jocular, and as a cardplayer he could beat the lot of them at "tresette." For this reason Boelle always wanted him as a partner. I remember now that I talked to him in the cemetery where they buried him, although he came to a bad end. But at that time he was full of life, and liked his glass of wine as much as Maestro Manca, although he could hold it better.

It is two weeks now since I broke off this narrative. It was Pietro Catte, and no other, who made my pen run dry. Boss-eyed Pietro Catte, bloated with wine, with his blubbery lips, appeared before me in all his utter fatuity. As futile as Boelle and Bartolino, as futile as Don Sebastiano and Don Pasqualino; as futile as Nuoro itself. Could I be wasting my time (and these indeed my last few years) in bestowing some substance on people who never had any, and could never have had any, who cannot be of interest to anyone, since their very existence dwindles down to a birth certificate and a death certificate? I have suffered terribly because of the sudden void that has formed around me. There is not the least doubt that Pietro Catte in the abstract has no reality, any more than any other man on the face of the earth. But the fact remains that he was born and that he died, as those irrefutable certificates prove. And this endows him with reality in actual fact, because birth and death are the two moments at which the infinite become finite; and the infinite can have no being except through the finite. Pietro Catte attempted to escape from reality by hanging himself on that tree at Biscollai, but his was a vain hope, because one cannot erase one's own birth. This is why I say that Pietro Catte, like all the hapless characters in this story, is important, and ought to be interesting to everyone: if he does not exist, then none of us exist.

And the same goes for Fileddu. Fileddu (the meaning of the word is "string") might be considered the jester to the "court" of the Caffè Tettamanzi, not to say the buffoon of the larger court of Nuoro. In effect, he was a peaceable simpleton who had taken it into his head to attach himself to the gentry, imagining that he was himself a gentleman. Life is a dream, and he was not awakened from his dream by the howls and catcalls that greeted him when he made his appearance at the top of the Corso, after emerging from the hovel where he lived in conditions that for others would have been those of the direst penury. He tended to weave as he walked, perhaps because of some defect in his sense of balance, but he always wore dark clothes, clothes that might have been considered elegant if they had not been four times his size: the size, let us say, of Boelle Zicheri, whose faithful spaniel he was. Every now and then Boelle gave him the job of putting up the shutters over the pharmacy windows, but this was simply an excuse for slipping him a little spare change, because hunger was sapping his strength. There were a few people, off in the wings, who took this middle-class calling of his in all seriousness, and therefore hated him (and I am thinking particularly of Casizolu, a simpleton like him, but who thought of himself as worse off). However, the gentlemen of the caffè took him into their circle, and with them he could live out his dream to the full. Who cared if the rascally boys, lying in wait at the corners of the alleyways, caught him as he passed and chanted, "Ting-a-ling-a-ling" and "Bottom of a slop pail!" which were two of the many taunts that the local genius for nastiness invented daily for his torture. He would sit at the same table as Boelle and Bartolino, being (gentleman that he was) on equal terms with them, with his beady little eyes, listening to the praises they heaped on him. Really a decent lot, the boys in the bar. And one evening it was Bartolino himself (or at least so I seem to remember) who gave him a great thump on his bony shoulder and said, "Francesco"—(this was his real name, which was thrown away on him—"you can't go on living alone like this, you've got to get married! We'll find you a wife. You must pay court to Carolina, Don Pasqualino's daughter!"

Enormous guffaws rose from one end of the caffè to the other. Robertino Caramelli, Francesco Casu and Don Gaetano Pilleri laid down their cards—one can't say more than that—and came up to the table. For you should know that if Don Pasqualino was the god of Nuoro, Carolina was a goddess in paradise, so lovely was she in her eighteen years. These three joined in the general chorus, and the cackles rose to the skies above. Fileddu was in his seventh heaven. That Homeric laughter seemed to him an indication of love, as if someone were urging him to venture along unknown paths. But were they really unknown? Had he not always thought of this marriage, as a dream within a dream, and today these gentlemen had made him aware of it? Tomorrow he would begin to walk beneath her windows, and would wait for the moments when she left the house. And in the meantime he was dazed with gratitude, while the gentlemen, all crowding around him (except for the glowering Don Ricciotti, in a corner), improvised an engagement party and ordered cakes and sweet wine, which he drank, though not much, because long fasting had shrunk his stomach, while the others raised their glasses in a toast to the bride and groom, Carolina and Fileddu.

Everything would have been fine if Fileddu's mother, who was also half-witted, had not been standing in rags in the wintry street, following the scene through the glass panes of the door, her eyes as pallid as a blind woman's. The same old story. She would certainly not have dared to go into the caffè, for she was afraid of those gentlemen, and was in awe of them, but she in-stinctively felt the injustice that was being done in there, and that she had to save her son. She waited for hours, until everyone had gone home, to collect this son of hers and take him protective-ly back to the hovel, where at least she would know he was safe until morning came.

12

I n the depths of her heart Donna Vincenza was alone, but she was not alone in her kingdom in Via Asproni, in the house which Don Sebastiano had built and left in her hands. The family was growing and taking on the form it would maintain forever, even when internal trouble undermined its existence, and in a material sense dissolved it, as with all the things of this world. But a family, this mystery in which our own person is multiplied, does not overcome solitude, but increases it. Donna Vincenza was not alone simply because other solitary lives gravitated around her, forming her little court.

The humble house in which she had lived before Don Sebastiano bore her off to the Santa Maria district was surrounded by even more modest dwellings, where poor women lived their lives and earned their bread by performing age-old tasks: making cakes to order, weaving cloth, grinding corn. Zia Isporzedda, whom we met on the occasion of my ghostly return to the cemetery, did indeed own a grindstone, and Parlamento, her blindfolded donkey, had been circling around it for five hundred years before Don Pasqualino stopped him with his steam mill. All these people looked with respect, and indeed with love, on the daughter of Monsù Vugliè, that Piedmontese who had died so unexpectedly. They were touched by her charm, and when Don

Sebastiano wanted to marry her, and bestowed a title on her, they gathered around her as if she were a daughter or a sister before whom a luminous future is opening up. And with the passing of the years they did not forget her. In fact, because of the changed circumstances, they almost felt themselves to be her satellites, and used to visit her in the immense house, bringing her their little gifts. Zia Isporzedda especially, who while sitting on the ground beside her donkey had learned to meditate, understood—although she understood nothing—the price Donna Vincenza paid for her riches, and whenever she could used to lend her a hand. While helping to shell peas or broad beans, she would tell her what was new at *Sa bena* so that, although she lived a cloistered life, Donna Vincenza was always up to date with events. Even the poor can give of their charity to the rich.

Don Sebastiano did not even spare a glance for these poor faithful creatures of his wife's when he passed them in the huge hallway of his house, while they drew back against the white-washed wall with the broad black wainscot that typified the dwellings of the rich. On the other hand, though without halt-ing in his stride, he used solemnly to greet Zia Gonaria, Donna Vincenza's poor cousin, who would come in with a smile and a greeting every day on her way to and from school. Gonaria (also named Sanna but not related to Don Sebastiano) was "Aunt Gonaria" to the family, because the children called her that, es-pecially the youngest, who was her godchild; and she used to tell how at baptism the infant had reached out to touch the flame of the candle she was holding. This was not true, of course, though she had most certainly seen it, because she lived passionately in a world of dreams. The dream was not only of the child reaching out of the swaddling clothes with his tiny hand, like a latter-day Hercules. No, it was the flame itself, in which the spirit was incarnated as in the Host: she saw it, and in a supreme hallucination saw her godchild take hold of the spirit between his little fingers, without getting burned. She had told the story many times in her life, even more frequently now that her godson was growing up, and already stood head and shoulders above her. For Zia Gonaria was a tiny little person, and would have seemed tinier still but for the perfect figure beneath her black dress, and the face of an angel under the big white kerchief that she bound tightly around her head like a bandage.

Donna Vincenza awaited her cousin's visit with a feeling of mischievous affection, because they were in a mysterious way complementary to each other. Gonaria knew all about God and nothing whatever about life. A virgin by absolute vocation, like the three sisters with whom she lived in a house rescued from past disasters (the memory of which was the pride of their solitude), it was with a joyful heart that she entered the house of a cousin who had brought forth so many creatures to the glory of the Lord. There she found, and as it were absorbed, the need for motherhood which every woman carries within her, and which every day she exercised on her pupils; for she was a teacher, and all the various generations of girls in Nuoro had come under her care. Mothers and daughters and even grandmothers had taken their turns for thirty years on the benches of that school, where those who had it in them learned to write, but all who left her were in love with God. Donna Vincenza knew all about life, and she amused herself by opposing it to the God of her cousin who, herself being nothing but love, was proof against all ironies; which in any case were good-natured enough, for Donna Vincenza also needed God, and for this reason was fond of her bizarre relative. Anyway, these innocent disputes ended with a cup of coffee, the only thing Gonaria was really insatiable for.

Gonaria, Zia Gonaria, was a saint. Her name, naturally, does not appear in the calendar. No one can become a saint without the backing of an organization, and so her spirit still drifts about the cemetery of Nuoro, like the souls of the sinners, and mingles with them. There she came to me and clasped my knees, as I would clasp hers as a child; and she begged me desperately for love.

That sullen God who had made Don Pasqualino and Dirripezza, Don Sebastiano and Boelle and Bartolino live on the soil of Nuoro, along with a hundred others whom we have met or will meet, in a moment of joy, with His own hands, had molded Zia Gonaria. Without doubt He had created her for her to adore Him, and in fact ever since she was a child He had made Himself known to her, in the form of a firefly entering a dark room, in the form of a new-born lamb that the shepherd carried by the feet, with its umbilical cord still attached, in the form of an egg laid in the strawstack, in the form of the sun or of the infinite stars that glittered in the sky. The house where God decreed she should be born was large and affluent, but in a few years it became small and impoverished. Her father (the usual story) had seen the Continentals amassing money by cutting down the forests, and although he had a university education, he thought he could do the same thing, and to start with he did quite well. But then, one time in the month of August, there was a storm that lasted for three days, in a part of the country where rain is unknown. The bark that he had stacked in the open, waiting for the buyer to collect it, rotted away completely. Her father trudged in dismay from stack to stack, staring at the red rivulets of tannine flowing down the hillside. In desperation he took ship to Leghorn, center of the trade, and never returned. He was carried off by a stroke as soon as he got there.

This at least was the tale passed down the generations. Her mother died shortly afterward, and Gonaria, Battistina, Tommasina, and Giuseppina, four little sisters, with a brother named Ciriaco, were left on their own. That God who had created Gonaria for His joy, or for His sport, entered and became used to the little house where they were forced to shelter, left with nothing except the brazier in winter, on the lid of which the cat with singed fur used to purr. And this also was God. Supper was meager, but the young girl found her nourishment elsewhere, and it may have been then that by an unconscious vow she got used to doing without food, aided in this by continuous headaches, which were also a manifestation of God, and which as a grown-up she symbolized by the white kerchief binding her hair. But God manifested Himself when she was a young woman, for—endowed with intelligence as she was—she soon managed to become a schoolmistress, with a salary of ninety-three lire a month, on which the little family's new home was built.

Gonaria would not for the life of her handle the money, because the devil was hidden in every coin, and just as she saw God, she also saw the devil. Her ninety-three lire ended up in the hands of Giuseppina, the sister who by vocation had taken on the role of Martha, and looked after the cooking and other small expenses. The other two sisters, Battistina and Tommasina, lived in the past, that is, on the memory of their lost wealth, which meant that Gonaria and Giuseppina did all *their* work as well.

But there was no harm in this, because each in her own way followed her destiny, which the others accepted. In any case, they were very different from one another, because Battistina to some extent shared the ecstatic soul of Gonaria, while Tommasina was sanguine and fat, and perhaps she underwent, rather than underwrote, the vocation of celibacy which they all shared. No one could then have known that God would make use of Tommasina for the trap He was preparing for His creature.

They all slept in the same room, because they were scared. The "butterfly" (the wick that circled continuously in its dish of oil) attenuated the darkness of night, and helped Gonaria to remain awake, because sleeping seemed to her to be time stolen from God. The shouts of the drunkards reached her every so often from the street, and more than once she had recognized the voice and the curses of her colleague Maestro Manca, hunted down by the savagery of those townspeople who kept him in terror of death. Then she would pray for him, even though at school in the morning, when the fumes of alcohol had abated, he would make dirty remarks to her, teasing her for her chastity; but he did it affectionately, and as if to make a display of his baseness. When exhaustion silenced the street noises, from the room on the other side of the corridor she heard a gentle snoring sound that filled her with consolation; for it was the breathing of her brother the priest, sleeping soundly until dawn broke and summoned him to say Mass.

Ciriaco (which was his name, if you remember) was the only man in that household of women who had an instinctive horror of men. What could he do but enter the seminary and take orders? It was the only way for him to live with his sisters—to become half woman himself. It is doubtful that he had a real vocation, but that was of little importance. What is certain is that in the dedication of her brother, her only brother, to the priesthood, Gonaria saw the sign of Grace. God had come in person to live in her house. With ecstatic eyes she looked upon those hands which had the magic power of touching the untouchable, the sacred Host in which the body of Our Lord was hidden—but not so hidden as to be invisible to her. And she surrounded him with attentions, put up with his quirks, and accepted the unkind words that he sometimes answered back with. Ciriaco was a simple man, had studied only to a very limited extent, and understood little about those sisters of his, who lived like nuns without taking the veil. On the other hand, there was nothing worse than seeing himself surrounded by a love that transfigured him, because when it comes down to it everyone wants to be himself with his familiar mediocrity. What he was interested in, and rightly, was that Gonaria should get a good hot cup of coffee to him in the sacristy when he came out from Mass, having had nothing since the evening before; a service she performed lovingly, with the help of a small girl, a little pupil of hers from a very poor family, but full of intelligence, who came to do little chores for her teacher out of gratitude. Her name was Peppeddedda, which means Giuseppina.

A house with four unmarried sisters is never lonely. With un-flagging constancy the other unmarried old women would come in from the neighborhood, dressed in local costume. At a certain hour they would lock up their little houses, put the key into their large red-bordered pocket, and enter the living room without knocking. They would all sit motionless in the evening that filled the room, saving on lighting, and eventually they were reduced to shadows, mute witnesses to meaningless vigils. Gonaria, back from school, was the only one who would wander around, complaining about her headache, which no one believed in any longer. The priest would sit in the corner between the sideboard and the door onto the terrace, his biretta on his head. Occasionally he would lose patience and shout at his saintly sister, "Can't you ever keep still? Anyone would think you were a top!"

A light arrived when darkness had eliminated the shadows, and nothing was left alive except the glow of embers, if it was winter. From time to time Gonaria would throw a lump of sugar into the brazier, because it gave off a good smell, but also because she could think of the smoke it produced as incense. The priest lost his temper every time, as he had quite enough of incense in church; and anyway, he was a man, and had no truck with these hallucinations. In the lamplight the visitors began to stir, and one by one they went away for the same reason they had come: they had used up two hours of their lives, and had helped others to do so. Tomorrow would be the same. They did not know it, but this also was an exchange of charity.

The greatest difficulty I find in this return to the past is keeping things in perspective. And one can see why. Each of us, even if he confines himself to looking within, sees himself as if in a fixed portrait, not in the successive pictures of real existence. This movement is a continuous transformation, and it is impossible to grasp and stop the individual instants of this transformation. From this point of view we may doubt our very existence; or else our reality resides only in death. History is a waxworks. I have just halted the four sisters in the immobility of a single twilight, because that is how I see them after so many years. But in fact they used to move, and indeed to become agitated, since their secluded life was not peaceful. The family had become more prosperous because Gonaria's earnings had been swelled by those of the priest, but nature reacted differently in each of them; and then, one cannot live on memories as Tommasina did while (apart from Battistina, who was a mere shadow) the others were working. Therefore storms erupted from time to time, but died down at once, because those who go humbly to work have far more sense of the past than those who sit and contemplate it in idleness. And then there was the priest, who when things went wrong would retire to his room, the only real room in the house, lovingly prepared for him by Gonaria with a large crucifix surrounded by wreaths of artificial flowers. When this happened they all fell silent, or blamed one another in low voices, almost in whispers. They never ate together, because each would go and help herself to a ladleful of the soup which Giuseppina had made, while Gonaria would walk around nibbling a piece of bread. Only the priest used to sit at table with everything laid out in front of him. Tommasina and Battistina always wanted to use the same plate, and sometimes hid it without even washing it. These were signs of the sickness which lay smoldering in them, and which later burst out most terribly.

Gonaria and Ciriaco left home early in the morning, one to go to school and the other to go to Mass. Tommasina grumbled that they were running away, for it did not occur to her that the little money that enabled them to live came from there, because in her dream she obtained her riches from the coffers of the past. "We are rich, we are rich," she would say in her powerful voice to the poor women who came to visit Gonaria (for no one would have bothered to visit Tommasina). She was also quite capable of taking the money from the pot where it was kept and distributing it to the poor, throwing Giuseppina into desperation, since she had only this to count on to keep the wolf from the door. She boasted about her riches as she prided herself on her health, or as she would say it was not Gonaria but she and she alone who believed in God, because she surrounded herself with holy pictures and in her chest of drawers kept a piece of wood from the true cross of Jesus, brought to her by a missionary from Jerusalem. The world revolved around her, in fact, and with the world turned everything else, her sisters, her brother, the neighbors; because as everyone knows, one mustn't wake sleepwalkers on the edge of a precipice.

My problem is, whether there is any sort of connection between these women and the drinkers in the Caffè Tettamanzi, regarding them both as I do, from my old age. They lived beneath the same sky, and they sleep, in the same grave. This is all I can say, and it is something they have in common, quite independently of whether God or the devil took their souls. In any case the priest, their brother, kept himself apart from his sisters' way of life, even though he profited from the comforts they procured for him. In his simple heart he cherished a great dream, the dream of becoming a canon. For this reason he steered clear of his underprivileged colleagues, and frequented the curia instead, gaining the trust of the bishops as they came and went one after the other. One day his hat would be adorned with the red cord, and a new life would start in the poor house that it had taken so much to rebuild.

Gonaria was waiting for the day, because a canon is closer to God than an ordinary priest. She had confided in Donna Vincenza, who teased her about it but promised that when the day came she would make her a great cake studded with chocolates. For it would be a grand occasion.

Donna Vincenza knew nothing about philosophy, and indeed she had never heard it mentioned. But she lived nailed to her chair, and this led her to meditate. When at the other end of the courtyard Don Sebastiano mounted his horse and left through the gateway without saying a word to her, a scene that occurred daily immediately following the afternoon siesta, Donna Vincenza was left alone, and sank into the abyss of time, which was as motionless as herself, hanging over her comfortless figure like the grapes on the pergola, which her shortsighted eyes saw forming and growing every year, enormous stalactites in a lightless cavern. She would count them one by one, ten times or a hundred times over, to keep at bay the ghosts that assailed her on all sides. But there were certain fixations that some malicious being had driven into her head. Over the boundary wall she could hear the voices of her neighbors, who at one time had been friends, and then had let her down, because they had not been prepared to give up a right of way. Don Sebastiano held all the cards, and could have forced them to give it up. But as usual, because she wanted it, and because he was accommodating toward outsiders, he had done nothing. She had been left with the fierce smart of a defeat, which still persecuted her. But what did she really care about a right of way? The truth of the matter was that those neighbors were content with their little lives, and she measured her unhappiness against their contentment. At one time, when old Donna Angelina was alive, they used to come and visit, and in fact they were distant relatives. Their house was small, rather like a Sèuna house, although it was in the middle of town. There was the courtyard and the well, and beside the well stood a fabulous bush of lemon verbena, which spread its perfume in all directions. Don Sebastiano, who never set foot in any house, felt drawn toward the scent and occasionally asked if he could pick a sprig of it. Then Donna Angelina had sent to Oliena for a girl to keep her company, and Donna Vincenza also had welcomed her as a daughter, and there were no secrets between them. But in fact there was a secret. For the girl, who seemed destined to remain a spinster, at a certain point gave them all the slip and attached herself to a ludicrous "master of cloth," alias a tailor, who married her. As he had money, he turned the cottage into a miniature palace, with a smart shop on the ground floor. The dispute over the right of way started at that time, because in order to do the construction work, they were obliged to carry lime across a piece of Don Sebastiano's land, thereby giving him the upper hand. Donna Vincenza understood the whole business clearly, but she raised her voice in vain. The end of it all was that she lost the company of the girl and was left saddled with the right of way.

These things might seem absurdities, and maybe they were, but they ceased to be so the moment they filled the life of a lonely woman tied to her chair. Don Sebastiano had none of these nightmares, because he lived for the future. He was not even really interested in the present, meaning this woman from whom he had already harvested all he could, but who on the other hand was as concerned as he was, and more so, with the conservation of what he had built up; and in those sons who were destined to grow like the vines he had planted in arid soil, each with his own character, and all of them in awe of his example. For them he had done what he had to do, had watched over them, and straightened them up like young vines. Now they formed a small community, in which they taught each other, and he could keep his distance. And in fact they were almost grown men. They attended school, and some of them went to Sassari or Cagliari, the unknown, distant cities, because at that time Nuoro offered only five years of secondary school—the world had not yet turned upside down. Everyone in Nuoro envied Don Sebastiano his children, especially those shepherd families who thought that it was enough to send one's children to school for them to escape from the tribe. His sons grew up bound to one another by the most intense bond of love, well aware of their responsibility, and therefore organized on the basis of a law (even if it was only that of becoming lawyers or doctors or engineers) that none of them could fail to observe. The most interesting moment in the life of a family is when the children, as they grow up, recognize each other, discover diversity in unity, like the figures in a picture composed and held together by a strong frame. Each of these young Sannas seemed to bear the stamp of the destiny that awaited him, but whatever it might be, none of them would ever be able to erase the mark he had received at birth, the physical resemblance he shared with the others, and would never be able to be just himself and nothing more. The real mystery of the family lies here, in the relationships between the children, more than in the one between the parents and the children. Nor is it only a question of the people involved but also of the property, because the brothers possess nothing but are mystically invested with property, with Ísporòsile, with Locoi, with Lardine, an investiture that has roots deeper than in the Civil Code, because it is a spiritual thing destined never to perish.

With her intelligence heightened by solitude, Donna Vincenza transferred the distresses of the past into the present, which was the future. In her hallucinations she saw her grown-up sons as they were when she held them in her arms, or laid them in their cradles, when with her body she shielded them from harm. These boys existed solely because she had created them, and the family would hold together as long as she and Don Sebastiano were there. Even Cain and Abel, she told herself wildly, had grown up together. As long as Don Sebastiano held the reins, even slackly, the unity would be preserved. But for how long? For this reason she harbored none of the sugared illusions of Don Sebastiano. For her nothing existed but the boys, one by one, and they were as the day they were born. From the armchair she had been reduced to, she anxiously watched over the character and tendencies of each one of them, and first and foremost she kept an eye on their health, because some of them were delicate. Peppino, for example, who had had typhus as a child and had survived by a miracle—so much so that in gratitude they had dressed him in a tiny Franciscan habit for a whole year—seemed never to have recovered, with that pinched nose and those frail hands of his; and Ludovico, the constant invalid, the wise man of the family, who had trouble with his intestines and had to be cosseted with bowls of broth which she prepared with her own hands. What would have become of them without her? And the time would come for them to choose careers. Would they succeed? Everyone said they would, but she had her eye on Giovanni, the eldest, who had some odd ways. Unlike the others, who were unpredictable but merry, he took advantage of the difference in age to isolate himself, to shut himself in his room, and to sink into terrible silences that turned to yells if anyone, even his father or mother, asked him why. Even worse, it seemed that he suffered from the same thing at school as well, for he was no longer the steady-going student he had once been. There was a rumor that he was in love with Don Pasqualino's eldest daughter, who was wonderfully beautiful but incurably sick. Donna Vincenza had learned this from Gonaria, who, like all saints, had a nose for this sort of thing. And then, for some time he had poured scorn on the house, finding everything wrong with it, and it seemed he was even ashamed of his mother, because of her great fat legs, deformed by arthritis and child-bearing. One had to be blind, like Don Sebastiano, not to see it. And then there was Pasquale, the third from youngest, who had never had a passion for study like the other brothers, who punished him in vain, hiding his shoes or shutting him up in the loft. And Michele... And Gaetano... There was only the youngest, the one she loved, who still clambered onto her lap, and would have covered her with kisses if she had allowed it; but he was little, and troubles had not yet touched him.

These were the envied children of whom Don Sebastiano was so proud. But she knew that the touchstone for children is not the family, but outsiders; it was this Nuoro, populated largely by drunkards, but also by forceful people ready to fight and to conquer. She thought about them one by one, these lawyers who triumphed in the tribunal, for they were all a bunch of pettifoggers and the tribunal was like the town gym. She had never seen them because she did not leave the house, and her eyes were as if covered with a veil, but word reached her from the law courts, passing by way of the Caffè Tettamanzi. The prince of the tribunal was Paolo Masala, a slightly hybrid offspring (since his father was not Nuorese) of the Mannu clan. Every delinquent in Nuoro, and many from Sardinia at large, had been through his hands. His voice was like a song, and he cast a spell on the judges and the *carabinieri* so that they let the accused go free, accompanying him to the door with a thousand apologies. Naturally, Donna Vincenza had never been in the tribunal, but she had heard him, because he nourished political ambitions, and so every now and then would give a speech in the little piazza near her house. Her heart was full when the echoes of the applause had died away. This was not due to envy, but to fear. She realized that to speak like this, and to act like this, one had to have immense, hidden powers, which her sons could not possess, because neither she nor Don Sebastiano, with his pen and his notary's deeds, could have given it to them. The world seemed to her to be hostile, a stage where only a handful of initiates were able to perform. And her sons were certainly not among this number.

Sunset often found her wrapped in these thoughts. Don Sebastiano was in his study, lost behind the headlines. She was waiting for the boys to return. What should be done? What should be done? She needed a loving voice to persuade her that in this world there is something else, something outside reality, in which we must believe so as not to die. But Donna Vincenza transferred her past into the future, and in her past there was no place for Providence. Meanwhile, the days passed, slowly, inexorably, over her immobile form. As winter set in, at sunset she would rise very

very slowly from her chair, and walk unsteadily over the cobbled courtyard toward the dining-room fire. There she knew she
would find Don Priamo, that brother of Don Sebastiano's whom
we already know, and who was already well on in years. He would
appear with the first cold days, sidle into the room, and sit at a
corner of the fire, which shed light on his great beard. He stayed
there for hours and hours without uttering a word. When he was
well warmed through, he would go away exactly as he had come.
This was why Donna Vincenza hated him.

13

D on Ricciotti, alias Maestro Bellisai, was sitting by himself, his bottom overflowing from the wicker chair in the Caffè Tettamanzi, but his brain was working with the feverishness of someone who feels that he is on the point of achieving the aim of his whole life, but also knows that his life is near its end. With his eyes he poured disdain on all those revelers, and with words as well on feeble Maestro Manca, who sold himself for a glass of wine. In fact he wouldn't have gone to the caffè at all if his home, his wife included, hadn't turned his stomach. His mind was paying close attention to certain scraps of information that were going the rounds. Apart from the business of teaching and Maestro Marinotti, and apart from the boys scoffing at Maestro Mossa's Lord's Prayer, on the previous day a gang of youngsters had poked fun at the priests who, with the bishop in their midst, were taking their evening walk through the gardens. Worse still, the youngsters—recognized at once—came from San Pietro, and within living memory no one had ever dared to cross the frontier of the middle-class town, the district of Santa Maria. At the *estanco*, Don Gaetano's tobacco kiosk, there were newspapers never seen before, such as *Avanti!* And more than one student flaunted them in the caffè, as if to challenge Boelle and Bartolino. He had cautiously sounded the students out, and had heard them talk of a certain Marx, and of revolution and socialism, but he had realized at once that these were indolent dreamers, useless in the struggle to force Don Sebastiano to give up the house at Loreneddu. All the same, there was something in those ideas, something that had not existed before. It was just that it had to be translated into Nuorese; that is, by replacing the ideas with the facts and personalities of Nuoro, leaving out the rest of the world. He began to rave, to stay awake all night. And thus it was that troubled times began for Nuoro.

This joyless town in which it had been his fate to live, which was indifferent to everything, which had turned a blind eye to all the pillages inflicted on him, slept the sleep of centuries, and was only a town in a manner of speaking; because a town is a place where you have a neighbor, not one where everyone goes through the motions of living, in houses as impregnable as castles, or at the pharmacy, or at the caffè. The only meeting point is the cemetery. The essential was to awake these dead and set them against Don Sebastiano. In the course of the year there were going to be political elections. He would put himself up as a candidate. It was an insane idea, because the deputies from Nuoro had always been lawyers, and the Nuorese would be ashamed to be represented by an elementary-school teacher. On top of this, the perpetual deputy was that same Avvocato Paolo Masala, the formidable orator whose speechifying Donna Vincenza had heard with her heart in her boots. Who cared? Times were changing. It was a question of knowing where and how to start.

With San Pietro, clearly, there was nothing to be done. Those people were either rich or robbers, or both at the same time. They did not need him. The town center, Santa Maria, was the stronghold of the enemy: Don Sebastiano, Don Pasqualino, Don Gabriele, Don Serafino, and all the others of Don Sebastiano's ilk. There remained the peasant suburb of Sèuna, that small group of harmless souls whose houses hung in the air, with the cart and the yoke for the oxen in front of the house. They all lived hand to mouth, and did not know they were poor because they did not know what wealth was. The landowners of Santa Maria, and even a few individuals from San Pietro, used to go there to search them out whenever they needed a day's work done, and were respectfully received in the room with the fireplace in the middle and the smoke that went up through the roof and was lost in the blue. This was the defenseless place he could put pressure on. He mentioned the idea to a few of those fops who were flashing *Avanti!* around, but needless to say, they took fright. It was easier to say boo to the priests when they were taking their walk. He swore to himself that the peasants of Sèuna would get him back his house at Loreneddu, with its garden, its orchard, and at the far end, the copse of laurel that his father had planted (or so he imagined).

Sèuna was the home of many of his old pupils, who had failed at school and gone back to wearing local costume. They had taken up the reins of the oxen which their aged fathers, now seated on the stone "street" outside their doorways—if they were alive at all—had let drop from their hands. He made up his mind to pay them a call.

He arrived toward evening, when they were coming home after their long day's work and getting ready for a supper of barley bread moistened with oil. At first they were astonished, because although he was a schoolteacher he was by birth a gentleman. Then little by little they got used to seeing him, and offered him bread, which he declined. It was like being back at school, after so many years, except that now it was not a matter of that incomprehensible alphabet, but of simpler things more accessible to their simple minds. It was a question of the injustices that they suffered without knowing it, of God who had created the earth, and of those who owned it and those who scratched at it with their rudimentary plows; and of some possible resurrection. His speech was soft and gentle, because he knew that those numbskulls were satisfied with their lot, and would never have dreamed of rebelling against Nuoro and its laws. His aim was merely to open a door to hope in their hearts. Later on they would come to hate Don Sebastiano, Don Serafino, Don Pasqualino, the natural obstacles standing in the way of hope, both for them and for him.

There was great talk in the cottages about this man who spoke like a messiah. In vain did Father Porcu, whose heart was brimful of rancor, declare that this petty schoolmaster was as false as the dean himself, and he could scarcely say more. People were becoming excited, and toward twilight, when Don Ricciotti arrived along with the cooler air, he began to be greeted by swarms of barefoot children who escorted him as far as the forecourt of the Grazie, where he now made it his habit to address the throngs. Even Ziu Poddanzu, who had his fixed abode at Sèuna although he spent his life at Locoi, grew pensive once he had heard him, and among the undulations of the vines that he had planted with his own hands he put in a bit of thinking. He decided to set the matter before Don Sebastiano the next time he came, for he was at that time busy making new embankments for the torrent at Isporòsile. When he came, Don Sebastiano said, "Friend, by the holy bond that there is between us, I tell you that this Ricciotti

Bellisai is a load of rubbish." Ziu Poddanzu accepted the description, and thought no more about it. But he was alone in this, not only among the people in Sèuna, but also in San Pietro, and indeed in Santa Maria, for word had spread to such an extent that certain landowners informed the police. An officer was sent down to take a stroll among the boulders of Sèuna, but he found nothing irregular.

With an infallible finger on the pulse of his listeners, Don Ricciotti measured the growth of hope. He had nothing to offer, but there was no need to offer anything. He had set their imaginations in motion and that was enough, at least for the moment. To coax them toward his own purpose, that is, to get them used to the idea of individual injustice, the injustice of Don Sebastiano, who was usurping his house at Loreneddu, he thought that the easiest and least dangerous way would be to act through the *res publica*. Public business and no one's business come down to the same thing. And Nuoro, the town that belonged to them as well as to others, possessed immense pastures which those rogues in San Pietro rented for a song, just as it possessed the endless plain of the Prato, grazed over by the sheep of a few privileged persons, but which in their hands would have produced mountains of wheat. Why should Nuoro, which meant the mayor and the aldermen, have its hands on all that property, which belonged to God and therefore to the poor? Maybe in law this argument was a bit oversimplified, but the law was an invention of the rich. The idea he put forward—rather in an undertone, since he didn't want to run into trouble—was in fact nothing new. Many years before, no one remembered when, they had divided up the vast plateau of Sa Serra between the families of Orune, and at Nuoro itself the Mountain was the property of the commune, and had been split up. It is true that the result was that the poor got nothing and the rich grew richer, so that the Mountain, with its gigantic oaks and crystal springs, was today part of the Corrales estate, and all the poor could do either at Orune or Nuoro was get it off their chests by setting fires every now and then. In fact at Orune, where people are more unruly, as soon as they realized they had been tricked, they went rushing around the streets yelling, "A su connottu" ("Back to what we know"), in an effort to destroy what was already law, and therefore indestructible. This act of daring, which ended in exchanges of musket fire with the *carabinieri*, gave an undying name to that year *(s'annu e su connottu)*, but the *tanche* remained in the hands of those who had managed to grab hold of them. Ah, but in those days Don Ricciotti had not been there, and if land were to be divided up today, things would be done properly, and every man in Sèuna would plow his piece of land, would plow his own. It was in the midst of such speeches that he launched the idea of forming an association, one that would lend substance to their demands and direct them toward their common goal, with himself, Don Ricciotti, at the head, but purely as a brother and a guide. At the next election (though this he did *not* say) the association would automatically be transformed into a party. The following day he sent Dionisi, the town crier, out with his drum *(duradum duradum duradum)* to announce throughout the length and breadth of Sèuna (but also in San Pietro and Santa Maria) that whoever wanted to join Don Ricciotti's association should come and sign his name or make his mark the next Sunday in the storeroom on the ground floor of his house. There was nothing to pay.

Dionisi's drum caused consternation among the people of Nuoro. In the old monastery Maestro Mossa and Maestro Fadda wondered whether an elementary teacher was allowed to "go public" in such a way, setting the boys a bad example. But in the houses of the nobility and the middle classes they trembled, thinking that no good could come of that loafer, a worthy son of his father. That evening Don Pasqualino, Don Gabriele, Don Sebastiano, and the rest of them met earlier than usual in the pharmacy for a consultation. It was perfectly clear that that hot-head wanted to turn the place upside down. But why? Each of them felt under attack, and Don Sebastiano felt (though he did not show it) that this scum-of-the-earth was plotting to get his hands on Loreneddu. At the caffè Maestro Manca coined a nickname for his colleague: "the unquiet king." It became popular at once. But Boelle and Bartolino and the other gamblers just wrote him off as a buffoon, worse than Fileddu. Giovanni Maria Musiu (who in the depths of his heart was thinking about Isporòsile, although on that result of his father's gambling Don Ricciotti had never made any claims) said that he wouldn't allow him to sit in the caffè any more, especially as he never ordered anything. Anyway, everyone was unanimous about one thing: that this association (to which some attached the term "criminal") was a storm in a teacup and wouldn't last more than three days. The only ones who in their sneaky way kept an eye on the agitated citizens of Nuoro were the youngsters who made catcalls at the priests, and were waiting to see how the wind blew before joining in the game.

Meanwhile, in Sèuna, in the house of the Perra sisters, the only one with two rooms one above the other, and flowers on the balcony, they were working on the great surprise. On Sunday, when the Seunese went to sign up, they would deliver the banner of the association to Don Ricciotti. They had scraped together a bit of money and bought some red, white, and green material, and now they were sitting up till all hours embroidering in large gold letters the motto which Father Porcu (swallowing his own repugnance for Don Ricciotti) had dug out of a schoolbook: "Ascend the mountain gazing upon your sun." The letters sprang into place very quickly indeed, because all the neighbors took turns, and on Saturday evening the work was ready. Nuoro stood at the threshold of its great awakening.

The bells rang madly that Sunday, because—though by sheer coincidence—it was the day of Pentecost. The caffè was already full first thing in the morning. Don Ricciotti had set up a table in his storeroom, with a register and a pencil on it, and sat down to wait, full of good spirits. The Sèunese would turn up one by one, and would fill the book with their crosses, because most of them were illiterate, even those who had been in his class. Suddenly Maestro Manca, who already had two glasses of wine inside him and lived in fear of hallucinations, saw advancing from the bottom of the Corso a Sardinian cart all bedecked with flowers, and drawn by two vast oxen with wreaths of flowers around their necks. It could only be Buziuntu's cart, because he had the finest yoke of oxen in the whole of Sèuna; and indeed, there he was walking beside them, with his goad bedecked with ribbons. Maestro Manca beckoned to Robertino Caramelli, who had started his everlasting game of "tresette" with Bartolino and Boelle, and they were already quarreling. All eyes turned toward the Iron Bridge. "St. Isidore is here early this year," said Maestro Manca, raising a laugh. And in fact, after Buziuntu's cart, which was laden with people in special feast-day costume, came Torroneddu's cart, also decked out; then the cart of Ziu Seddone, who was old but still full of spirit; then the cart of Peditortu, who limped along solemnly; then the cart of Palimodde, who was cross-eyed; and then all the rest of the carts, with the whole of Sèuna on top, followed by a rabble of barefoot children yelling, "Hooray for Don Ricciotti!"

This strange procession passed in front of the caffè, dotting the Corso with the odorous leavings of oxen. Everyone was struck dumb. It was Bartolino, who was Continental though Sardinianized, who shouted the first insult: "Louts!" Among the herd of them he had recognized some of his day laborers, to whom he never failed to give a cigar with their pay. And his shout prompted an outbreak of rude noises and gestures. "Buffoons, boobies, bumpkins!" they shouted, and a few voices taunted them with "Seunese!' accompanied by a cackle. On the other hand, the free-thinking youths began applauding, and it was a miracle that the tables didn't start flying. In the nearby pharmacy the gentry had retired to the inner room, to avoid the sight. The Seunese continued unruffled on their way, filed in front of Don Ricciotti's store (and he was the most astonished of all), and stopped at the far end of the little piazza, where they climbed down from their carts.

Not one of them knew why they were forming this association, but on the other hand no one asked. They were associated in a mysterious hope which the schoolmaster cherished in the tabernacle of his heart. One by one they stepped up to Don Ricciotti's table, were greeted by their names or nicknames (for the nickname was not considered offensive), and there they made their mark in the book as best they could. Many of them left a lira on the table, as they did in church.

They are children, he thought, but I will make them into men. At the end, when he was asked to come outside and see "something," and they showed him the banner with the golden writing on it, he was truly moved, and plunged his face into the flag to hide his emotion. At that point he felt that he ought to speak, to say in public what he had so often whispered in the houses in Sèuna and in the forecourt of the church. So, mounted on the table which he had carried outside, he spoke as follows. (The news that this unimportant schoolmaster was making a speech spread like wildfire the length and breadth of Nuoro, and people of all sorts and stations came running breathlessly from every direction. Don Sebastiano's children were among the first to get there, because their house was not far off.)

"People of Nuoro, my brothers," he began, and it was enough to hear that first apostrophe to realize that he was a great orator, and so a vast wave of applause greeted it. "Ascend the Mountain gazing upon your sun. Yes, that Mountain that is no longer ours, that until yesterday you climbed with your eyes turned to the ground, backs bent with toil, from now on you will ascend with heads held high, for you are no longer the forsaken peasants of Sèuna or the minion shepherds of San Pietro. With your bedecked oxen, anticipating the day of St. Isidore"—the same idea that Maestro Manca had expressed as a joke—"you have come to found your association, the association that will set you free from slavery forever." The cheers and the clapping rose to the skies. "Yes, because until today you have been slaves, though you have never known it. It is not true that slavery has been abolished. No one without his own land is free; he is not even a man: he's just a hand, a laborer. This is what they call you."

The peasants of Sèuna hearkened to that resounding voice, which filled all the neighboring streets. They did not know that they were slaves, or even what slavery was, and were therefore dumbfounded. Don Ricciotti saw that he would have to tread carefully, and above all make himself clear to these overgrown children. "We, joining together in poverty, wish to become men, and men we shall be, without harming anyone else. We want the drops of sweat that drip from our brows to fall on soil we can call our own, and to achieve this aim I will lead you to victory. Peditortu, Palimodde, Buziuntu, all of you, brothers and sisters alike, have made a cross as your mark in the first register of the association. This mark is a symbol, and this cross will shortly make you masters of your own destinies. Follow me then, and together we will reach the summit of the Mountain, where the sunlight strikes!"

And he kissed the banner. An immense shout rose from the far end of the piazza. However, it was not the peasants of Sèuna who were frantically applauding the speaker, but the children of Don Sebastiano, of Don Pasqualino and the other bourgeois gentlemen of Nuoro.

After this no one talked about anything else. At table, Don Sebastiano would "chew his soup," as he was wont to say to his boys when they were eating too slowly; and family meals became gloomier and gloomier. He could have imagined almost anything, but not that that good-for-nothing Ricciotti Bellisai could gain credence in his own family. At last one day, as if talking to himself, he spluttered, "We've come to this then, that a downright degenerate comes and upsets the peace and quiet of the community with his politics." He then added that it was not correct to call Don Ricciotti a degenerate, because he was nothing but his father's son. This started an argument in which the boys went so far as to question the legitimacy of their father's possession of Loreneddu; at which Don Sebastiano rose, left his half-eaten plate of boiled meat, and went out, banging the door behind him. Donna Vincenza had not opened her mouth. She was following another train of thought. The way her boys reacted in favor of the poor she saw as yet another sign of their inability to face up to life, and she withdrew into gloomy forebodings. It was not that the poor ought not to be helped; what frightened her was the weakness of character, the inability to stand up to others. Ricciotti was certainly a scoundrel, for she had known his father well, and knew all the stories about him. But he was a man of some force of character, and a clever speaker, and this worried her for the sake of her sons; all of them, but especially Ludovico, who was so delicate in health and so sententious in his manner of speech. Loreneddu was important for this reason, and not because of the four walls that she had never seen, or remembered only as in a dream: it was important because her sons were prepared to renounce it after hearing half a dozen words. As if Giovanni, the eldest, wasn't enough, getting more sullen day by day, avoiding everyone, and constantly bickering with his brothers, who poked fun at him. What next?

But family dissension was widespread, and the Sèuna movement came close to becoming the movement of the sons of the rich, who joined the association *en masse*, not without causing Don Ricciotti some alarm. As for him, he went on giving speeches, each more successful than the last. Even at the caffè they no longer knew what to think, and began to regard him with a certain preoccupied admiration, all the more so because the priest-taunting youths, who had swelled in numbers, had already joined his ranks and set him up in their midst. The chaos was at its height when news arrived from Rome that the Chamber of Deputies had been dissolved and that new elections were announced for November 23. Everyone held his breath and waited; Don Ricciotti sensed that his moment had come.

In the caffè they all swore that he would never have the nerve to stand as a candidate, not only against Paolo Masala, but against those eternal rejects Avvocato Orrù and Avvocato Corda. The vicar, who you will remember had the mandate of all his relatives from Orune and Olzai in supporting the candidature of his nephew Dr. Porcu, the first Catholic candidate in all Sardinia, from the depths of his presbytery leveled curses against this paltry schoolmaster who had come and upset his plans. Don Ricciotti went twice as often to Sèuna to sound out his faithful flock, who were expecting the distribution of land on the Prato. He calculated the risks, and decided that if he lost it would be the end of him. Perhaps it was worth making one last bid.

It was late at night, an almost winter's night such as you get in Nuoro at the end of the summer, when the skies break open and rain ravages the fields. The roads were deserted and the first rolling mists shrouded the town. Don Ricciotti, who had spent four sleepless nights, approached Don Sebastiano's front door and raised the brass knocker. He paused a moment with hand uplifted, and then left destiny to take its course. A sound that seemed to him funereal boomed in the immense hallway.

"Who is it?" said a woman's voice.

"Friend," he replied. A crack of light showed, and the maid recognized the tubby dark figure of the teacher.

"Wait a moment." With her heart in her mouth she entered the dining room, where the master of the house was reading the paper, surrounded by his sons doing their homework and Donna Vincenza in her corner.

"Don Ricciotti is here, and wants to speak to the master."

There was a moment of panic. But Don Sebastiano, who knew no such thing as fear, said at once, "Ask him in and send him up to the study, where I am now going." Declining the presence of his sons, he went to the bedroom next to his study, opened a drawer and took out a pistol, which he hadn't touched since the days when he used to ride all over the countryside to draw up deeds. He slipped off the safety catch and hid the gun under a sheet of official paper on his desk. Then he said, "Come in."

The flabby figure of Don Ricciotti entered, and Don Sebastiano at once realized that he was in no danger. "What is it, then?"

"Sebastiano," he said, "we have known each other for a long time. We were boys together."

"True."

"You have seen what has happened. I am only an elementary-school teacher, but in a few months I have managed to bring the whole of Nuoro to my feet."

"So I have seen. You are good at talking and even better at making promises."

Don Ricciotti did not catch on, and proceeded: "Now I am running for deputy. I have nearly three thousand members in my association and am sure to win. And do you know what?

If I become a deputy you will all live to regret it. You have no idea what I am capable of."

"And so?"

"So, I have no wish to fight, whatever they may say. I am old and tired. The Seunese don't matter a fig to me. I have come for reasons you very well know. Once again I ask you to give me back the house at Loreneddu, before I take it by force."

Don Sebastiano glanced at that sheet of stamped paper covering the pistol, and decided to give him rope. "Listen here," he said. "If you give me a single reason why I should give it to you, I'm prepared to do so."

The rain was lashing against the windowpanes; the light of the oil lamp fell on the teacher's white face, and seemed to put new life into it.

"You bought that house at auction," he replied.

"And so?"

"So it means that my father didn't sell it to you. You bought it without his wanting you to. It's as if you had stolen it."

"You're mad."

"No, I'm not mad. Listen to me. My father gambled away Ispor- òsile, and that land, worth a million, is in the hands of Giovanni Maria Musiu. But from him I don't ask anything. So much the worse for my father, who threw it away. But your case is different."

"Why is it different? Your father was up to his neck in debts to the bank, and no one wanted to buy the house when it was put up for auction. He came to me in tears and begged me to bid for it, otherwise they'd have had the shirt off his back."

"I know that perfectly well, and it's exactly what condemns you. If no one had made an offer, he would have kept the house."

Don Sebastiano was on the point of telling him that he was as mad as his father. But he held back a moment.

This man's madness had a germ of truth in it, one that he, as a notary who had attended so many auctions, had never thought of. A debtor who does not pay is subject to the confiscation of his property. This was written in the Civil Code that lay before him (an old miniature edition with yellow-blotched pages, which he never opened because he did not need to), and it was more than just: it was the very basis of living. But it was also true that the debtor had no part in the matter: his property returned, so to speak, to the community from which it had come, and which saw to the sale. From this point of view every confiscation was a theft, and for this reason people who bid at auctions were frowned upon. No friend would ever take part in the bidding, and he too had always respected this prejudice. This was even a cause of disagreement with his wife.

Don Sebastiano's silence had lit a small flicker of hope in the schoolteacher's sullen spirit. "Well?" he asked.

Don Sebastiano's face regained its confident look. "You might have some vague right on your side," he answered. "But sitting on that very chair where you are sitting, and at this same time of day, your father implored me to put in my bid, as I told you. I didn't want to, and in order to oblige him I had to get into debt in his place. This happened twenty years ago. Your father is still alive, so why doesn't he come and ask me himself?"

"My father is an imbecile," replied the other. "This matter must be arranged between the two of us."

"As far as I am concerned, it is already arranged," said Don Sebastiano, casually eyeing the sheet of stamped paper.

"Is that your last word?"

"The very last."

"I'll make you weep tears of blood," said the schoolmaster, rising to his feet. And he went out into the night.

"I speak to the poor, the poor of Sèuna, the poor of San Pietro, the poor of Santa Maria." These were the opening words of Don Ricciotti's first electoral speech after his nomination. The Piazza del Plebiscito was like a *tanca* in flower, for everyone was wearing the red jerkin of the local costume and had come swarming to hear the "speechifying" as soon as Dionisi had announced it. Don Ricciotti felt like a hunted boar. He had therefore reduced the political problem of Nuoro to the simplest possible terms: to defend himself by goring, one by one, those savage hounds, those vile plutocrats fat with the spoils of thievery, who lived by sitting on the money they and their ancestors had stolen; to hurl the poor of every district against them like stones from a sling; and to reduce the political struggle to the struggle of one man against another, the only kind that the Seunese, and all the poor in town, were capable of understanding. In fact, it was the only kind he could understand himself; though who knows if all disputes are not based on hatred. The only danger was that the poor were dependent on the rich, as ever; but it was here that he had to strike, if he wanted the rich to come begging for mercy.

"Hear me, poor people of Nuoro. The day of your redemption is at hand. Until now you have lived in darkness, but now together we shall ascend the Mountain, gazing upon our sun, for it is written here, on the banner of our association. They have cast a spell on you, these moldering misers, these retired robbers, and you are unable to walk. So it is my task to raise you; like Jesus I tell you: Rise and walk. See there the Mountain, the divine Ortobene! It abounds in oak trees—And you? You cannot gather one acorn for your pigs. It abounds in water, but you cannot stoop there to quench your thirst! Yet no more than fifty years ago that Mountain was yours, and you were rich and free. Who took it from you? Mayor Mereu was full of good intentions, and wanted to give each man a plot; but the Corrales, who lived like hermits in those days, very well knew how to shuffle the cards, and the Mountain, the whole Mountain, now belongs to those bandits, and you have to ask permission to cross the *tanche*. As for the Prato and the pastures of the Serra, they were even more cunning. They prevented them from being shared out, and rented them from the local government for next to nothing, making it impossible for you to cultivate them."

This, of course, was merely the preamble. Don Ricciotti cared nothing for the Mountain or the Corrales, apart from the fact that the Corrales were people who handled rifles like toys and were crack shots. "When you have given me your vote," he continued, "I will repair the injustices which you have suffered and which your fathers suffered. But"—and here his voice took on a note of profundity—"the masters of Nuoro are not at San Pietro and they are not on the Mountain. They do not wear costume. No! they are gentlemen. It is they who exploit your labor and live on your backs. They keep you hidden under a bushel lest you should realize that the sun shines on all alike. Look at them there, all together!"

And with a gladiatorial gesture he stretched out his hand toward the pharmacy, where Don Serafino, Don Gabriele, Don

Pasqualino, Don Sebastiano and the others were innocently seated. The excommunication of the Corrales had given them some amusement. When it came down to it, he was not altogether wrong, and if he got his teeth into San Pietro, so much the better. When they saw him taking a new tack, they stiffened.

"That smoky old lamp, Gabriele Mannu," he shouted, raising a great laugh, especially from the nearby caffè. In fact, Ingegner Mannu was about five feet tall, hid his hairless pate under a sweat-stained bowler, and had eyes as yellow as his wrinkled skin; but no one had ever thought of him as being an exact replica of an oil lamp, one of the brass kind, with the blackened wick, still used in kitchens to save money. "That old oil lamp, Gabriele Mannu, is the owner of the house across the road, with its crumbling walls and windows that are never opened. You, Cosimo Marche, pace out the front of this house and tell me how many times it is bigger than the hovel where you and your family take refuge from the rain. Inside that house, where a lamp is never lit, between collapsing walls, on floors that have never known a broom, wander this man's two children, whom he has driven out of their wits, being a half-wit himself, by giving them nothing to eat. Peasants of Sèuna, answer for yourselves: have you ever got a day's work out of Don Gabriele? But leave work aside! You, Dirripezza, or you, Baliodda, or you, Poddanzu, have you ever had a penny from him when you stretched out your hand?"

Don Gabriele Mannu, whose only fault was to have designed Don Sebastiano's house in the manner which we already described, curled up like a frightened wood louse. Don Sebastiano ostentatiously shook him by the hand. As the crowd was laughing, they were helpless. And then, unfortunately, what Don

Ricciotti was saying was true; or rather, it was false only because it came from his mouth. The stinginess of the Mannus was not of the usual sort, because we are all stingy. There was something dark and sorrowful about it. For those who take my point, it was a Nuorese stinginess, the stinginess of people born without hope. There are so many poor wretches who hoard up rags and empty cans, the refuse of the world, and live among this in their dens, clasp it to them and gloat over it, because they are without hope. Don Gabriele was one of these wretches, even if his rags were worth millions; and so were his brothers, his cousins, and everyone of his relatives. But did he therefore deserve to be stripped bare and thrown to the wolves of Nuoro by this third-rate intriguer, whose own character could more justly have been pulled to pieces by anyone having such power of brazen speech? I find it unjust, even apart from penal law, because a man's private life is a matter between himself and God.

"But you, Predu Fois," continued Don Ricciotti as soon as the roar of the crowd broke off, and remained suspended between heaven and earth, "you, Predu Fois, you see that other one over there with the little white beard, enjoying the cool air in the pharmacy? That is Avvocato Porru, the glory of Nuoro, whom we all revere. But you, who are a blacksmith, did you know that your father, God rest his soul, owned the farm at Monte Jaca which produces the wine you pay through the nose for in Mucubirde's cellar? That farm would have been yours, yours! And instead it belongs to Avvocato Porru, because your father had a little lawsuit, and this generous lawyer not only caused him to lose it, but made him hand over the house in lieu of fees, as your father didn't have a penny to pay him with. All this gentleman's properties came to him that way, and this is the gentleman whom you all respect and honor because he wears a hat."

The hubbub was now at its height. "Don Pasqualino, they say you are my blood relative. But your only relatives are the electricity bills you sting the poor of Nuoro for, and the profit on flour that like a feudal overlord you collect from the luckless women who come to your mill with bushels of grain on their heads. And you, Pascale Gurture, an honor to your name, always in a bowler hat as if you were a minister, what do you do with the enormous *tanche* of Su Grumene, grazed over by thousands of sheep that you do not own, since you would never risk a single penny? Are you keeping the money for the crows to eat?"

All this was a facile play on words, because the name Gurture means "vulture," but there was also an allusion to the fact that, like so many Nuorese, Pascale Gurture was a bachelor and kept a woman at home, whom he called his housekeeper, by now an old stick like him, and he fed off her carcass. The tension of the audience therefore burst out in a great yell of laughter, much to the relief of everyone.

Everyone laughed, but not Don Sebastiano, who knew very well that his own turn was coming soon, and that all these infamies were nothing but an excuse to commit the greatest infamy of all, the one against himself. If he could have left, he would have done so, but the crowd was so thick he could not reach his house, although it was only a step away. And sure enough: "All these parasites, poor people of Nuoro, I will sweep away as soon as you have elected me your deputy. But from one of them I wish to exact justice in a more entertaining way: from the most upright, the most honored of all, the diligent worker called Notary Sanna, the noble Don Sebastiano. All of you honor and esteem this man, because he has reclaimed tracts of land with the sweat of your brows, paying you a miserable daily wage. Well then, I will tell you how he made his money, because it concerns me personally. You are aware that he is the owner of Loreneddu, the great domain which now houses the barracks of the King's *carabinieri*. Well then, what you don't know is that that house belonged to my father, and was put up for auction on account of the debts he had with the usurers. Not a soul in Nuoro would have acted as an accomplice of the usurers, and in fact no one turned up at the auction. Only this hypocrite, cloaked in virtue, had the nerve to exploit the misfortunes of others. I offered to buy back my house and give him the miserable sum that he had paid, but he laughed in my face. Don Sebastiano, today you must tremble! The whole people of Nuoro will take revenge on you, because the whole people of Nuoro has until today been victimized by you and your worthy friends; but now at last it has learned that justice can be obtained in this world."

Such was the speech with which Don Ricciotti opened his electoral campaign. No one noticed the fact that Boelle Zicheri and Paolo Bartolino and Giovanni Maria Musiu, about whom there was also much to tell, were spared his cannonades. Don Ricciotti, for all his ranting, did not lose his sense of what was prudent, and knew that he had to keep his place at the table in the Caffè Tettamanzi, from which he would otherwise have been ignominiously expelled.

Canon Pirri, the dean, who was also the uncle of the Corrales clan, called his oldest nephews to his bedside—the ones whom he knew to be most quickly roused to anger and unthinking acts. There were no loudspeakers in those days, but Don Ricciotti's voice had nevertheless, word for word, reached the stuffy room where for a hundred years he had been waiting for death. With his prodigious gift for reading the minds of his nephews, he realized at once that they were not going to stand for the insult, and that Don Ricciotti's days could be said to be numbered.

"You will do nothing," he said, wasting no time in getting down to business. "Your father might have been able to do it, but you have children who will be going to school and will give up wearing costume, and you cannot send them into the world as the sons of murderers, even if the hand of justice does not reach you. In Nuoro, everyone knows everything. Get this into your heads: the Corrales are finished, and the time has come for the Faddas of this world, who will be lawyers and doctors, and will go and live in Santa Maria. Our race must be forgotten. As for Ricciotti, leave him to me."

That morose company decided that *tittiu* (for so the family called their priestly uncle) had gone gaga, but there was the matter of his fortune, which was considerable, so they had to resign themselves. They would get to Don Ricciotti all the same, by roundabout routes.

In his solitude the dean possessed a redoubtable informer, Dr. Nurra, or more simply, Zizitu (that is, Franceschino) Nurra. He was one of those innumerable doctors of law who made up the fresco of Nuoro, and who, once they had qualified, never looked at a law book again. Like the late Avvocato Orecchioni, simply in remembrance of him now that he is dead. I believe that he didn't even know when and where he had qualified, but he had exploited his degree in order to marry a rich, ugly spinster and live in comfort. A fate common to many, after all. For a reason that I have never been able to understand, these Nuorese graduates became misanthropic. Dr. Nurra had only one friend, and this was the old dean, and every evening as twilight was falling he would go to visit him, sidling along near the walls, ready to dart around the corner if he saw some acquaintance approaching. He was a handsome man, with long gray whiskers, and he always dressed in black, as the fashion then was. Dr. Nurra never spoke to a soul, but he had a lot of curiosity in his temperament; and as he lived on the top floor of the house above the caffè, toward evening he would open a tiny window, stick out his head, cup his hand behind his ear, and listen to the conversation of the customers seated at the tables.

In this way the dean came to learn that Don Ricciotti—who was piling speech on speech and no longer sparing anyone at all, even reaching the point of having himself carried in triumph on the shoulders of those creatures from Sèuna—had been dubbed "the honorable member" by the habitués of the caffè, though he did not know whether in earnest or in jest. Fear had certainly lodged in the hearts of everyone who had anything to lose, partly because by this time Don Ricciotti was talking openly of revolution, backed by the youths who read *Avanti!* The upper and middle classes had vanished from the nearby pharmacy and withdrawn to their homes. Canon Pirri listened gravely to these accounts, without asking for advice, which Dr. Nurra would have been powerless to give him. He had to find the way out of it, but without noise or fuss, because there might be some truth in Don Ricciotti's slanders.

The following day, summoning up his scant remaining strength, he sent a message to Canon Monni, the parish priest, assuring him that San Pietro would vote *en bloc* in favor of his nephew Dr. Porcu. Then, one by one, he began to send for all the shepherds of San Pietro, masters and minions alike. In the course of sixty years he had heard the confessions of the grandfathers, the fathers, and the sons, and held weapons more powerful than anything Ricciotti had, which for the most part was nothing but gossip. What he said will never be known, but it was most certainly a procession such as had never been witnessed, even on the Day of the Redeemer.* As regards the Seunese, he could do nothing, since they went to confession with Father Porcu, who had sided with Don Ricciotti. But the dean knew them well: they were like straws that the wind blows where it listeth. Then he had an idea. He sent for Paolo Masala, the formidable orator, who was also a candidate, and who had defended so many Nuorese in court—for the Seunese were also Nuorese, and were constantly entangled with the law. After reproving him for his indifference toward the Mannus, whose relative he was, he arranged for him to make a counterspeech. The following Sunday Ricciotti would throw open the window of his house on the Piazza del Plebiscito and would vomit forth his remaining hatred in front of the applauding crowd. After the last word, Masala would appear at the window of Maria Sechi's house immediately opposite, and throw Ricciotti's whole life in his face. The dean, who knew his people, was certain this would do the trick.

And it so happened that on Sunday, when Don Ricciotti was mopping his brow and rejoicing in the sound of the applause of

---

* August 29; celebrated with processions, dancing, etc., throughout Sardinia.

his electors, whose eyes he had finally opened to the crimes of the landowning classes, another window was flung open, and Paolo Masala shouted in his full-throated voice, "Stay where you are! Now it's my turn to speak."

It was like a thunderclap. In one hour Don Missente Bellisai lit himself a hundred cigars with a hundred hundred-lire notes, this paltry schoolteacher had neglected his duties toward his pupils in order to follow the promptings of insane revenge, had promised the impossible to poor people who were happy in their work, and had neglected his duties to his own family, who were languishing in poverty because of him. The winged words entered at once into every heart. In vain did Don Ricciotti, withdrawing to the back of his balcony, put two fingers in his mouth to incite his loyal followers to whistle. The Seunese applauded Paolo Masala for the same reasons that they had applauded him: because what counts is the gift of the gab, something not one of them could have achieved, the very voice that issued from those robust chests. All the same, Don Ricciotti lost the election not because Paolo Masala had overwhelmed him with his eloquence, but due to a simpler thing, which not even the dean would have credited.

The news that that "load of rubbish" had insulted Don Sebastiano had even reached Ziu Poddanzu at Locoi among the vines. He was Seunese, even though he went home only two or three times a year. The day before the election he set off on foot for Nuoro, and when he got to Sèuna he grabbed the first man he met by the jerkin and put him to shame in front of everyone. He threw in his teeth the days of work that Don Sebastiano had never failed to give him, and the festive grape harvests in his vine- yards, with meals of macaroni and roast lamb, and he threw in his teeth the humility of his old companion, who was closer to the poor than anyone had ever been. And now he and the others were allowing Don Missente's son to spit on him.

It was Ziu Poddanzu who really won the election, not Paolo Masala. Don Ricciotti got 290 votes. The members of his association numbered more than 3,000.

The year of troubles was over.

14

The hands of the clock on Santa Maria turned inexorably slowly, while Don Sebastiano drew up his deeds, Don Pasqualino did the accounts for his scores of firms, Don Ricciotti ate his heart out pursuing the dream of Loreneddu, Poddanzu and Dirripezza waited for charity, the peasants of Sèuna rolled their carts over the stones stripped bare by the rains, the thieves of San Pietro followed the tracks of flocks among the unguarded *tanche,* and Monsignor Canepa composed his homilies. If in place of the enormous clockface that Bishop Dettori had had hoisted up the bell tower at around the end of the century there had been a great mirror, then the Nuorese would perhaps have measured time better by the ruin of their bodies; for there is no doubt that all the characters in this story were getting older. But it is possible that the life of a town occurs in a unity of time and place, like the ancient tragedies, and that the succession of events possesses the mysterious immutability of the cemetery. Seen by God, on the day of judgment, I think life surely must appear like this.

The social scene at the Caffè Tettamanzi had not substantially changed. There were more clients, because the tendency of the shepherds and peasants to become middle class was creating unemployment, but the distribution of roles was still the same, with Bartolino and Boelle Zicheri, the pharmacist, pulling the strings, and Fileddu and the rest of them bearing the brunt of it. If one could have stopped the action, as when a film breaks down, one would have seen a lot of hands raised in the air, a lot of ecstatic faces staring wide-eyed at the "tresette" cards, Fileddu lost in his oversized coat, with his doglike eyes fixed on his own dear Boelle, Pietro Catte with his bulging eyes fixed on the full wineglass on the table, and Don Ricciotti—who had returned to the caffè after his mad adventure—wearing his sarcastic smile. All was the same as ten years earlier, twenty years earlier, or indeed since the beginning of time.

Things, however, were not as they seemed. For example, anyone looking closely at Boelle Zicheri's hands, even when he seemed at his most carefree, organizing the fun at the expense of Fileddu or Maestro Manca, would have noticed that for some time now they had begun to tremble. And not just one but a hundred eyes were fixed on them, the eyes of all who laughed at his jokes and followed the progress of the tremor. Now he couldn't even raise a glass to his lips (although he drank little) without spilling several drops on his impeccable suit. When he left, people would wink at one another (while some swore that he was unsteady on his feet), and there was an exchange of diagnoses. "He sowed his wild oats when he was young," they said, "and now he's paying for it." And they spoke with relish of general paralysis, or of other worse afflictions, if there are any. Boelle, on the other hand, had never been so gay as since the symptoms of the disease first appeared. He seemed to be seized with a frenzy to live. For this reason Maestro Manca, following him with an eye dimmed by the latest glass of wine, from the heights of his culture loudly declared: *Et exsultabunt ossa humiliata.* There was a sort of ferocious sadism, or worse still a feeling of revenge, against this tortured frame. Each one of them felt smitten in the person of Boelle. Now that sickness had seized him, the jovial pharmacist reflected the uselessness of each one of their lives; and therefore they hated him, because they hated themselves. "He's going to die, he's not going to die, he's sure to die, he'll only last three months." Even Fileddu, in the darkness of his mind, had a dim feeling that Boelle was in danger, and when Boelle got to his feet he followed him step by step all the way home.

Worst of all, the person who noticed the trembling of his hands more than anybody else was Boelle himself, and as pharmacists are doctors in a small way, he had at once made the fearful diagnosis. In the midst of all the rowdiness at the Caffè Tettamanzi, perhaps he had been expecting it for some time. And maybe he was aware from other signs, not evident to the idlers in the bar, that his life was drawing to a close. And a strange thing was that he felt toward himself the same hatred that others felt for him. It was as if that God who was preparing to destroy him was destroying Himself, as one day long ago He had created him; and this gave Boelle the sadistic joy of nonexistence. According to his calculations, he still had a few months to go. He had to arrange everything, because he wanted to take it all with him. Just as with him would die all his friends in the caffè, all the Nuorese, and the whole world, so he wanted all his property to die, so that no one might henceforth say, "This is Boelle's house," or "This is Boelle's *tanca*." He was dying a bachelor; therefore it was already as if he had never lived. The next morning he would go to see Don Sebastiano and ask him to help him with his will. But first, at once, he wanted to write something himself, with his trembling hand, two lines that would be his real will and testament. Like all the bachelors in Nuoro, and they were legion (as I think I have said), he hated the priests. He reviewed them all, one by one: Canon Floris, Father Porcu, Father Delussu, Canon Fele... These men, for him, were the Church. But even as they were, boozers, swindlers, hypocritical and quarrelsome, they were witnesses of God, of a life without end; and this he could not stand. He went to the desk, dipped his pen in the ink, and wrote in a hand that seemed to him steady, on account of the effort it took: "At my funeral I want neither priest nor cross. Let my body be cast into the bare earth, without a name." Then, recalling the fears of Don Gaetano Pilleri (who had seized a whip and chased away the priest who dared to enter his tobacco shop for the Easter blessing), he added: "I am in full possession of my mental faculties. But if, with the progression of my disease, I should change my mind, it is today's wish that counts. That is: I want neither priest nor cross." He put the paper into an envelope and went to bed.

At seven o'clock the next morning he was already at the pharmacy. But he was not there to arrange the decorative jars that made such a show behind the counter. He was waiting for Don Sebastiano to pass the door; for like all the gentry at that time he used to go in person to buy the meat, nearby in the Piazza San Giovanni, where the market then was. And sure enough, a little while later Boelle saw him coming down the road with the brown-paper package held out in front of him like a bunch of flowers (how sweet life could be, it seemed to him at that moment), and motioned to him to come inside. In the empty back premises they whispered for a quarter of an hour. Don Sebastiano said that he would go to the land-registry office and make a list of all Boelle's properties, because he had had two legacies from old aunts on his mother's side, and not even he knew what he owned. They arranged to meet again the following Saturday evening.

"Listen, Sebastiano," said Boelle, getting to his feet. "Look at this envelope. It contains my true wishes. I entrust it to you. You must open it in the presence of my corpse. But you must swear to me that you will do what is written here. I'll expect you on Saturday."

Boelle's idea was simplicity itself. He wished to disinherit all his nephews, and he had many, both rich and poor. He did not want to connect his life to anyone. For this reason he had even decided against leaving anything to poor Fileddu. He would leave all his property to the hospital, thus throwing it into the common grave, or restoring it to the community at large, where it would lose all individuality. It was even likely that the hospital would put the properties up for auction, which is like scattering ashes to the winds. The thought that this was giving charity did not even occur to him. There was no question of benefiting anything or anyone: it was simply a matter of disappearing, with the same indifference with which, on one distant day, he had appeared. He felt satisfied with this decision. The important thing now was that no one should realize that he was so far gone. He therefore started frequenting the caffè again, indulging in pranks that grew noisier and noisier, and that made him breathless and purple in the face, never noticing the winks passing from one end of the room to the other.

He died suddenly in May, on a night so warm that he had left the windows of his room open. It was because of the open windows, and the locked door of the pharmacy, that they realized something serious had happened. They broke down the door and found him lying quietly stretched out. His relatives appeared at once, and wept, and sang the praises of the dead man. Don Sebastiano was informed, and came and opened the envelope that had been entrusted to him. There was a chorus of protests—the shame it would mean for the family, the damnation of his soul. Then Don Sebastiano told them that he had left all his property to the hospital, and that was the end of the protests.

The funeral took place the same day. People had come from all sides to see a burial without priests. The silence of the bells weighed heavily on the town as the coffin passed among the few bystanders, who even forgot to take their hats off. In this way they reached the cemetery, and then the people turned back; or so they thought, because they did not know that Boelle had taken them with him to the grave. But right at the entrance an unexpected episode occurred. Fileddu had done his duty by accompanying Boelle to the graveside, but he had the misfortune to bump into Casizolu, his envious rival. Casizolu gave vent to the rancor he had been nursing for years, and began to yell, "He's dead! He's dead—the man who used to give you his old jackets!" Fileddu, who had understood nothing, was already in the distance and the other was still crying out, "He's dead! He's dead!" That evening in the bar the jokers tried to coax Fileddu into challenging Casizolu, but Fileddu was sad because his great friend had not come.

The last wishes of Boelle Zicheri were respected only in part, because some ass at the hospital thought it wrong that such a benefactor should be left to rot in the same earth as Poddanzu or Dirripezza, and (with the dead man's money) had him built a marble-flagged sepulcher, with an enameled portrait held in place by two bronze bosses. It is hard to find, because the mausoleums of the *nouveaux riches* have sprung up around it, but when you manage to part the wild grasses that have overgrown the tomb, his faded eyes look at you sadly, because you don't know him, but he knows you very well indeed.

But these are things of no importance, because no one will go to look for the pharmacist in the old cemetery. On the other hand Boelle's death had an odd sequel, if indeed it was not a coincidence. The Caffè Tettamanzi returned to normal: the void left by the dead man was soon filled. For a few days people spoke ill of him, mostly because he had left everything to the hospital. That swarm of disinherited relatives could understand anything except charity. Bartolino, left on his own, continued to flaunt his towering Continental stature, and played twice as many pranks, although he had become more quarrelsome. The only one who gave signs of being upset by Boelle's death was Maestro Manca, but this was because the young fellows who surrounded him, knowing the terror he had of death, would tell him it was his turn next. He gnashed his teeth, and pressed his index finger on the vein in his temple, which seemed to get larger every day. Pietro Catte rolled his ox-eyes around, and everyone knew that he was waiting for his aunt to die, so as to inherit her house and vineyard, and they insinuated that she would do the same as Boelle.

From the little window at the top of the building, Dr. Nurra still strained his ears to catch the latest news. The customers who had noticed this began to invent the wildest stories imaginable, but above all they spread the word that he had a tumor of the throat—no, the lung—no, the intestine; and that his hour had come. The result was that, terrified and full of aches and pains here, there, and everywhere, he pulled in his head and shut the window amid the laughter of all present. And so the hands of the clock went round and round, and all seemed to be as usual. Except that one day, when Boelle had been dead for a month, a few people began to notice that Fileddu had not been seen. Where could he have gone to? Even Casizolu, who always waited for him at the corner to shout, "He's dead! He's dead!" was surprised, and scented some mysterious treason. Finally someone went down to inquire around the hovel where Fileddu lived, but no one knew anything. Then they called the *carabinieri,* who barged down the four planks that served as a door. A fearful sight met their eyes. Fileddu was lying on the rush mat, covered with rags, motionless, with staring eyes. By his side was his almost-blind mother, gazing at him with whitened eyes, waiting for her son to wake up. When she noticed such a crowd of people, she seemed to understand, and went groping her way out into the sunlight.

The news that Fileddu was dead went through the town in a flash. And then the strangest thing happened, one that even now I cannot account for. It was not even a case of following the body of Don Pasqualino or Don Sebastiano, but from their houses at the upper end of San Pietro the ordinary folk began to move, and then the shepherds, and then even the bigwigs of the great dynasty of the Corrales. Fileddu's hut was on the very edge of Sèuna, practically out in the cheerless countryside, and they had to traverse the whole of Nuoro to get there. Along the route the gentry of Santa Maria left their respectable homes (except for Don Pasqualino, who was immobilized by gout), and it was as if a torrent were pouring down the Corso toward the hovel where the coffin, donated by a carpenter in Sèuna, rested on the ground waiting for the burial. Someone had given orders for the bells to ring slowly, as was the custom for the rich, and the funeral chimes kept time with the thoughts of all. At last Father Porcu arrived, with the young deacon. He was beside himself with rage, because he had not been expecting all those people, who would make the business drag on and on. Finally four stalwarts hoisted the coffin on their shoulders and Father Porcu set off, chanting away. He tried to hurry things along, because it seemed to him a waste of breath, but the Nuorese were cramming the roadways, while the women stood weeping on the balconies. They followed a stretch of the Corso, but at the Alberetti, where the cobbled road leads up toward San Pietro, the priest motioned for them to turn off. The bearers stopped in their tracks, and so did the whole procession.

"Let's carry on along the Corso," said Pascale Farranca.

"I have the right to go the shorter way," replied Father Porcu. And on he went, without looking back.

Then an incredible thing happened. Pozeddu, who you may remember was sacristan at the Grazie, but had learned the priest's job, exchanged a glance with Pascale Farranca and stepped up to the head of the procession. *"In paradisum perducant te angeli,"* he began in his sonorous voice; and while the priest went off toward the cemetery with never a dead man behind him, Fileddu with his immense following passed along the Corso, of which he had at last and in truth become the master. With increasing solemnity Pozeddu advanced, in his threadbare cassock instead of surplice and stole. Perhaps the priest would expel him from the church as soon as he got back, but for this very reason he sang all the louder. *Dies irae, dies illa…* In the deep, deep silence of men and of things, it seemed as if the Nuorese were offering up to God this half-witted child of theirs, in expiation for the sin of being either good or bad, rich or poor, in sickness or in health; for the sin of living.

So it was that Fileddu had his moment of glory, even if it lasted only until the last of the shovelfuls of earth that Milieddu hastily and noisily threw onto his coffin lid.

15

That evening, as usual, Don Sebastiano sat reading in his now deserted study by the light of the huge oil lamp, which he had not chosen to replace with Don Pasqualino's electric light because, he said, it tired the eyes. But there was no need for much light or strong spectacles for those banner headlines announcing the brutal killing of an Austrian archduke in an obscure town in Serbia. Don Sebastiano read, and at every line he wiped his eyes with the large handkerchief he wore between his neck and his shirt to absorb the sweat while out in the country. Like every Nuorese, he was used to hatred and killing. Not a month went by without news of some slaughter from Orgósolo, and even the Orgolese who took refuge in Nuoro did not escape their destiny. Only a week or so had passed since they had stretched out Antonio Bussu in a pool of his own blood, and he was a decent man, who had fled from Orgósolo to the house of Franziscu Sole, of whom he was an *amico de posada*. He stayed shut in the house for days. That morning he thought he would take a breath of fresh air, and ventured as far as the Alberetti of Sèuna, no more than two hundred yards away. Two shots reduced him to nothing in a moment. Even I remember it, because we played truant from school to go and see the gore still trickling among the stones. But Antonio Bussu knew who had killed him, as Abel knew Cain.

This archduke knew nothing, any more than did the King of Italy whom they had killed fourteen years before. The notary did not understand the eye-for-an-eye of hate, and therefore he wept beneath his reading glasses. Through a film of tears he read that Austria was threatening to make war on Serbia, and that this war would inevitably drag in the whole of Europe.

In 1914 Don Sebastiano was sixty-four, which was a lot in those days; but he bore his years very well, with that health-giving to-ing and fro-ing from desk to vineyard, which after so much work was now paying well. He was still the head of the family, even if the family had split up. Only little Sebastiano and Peppino were left in the old house (though the next year even Peppino would be leaving the nest for his lycée studies in Sassari or Cagliari), while Ludovico spent long periods there. He had qualified at the lycée with a thesis on *Quisque est suae fortunae faber,* maintaining that it wasn't true. This had been discussed at length, and still was. Unfortunately, as a result of his efforts, his nervous condition had worsened, and he did not often attend the law school, in which he was enrolled. It may have been (but perhaps this was part of his neurosis) that he was upset by the sight of those strapping fellows in Sassari, who took life with such impetuosity, almost with scorn, and set about learning as they set about having a binge. Many of them came from out-of-the-way villages in the interior, and had all the drive of the underprivileged discovering the world. The delicate web of his programmed life was upset by this. Anyway, he spent a lot of time in Nuoro, as if to prolong his childhood, and there, alongside his literary library, he began to put together a law library, buying treatises and monographs that he would read when the time came. Little by little, because of his studied way of speaking, the prudence which masked his basic insecurity, the everlasting maxims which he used to avoid the dangers of action, and even because of his precarious health, he was becoming the family authority, and even Don Sebastiano began to consult him when he ran into a problem—the very man who had never asked for or listened to advice from anyone in the family, as in her misery Donna Vincenza knew. And still she cradled this child, anxious about his health, and resentful against Sanna, who noticed nothing.

Neglect of her body had not only caused her legs to swell, but had ruined her teeth and, what is worse, her sight. People and things became shadows for her. The acuteness of her understanding compensated for the decline of her faculties, and so from her armchair she was intensely in touch with the life of the house; she read the face of each of her sons, and from the window at which she stood on the long dull evenings she recognized, by their voices or their footsteps on the cobblestones, all those who passed by without looking up for fear of having to greet her. Playing with her two youngest, Sebastiano and Peppino, who were still very close to her, she regained the liveliness of her girlhood. Sebastiano would still have jumped on her lap if she had not held him off. Peppino, whose fine-drawn face revealed the almost feminine delicacy of his spirit, in response to some unknown call had discovered a mysterious world, the ancient epics of the Orient, and when the three of them were alone together he read some passages in the translations of Michele Kerbaker or Italo Pizzi, and she would pretend to understand; or maybe she really did understand, prompted by motherly love. She too had her moments of happiness. Sebastiano was proud of this brother little older than himself, and together they created distant, iridescent worlds in which they would live when they grew up. It is what all children do, except that these dreams were made in Nuoro, where no one dreamed.

I have to admit that this is not quite true. In fact, the truth is the opposite: everyone dreamed. But the dreams of the Nuorese were like those of Antoni Mereu. Antoni Mereu (and I seem to see him before me) was a peasant who lived on the edge of Sèuna and worked as a day laborer like all the rest, except that he had a little field with half a dozen olive trees and a handful of vines, and this set him above the others, because he moistened his bread with his own oil and drank his own wine. He was, like so many others, "related" to Don Sebastiano, who was godfather to his only son. The boy grew up skinny and stunted, with a pear-shaped head, and he would have made a perfectly good Seunese if his father had not started dreaming, as I said. And his dream was to get his son an education. He spoke about this to Don Sebastiano, who told him he was mad. He didn't know what it meant to maintain a son as a student; and in any case, everyone ought to follow his own destiny. Antoni dug his heels in. He sent his son to school, and as if to spite Don Sebastiano the lad did not do badly. Though he had to repeat a few years, eventually he would have received his diploma. Antoni Mereu worked like a beast, waiting for the day. Suddenly the boy began to cough, to get thinner and thinner, and then to spit blood. Antoni went wandering around the streets like a lost dog. It was heartbreaking to see him, but the fault was his, because he had chosen to dream.

But I am straying off course with these memories that come crowding into my head, and I have no time to lose. Don

Sebastiano's sacrifices were beginning to bear fruit, and in fact the time had come when the family goes ahead on its own and the parents are left as impotent spectators, watching and suffering. In addition, the lofty example of Don Sebastiano weighed on his sons. Too long had they seen him working and depriving himself of everything, not to feel the need to lighten his load as soon as possible. This was the height of unfairness, because the father asked nothing but to crown his sacrifices with the success of his highly gifted sons. Although he had not traveled, he knew that there were such things as meteoric careers, goals higher than those of the lawyers and doctors who populated the town. There was the university career, which brought one fame, and even in Sardinia there were some examples of this, such as Chironi and Fadda, whom he had known as boys. Poor notary, he also had his dreams. But Gaetano, who had qualified with excellent results in medicine, had immediately competed for a post as medical officer in a far-off village in Campidano, because he wanted to earn his own living. And Michele, who was studying engineering, was destined to do the same thing. But one has to admit that this spirit of independence on the part of the boys had its positive side, because the commitments were not yet finished: there were still the two youngest, who would also leave home soon, and there were Pasquale and Giovanni, who gave food for thought.

In fact Pasquale, who seemed destined to go off the rails, had been rescued by Ludovico with a bold stroke that had contributed not a little to gaining him that reputation as a sage that would be with him all his life. Pasquale was certainly intelligent, like his brothers, but he had no desire to study. In the rigid secondary-school system of those days, he failed every year.

In the family there was an atmosphere of tragedy, because Don Sebastiano's plans were upset by this. All the most violent remedies had been attempted, but without success. The family was threatened with the shame of having a member who was a flop. It was then that Ludovico, who had kept in touch with the headmaster of the school, went and had a talk with him, and together they made the great decision: Pasquale was not suited to classical studies, but should turn to technical studies, thereby losing his chance of getting a degree. These were days of mourning for Don Sebastiano—bow was it possible that any son of his should not get a degree? But there was nothing to be done about it, and Pasquale had to take the road to Sassari, where he was to study accountancy. And it seemed that in one way or another he got by. Proud of this success, Ludovico returned to his uncut books. But he had gained moral dominance over the family.

The real anxiety, the great anxiety, was Giovanni, the eldest. You will remember that from youth up he had lived a life of his own, almost looking down on the rest of his brothers and immersed in some dark dream; and you will also remember that there was a rumor that he was infatuated with Don Pasqualino's beautiful daughter, who was hopelessly ill. Well, she died, and from that moment on, it seemed that Giovanni had entered a kind of nimbus of insanity. He had got into university, also in the law school, but had then failed to take his exams in time. People murmured that not everything could be expected to go right for Don Sebastiano. And Don Sebastiano, who was not really abreast of things, wrote letter after letter to no less a person than the Rector of the University of Rome, to find out if his son, who never got in touch, was keeping up with his exams. He wrote with the same wretched pen he used for drawing up deeds. But the Rector did not answer. Unless it was that his sons hid the reply so as not to upset him. He blamed the mail, and said that one of these days he'd go there himself to find out.

The tragedy came when, after the fiasco of his exams, Giovanni returned home. He arrived without warning, as if at a hotel where one has a room permanently booked. His arrival was marked only by his heavy step on the stairs and the slamming of the door of his room. Peppino stopped reading, and Donna Vincenza told her beads. Ludovico said they should let him be: Giovanni was a fake neurotic: the real invalid was himself, and *he* never gave *anyone* any trouble. And so he spent his days. When he deigned to come to table the meal became funereal. No one even knew what they were eating. Don Sebastiano, who was dying of hunger because he ate only one meal a day, would chew furiously, and the noise of his dentures clicked the silence away. The wretched boy appeared to detest his family: this father who fed his horse before the meal and brought with him the smell of the stable; this ignorant, gloomy, prematurely aged mother; these badly dressed brothers, who passed their exams without batting an eyelid…As soon as he had finished eating, Don Sebastiano would mount his horse and set out for his sun-drenched fields: let them all go hang! Donna Vincenza wept without shedding tears, and amid the protests of her sons she would climb the stairs as best she could and stay motionless for hours outside the door of Giovanni's room, not daring to knock.

Into this family, which was forming and disintegrating at the same time, as is the law with all families, Don Sebastiano that evening tossed the news of the assassinated archduke, and the possible declaration of a war that might involve Italy. The boys' eyes shone, as they did when they read a story from Plutarch. Ludovico said that if he didn't have that nervous stomach he would volunteer. Don Sebastiano read the paper out loud, and not without a touch of pride. Only Donna Vincenza, in the depths of her gloom, understood a very, very simple thing: that people die in war, and that of her seven children five would be exposed to death if Italy were to enter the war. With her heart in turmoil she shouted—and no one had ever heard her voice so loud—that Italy was in no condition to go to war. They were all taken aback, and Don Sebastiano, always ready to be emotional and to see things through rose-tinted glasses, was on the point of saying that she was in the world just because there was room for her, but luckily he restrained himself. Instead, he driveled on about old people who can make themselves useful in wartime, even if they don't go to the front line.

Enough of that. As everyone knows, the world did go to war, and for a year Italy was hanging on the edge of the abyss. In the Caffè Tettamanzi, where they all hated Italy because it had turned Sardinia into an outpost (as if this had not been its fate since Roman times), between one drink and the next they said that if Italy went to war the Sardinians ought to refuse to fight. Words, words, words: especially when unknown people arrived from Italy, made contact with the socialists and (naturally) with Don Ricciotti, improvised meetings in favor of the liberation of Trento and Trieste, and drew crowds to the Piazza San Giovanni; and these applauded frantically in spite of the fact that no one had ever heard of those cities. Even Commissioner Palazzi, who clearly had orders from the government, put on his tricolored sash and had three bugle calls sounded to disperse the crowd. But he did so without enthusiasm, because the fever had gripped even him.

Consumed with anxiety, Donna Vincenza dwelt on the fact that the first to be called up would be Pasquale, since he was due for conscription. After that would come the others, because the war wouldn't last only two months, as those imposters said. At least five of the boys might run the terrible risk. Only Sebastiano and Peppino would be exempt because of age. She had started to pray again, and she did not get even those few hours of sleep that her perpetual sufferings allowed her. Her sole comfort was Gonaria, who had no sons, only her brother the priest, but who knew that war had its origins in original sin and could bear no fruit other than sorrow. They spent long hours under the pergola, which was already covered with vine shoots. Will they still be here when the first bunches sprout? Suddenly came a hope: the newspapers said that there had been a disastrous earthquake in a place called Avezzano. The papers came out bordered with black, the King visited the scene, and dismay filled every heart. Italy could not make war under these conditions: this was the thought that came into her mind, and she clung to it with desperation. Even Gonaria said that God had sent a sign of His power to warn the Italians.

But war did come, as everyone knows, because men are more powerful than God. If we really think about it, God exists for any single individual who puts his trust in Him, not for the whole of humanity, with its laws, its organizations, and its violence. Humanity is the demon which God does not succeed in destroying. And so Donna Vincenza's sons started for the front line, which for Sardinia began at the port of embarkation, Terranova, on account of the submarines. She remained in the old house, custodian of the years, with the two youngest and with Ludovico and Giovanni, who had been rejected.

Her relations with Don Sebastiano grew worse, because (prey to his sentimentality) he had done nothing to help his boys avoid military service, and in vain did Donna Vincenza reproach him with the examples of Don Pasqualino's sons, who had stayed in Nuoro because they worked in industry, or those of the Corrales, because they were employed in agriculture. But he was thinking of doing even worse. As the government was issuing one loan after another in the name of "the Country in Danger," he wanted to sell all his property to underwrite bonds at 5 percent. Rescue came, as ever, from Ludovico, he who would have volunteered except for that damned neurosis, but who had enough balance (as well as having studied a bit of economics for his exam) to understand that wars produce inflation and that those shares would have become worth no more than the paper they were printed on. Don Sebastiano had done his duty to his country by way of his sons, and when they came back they would ask him to account for Isporòsile and Locoi—their patrimony as well as his. Giovanni continued to be the way he was, if not worse. When the newspaper arrived and little Sebastiano was reading it aloud under the pergola, while Don Sebastiano sat listening with moist eyes, Giovanni sidled up as if in a trance, snatched the paper from his brother's hands, and rushed up to read it in his lair. No one had the courage to protest, partly because Donna Vincenza held up her hands in supplication, as if to ward off disaster.

Well, if he snatched the newspaper it meant that he had some interest in life. The war reached Nuoro in the form of telegrams bringing news of those killed at the front. Buziuntu's son died, and the sons of Palimodde and of Zia Tatana, people from Sèuna, San Pietro, and the Corso, all together in a heap, like sheep at the slaughterhouse. The Caffè Tettamanzi was depopulated. The young socialists who gave themselves airs with *Avanti!* sticking out of their pockets had all followed Mussolini's example and volunteered: those loafers who aimed at getting into the middle classes had either taken the little train that would carry them to the other world, or had hidden away in the civil services and dared not show their faces for shame. Only Bartolino, Giovanni Maria Musiu, Ricciotti, and the other old men were still left, to keep up the card games and play at defeatism. Anyway, the war was a long way off, and there was still white bread to eat, and ration cards were useful only for those who were unable to fend for themselves. Meanwhile, the years went by and the end was not in sight. At Don Sebastiano's house, on the other hand, two sheets of paper arrived, calling up Peppino, who was eighteen, and Giovanni, who was over thirty. If there was nothing to worry about with Giovanni, because he was assigned to the territorial services (and his departure would remove a nuisance), Peppino was scarcely more than an adolescent, and they wanted him simply to get him killed. Things had gone that far. Donna Vincenza, her heart already turned to stone, filled his suitcase with sweet buns that could last as long as a month, and he took the little train, accompanied to the station by Don Sebastiano, who walked with his chest thrown out. Young Sebastiano remained alone in the deserted house, because Ludovico had gone off to Sassari to take his exams, which the war had made much easier to pass.

*

Letters from the front arrived fairly regularly, and they were always cheerful, even when they contained the news that this person or that person was dead. They were like messages from nowhere, because there were never any signs of where they came from. Donna Vincenza called on Gonaria to read between the lines for her, knowing that the letters were (as they said) censored, and that Gonaria was incapable of telling her a lie.

And so, day after day, the war became a habit. It was a distant thing, that perhaps might never end, just as there had seemed no end to the state of peace in which Nuoro had lived until then. Terrible things would happen from time to time. For example, one of the ferries between Sardinia and the Continent had been torpedoed, and five hundred people had been killed. One stunned moment, and then nothing. Many people didn't even know who the war was being fought against; and as for the places mentioned daily in the bulletins displayed in the windows of the Caffè Tettamanzi, they had no notion where they were. Right at the start the government had sent over about twenty internees, who were dotted around the town. No one could imagine who they were, but later it was learned that they were Austrian and German Jews resident in Milan, who had not wanted to leave Italy. Until then no one had ever heard of the Jews, except in the Bible. They were men like any others, but they were gentry, and had money, and if some of those draft-evading socialists said that when it came down to it they were traitors to their countries, the aristocrats, who had a good nose for such things, opened their houses to them as guests of honor.

The only penniless exiles were a family of semi-gypsies, two sisters and a brother twelve years old and scarcely less than a moron, who as soon as he got off the train started trotting about like Raffaelle and shouting "Chuff-chuff, chuff-chuff," and "Chuff-chuff" became his nickname. They must have been Slavs, and no one could imagine why anyone had bothered to send them all that way, since they didn't even know where they had come from. The sisters could earn a bare living, and earn it they did, competing with Giggia up in the bushes at Sant' Onofrio; the boy lived on air. Don Gaetano Pilleri the tobacconist, who also sold newspapers, took pity on him and employed him as a news vendor. It wasn't much to live on, but it was something. And he would trot about, alternating between "chuff-chuff" and the news headlines and making everybody laugh. Except that winter came, the bitter winter of Nuoro. Chuff-chuff, who was half-naked, began to cough, then to spit blood and run high fevers. In a short while he died. The cemetery of Nuoro, with ever-open arms, received him. No one knew where he had come from, just as no one knew where he was going. And as he had no name, no one even knew if he had really existed.

The war was extraneous and distant, but it was to have enormous influence on Sardinia, because the Sardinians discovered Italy, if indeed they did not discover mankind at large. All that, however, was still in the future. Meanwhile, the news of Peppino seemed good. They had sent him to an officer-candidate school, and such was their rapacious hunger for men that in a fortnight he was given the specially created rank of "cadet," which was one of those bureaucratic compromises made to create *de facto* officers and hurl them into the fray. What Donna Vincenza did not know (he himself was to tell her afterward) was that Peppino, half in officer's uniform, wearing his civilian shoes because the army was short of everything, with the lines of the Rāmāyana still in his head, was sent at once into the war zone. There he reported to a bewhiskered general who said, "So you're dying to be an officer? Well, go to the trenches and die." Peppino had set off on foot in the pouring rain, over mountains of red mud that left him breathless. After half an hour the soles of his shoes were torn clean off. He went on barefoot all night long, and when he reached the trenches in the morning he was a mass of cuts. Among the soldiers there were a few from Nuoro, who recognized Don Sebastiano's son, and bandaged his feet and gave him something to eat and drink. He was in a dugout all day, and toward evening he began to run a fever. The next day he was worse. They came for him with a stretcher and took him to hospital.

From the hospital he wrote home and told them about the slight ailment that was keeping him out of the front line. But he would soon be better, and would come home on leave. Donna Vincenza told Gonaria that she was very uneasy in her mind, but Gonaria, who spoke with God, reassured her. At the arrival of each letter Don Sebastiano would ride off, Ludovico would say that it was all nothing in comparison with what he was suffering, and Sebastiano would look at the books that Peppino had left in his keeping, and weep. At last a telegram arrived from Peppino, saying that he would soon be back on long leave.

Dawn illumined Donna Vincenza's harrowed face. She summoned all those women, witnesses of her childhood and her happy days, and threw them into preparing all manner of Nuorese delicacies: *sas casadinas* and *sas sebadas*, the traditional sweetmeats made with carefully worked fresh cheese; *sos culurjones*, made of almonds and lemon; *sos maccarrones cravàos*, which are little gnocchi pressed flat with the fingernail... For the day of his homecoming Gonaria had promised one of the sweetmeats for which she was famous. For a week the whole house smelled of dough and honey. And at last the waiting ended.

It was an April morning, so mild that the war became a bad dream dissolved in the clear air. Borghesi's orchard, where the offices of the province now stand, was all a cloud of almonds in blossom. Don Sebastiano set off in good time for the station, dressed in black and wearing a gold chain across the front of his waistcoat, something he had never done before when his sons came home. But this one was returning from the war. When the train stopped he stood rooted to the spot when he saw a sort of specter emerge from the single rust-red carriage and stagger toward him. But he pulled himself together at once and realized that the boy could never make the short distance home on foot. So he sent to Giovanni Maria, the same nephew whom Donna Vincenza had turned out of the house, asking him to send a carriage, and Giovanni Maria could scarcely believe that he was back in his uncle's good graces.

In Don Gabriele Mannu's ridiculously immense entrance hall Peppino appeared even more spectral to his mother as she came, almost nimbly, to meet him. There was nothing for it but to put him to bed, carting him up the stairs and into the room he had shared since childhood with his younger brother. Ludovico put in a moment's appearance to say that it was nothing serious, and that the real invalid was himself. And there he was, left alone with little Sebastiano, who seemed not to have noticed anything, and was proud of this playfellow and fellow student who had been to war. In the kitchen, which was piled with the cakes prepared for the homecoming, Don Sebastiano said that as far as he could see there was no hope. Donna Vincenza replied with some violence that he knew nothing of hope except concerning himself.

And so began the gradual descent toward death.

In the dismissal form issued by the hospital they had written: "Fever caused by over-exertion in an already delicate organism." Dr. Manca, Pedduzza's brother, who when he was not drunk was an excellent doctor, said that he would soon be cured, but he did not say from what disease, and this remained forever a mystery. In the first month it really seemed that he was getting better. The air of home, the constant presence of Sebastiano and of his mother, who had in his case returned to the caresses of earlier days, twice a day climbing the terrible stairs (and with bated breath he listened to the thud of her feet on step after step) had restored some measure of strength to him; so much so that, though unsteady, he was able to get down to the courtyard, where he rediscovered the little things of his childhood and looked at them with fresh eyes. He leaned on his brother as on a young sapling. Sometimes, in the small room where they had set up their little laboratory, he took delight in looking at the books that they had bound up when they were boys, and managed to follow Sebastiano when he read passages from his Oriental poets. How far away the war was, and the trenches, and the mud . . . All would have been well if the fever had not returned with dreadful regularity every evening. At such times Sebastiano, who suspected nothing, stayed on at his bedside as if to help him fight it. "When I get better," Peppino told him, "I want to buy you a lovely present."

July arrived, punctiliously withering every blade of grass in the landscape and covering Nuoro with its dusty skies. Dr. Manca, who understood less and less, however good he was at his job, advised a change of air for the patient. For those times this was an almost inconceivable idea, because everyone, rich and poor alike, accepted the seasons as they came. They thought of Locoi, where there was that locked room which I spoke of before. They cleared out all the equipment and put in two camp beds, and there the two children (for Peppino's illness had taken them both back to childhood) lived out their last fairy tale, in the shadow of the great pine tree, amid the waving vine leaves, and in the company of lizards which Ziu Poddanzu amused himself by taming. The old peasant, whose face was now completely framed in white, was always at the invalid's side, and told him about the times when he himself had been a soldier. They were simple, happy days, except for that inexorable fever. Ziu Poddanzu laughed, and made the others laugh. But one evening (it was already late September) he announced that he was going to Nuoro and would be back a little late. The boys were left alone, mournfully waiting. Ziu Poddanzu went to Nuoro to tell his employer that his son was in a bad way and should be taken home. This is what he thought, in his ignorance. Don Sebastiano, who had not forgotten his first fearful diagnosis, once more asked for a carriage from Giovanni Maria, and so they returned home. The patient was put to bed at once, still side by side with his younger brother, to whom he had promised a lovely present when he got well. The next day Don Sebastiano went to the post office, where Peppino had deposited his paltry earnings as an officer, and by asserting his authority he had them transferred to his own account. When the boy died it would be impossible to cash them without paying the death duties, and there would have been a thousand difficulties because of the heirs.

October passed. Peppino by this time never left his bed. Clear signs were in the air that the war was about to end. Drop by drop there still came news of the dead, but people felt that these would be the last. On the night between the third and fourth of November Sebastiano, still uncomprehending, was told by Ludovico to leave the invalid's room, and Don Sebastiano and Donna Vincenza sat themselves down on either side of the bed. The sick boy's breathing was already a deep rattle. Suddenly, from the Piazzetta Mazzini, where the town band assembled, the patriotic notes of the "Hymn of the Piave" struck up amid the yelling crowd. The war had ended in victory. "Listen to the music!" These were Peppino's last words. No one knew whether he meant the hymn, or his own labored breathing.

16

So death first entered Don Sebastiano's house, for time had swept away the memory of the two little girls who had died thirty years before. A wave of panic seemed to strike the whole family. Don Sebastiano's withdrawing the savings from the post office was held against him by his sons as an act of betrayal; but Ludovico, who in the meantime had taken his degree, silenced them all by enumerating the laws and regulations governing post-office deposits, which seem expressly designed to take your money and not give it back again. Donna Vincenza had no need to add still more black to the black garments that already enshrouded her. Her childhood friends had come to see her, in their Sunday best and with long faces, and they told her she ought to thank God it had been possible to "layout" her son, whereas all the others had been dumped heaven knows where. Donna Vincenza put up with this for a little while, and then got tired of it and returned to her solitude, clinging to her youngest, who was to live with the shadow of that loss all his life long. What is more, so harsh was the nature of the old Nuorese that not a Mass was said, not a cross was raised over the grave; and Peppino was left alone forever.

The end of the war brought the return of the survivors, and naturally posed many problems. Basically, the families who were mourning dead sons were better off than those who were expecting them back alive. Among the latter was Don Sebastiano's family, expecting and fearing the homecoming of Giovanni. As a matter of fact, the latest news from him had given rise to some hopes, since he had managed to take a degree, albeit in a more or less improvised university for military personnel; nonetheless, he had taken it. When at last he arrived, without so much as a word of warning, he was clearly a radically changed man. He had become stout and loud-mouthed, and what struck them most was that he had become slovenly in his dress. All that tramping from barracks to barracks, living shoulder to shoulder with people whom the call to arms had provided with a profession, who swore and talked about women from dawn till dusk, had weaned him from the rarefied atmosphere of home, and dispelled the phantom of the dead girl which had formerly conditioned his existence. Not that he had changed his attitude toward the family, for whom—and especially the ruin that was Donna Vincenza— he appeared to nourish inexplicable rancors; but at least he did not stay bottled up in the house. On the contrary, he seemed driven to continual escape, to mingling in that bastard world that had emerged from the war. For those migrations of peoples which wars always produce had their reverberations even in Nuoro, and if the Jewish internees, and the white-collar workers who had stayed on in order to escape the stringencies of life on the Continent, had by now departed, hordes of adventurers had drifted in, not only from remote parts of Sardinia, but also from various regions of Italy, especially from the south; and no one knew what they were after. Nuoro impassively absorbed them all, cut them to its own cloth, and after a while they forgot their own way of speech, like immigrants in America. The Caffè Tettamanzi had been refurbished and "improved." Maestro Manca began to include the newcomers in his melancholy clowning. It was into the midst of this crowd that Giovanni had plunged, and he seemed to get a kick out of cheapening himself. But when he got home he grew surly again, and shut himself up in his room. Ludovico said that it was another form of neurasthenia, a manic one, just as the previous form had been depressive. Indeed, since in order to cultivate his own neurosis he had amassed books on medicine, he explained that there was a typically family form of neurasthenia, meaning that it was not shown in front of outsiders but only in the family, where there was less opposition. In short, he advised them not to make an issue of it, to pretend not to notice him. There was no other remedy.

But Donna Vincenza did not let things ride. This son, who had come home so noisy and boisterous, frightened her even more than the one who used to languish in the solitude of the house. When evening came she would grope her way up onto the platform that enabled her to get to the dining-room window, and there she would wait for hours, hidden by the shutters, listening for the voice or footstep that announced his return. The frivolous noises from the caffè, among which one could always distinguish the voice of Bartolino above the others, surrounded her shadowy figure like the buzzing of a beehive; but she was deaf to them. As soon as she recognized his step she climbed down into the darkness and obliterated herself in her armchair. She knew her son would go into the kitchen, because neurasthenia does not abolish hunger, and she always arranged the leftovers from supper for him on one corner of the table. He would eat, he would take his fill, and when she heard him hurrying up the stairs she would come out from the shadows and start the ordeal of the steps which she had to conquer, one by one, to get to her room.

It was like this every evening, with the other boys protesting against this absurd privilege. And the brothers were right to protest, because brothers are like the sailors in a ship: whoever does not pull his weight on board is a traitor. But it was also right for Donna Vincenza to live in trepidation about this son who ignored and maltreated her, because her eyes saw what the others did not see; and it may have been that in the destiny of someone chasing after the shadow of a dead girl she saw her own destiny. Maybe... for Donna Vincenza certainly did not reason about these things. It is I who am reasoning, now that the earth covers them all, and they are all condemned or absolved together.

In fact, this process of debasement that Giovanni was undergoing was the inevitable outcome of his previous way of life. The stakes are always life and death. That long-lost girl whom no one remembered, not even her parents, had for a long time beckoned Giovanni to follow her; and one way of following her was the vacuum in which he had confined himself, the desperation he had inflicted on himself and others. Life in the barracks had stripped him of his personality as a snake loses its skin, but it had prevented him from dying. There was nothing for it but to live; that is, to brutalize oneself with work, which gives one a carapace of money that ghosts cannot penetrate. This is what he had done, for without breathing a word to anyone he had taken his exams to become a notary. He saw that Don Sebastiano was getting old and needed an assistant. Later on, he would step into his shoes. Suddenly coming to his senses again (Ludovico had been right), he went around the place with his clothes covered with stains and his beard unkempt, indifferent to himself and others. He still retained his tall figure, his aristocratic features, and the slender hands which now wielded the same pen as Don Sebastiano. In the evening he would count up the money earned, before locking it in the safe. This did not assuage Donna Vincenza's fear of him, for when some client came she had to send someone to look for him all over Nuoro, which made him fly into a rage. One fine day he announced that he was going to marry. There was a lot of grumbling in the family, because his brothers thought of this also as an imposition. Don Sebastiano, who was an upright man, went to the bride and told her what his son was really like. But she, who was getting on in years, said she would marry him all the same.

This marriage of Giovanni's might have been a liberation for Donna Vincenza, as the cross passed out of her hands into another's. But Donna Vincenza, whose blind eyes saw what Don Sebastiano did not see, immediately understood that Giovanni's departure was the beginning of the end. The house in which her husband had shut her up was nonetheless still a house. The war (which had virtually not been felt in Nuoro) had emptied it out, and it would never fill up again. It was not simply a matter of Peppino, for the dead never leave home. No, it was a question of all the other boys, whom the war had not restored to her, even though they had survived, because she now had to measure up to the enormous events they had witnessed, and she did not feel equal to the task. They were different people, in short, as Nuoro was different, launched as it was toward the absurd adventure of becoming an overpopulated provincial city, where people were beginning not to recognize one another in the street. A gulf of solitude opened before her. If only she still had one of those dead girls…Or (for Michele also had married, far from Nuoro) if her daughters-in-law had not started having children…One of them might have helped her to bear the weight of the house, the weight of life. Ludovico, after consulting his oracle, thought of starting a law firm. Pasquale, the only one who had seen the war from beginning to end, because he had been due for call-up anyway, had now returned and, after giving vent to his *joie de vivre* in all the drinking dens, seemed to want to go into business. She was left with her youngest, who was still at the local school but in the autumn would be off to study in Sassari or Cagliari. How she dreaded the approach of that day! And she was right, for when the day came, she prepared him food for the journey, with tender meat coated with bread crumbs, and pancakes sprinkled with sugar. Sebastiano left it all behind, ashamed of his mother although he adored her, and left home in the darkness as if anxious to belong to the outside world.

Don Sebastiano went to the station with the last of his sons, as dawn was barely beginning to tint the sky. He had noticed nothing. Donna Vincenza was left with the maid in the kitchen, staring at all those good things to eat. She would have to unwrap them from the package she had made. Someone would eat them. But this was not the problem. The problem was the refusal of an act of love. Her son would understand it many years later, and remember it all his life. But Donna Vincenza did not know this. She felt the void surrounding her. The old wound began to bleed again. Once more she became the young girl whom Don Sebastiano had taken as a bride, who was unable to step out of the house because there was no hand to help her.

17

The news had spread in a flash among the habitués of the Caffè Tettamanzi. In the old-fashioned rooms, with mirrors on the walls and sofas covered in red velvet, between one game of "tresette" and another, they would now discuss politics; not because the priest-eating youngsters with *Avanti!* in their pockets had turned up again, but because the war had somehow brought the town closer to things, and one heard the echo of what was happening in Sassari and Cagliari, and of certain new ideas that were in the air, the most bizarre of which was the notion of making Sardinia into a republic, separate from Italy. Maestro Manca said that they ought to nominate Don Ricciotti as President, while Don Ricciotti thought that if there was a republic it would change the laws and he might at last lay his hands on Loreneddu.

But there was only one piece of news that day, and it was this: after years and years of being confined to an armchair, Pietro Catte's aunt had died and left him heir to all her properties. These consisted of the two-story house (two up, two down) where she lived, and of a piece of "open land," meaning an unfenced strip of grazing land that must have been what was left over after the building of a road. And in fact it bordered the dirt road to Locoi, and the vagrant shepherds used to drive their sheep in there at night. The total value, with the inflation produced by the war, was a hundred thousand lire.

Pietro Catte was not seen at the Caffè Tettamanzi for a week. When he reappeared he was wearing a black suit bought from Carobbi, the Tuscan tailor (who had three assistants), with the cash he had found in one of his aunt's drawers. When he was dressed in all that mourning, his cross-eyes looked more pronounced than ever, but you could bet that they had shed not a tear. Zia Mariantonia had in any case been in two minds whether to leave her all to the hospital rather than to that nephew, who had never managed to master more than the alphabet, and who had been ignominiously sacked from his job as bus conductor. Then the memory of her only brother had prevailed, and perhaps some hidden maternal feeling. Francesco Casu, the one whose means of livelihood was so mysterious, went right up to him and said loudly, "Pietro, your aunt is dead, and good health to us until she comes back again! But now that you're rich, don't turn your back on your old pals. Stand us all a drink!" Pietro was a trifle nettled by this familiarity, but he didn't mind standing a round, because for the first time it gave him a chance to show off his altered circumstances. Everyone crowded to the bar, and when the time came he reached into his waistcoat pocket and pulled out a silver scudo, a coin that the war had swept away, and everyone was left gasping. He pocketed the change with perfect sangfroid and left the bar.

After that, Pietro Catte never missed an evening in the caffè, and even joined in "tresette" with Bartolino and Robertino Caramelli. But it was easy to see that he was not the same person as before, and that sudden wealth had put a barrier between himself and ordinary people, whose jokes at his expense he did not appreciate. The fiend was beginning to whisper in his ear. Unlike Don Sebastiano, who said that only the cemetery is rich, Pietro went around saying "I am rich," and he said it so often that he ended by becoming a kind of myth. Who would have thought that Zia Mariantonia had so much money? And it can't have been an old wives' tale, because he even went so far as to give a lira to Poddanzu or Dirripezza, when everyone could see him do it. "St. Peter the Rich," Maestro Manca called him in one of his blasphemous ballads, invoking his intercession with the Lord. In a word, Pietro Catte was on everybody's lips. But the trouble was that at a certain point, as his folly progressed, he got bored with the Caffè Tettamanzi, he got bored with Bartolino, he got bored with the useless life of the Nuorese, and he began (but it was the devil still whispering in his ear) to conceive a grandiose scheme. A man of his stature could not stay in Nuoro, and his wealth ought not to remain inert. The fame of Milan, where money multiplied if you only looked at it, had reached as far as Nuoro. There he would go and start a good business, and after a few years he would return with one of those automobiles that were beginning to be seen around even in Sardinia, and he would buy a house in the Corso and a *tanca* like Don Pasqualino's. One evening (it was in early autumn) he knocked at the "little" door of the house of Don Sebastiano, who had been a friend of his father's, and offered to sell him his house, his land, his whole inheritance. Don Sebastiano was getting ready to read the newspaper, but nevertheless listened patiently to the other's plans.

"You are looking for bread made from better things than wheat," he told him. "Swallows leave the nest because God urges them to, but the man who leaves his home is egged on by the devil."

It was ancient wisdom speaking in him, but it was also reading the newspapers that informed him of the hell caused by the war in those distant cities, quite apart from the fact that he thought of Pietro Catte as subnormal, a *"minus habens,"* as he was accustomed to say.

"You have been fortunate in that your good aunt left you a roof over your head. There are jobs here to give you enough to live on."

Don Sebastiano knew that madness is always lying in wait, and had not forgotten that early in the war he had been on the point of selling all his land to buy pieces of paper that today would have been practically worthless.

"So you don't want to buy?" asked Pietro Catte.

"No," replied the notary, "because your property does not interest me, and I do not wish to suffer from remorse."

The house and land were sold to someone who had come back from the war with a pile of money: rumor had it that he had rifled a shop during the retreat. And so Pietro Catte found the incredible sum of a hundred thousand lire in his hands, in glowing thousand-lire notes. The deed was drawn up by Don Sebastiano, who never once raised his eyes from the desk while he was writing it.

Pietro Catte was not an emigrant. He was a rich man in search of a world worthy of his enterprise. For this reason he traveled second-class, among the real gentlemen, whom he did not hesitate to inform that he had received a large legacy and had a hundred thousand lire in his pocket. Everyone listened with curiosity to his broken Italian, but one gentleman in particular, with the pince-nez fashionable at the time and a very distinguished air about him, seemed to take to him particularly, and asked if anyone in Milan was expecting him. Well, actually no, he hadn't thought of that. And it seemed strange to him that he had overlooked such a basic thing, what with all the Continentals who came to Nuoro and frequented the Caffè Tettamanzi. But no matter: the gentleman had a little place which he never used. He would be only too glad to put it at his disposal. It was just a stone's throw from the Duomo. Pietro Catte relished this kindness as the first taste of the El Dorado that awaited him. He thanked him very much, and went to his suitcase for the *casadinas* he had been given before he left, which he offered to all present. Everyone had a taste, and sang the praises of the distant country which the war had brought into the limelight because of the Sassari Brigade. He ate his fill of them, because he had had nothing for twenty hours, and then went noisily to sleep, among the ironic whispers of the gentlemen. Finally he was awakened by a big jolt, amid a babble of voices, like the one on the Feast of the Redeemer. Everyone got out, and the kind gentleman remained behind for a moment as if he had lost something. When they were alone, he wrote down the address of the house and gave him the keys. He told him to make himself at home, as there was no one else there. He would call on him the next day.

Deeply touched, Pietro Catte made a mental comparison with the presumptuous antagonism of Don Sebastiano, and set off toward the exit with his suitcase, making his way with difficulty through that sea of people who seemed to be constantly celebrating something. In the station square Milan met him like an immense wall, closing in to suffocate him. For a moment, but only for a moment, he thought of his aunt's little house with its flowering balconies, all sold now. Even the air was different from the air of Nuoro. Luckily a yellow vehicle drew up beside him, and the driver asked if he wanted to be taken anywhere. He produced the paper with the address, and the chauffeur, as they were called in those days, told him to get in. They went around in circles like people with nowhere to go (or so it seemed to him) until the taxi stopped outside a little low house, such as then still existed in the heart of Milan. Twenty lire! He thought it an enormous sum, because in Nuoro he lived for a month on twenty lire. His hundred thousand lire shrank. But perhaps he was tired; he hastened to let himself in. In the first room he saw a divan; he threw himself on it and fell into a deep sleep.

The next morning he was awakened by the presence of someone in the room. He roused himself at once. It was the kind gentleman from the train. Why ever had he slept on the divan? He must have a shower and a shave. And as he had never seen a shower, the gentleman showed him how it worked. That rain falling on his tubby body, and on the almost African face which he saw reflected in the mirror, at once restored his faith in Milan and the world. The gentleman told him his name: Ingegner Ambrogio Fappala. And he made an appointment for midday, in the Galleria. They were to lunch together at Savini's.

He immediately regained his euphoria. With confident steps he left the house and set off at random along one of the innumerable streets which spread before him. The buildings made him dizzy to look at, but the wallet with his money in it, which he constantly patted with his hand, gave him a sense of security, as if he were not excluded from so much grandeur. People turned around to stare at this strange wild man of the woods, but he proceeded firmly on his way until he found himself in an immense nave, full of a gaily colored throng. At first glance he reckoned it could contain the whole Corso of Nuoro, and it was covered with panes of glass that glittered in the sunlight. He felt more and more excited and sure of himself. At a certain moment, in the midst of all that bustle, he heard his name called. He turned in amazement. It was Ingegner Fappala calling to him, though how he had managed to recognize him in that crowd was more than he could understand. With him was an elderly gentleman whom the engineer lost no time in introducing. He was Dr. Rossi, an important business-man who was keen to make his acquaintance. They all went into Savini's through a door that revolved without stopping, and in which he got stuck. In the thousand mirrors all around him he saw his own grotesque figure, almost as if it wished to stay his steps on the fatal path.

However, I must hurry on, because by now the reader will have understood everything. It was one of the usual confidence tricks that the papers are full of, but with this very relevant difference: that it was Pietro Catte who was tricked. Perhaps if those gentlemen had known this, they would not have done it. As soon as he became aware of the deception, the ground began to spin dizzily under his feet. In this terrifying maelstrom there was only one fixed point, and that was Nuoro. Nuoro was the reality of the world, and his bulging eyes were riveted on it and saw nothing else. It was the moral reality, the place and the day of judgment: the conscience that resides in the stones and in the people. All the good or ill that you do, you do for Nuoro. Wherever you go, Nuoro follows you, waits like a brigand at the corner of the street, or like a tax man demanding his taxes. "You are looking for bread made from better things than wheat..." The old notary's words roared in his ears, and deafened him, and prevented him from hearing the din of the city in whose streets he groped like a blind man. At this time of day Bartolino dealt the cards for "tresette" in the Caffè Tettamanzi. But it was not a question only of the living, of that handful of beggars in San Pietro or Sèuna; there was also *Sa 'e Manca*, the cemetery watched over by that granite crag resembling a mourning woman; and there were all the dead of all the generations crying out to him, "Pietro Catte, what have you done?" And one of these was Zia Mariantonia, who had left him the house so that it should rest firm on its foundations, not for him to take it to Milan in a wallet.

Pietro Catte, Pietro Catte, Pietro Catte... One morning they found him in a faint on the steps of a church where he had sat down to rest his swollen feet. He was unable to say what had happened to him, because he remembered nothing. All he could see was a white something, dazzling and distant. And toward that something he was sent back, either with a travel order or with the paltry sum left in his pocket.

At midnight the thunders of Corrasi, of Supramonte, of Sa Serra, of Montalbo, the four cardinal points which had arranged to meet above the Corso in Nuoro, burst forth in a single, terrifying roar. However, they did not succeed in drowning the bell of Santa Maria, which was chiming either the time or the slow knell, *su toccu pasau*, that announces the death of the rich. From the open hatchways of the skies the rain came down on the rooftops as if to crush them. The people of Nuoro hid their heads under the blankets, thinking that the end of the world had come.

And in fact it had.

At the top of the Corso, where the road from Orosei and the sea comes in, and right at the spot where Tortorici's kiosk at one time stood, the bus that brings passengers and mail from the Continent had stopped. How it had got there, at that hour and in that weather, it was impossible to tell. The first to get out was the driver. It was the devil in person, with his horns and pointed beard and twisted tail, surrounded by a fiery nimbus on which the water hissed as it fell from the sky. He stood still a moment, then grabbed a flute out of thin air and started down the road. In answer to a long note, the next off the bus were *sas surbiles*, the witches who live in the mountains of the Gennargentu. No one has ever seen them, but I can assure you they exist. With sneers and with cackles they followed the devil, who continued his darksome summons. Four Furies then obeyed the call and joined the procession, howling and gnashing their teeth. The wind roared in the Corso as if in an enormous tube, and Don Pasqualino's lamps jumped around like maddened things. Many of them smashed, casting the world into darkness. As in the funerals of the rich, the procession made a pause, and lo, from the flute (or perhaps it was no longer a flute) there came a lacerating note, and at that note Pietro Catte fell headlong from the bus as though someone had pushed him out. Of what he had once been there remained nothing but a death's head, the eyes more asquint than ever, the fleshy lips frozen in a grimace. His black coat hung on him like a sack, and his trousers were held up by a belt fastened at the tightest hole. Like an automaton he joined the procession, and at once a gap appeared between him and the others before and behind, so that he was seen to be what he was: the king of the feast.

The devil had now thrown away his flute, and as he walked he put two fingers crosswise in his mouth, as Sardinian shepherds do; and he emitted piercing whistles. Then out of the bus came a countless swarm, more numerous than it seemed capable of holding. The first was Boelle, who had died most recently and who watched the scene with a sneer. He was followed by Fileddu, ever faithful, with his jacket hanging from his skeletal shoulders. The entire cemetery appeared to have emptied out to join the procession. Zia Mariantonia was dragging herself along, and would have liked to turn off and see her house again, but that was not possible. Dirripezza was there, and Baliodda, and there were also important skeletons, who could be distinguished by their solemn gait. But not all of them were dead: there were all the tavern keepers in Nuoro, with their retinue of puce-faced drinkers; there were the cardplayers; and there was Bartolino, impressive as ever. Last of all came Don Sebastiano, scattering wheat on the flagstones of the Corso; and the wheat grew tall at once and produced ears. Another stop was made in front of the Caffè Tettamanzi. The din of the thunder seemed to redouble. Pietro Catte opened one eye, and when he saw that as usual the tables had been left outside for the night, he felt like crying. The rain was coming down in sheets, but the strange thing was that it seemed he was the only one getting wet, while all the others were left immune, in the dry. Or maybe it was sweat that was streaming out of his hair. They passed over the Iron Bridge and through the trees of the Alberetti, which the wind seemed likely to uproot. Then came the Quadrivio, and then the great *tanca* of Biscollai, the one which he had been going to buy when he came back from Milan—that, or another like it.

At the top of the hill there was still the huge oak under which he had so often had a picnic as a child, on Easter Mondays, with Zia Mariantonia and friends from the neighborhood. In fact, it seemed to have got even bigger, to have grown out of all proportion, and as the crazy procession approached it, the hurricane seemed to hoist it upward, as if about to tear it from the centuries-old roots resembling veins that gripped the ground all around it. The living and the dead arranged themselves in a circle, *sas surbiles* and the Furies intoned a funeral dirge, and Pietro Catte stepped up to the trunk. Here the devil grabbed hold of him, ripped the belt from his trousers, wound it around his neck, and then flew up to a branch, from which he left him hanging with staring eyes.

Dawn was beginning to whiten the sky, when a young shepherd roused the sheep which were still in the fold and drove them out onto the hillside, where they started to graze once more to the tinkle of sheep bells. The boy, too, took a bit of bread and a piece of cheese from his bag and set off toward the oak, where he was going to wait until the sun was high, and then take the sheep in for the first milking. The morning, as happens in Sardinia in late summer, was as clear as crystal. Every blade of grass was beaded with that wholesome dew that makes up a little for the drought. As he neared the tree, he saw the hanging body slightly swaying in the morning breeze, and he stood speechless. Then he threw away the bread, abandoned the sheep, and ran madly toward the town, which was just awaking.

"Pietro Catte has hanged himself! Pietro Catte has hanged himself!"

From every window tousled heads poked out. Pietro Catte has hanged himself! Then the procession began. The magistrate, the *carabinieri,* Father Delussu still stunned by wine...they all followed the shepherd. Everyone recognized him. What should be done? Father Delussu declared that he was mad, and so it came about that Pietro Catte, who had chosen to look for bread made from better things than wheat, was buried in the consecrated ground where all the other Nuorese sleep, or lie awake.

18

With the return of the fine weather, Donna Vincenza had her big wickerwork chair carried out under the pergola in the *corte*, and there, motionless, she would spend her day. What she had been afraid of all her life, with the birth of one boy after another, had come to pass. She was left alone in the great tomb of the house. Boredom began to engulf her. The mulling-over of memories that had filled her existence—the recollection of a brief, happy past, the slow destruction of her being—had become quiescent, just as her eyes had clouded over. The house of which, by some supreme irony, she had been the mistress, began to suffer for it. Peppedda the maid, on the threshold of old age, had been discovered by a smallholder who had lost his wife, and she had married him. Since then there had been a string of healthy, happy, lively girls on whom Donna Vincenza vented her resentment, so that after a little while they would leave. The rooms were no longer swept, and there was a film of dust on the furniture. One day Don Sebastiano had warmed up the coffee, the only thing he was particular about, and had tasted something unfamiliar. "This coffee's made of barley!" he yelled, loud enough for Donna Vincenza to hear him. It was true… or rather, it was not true, because she had simply forgotten to add the fresh coffee to the boiled dregs. In former times her rancor would not have prevented her from reddening to the roots of her hair, but now she listened to her husband's complaints with indifference, almost with pleasure. In fact, it had come about that Donna Vincenza, in her infinite misery, had realized that time was on her side. The difference of ten years between herself and Don Sebastiano now began to make itself felt, and her husband, though still in good health, gave many signs of feeling the weight of age. The scepter was at last handed to her, and she used it to wreak the cruelest revenge; that is, pretending not to notice him, not answering when he addressed a word to her, refusing his overtures of kindness and forgiveness. The poor old fellow did not understand it; he aired his grievances to his sons (when he saw them) and let off steam at Locoi with Ziu Poddanzu, who would shake his head and (out of respect) say nothing. "Vincenza is mad, she's mad," Don Sebastiano would say, "and if she goes on like this she'll ruin the family." He did not realize that for all of us the time comes when we are in the world just because there is room for us, and the moment had now come for him.

The tragic thing was that the boys, those who were left, and those who came back increasingly rarely to the old home, all took their mother's side; and the most hostile to him was that "filthy puppy," as Don Sebastiano called his youngest son in moments of rage, that same Sebastiano who had nonetheless broken his mother's heart by refusing the food she had so carefully prepared for his journey. Ludovico, who had finally opened his law office and knew his Civil Code, said that when two married people cannot get along together they should separate; and it was the only thing he could say, seeing that in the law he had discovered the self-confidence that eluded him in life, and was naturally led to mistake the law for life itself. One had to make allowances for him because he was a bachelor, and perhaps had never loved anyone, and could therefore not understand that hatred makes marriage more indissoluble than love. Also against Don Sebastiano, of course, were those impoverished satellites of Donna Vincenza's who occasionally—though less and less often—were around the house doing little jobs for her.

But in Donna Vincenza's long day there was one hour of joy which the Lord had not deprived her of. This was when, at about five o'clock on summer evenings, her cousin Gonaria would call in on her way back from school. Being in love with God, Gonaria respected Don Sebastiano, who in her eyes had something of God in him, if only the fact that he was a man. But for Vincenza, whom she thought of as far more important than she was herself, because she was a mother, she had the ecstatic feeling that comes of a common frailty: they were both frail because they were women and therefore by nature subject to the dominion of others. Gonaria came from a house of sorrow and entered a house of sorrow, but her simple faith transfigured everything, cheering even that cousin of hers who did not grumble about her woes. She would come into the great hall without knocking, hurry straight through to the pergola, sit down practically at Vincenza's feet, and speak at once of the only thing she knew about, which was God. I am sure that God, there above the pergola from which the milky bunches of grapes hung down, would listen to these monologues which directly concerned Him, and forgive Donna Vincenza if she followed them with a smile on her lips.

That day, however, Gonaria had arrived almost at a run, enveloped in her black skirts, because she had more substantial things to tell her venerated cousin. This was the news that had been so long expected, the event for which Vincenza had promised a cake covered with chocolate. It now seemed certain that within the week the bishop would announce her brother Ciriaco's appointment as a canon. The hat with the red cord would enter their resurrected house; that is, there would be more of God in it, because there is no doubt that the presence of God increases with a rise in rank. Immense was her joy. Ciriaco was becoming more and more demanding and intolerant at home. He especially had it in for her, because she used to pray out loud; or sometimes out of absolute silence, with her eyes raised to heaven, she would cry out, "Where is God?"

"Stop it!" he would yell. "This place is a madhouse!"

He had become difficult about his food as well, so that she, Gonaria, would see to making him the choicest delicacies, biscuits to dip in his milk, lighter than the sacred Host. But what did it matter? When the red cord came, all troubles would fade away, she would serve him with greater faith, and she would make his very room into a tabernacle. Donna Vincenza was pleased, too. Gonaria's family were the only relatives she had left, and she remembered the precise day on which the catastrophe had occurred, leaving the little girls and their brother in the direst poverty. Now everything was back together again, thanks to the work of this gentle creature who sat at her feet and who had never known what evil was. Although Ciriaco was grumpy, and took no notice of his sad cousin (perhaps he had enough on his plate, with all those sisters), his appointment as a canon crowned the hardwon resurrection of the household. And then, even she needed to give herself to some dream, and having none of her own, she welcomed Gonaria's. This was why she repeated her promise of a cake studded with chocolates. Who could tell if Sebastiano, the youngest, who had gone off to study and was Gonaria's godson, would come for the celebration. He never wrote, and they had no news of him except from the tales of schoolfellows who came home, and she no longer even dragged herself to the door, as she had done for so many months, to wait anxiously for the postman.

The red cord arrived a little later than Gonaria had said, but arrive it did; and for three days the house was full of people. The relatives from Galtellì came on horseback, and from Dorgali came the Mariani spinsters, owners of that fabulous villa with a loggia looking right onto the sea, that was called La Favorita, where Gonaria had once been, and had remembered like a lovely dream. The canons of Nuoro came, of course, and also the parish priests from Orune, Oniferi, Oliena, and the other nearby villages, and each of them brought nougat, or a lamb, or bread glazed with egg, like they make at Easter. The parish priest of Oliena arrived, needless to say, with a demijohn of wine, saying: "With Oliena wine you can say Mass, even though it's as black as sin." And the neighbors who called every evening came, and they were welcome although they brought nothing, because they were poor. Of the sisters, Battistina and Tommasina were already in the grip of their affliction, and withdrew into a corner, in almost total darkness, because they were afraid of having to shake hands with anyone. Ciriaco sat with his hat on his head, his cassock trimmed with red, and his feet on the pan of the brazier, which contained last year's ashes because it was never removed from the room.

Toward evening the bishop was announced. They opened up the room they called the sitting room, which no one ever entered. Here were the portraits of their ancestors who had known prosperity, and here also was a large portrait of Ciriaco, which Gonaria had hung among the pictures of the saints. On the few pieces of furniture saved from the shipwreck glittered wreaths of artificial flowers with a baby Jesus in the middle. From the permanently closed windows came a long ray of dusty sunlight. Gonaria did the honors, neatly serving the cordial she had made herself and Donna Vincenza's cake. Ciriaco had risen to his feet beside the brazier, and the bishop went over to him and embraced him. He complimented him on the honor that he had so well deserved, and finally dropped a hint that things would not end there, even though only heaven can appoint bishops. The new canon held up his hands in a modest gesture, Gonaria kissed the bishop's ring three times, and then it was all over. A new life was beginning, and one had to make ready for it.

Night enveloped the house and cut it off from the world. Gonaria alone remained awake, as if suspended between heaven and earth. God had come nearer to her. From the canon's room from time to time she heard the sound of a rasping cough, but she thought nothing of it. Outside, the youths of Nuoro were serenading Maestro Manca, chanting, *"Portantina che porti quel morto."** And Maestro Manca, scared out of his wits, threw open the window and swore to high heaven.

The months went by. The canon continued to spend his life between the church and the curia, as he had done as a priest. While

---

* "O litter bearing that dead man…"

Giuseppina looked after the rest of the family, Gonaria had taken her brother into her care, and made him those delicate sweet-meats as only she knew how.

Everything seemed to be set fair for a happy future, but the cough did not go away. It tormented him when he said Mass, and in the choir stalls, annoying the other corpulent clerics who took advantage of the monotony of Gregorian chant to take a short nap. He came home in the evening worn out, paler and paler, until one day he started to run a fever. In the house of the four women, still full of the celebrations, madness broke out. No one had any illusions: the terrible disease that at that time had no cure had seized hold of Ciriaco; but no one wanted to admit it. Tommasina, who had a phobia about microbes, rose up like an angry serpent, shouting that it was nothing, that he, like her, was perfectly healthy, that none of the Sannas had ever been sick, and that but for that catastrophe their father would still be alive. At the same time, behind his back in the kitchen, she scorched all the plates he ate from, while Giuseppina, the busy bee of the house-hold, who if she had been strong enough would have torn them from her hands, wept. Battistina had withdrawn even more into her dark corner, and there would keep her hands in the air so that they touched nothing; but she was no trouble to anyone. Gonaria, who was in constant touch with God, spoke of a neglected cold, and strained every fiber to care for the invalid. Her tiny body hov-ered in the room in search of some comfort, while she cried out that the patient was getting better every day, and prepared him concentrated broth that gave nourishment without lying heavy on the stomach. For the first time in his life Ciriaco looked kindly on this winged sister whom he had always thought of as mad, even though with her ninety-three lire a month she had been able to put the house back on its feet. He stroked her hair and told her that they would take his first outing together, and that they would go to church to give thanks to the Lord. As on the day of the celebrations, he was sitting in the small space between the sideboard and the French windows which opened onto the balcony, with his feet on the pan of the brazier and his biretta on his head. And between one fit of coughing and the next, he was saying litanies. The neighbors no longer came to visit the sisters, because they were afraid of letting out what everyone was thinking and saying. And in fact when Dr. Manca, whom you will remember as a good doctor when he wasn't drunk, put forward his first suspicions, Gonaria turned on him like a scorpion and chased him out of the house, yelling after him that he was a drunkard, that Ciriaco was in the best of health, and that the fever would go away when the fine weather came.

The truth was that for Gonaria Ciriaco could not die, because he was a priest, and indeed a canon, which meant that he was the very presence of God in the house, the proof that God, to whom she had offered her whole life like a burning candle, did indeed exist. With her frail body she engaged in ferocious combat with something incomparably stronger than herself. She was always at his bedside, she soothed his cough with an infusion prepared with her own hands, she held it to his lips, and at times when he felt better she read him the breviary, and as he listened his eyes grew huge. The days passed and the nights passed, and in the whole of Nuoro, in the whole darkened world, there was nothing but the little flame of her ludicrous hope. She did not know that the Nuorese had already condemned Canon Sanna to death, and therefore scoffed at her faith. Death was bound to come. And in fact it came, one evening as dark was falling, while she was talking to him and telling him that the next year they would go to the Madonna del Monte together. With the reed of a voice remaining to him he asked her forgiveness, then turned away his face.

Contact with real life began at once, because she wanted the whole Chapter at the funeral, which had always been the right of canons, but Father Medde, who was the accountant of the confraternity, said that it had been decided that no funeral should be free of charge any longer, and asked her to put down a deposit for the expenses, which were not small. Where could she find the money, when what little was left had been thrown away by Tommasina because it was infected? She sent to Donna Vincenza to ask for some, but Donna Vincenza told her not to be silly and not to waste money on absurd displays. Well, Ciriaco was buried somehow or other, and then, when even as a corpse he was not there to keep the sisters in check, Tommasina's madness flared up. Those microbes that she had kept at bay with a thousand stratagems, not shaking anyone's hand, not turning door handles except with a cloth which she always kept in her pocket, even avoiding washing her face with the tap water that came from heaven knows where, had entered the house victoriously and had brought death. Some of them were as big as oxen running around the room, others were as small as scorpions, and were the most frightening, and came in black, red, and violet; her pupils dilated as she stared at them. Battistina saw them too, but confined herself to holding up her bony hands to ward them off, almost as if resigned to perish. But Tommasina, with her sanguine temperament, did not intend to go down without a fight. She began by smearing her hands with soap, rubbing it into the dining table, especially where Ciriaco had always sat, and then went on to alcohol, to terrible disinfectants that polluted the air and cracked the skin on the fingers; and finally she resorted to fire. She lit pages of newspaper and rubbed the floor with them, she scorched the soles of their shoes, and would have set fire to the house if—as happens with such diseased minds—she had not had some sense of where to stop. In a short while, through wanting to become too clean, she became filthy, because she never dried her skin, and soaked her clothes ten times in the same water. Giuseppina, busy bee, wept over the ruin of the family, over their shame in the eyes of all Nuoro. "*Ghettadommos, ghettadommos*" (home wrecker), she would say to her between one sob and another, but it was like talking to the wall. What she could not understand was how so much grief could be heaped up on one tiny corner of the world, and so much suffering overwhelm creatures as insignificant as they were.

When Ciriaco was taken away, and the sisters fled from the plague-stricken room, Gonaria crouched down in a corner with her eyes fixed on the bed, enormous in its emptiness. She thought she saw his form impressed on a shroud. She made up her mind that this was a temple, and that no one would ever again enter the room where the sacrifice had been consummated. Her task was now to adore the God who lived hidden in the room, to prevent anyone from defiling it and making it what in fact it was, a place for the use of the living.

She tidied the bed, destroyed the medicines which were still on the bedside table, dusted off the hat with the red cord, put it in the cupboard, and laid the breviary on the pillow. Then she tiptoed out, and turned the double lock of the door. As soon as she got outside she felt herself falling into a great pit: she was without God, God had been left inside, in the empty bed, in the hat with the red cord hanging on a hook, in that death without resurrection. She had loved the Creator in the person of one of His creatures, and now His creature proved to be a phantom, or worse, a cruelly real thing. Suddenly she felt the unimaginable smallness of her body, the uselessness of her hands joined in prayer. She thought of her big cousin Vincenza's smile, when she was talking to her about God. Like herself, though in another way, Vincenza had sacrificed her life, and only to be rewarded with a body that was scarcely less than deformed. She thought for a moment of reopening Ciriaco's room, but had an instinctive fear that God had gone away even from there. She went into the room they called the dining room, and thought she must be seeing things. Tommasina was circling around the table with a burning paper brand, Battistina was raising her arms, useless as stumps, to heaven; Giuseppina was in tears.

Had a day passed, or a month, or a year, when she came to herself on the bed where they had placed her? Eternity had passed. She listened carefully, but she heard no cough from the room across the passage. Automatically she rummaged in the pocket of her wide skirt, and felt the bulk of a big key. At that she jumped up from the bed, went into the dining room, and found Tommasina asleep in a chair, curled up so as not to touch the floor with her feet. The chair beside the brazier, where Ciriaco had sat waiting for death, was still in its place, and not only was it empty but half burned. At that precise moment she realized that God did not exist. God did not reach that little town where the seed of her being had been sown, He did not reach her tiny person, and the Nuorese, who all lived without God, were right. Except that she had had Him in the house, first as a priest and then as a canon, and in her house He had died. There remained that locked room that would never again be opened, the very room where God had died, or where perhaps she could persuade herself He was still living. But meanwhile, what was to be done? She could not die, because her ninety-three lire were now all her unfortunate sisters had to depend on. She had to go back to school. But what would she teach, since what had she ever spoken about to those girls except God, even when explaining arithmetic or history? It did not occur to her that God was her suffering, and also the suffering and madness of Tommasina and Battistina, or even the very sickness and death of Ciriaco. Yet she had read it in the book, she had said it so often to her pupils, to bring them hope, to the point of being reproached and laughed at by the new headmaster.

The first time she left home to go to the monastery she took the hem of her outermost skirt (in those days there were lots of skirts, with a mass of pleats, as there are still petticoats today) and pulled it over her head, so that nothing could be seen but her waxen face and her glistening eyes. At school the girls had prepared her a huge bunch of wildflowers, which she hugged to her breast as she fought down tears. Then she spoke, and she seemed the same person as ever, the teacher who had known and loved the mothers and grandmothers of the girls now sitting on the benches. The only difference was that she didn't want anyone to see her home after school, nor did she call on Donna Vincenza, whom she never saw again.

If you don't die, you live. And this truth, which seems obvious, is on the contrary pregnant with consequences, because life transforms everything, and nothing resists its implacable will. The years that followed (I have to hasten to the end, for brief is the time remaining to me) saw the death of the only one who ought not to have died, Giuseppina, the busy bee of the house. She went off just like that, of a banal attack of influenza, and her end was peaceful, because she said she didn't know why she had come into the world. This event, which should have caused even worse disaster, turned out to be the salvation of the household, because Tommasina began to get better. She started to say that it was all nonsense, that they were all in the best of health, and that she was the healthiest of the lot. And in fact she began to put on weight, regained her ruddy complexion, and stopped disinfecting and burning things; except that whenever someone came she would rush to shake their hand before anyone else did. In compensation, she went back to the old *folie de grandeur*: "We're rich, we're rich."

The fated victim was, naturally, Gonaria. Since Ciriaco's death, Gonaria had never been to church, and had a horror of seeing a priest's cassock or hearing a priest's voice. Tommasina put down her return to health to a very special act of Grace conceded to her, and she therefore felt it her duty to safeguard the rights of God, or at least those of the Blessed Virgin. "Traitor to the Church, traitor to the Church," she would bawl at the poor creature who had not so much abandoned God as she had been abandoned by Him (if indeed it doesn't come to the same thing). "Traitor!" And that poor creature, who by this time lived on nothing but air, took refuge in front of the door of the room where Ciriaco had died—the key to which she jealously guarded. Perhaps God still existed there within.

But Gonaria's crimes were not committed only against religion, which had been the salvation of Tommasina. For some time the latter had started complaining again about the ridiculous penny-pinching which Gonaria had forced her into with her ninety-three lire a month. They were rich, because they owned the house they lived in, and the house was too big for them. It would be no trouble to rent out a room—the room that Gonaria had insisted on keeping locked ever since Ciriaco died. All that was needed was to open it up and disinfect it from top to bottom, because it was still full of microbes. There was no need even to furnish it, because everything was already there. They had done it up completely when he was made a canon. What were they waiting for? That would be at least forty lire of income to add to the paltry ninety-three.

Gonaria saw the danger at once, and withdrew into her shell and prepared to defend herself. No one would ever get into that sanctuary as long as she lived. She said she would give her ninety-three lire to her sister, and she herself would eat only a sliver of bread, and not every day at that. For some time, in any case, she had suffered from a constriction in the throat that prevented her from swallowing food.

But Tommasina would not let go of her prey. It was not a question of eating. Those forty lire represented an income and therefore a sign of that wealth with which she had nourished her imagination. As her sanguine constitution made her an extrovert, she began to tell the neighbors who had started to call again that Gonaria was mad, and that she was leaving her in poverty after turning her back on the Church. Only a madwoman could lock up a room—which after all was hers as well—for ten or fifteen years. And those women thought she was right, and since they also gossiped and spread Tommasina's complaints the length and breadth of Nuoro, all Nuoro began to take her side. Even the bishop put his oar in, though he was not Monsignor Canepa and had therefore never known Canon Sanna. To persuade Gonaria he sent his secretary, who found himself face to face with such a minuscule creature that he was at a loss to understand how she could have caused such a to-do. But he was quick to realize that that birdlike frame contained an immovable will, though it was uncertain whether this had its roots in hope or in despair. He returned to his superior saying that in any case they were dealing with a madwoman, so the bishop thought no more about it.

Gonaria was mad, but not so mad as to be unaware that the writing was on the wall. Beneath her white kerchief her brain was at work. It would have taken an angel with a flaming sword to guard that door. But not even he would have been capable of it, faced with human needs. And then...If the God she had lost had really remained within, unchanged by the passage of time, and if when the door was opened He re-entered her soul...Several times she caught herself thinking such things. She was getting old, even though time had left no mark upon her person, and perhaps she felt weary of living without the One who had sustained the purity of her youth. In any case, it was the beginning of surrender.

Seated on the bed, she listened to the night sounds of Nuoro. Ever since she had stopped praying she would spend the nights like this, without sleeping, without even getting undressed, as if waiting for a sudden summons. This night she was living through might be the last one of her life, because the next day she had to open that door. After exhortation they had turned to threats, and it was obvious that she could hold out no longer. She still expected the night to give some mysterious sign. Who knows, the song of a bird that in her superstition she could interpret, the wail of an infant that would take her out of time, or the rumble of a cart to give her courage to pursue her destiny. The reveries of one forsaken, who will not yield to necessity, who forgets that night is the sequel to day, and that if the day has been cruel the night also cannot fail to nurture cruelty in its shadows.

The first sign (though she could not understand it) came from the street in the early hours of the night. It was as if a fleeing army was pounding past on the cobblestones: not a voice, not a cry broke the silence, which the rattle of footsteps made even more sinister. What could have happened, at an hour when the Nuorese are shut up in the caffè or the drinking dens, finishing a binge or starting out on one? She went to the window, trembling, and someone excitedly told her that Maestro Manca was dead.

In these last months his terror of death had become even more acute. He kept his finger constantly pressed against the swollen vein in his temple, and could not stay on his feet without a glass of wine in him. "*Portantina che porti quel morto…*" The lugubrious song that the youths would chant whenever he appeared, drove him out of his mind. To escape from this teasing he had taken refuge that evening in a dive in San Pietro, and there, while reaching out a trembling hand toward his glass, he had slipped out of his chair and under the table. If only he could have imagined that dying was such a simple thing! The news spread through Nuoro like lightning: it entered the Caffè Tettamanzi and interrupted the games of "tresette," it entered the low pothouses and froze the blood and wine in the veins of the drinkers, it entered the houses of the rich and the poor, of all those who had made judgments on Maestro Manca during his lifetime. At once the great cavalcade began through the deserted streets. They dashed to San Pietro and did not find him; they dashed to the cemetery and no one was there; they dashed to the hospital, and there they found him lying on a iron bedstead in a room as bare as a warehouse, unmindful of himself and free at last of his vicious habit. A hundred, a thousand eyes gazed at him with fear, as if Pedduzza had skipped out on them, and with the mystery of his death had squarely faced each one of them with the mystery of his own life. *"Portantina che porti quel morto…"*

Gonaria went back to the bed and lost herself in the far-off years when she had so happily begun work at the school. Maestro Manca was young in those days, like her. He had a little pointed beard, with a little curl at the tip of it, and mocking blue-green eyes. He was short and already tubby, and it was then that they called him "Pebble," the nickname that stuck forever; but he was a merry soul and amused himself by teasing her about her nunnish calling:

Butta alle ortiche il soggolo
*e parlami d'amor…**

He wrote his verses in Italian, for he had not yet acquired the drinking habit, and she must have felt flattered by them, since she still remembered the ridiculous doggerel of youthful days

---

* "Throw your wimple into the nettles / and speak to me of love…"

that maybe had never existed. Later on, what had happened had happened, and now Maestro Manca lay motionless on a bed in the hospital, as she lay on hers. What message came to her from that sinner? Both in their different ways had destroyed their lives, and there was precious little to choose between them. The destination was nothingness, the void, the longing for death...There was only that key which she fingered in her pocket, and to which she clung as to an anchor. Perhaps it held the secret, for her, for Maestro Manca, for everyone...

In her wearied mind her thoughts ran wild. The night seemed to have reabsorbed that sudden burst of activity into its silence, when from the top of the street she heard the howling of a dog. But it was not a dog, because as it came closer the cry split up into incoherent words, becoming the lament of a human creature. The lament poured down the street, but awakened no echoes around it: no one opened a window and no footstep sounded on the cobblestones. Everyone knew what it was. Do you remember Giggia, who when she was young and beautiful was the girlfriend of the woodcutters who came from the Continent and had her naked serving them at table? I also told how when she was old and alone she worked as a prostitute in San Pietro, without being aware of it. And this is the truth. When the woods had been destroyed and those gentlemen had gone away, Giggia had no choice but to continue in public with the way of life she had begun in private. But if reverential awe of the bosses had rubbed off on her, making her respected and maybe even envied, once she was left to herself she became the laughing-stock of all Nuoro. It has to be said that it is hard to be a prostitute in Nuoro without going mad. With the passing of the years, in fact, Giggia seemed to lose all awareness of herself. The mature bachelors of the Caffè Tettamanzi, who perhaps in early days had gone to find relief with her, as if stepping into the shoes of the Continentals, seeing her so lost and unthinking when she meekly yielded her body, had made her up a nickname that became popular: "Giggia the guileless whore of fifteen," They were of course unable to imagine the profound truth embodied in this phrase. They laughed, and the whole of Nuoro laughed with them. The young lads and even the small boys would run after her shouting these words, but she noticed nothing. In time she grew old, and was covered with sores, and became a specter frightful to behold. But she was still a woman, and as she left the door unlocked the night-prowling drunkards would reel in and possess her in her sleep. Anyone who remembered left two lire in a dish on the bedside table.

Now Giggia, the guileless whore, lived in a hole in the wall without windows or anything else, but to her it was immensely valuable because it gave her shelter from the wind and the rain and enabled her to feel alive, to feel that she was herself, even in her infinite poverty. Except that this hole in the wall, like every-thing else in this world, had an owner, and he was an illustrious lawyer who, in spite of being a big property owner, professed to be a socialist. But socialist or not, the word "owner" meant that the house or the hole in the wall was his, and anyone in it had to pay rent. Giggia did not know what rent was, or even remember how she had come to occupy this cavern. So one day, when she received a sheet of paper covered with all sorts of stamps and seals, she simply put it on the bedside table, partly for the very good reason that she couldn't read. Then came another, and then a third, which suffered the same fate. Nor indeed could she have imagined for a moment that the avvocato needed his cavern. And so it came about that eventually a person turned up brandishing yet another sheet of paper, with two porters who without so much as a why or wherefore carried the bed and the bedside table and the other few sticks of furniture out into the street, fastened the door with a padlock, and went away. Giggia can't have realized what had happened, because she sat down on the bed as if in expectation. Out in the open or in her cave made very little difference to her. But when night began to fall, and she saw the door tight shut, she felt the enormous emptiness of the world all around her, and she was afraid. In desperation she grabbed the padlock and tried to wrench it away, but not even the doors of the nearby prison were so unyielding. So she gave up hope, and wept, her face buried in her loathsome pillow. Then suddenly she stood up like a robot, and clad in her few rags started on her wanderings through the deserted streets of Nuoro. Aimlessly she walked howling down the alleys of San Pietro, turned into the Corso, where by this time there was not a soul, and passed in front of the Caffè Tettamanzi, where the clients had already retired inside because of the chill. Only Giovanni Maria Musiu went to the door, but when he saw Giggia he blushed, because he had been a client of hers, and he pulled in his head at once. "What have they done to me tonight," she wailed. "They've ruined me. They've taken away my home. Carabinieri, help me! I'm a dead woman..." Her cry broke against the shuttered windows, and the Nuorese turned over in their beds. "Help me, help me! Tonight they've killed me..."

Her wail lay upon Nuoro like a cloak of lead. Instead of wandering around the streets, Giggia would have done well to go to the cemetery and dig her grave with her own hands. She was bound there anyway. In the meantime it was her howling, echoing down the narrow street, that Gonaria heard as she sat on her bed. It was the second message brought to her by the night. If she went downstairs, she could open the room that had been shut for twenty years, and put that luckless creature into it...But one cannot even consider such things. Perhaps that drunkard Canon Mocci would have done it. Her hands clasping the white kerchief binding her head, Gonaria nonetheless had enough sense to understand what Giggia, the guileless whore, was telling her with her cry. It was not a question of human nastiness; it was not a question of that socialist lawyer, who was probably already peacefully asleep. Whether him or somebody else, it would have come to the same thing. What that poor woman was giving voice to was the sense of the ineluctable. What has to happen happens inevitably, and God can do nothing to help us. In the morning she would open the room, and destiny would be fulfilled.

Crouched in front of the door (she had insisted that Tommasina should go into the dining room), she gripped the key in one small hand and rocked her body, almost transparent from perpetual fasting, with the rhythm of women at wakes. How many hours had passed, how many were passing, in her solitude? Even if she was not mad, the stakes were high. Twenty years earlier she had stopped time in that room at the hour when Ciriaco had died. In her mind's eye she saw things one by one, just as she had arranged them: the pillow, the breviary, the hat with the red cord. It was all there...on the other side...But stopping time means stopping God, fixing Him eternally in one of the countless moments into which life is divided. This was her terror and her hope: that the God to whom she had entrusted the whole of herself, and who in an instant had cruelly withdrawn Himself from her, had remained there within, so that when the door opened He would come back into her soul, and all the pain of all these years would prove to be a dream. It was fear even more than hope that had driven her to the absurd decision to keep the door locked, and so it would have remained if they had not used violence against her, if Tommasina, who had God within her, had let her alone. The truth would have been known after her death, which by now could not be all that far away. But now...

The bell of Santa Maria struck the hour. It must have been late afternoon, because the shadows were growing longer. She had refused all food, and not even wanted the cup of coffee that had become her only sustenance. She had to act, because at any moment Tommasina might appear, or some neighbor, and smother her with insults, or even snatch away the key. Slowly she rose, and put her knees to the ground, as if in a sudden spasm of prayer. Then she drew the key from the pocket of her skirt, and inserted it in the lock.

A stuffy smell, that seemed to her the smell of death itself, assailed her nostrils and offended her sharp senses. Stifling, she ran to the window, through which a dust-laden light filtered in, and tried to open it. The frame jammed, as if nailed shut. Then she turned, and looked around, and the first thing she saw was a mouse nest dug through the bedspread, which had housed who knows how many generations over the years. She would have let out a shrill cry, because she had a horror of all creatures that live in the dark, but she was afraid that people might come running.

She approached the bed. Of the breviary nothing was left but a scrap of the spine, and the bed itself was just barely balanced, for as she leaned on it the thing collapsed without so much as a creak. The woodworm, undisturbed, had eaten the thing away from inside, as termites do. Here and there she saw the little holes that were the doorways to their interminable catacombs. From the vaulted ceiling hung great bunches of spiders' webs, which looked untenanted, while the flowers around the Madonna beneath the glass bell had fallen into dust. On the peeling wall almost nothing remained—no more than a faraway shadow—of the portrait of the canon, that once had so proud a look. Dumb with terror, she looked at last toward the cupboard, where she had devoutly hung the hat with the red cord. Through the sagging door nothing was left to see. The mice and the moths (and what other horrors?) had eaten everything. In the inch-deep dust were a few woven threads, to bear witness to a past that might never have existed.

Then she knew for certain that she had made her bet and lost. She left the room slowly, closed the door but left the key in the lock, and went downstairs. She was overwhelmed by the notion of running away. She could stay no longer in the house where God had died. When she reached the street she felt like a dog without a master. Next door to her house was an old olive press, and the low rumble of the millstone, the muffled voices of the owners and workers, had at one time accompanied and punctuated her nightly ecstasies. Only on midwinter nights, when work was at its heaviest, did one hear the noisy bourgeois who met to eat bread moistened with oil straight from the press. But they did not disturb her, and in fact were a help to her visions, because the press, with the horse going round and round to turn the great millstone, with the men intent on their work by the light of a lantern, used to remind her of the manger at Bethlehem.

Two women who had come to their doorways saw her pass, but they said nothing. Basket in hand, they watched her for a long time, until she vanished on the other side of the Corso, which she crossed with bowed head. The lane on the other side, the one (for clarity's sake) where Marianna Secchi's shop was—a sort of combined dive and caffè—divided in two, one branch leading to the church and the other, through a maze of alleys, to the open country. She started along the latter, groping like a blind woman, and found herself at last on a broad dirt road which zigzagged steeply down into the valley. She recognized it at once, partly because she had not seen many roads in the course of her life. It was the one that led to the sea, to Orosei, to Gonone, to the villa of the Mariani sisters, which had remained in her memory like a dream or a fairy tale. She remembered that beneath it there was a beach of sand so mellow and fine that they called it Palmasera. It seemed to her that she had found, in all the earth, a place to make for. It did not occur to her that it was a vast distance away, something over thirty kilometers, and she started on the descent as if chasing a mirage. The important thing was not to look back. At first there seemed to be signs of life to keep her company: the carts, the oxen, the men who had stopped work, had left traces on their way back from their day in the fields in the valley. Tomorrow, for them, would be another day. Then, suddenly, solitude.

The road descended from the crest of the Mountain, which at that point loomed over the valley with enormous crags, and like a swelling serpent it engulfed her in its spirals and held her paralyzed against a low wall that she had leaned on because her feet were hurting. She had never been alone before, and from the depths of her being came the specters, the monsters, and the demons that had peopled the nights of her childhood. Coeddu came in person, and he was the Devil, so named because of the tail that was his symbol. In her terror a cry burst from her: "Help me, help me! They have killed me! They have chased me away from home tonight!" It was the same cry as Giggia's, and in the same way it was launched into the void, to a sky without stars or God. Then she was ashamed of herself, and started walking again in silence, treading carefully, because her feet were swollen. Utter darkness, and each step could easily take her into a chasm, but she went ahead, and passed the turning for Oliena, which she recognized by its street-lights, and these, in spite of herself, gave her a feeling of comfort. Her brow was running with sweat, and the white kerchief binding her head squeezed it like a vise. Her greatest fear was of losing hope. What time could it be now? Increasingly unsteady on her feet, she reached a place where the road ran flat, or was gently undulating. She was already in the warm lands, which get sun from Baronia, though Baronia is a long way off; and indeed she thought she smelled the odor of myrtle. She thought she recognized the place, though for thirty or forty years she had not passed by that way; and she felt like crying. But almost at the same moment the miracle happened: an enormous radiance spread from Monte Corrasi, and distant, inaccessible, yet close at hand, the moon appeared. The entire plain was drenched in its light, and as if in answer to a mysterious signal, the crickets began to sing, the myrtles to give forth perfume, the oleanders along the dry streambeds to sway with joy. It was a chorus led by God, the God of the woods, the God of the lentisc and of the arbutus, of the nightbirds already giving forth their melancholy song; but a God who lives not in the hearts of men, who dies with those to whom He brings death, who allows Himself to be devoured by mice and woodworm in a room under lock and key for twenty years. This joy at night increased her pain. What time could it be? She would willingly have stretched out on a heap of gravel, if she had been able to stop. But she had to get there. The animals are eternal, because they do not hope. Her feet were bleeding. Maybe she would die before she got there. But death also was an arrival. A faint light tinged the mountain of Galtellì, its dovelike form. It might be the herald of dawn, and this frightened her. She would hide, for they would certainly come looking for her. But it might be just an illusion. The birds fluttered in the hedgerows all around her, and began to twitter. She, who had never slept, then realized that she had never seen the reawakening of nature. If only she could have a sip of water. She dragged herself up a short slope and saw a faint light farther down the road. It could not be a shepherd's hut: shepherds do not keep fires burning at night, because they too are children of the dark. It turned out to be a roadman's house, one of those red buildings that punctuated the wilderness in those days. She knew that there was one of them every nine kilometers, which meant that in the entire night she had not walked more than nine kilometers. In great surprise, she went up to the door and knocked. In answer came a silence charged with fear. She knocked again. A window opened and a woman's face looked out. Gonaria asked for a drop of water, for the love of charity. The house at once filled with noise, and a pregnant woman, followed by a string of children excited at this unexpected event, opened the door.

"Oh, ma'am!" she cried. "You here? But how on earth? What has happened?" It was an old pupil of hers, one of the hundreds whom she had brought up in the love of God.

"Give me a little water. Help me...It's nothing...I have to get to Gonone."

The woman thought she was delirious. Her hands were hot, too. Maybe she had a fever. A solemn-faced man, yellow with malaria, arrived with a lamp in his hand.

"Come," he said, "come upstairs and rest a little. Your shoes are all gone to pieces. We'll see if we can find a pair of the girls' that will fit you. Then you can go on."

She let them lead her. They laid her down on the double bed, which was still warm, in a room full of tools. She could not imagine poverty worse than this, but it was a house full of human lives, which gave her a feeling of peace. Thinking that she was asleep, the pair of them left the room on tiptoe. She could hear them talking in low voices. A little later she heard the sound of a light cart fading into the distance. She at once realized what was happening. She cried out, "I want to go to Palmasera. Let me go!" She tried to get up, but fell back exhausted. It was the end of her flight from life and from death.

The last message came with a ray of light filtering through the ill-fitting shutters, slashing sideways through the shadows, and ending in a broad cone on the head of the bed. It was the ray of a dying sun, as if that night had turned back on its tracks, and it brought with it a restless dust, or perhaps it was wisps of cloud, slowly growing and taking on form and substance, until she saw (or did she see?) the shade of a girl seated on the bed beside her.

"Teacher, dear teacher! Don't you recognize me? I have come to get water from Obisti—I am dying of thirst. Why didn't you send it to me?"

She shook herself free from the nightmare of it, and recognized Peppeddedda. You will certainly not remember her, but she was the girl whom Gonaria used to send to the church in the morning, to take coffee to her brother when he came into the sacristy after Mass. Scarcely more than a child, the daughter of very poor parents, who lived in one of the many hovels to be found even in the center of town, she was intelligent and hardworking, but above all devoted to her teacher, who in return for little kindnesses would teach her some of next year's work, because she was ahead of the others. She was a happy soul, who brought light to all she saw, and even managed to bring a smile to the lips of those mournful women perched on chairs like hens roosting, so as not to let their feet touch the floor. She would come in with a jaunty step and a singsong greeting, and was ready at once to help her teacher get lunch for her godly brother. Gonaria would sometimes send her to Donna Vincenza's when her godson Sebastiano was there, bringing cakes she had made with her own hands—and she sent word that they were very clean hands indeed. There Peppeddedda would meet the lad, who was only a little older than herself, and they would talk, brought together by the mystery they shared. The poor girl even put light into the face of Donna Vincenza, who never failed to drag her limbs over to the huge sideboard, where she kept the change received from the trifling sales that Don Sebastiano allowed her to make, and give her a soldo. And let there be no mistake about it, a Sardinian soldo, which was ten centimes of copper bearing the image of Vittorio Emanuele II, with his long neck.

The appearance of the girl who took the canon his coffee struck her as a good omen. But as she went on crying "Teacher, teacher" in a voice that grew weaker and weaker, a wave of terror swept over Gonaria. Her mind went back to the day when Peppeddedda had left Nuoro for Genoa. It was snowing, but she skipped over the snow like a sparrow, delighted with the unknown world that was beckoning to her. The child had an aunt in Genoa, in service for years with a well-to-do family, and hearing that she was clever they had offered to pay for her education. Gonaria had made all the arrangements. The parting was a heartbreak, and even those two poor madwomen, who had grown accustomed to her voice, if they did not go so far as to take her hand, wept as they gave her their blessing. The house seemed empty, because nothing fills a house more fully than a young girl alive to her own poverty. She embraced her teacher, above whom she already towered, and swore that as soon as she became a teacher herself she would come back and work at her side.

So off she went along the path of dreams. Each week she wrote, ever more wonderful letters, because those schools had far better teachers than Gonaria. And Gonaria would read them in class, holding up the example of this poverty-stricken girl who was building her future with her own hands. Then, all of a sudden, silence. No one knew what had happened. Two months later a letter came from the aunt, saying that Peppeddedda had felt poorly, because she had been working too hard, the schools were tough, and the climate in Genoa was not as good as in Nuoro. The doctor had ordered her to be sent to Santa Tecla, and now she was a bit better. No one knew what this "Santa Tecla" was, but in fact it was the tuberculosis sanatorium, where in those days you went to die. From time to time letters would arrive from the girl, but they were increasingly rare and brief. She would tell them she was not too bad, and that she was still pursuing the dream that had taken her that far. If she hadn't had a touch of fever in the evenings she would have gone back to school, but the doctor said she should wait. In about October, after a summer of silence, came a short note in which she said that she had a terrible thirst, and begging the teacher to send a bottle of the water of Obisti, but that she should go herself, so that it would come directly from the source. Only that water could quench her thirst. Those were her last words. Not even the echo of her singsong voice was left. A meaningless journey through the world. Don Sebastiano would have said that she too had gone "to look for bread made from better things than wheat."

Gonaria roused herself suddenly. Perhaps her head had slumped down in her sleep. But dream and reality make no difference. The little girl who eternally carried with her the mirage of that water was none other than herself, with the thirst that had devoured her all her life. The water of Obisti, of that unassuming village spring, would have been able to bring about the miracle. It was only that no one had offered her the cup, as she had not offered it to Peppeddedda. What has to happen happens inevitably, and God can do nothing to help us. In the morning she would unlock the room, and her destiny would be fulfilled.

19

Summer that year arrived in the month of May. It was announced by gusts of scorching wind, a wind blown forth from
Africa over the whole of the Tyrrhenian Sea, halted neither by hills
nor by mountains. Nothing like it had been seen since the time of
the locusts. It swept over the flowering *tanche*, over the fields where
the wheat was already high, and at its passing everything appeared
to curl up and roast, as when forest fires broke out in August. A
dense rain of sand fell in the desolate town, forcing people to shut
themselves up indoors. The ominous lowing of bewildered cattle
could be heard from the countryside. Only toward evening, when
the sun set, could a few shadowy forms be seen in the pharmacy or
the caffè: Don Sebastiano, Don Serafino with a handkerchief between neck and collar, Bartolino and the others with open necks,
all of them resigned to fate. Bustianu Pirari said it was the fault of
those whores who had gone to Tunis to have their bastards.

The wind lasted four days. The first to give signs of life were
the stray dogs, which had mysteriously disappeared at the first
gusts. Then human beings began peeping out, with the air of
having survived the Flood. The streets filled up and everyone—
or at least all those who had property—set off for the fields to
see the damage which that scourge had caused. Don Sebastiano
mounted his horse and rode down to Isporòsile. The bramble

hedges on either side of the road to Mughina seemed turned to stone, such was the sand piled upon them. The little scattered vegetable gardens, which inveterate peasant idleness had already left neglected, looked like battlefields just abandoned by contending armies, for here and there one could see animals that had died of starvation or the intense heat. Lower down in the valley the olive leaves had all curled up, and Don Sebastiano thought gloomily that the next two years' harvests could be reckoned as lost. He was not given to meditation, nor did he concede too much to Providence, but that sight made him grieve inwardly, and the idea that crossed his mind was as old as the world: the idea of castigation. Personally he had nothing to reproach himself for, but a few months earlier they had killed Recotteddu, who was a good soul, and no one had got to the bottom of it. Not to speak of Francesco Mattu, whom they had reduced to beggary by hamstringing his cows for some unknown reason. It could be that everything is paid for, and that all must pay for the sins of one.

The horse had reached the end of the road, and was making its way toward the ford across the stream that bordered Don Sebastiano's enclosure. As you may remember, he had quite literally built this stretch of country, and not once but twice, three times, as often as there had been floodwaters to devastate it. For this reason he loved the little property as a child of his own, and he trembled at the thought of the destruction he would find there. Between the gate and the farmhouse was a dense olive grove, and he rode through it unable to believe his eyes. The trees were burgeoning forth luxuriantly, the soil was carpeted with grass, and the oxen were peacefully grazing on it. In a word, there was not a sign of the recent blight. He was astounded, and would have been beside himself with joy, except that the anguish of what he had seen along the way was still in his heart. By what privilege had his place been exempted from the slaughter? He thought of an interplay of airstreams that had pushed the harmful winds toward the north, or of the protection of Father Antonio's hillside, which shut the valley in. It was possible or probable that a vacuum had been formed at the bottom, and that this had meant salvation. He tried to remember one of the few scientific articles he had read, and was wrapped up in these thoughts when, almost under the belly of the horse, there appeared a spectral figure, followed like a dog by a youth of about fifteen, also looking wretched and with signs of malaria in his face. While dwelling upon his good fortune he had forgotten the sharecropper Nanneddu Titùle (which means Squalid Johnny, though it was of course a nickname), who had been working the farm for about a year. Seen from above in this way, it was as if the baleful wind had struck him and him only.

"Master," he said, "you are wondering how we have escaped the plague. Come and see."

Don Sebastiano dismounted. He detested this sharecropper, sent to him by a friend from Barbagia because labor was short in Nuoro. He had arrived with his load of penury and children, of whom that fifteen-year-old was the eldest. He didn't even have health to recommend him. Don Sebastiano had helped him, but could not disguise the fact that he didn't like him. He felt that he demeaned the farm, and on top of that he wanted to do things his own way. Poddanzu had been right in putting him on his guard. They went down the short slope under the oak, and stopped in front of the house. On the closed half of the double doors hung a dog crucified with its front legs stretched apart and nailed to the wood, and its head hanging slantwise on its chest.

"That's what saved the farm!"

Don Sebastiano stood as if turned to stone. His mind went back to the ritual sacrifices that, without really believing it, he had read about in the encyclopedia, or those crucified figures with asses' heads which the pagans used to paint to make fun of the Christians.

"He howled for three days, then he died, and the wind that was bending the trees double on the far side of the priest's hillside stopped at once."

Don Sebastiano would have liked to hurl him over the sustaining wall of the vegetable garden, but the peasant's eyes had a visionary look in them, which almost frightened him, though he could have squashed him with one finger.

"Take it down at once and bury it, and don't tell anyone about it. Just remember that!"

"Just as you say, master."

Don Sebastiano was not squeamish, but he was upset by superstition, as a denial of the faith he placed in reason. He really had to get rid of this savage.

But the latter, accompanying him with a disappointed face to his horse, lowered his eyes and said, "There's Ziu Merriolu, who works Pascale Martis's land above here. He doesn't let the water run on after he's used it for his vegetables. For the moment there's enough water, but in summer there's a chance of it running out. What should we do?"

"Work it out between you," said Don Sebastiano irritably.

Later on, he was to remember these words.

*

Nanneddu Titùle had one idea in his head: to overcome his own penury. He had been employed by a landowner in a village where the employers are worse off than their servants: a hundred lire and a pair of shoes a year to look after a herd of goats. And if he himself managed to live practically without eating, on two slivers of bread and a touch of oil, his wife and children had to depend on the charity of the neighbors, unless they wanted to die of hunger. When that friend of Don Sebastiano's suggested that he should go to Nuoro as a sharecropper, he thought that the Lord was at last taking notice of him. They arrived like gypsies, and when Ziu Poddanzu—who was overseer of all Don Sebastiano's properties, although his own place was Locoi—saw them with his own eyes, he advised his employer not to take on that "load of green wood." But Don Sebastiano, who was humane at heart, did take them on, settled them at Isporòsile, and helped them with some money in advance. Land! Land at last! That stretch of country cut through by the stream, the stream with its enormous boulders deposited there by the floods, had not one but two vegetable gardens, both fed by the channel that Don Sebastiano had cut. One blow of the mattock and he felt the place was his. Half the produce would go to the owner of course, as was only fair because he paid the taxes, but all the same, the plants that grew would be his as well: the tomatoes, the peppers, the lettuces from the garden, let alone the olives, the wheat, the almonds (not the vineyard, however, because Don Sebastiano was really particular about his wine, and had never shared the produce of his vineyards). Obsessed by this idea, the man worked like a fiend, deprived himself of everything, forced his wife and the son who was barely more than a child to do the heaviest of labor, and got up at night to listen to the growing of the vegetables which he had planted by day.

The neighboring sharecroppers looked askance at this sullen outsider who had got his hands on the best enclosure in the district, and put the blame on Don Sebastiano. The relationship of the Nuorese peasants with the soil (and I mean the peasants, not the shepherds) is a friendly one. When they hoe it they might be tickling it. And then, they know that the soil has its times of rest and of sleep; therefore when the Dog Star rages they sit under the fig tree, and everyone congregates there from all the farms around. They start work again when the sunlight, pursued by massive shadows, begins to climb the valley; then, when the first stars appear, they gather the fruits that the earth has ripened— and it is as if they asked her permission. That wretched foreigner wielded his hoe as if it were a pickax: at every blow, a wound. What was he aiming at? In early days they had tried to approach him, because in the country one cannot live without others, but a little because of the difference of speech, and a great deal because of his diffidence as a down-and-out, Nanneddu refused all contact.

After a year he was out of the red with Don Sebastiano, in the sense that he had paid off the initial loan, and was in credit to the extent of some thousands of lire. A little longer, and the life of hardship would be over. He would go back to his village and build a small house with his own hands. God would provide for the rest. And God did indeed provide, sending first that African wind which he had been able to overcome with magic, then a drought such as had never been seen before. It seemed as if the wind had polished the sky so highly that the clouds could no longer get a hold on it. There had never been a shortage of water at Isporòsile, because of the channels made by Don Sebastiano, but that year it began to get low. For a little while, working in the dead of night, Nanneddu managed to capture a small trickle that was enough to water four or five beds of vegetables, but toward six in the morning it shrank, it dwindled, it died out altogether. Beneath that metal sky the tomato plants bent their heads sadly over the furrows, the lettuces bolted, the soil turned to stone. Toward the beginning of July the trickle disappeared completely, and it was the end of everything.

He knew the source of that tragedy. Within living memory water had never run out at the Isporòsile farm. This was its great merit, the thing that set it above all other farms. But the devil was not to blame this time, as he had been for the wind. The water for the farm came from the stream that ran through Pascale Martis's holding. He—and this meant Merriolu, his sharecropper—had the right to use it for his vegetable garden, but then he had to let it flow on down, because this was both the law and the custom. But Nanneddu, spying at night, had for some time noticed that Merriolu had made a number of little ditches in which the water collected drop by drop, forming small deposits that served for other uses. Could it be true? Had it been a hallucination? More than once he had yelled at Merriolu to let the water flow freely, and the latter had replied that on his own land he did as he saw fit. He had told Don Sebastiano, and you have heard the answer he got. Meanwhile the garden died, and with it died all his hopes.

He would stay in it motionless for hours and hours. Even the oxen would have died in that fearful drought if his son had not taken them to the town drinking trough, where a few drops still seeped in. But what did the oxen matter? He had been forced to ask Don Sebastiano for money to feed himself and his family, and his capital was very nearly exhausted. He got thinner and thinner, and was unable to sleep. Yet there was water, there on the other side of the hedge. All he had to do was destroy those deposits...All he had to do was destroy...

During the night he got up from his pallet in the porch and called to his son in a low voice. "Get up," he said, "and come with me." He picked up his ax, and they started toward the neighboring farm. They climbed cautiously over the hedge. Not a dog barked. Perhaps even the animals were dead, or paralyzed with thirst. Slowly they approached the cabin. The door was open, and by the glimmer of the stars they saw Merriolu lying on his matting, fast asleep. Nanneddu glanced at his son. He crossed the threshold. As Merriolu made a slight movement, he brought the ax down on his head. "Work it out between you," Don Sebastiano had said.

If at that moment the skies had opened and rain had fallen in torrents, then his act would have had its use, like that of the cruci-fied dog. But the skies remained inscrutable. They had to conceal the body before daybreak. Between the two of them they picked it up, trying not to get blood on themselves, and with it made the return journey. They laid it on the ground in the vegetable garden, and by working all night they buried it, carefully smoothing out the soil above it. At first light they yoked up the oxen, because they had to take the wheat to be threshed at Ziu Lucca's threshing floor just outside Nuoro.

To unravel the crime was child's play for the police. Nanneddu and his son were led in chains through the streets of Nuoro, among the hostile shouts of the crowd. Merriolu was a good man who had never harmed a fly; and the two murderers were outsiders. On top of this, it was discovered that the water deposits had never existed, so that the crime had not even a shadow of justification. Shut up in his room, Don Ricciotti Bellisai listened to the voices that reached him from the street, and filtered them one by one through his consciousness. By this time he was a finished man, because he had a cancer that was eating him away, albeit slowly. After his political disaster he was left with no hope. He spent the long hours sending snippets of news to a Rome paper, which had recently begun to print a special edition for Sardinia and—heaven knows on whose recommendation—had appointed him correspondent in Nuoro. He had to cudgel his brains to find anything to say, in a town where nothing ever happened. He was in this glum state of mind when along came the news about Nanneddu and Merriolu. In a trice he grew twenty years younger. After so many illusions and so many defeats, and just when it had condemned him to an atrocious death, destiny again put Loreneddu within his grasp; or at least his revenge, which by this time was worth more than the house itself. He got up from the bed, smoothed his unkempt beard, and went toward the writing table.

Nuoro, 20 June, 19— A dreadful act of violence took place last night. A certain Nanneddu, known as Titùle, sharecropper of the rich landowner Don Sebastiano Sanna Carboni, murdered a certain Merriolu, sharecropper of the neighboring property, in the district of Isporòsile, with a blow from an ax. A blood-curdling detail is that the murderer enlisted the help of his fifteen-year-old son, with whom he carried away the body and buried it in the vegetable garden of the said Don Sebastiano, where it was found by the police.

The motive is to be sought in the shortage of water caused by the long drought. The murderer got it into his head that the said Merriolu was damming up the normal flow of the stream that crosses both properties. It is not known whether this is true.

So much for the reports. However, it is a persistent rumor in town that this Titùle, who comes from the remote parts of Barbagia, is a *minus habens,* who could not even have conceived of such an atrocious plan on his own. The more so because this interest in the water was not his concern, except at second hand. It is therefore thought that he acted for a third party. According to the commonly held opinion, the instigator is to be identified as the owner of the farm, the above-mentioned Don Sebastiano Sanna, a man who is extremely attached to his possessions. The police are maintaining strict secrecy, as the person concerned is not only wealthy, but very powerful.

He sealed the letter with a smirk, went to the mirror, and regarded his emaciated face. I am preparing my last will and testament for you, Don Sebastiano! Then he went back to bed and waited on events.

The "story" was read in the Caffè Tettamanzi and received with hoots of laughter. However much times had changed, Don Sebastiano was still respected by all, apart from which the memory of Ricciotti's rantings had not faded. In the pharmacy they urged Don Sebastiano to sue Ricciotti, but Ludovico said that it was better to do nothing. It was probable that Ricciotti, feeling that he was close to death, wanted to be remembered for something sensational. So a week went by, and then another short article appeared.

> Nuoro, 27 June, 19— The affair of Merriolu's murder grows ever more sinister. The impression we referred to in our last dispatch, that the sharecropper was merely the hired assassin of a well-known instigator, is acquiring increasing credibility. There are countless obscure elements, but one fact seems to us irrefutable. This is that on the very day of the murder Nanneddu Titùle was sent to thresh the wheat from the farm on a threshing floor at least five kilometers away, belonging to a certain Ziu Lucca. What motive could there be for this? It is contrary to all reason that the threshing should take place outside the farm where the grain has been harvested. But the judiciary, which is responsible for the investigations, is on the right path. In fact, it seems certain that this bizarre command can only have been given in order to create an alibi for the sharecropper, and thereby divert suspicion from his employer. Justice is on the right path. In the meantime, it would be best if the killer and his abettor were both in preventive custody, to protect the truth from being tampered with.

That ass of an editor at the Rome paper, who did not know Don Sebastiano (or he would never have done it), had printed this item under a banner headline in bold type. In spite of the atrocious heat, a chill ran through Nuoro. Confidence began to waver. The fact of the threshing floor seemed really and truly inexplicable. And why shouldn't it be true? Don Sebastiano felt that there was a slight uneasiness in his relations with others. But the most upset of all was the public prosecutor, who was a friend and admirer of Don Sebastiano's but was unable to ignore the accusation. He had not moved before because there was nothing to go on but the slanderous backbiting of a degenerate like Ricciotti. Now this question of the wheat was at least a clue, something that forced him to act, even though with the necessary caution. The poor man, who was a stickler for his duty, asked Don Sebastiano to call on him in his office. It was a terrible blow. Don Sebastiano had never come into conflict with the law, although his whole life had been spent filling up sheets of official paper. He left home early and walked up the slope to the court building, feeling that all eyes were following him. The prosecutor received him in his dusty den, and appeared grave and cold. He wanted to know the story of this wheat. The rest of it didn't interest him. Don Sebastiano looked at him in a bewildered way and babbled a few disconnected phrases: "I don't know, I don't know."

"What d'you mean, you don't know? Are you the boss or not? You must realize the position you're putting me in."

It seemed to him that Don Sebastiano might be going to faint, so he changed his tone and began to suggest the answers.

"Perhaps you have someone in charge of your lands, and he might know. Can you tell me who it is?"

As if rescued from a nightmare Don Sebastiano replied, "My bailiff is Giuseppe Chisu, known as Poddanzu."

"Very well, very well. I'll call him in. Now you may go, and keep yourself at my disposal."

Ziu Poddanzu was at Locoi when he received a summons to appear before the prosecutor. He put on his best costume, and then he too climbed the long slope, which he had occasionally done before, on his way to the church which stood opposite the law courts. He had even tidied his beard. Shown in at once, he found himself in front of the prosecutor, who did not even raise his eyes from the desk.

"So then," said he in a voice which sounded threatening, "do you know why, on the morning of such and such a day, the wheat was taken by this cursed Nanneddu to be threshed a long way from Isporòsile?"

"I don't understand," replied Ziu Poddanzu. "We have done this every year, because there's no threshing floor at Isporòsile."

The public prosecutor leaped to his feet. "What are you saying? Every year? There's no threshing floor?"

"Yes. It's always been that way."

The prosecutor was a man transfigured. "Give me your hand, my good man. But why didn't that silly fellow say so? Such a simple thing! Give me your hand."

And the callused hand of Ziu Poddanzu shook the slender hand accustomed to signing arrest warrants.

"You may go. Here is half a cigar for your trouble. And give my regards to your employer."

And so for the second rime, and the last, Ziu Poddanzu saved Don Sebastiano's skin.

20

The escape in which her cousin Gonaria had failed was achieved by Donna Vincenza, ever more securely nailed by arthritis to her big chair under the pergola. But Gonaria was urged by love, Donna Vincenza by hatred. Her indifference toward her husband, which we have spoken of, had developed into an absence. By this time she no longer saw him, even as the shadow her dim sight allowed her, and she did not hear him either. She came back to life only in the rare periods when her youngest son, whom she loved even though he had rejected his viaticum, came home for the holidays, and clung to her, and lamented her plight. Then he would go off again and send no news of himself. After one of his joyous appearances, overcome by grief and tedium, she had found a postcard and written as well as she could: "Out of sight, out of mind." But she got no answer. The dispersal of her sons was practically concluded with this youngest one, even though he was still studying. He would certainly not come back to her, because he too would "look for bread made from better things than wheat." Anyway, she did nothing to hold him back. If her troubles failed to stop him, what could her entreaties do? She realized that he was following his destiny, like a bird leaving the nest, and she too had followed her destiny, although this did not exonerate Don Sebastiano, who had been the blind instrument. She knew that in a little while it would all be over, because a woman in her condition can only live so long, and all would be as if she had never been born... That would be wonderful; but an obscure feeling warned her that it would not be all that easy. After her flesh her sorrows would remain, her life of sorrow, which no God can cause not to have happened. This is why for centuries the Church has continued to say *Requiescant in pace,* words that have no meaning if the dead are really dead. A short while before, she had had an experience she could not forget. She was fast asleep in her bed high up on the top floor when she was awakened in the dark by a rhythmic sobbing that seemed to come from the top of the wardrobe where she kept her few possessions. It was like a word that could not force its way out of a strangled throat. For a long time she lay there listening, bathed in sweat. The thought came into her mind of an elder cousin of hers and Gonaria's, a man who had been a formidable orator and had been struck by paralysis of the tongue. Perhaps he had come to tell her something, and was unable to. Groping in the dark, she made her way to the next room, where Sebastiano was sleeping, and woke him up. "Listen... listen..." The boy came to in a flash, and they clung together to pluck up courage. Then he got up and put on the light in his mother's room. Two snow-white doves had come in through the window in the evening, and had perched there, and were cooing softly. As soon as he opened the window they took flight toward the moon. Sebastiano fell back to sleep at once, but in his mother's room there remained a touch of magic, the anguish of a spiritual presence, and that maimed voice that stayed with her as an omen for the rest of her life.

But maybe these were ravings, like those of her cousin Gonaria. What can a woman think when she has been abandoned in a chair, with only her past before her? For the dispersal did not only involve the sons who had gone out into the world. Those who had willy-nilly stayed behind were no longer present either. Giovanni was glumly going after money, while Pasquale was busy trading in almonds and other products of the island. Both had departed far from her own being, and had forcibly introduced into their mother's life women and children whom she rejected as foreign bodies. One cannot love if one has not been loved. And then...there was Ludovico.

If I remember rightly, I was speaking of him when Gonaria came to me, begging me to help her to set herself free from her life; and I traced her steps until the day she tried to escape. So everything has got behind schedule, events have piled up; and in addition I have been in such pain that for a number of months I have been unable to approach these pages. I was saying that Ludovico had opened a law office. This had not been a sudden decision; in fact, not a decision at all. In the program he had drawn up for his life there was no room for decision, because like all actions it always involves an element of irrationality, and this was incompatible with the type of character he had built up, and that had grown as he grew. If he had decided to open an office, what difference would there have been between him and those self-assured young men from the villages, who came up to Nuoro to conquer the law courts and the women? But this was not all. He had inherited from who knows what ancestors, or perhaps simply from the observation of his own uncertain health, a magical sense of things, on account of which every act was a rite, every word an echo of another word, and every fact a mystery. And one cannot say that he was wrong. For instance, the birth of thought in the depths of the spirit, the shaping and ordering of it into periods, the translation into signs, and above all the transference of it from one spirit to another, the communication that is, if only for an instant, the meeting of two beings, with the unforeseeable consequences that such a meeting always causes, is in fact a miracle; except that the moment one stops to think about it one can't even write a letter. And indeed, the letters which Ludovico wrote seemed to come from such infinite distances, like messages set afloat in bottles; and this was reflected in his style, which wound and unwound in archaic evolutions, as if afraid of facing up to the reasons for writing, however banal these might be, in the studied consideration of what was appropriate. It even affected his handwriting, which was fine and dense, with the regularity of ideograms, stripped of the least concession to the imagination, and therefore without second thoughts or cancellations.

Ludovico had opened his law office purely and simply because it enabled him not to leave the house in Via Asproni, not to put his own personality to the test of the world. He was already twenty-seven, and the books he had accumulated had remained uncut, waiting for him to start the first of them. This was his vocation: to be forever waiting to begin, standing apart from real life, as if beginning things had nothing to do with this and did not depend on us. At bottom it was the attitude of the ancients who studied the phases of the moon or consulted soothsayers. And in fact, when anyone demanded action from him he would gaze into the distance and solemnly declare, "Everything in its own time." This had become the motto of his life. It is hard to say how much of it was spontaneous and how much was studied. It is certain that he knew himself extremely well, and knew that he was not equal to action, and therefore circled around it, carefully avoiding any confrontation. But long practice, carried out (as I said before) since childhood, led him to deceive himself rather than others, or else to deceive others in order to deceive himself. In any case the danger was other people, who might force him to show his cards, or even lay him out stark naked on the table. Therefore, he had instinctively woven a cocoon around himself, had succeeded in surrounding himself with an aura of respect, veiling himself in mystery. And it must be admitted that he was seconded in this by the environment, because the enraptured town of Nuoro had a need for idols (like all other towns in Sardinia, if it comes to that), and by backing Don Sebastiano's son the Nuorese felt they were acquiring a bit of nobility.

When I was a boy there was a certain Don Antioco Mores, who lived in Orotelli. He was an old "doctor of law," and like the rest of them lived off the rents of his *tanche*. Always wrapped up in his own thoughts, if he happened to have any, as a young man he had taken out subscriptions to two magazines, one German and the other English. Every month for twenty years the postman faithfully delivered them, and he stacked them up unopened in his room. But the citizens of Orotelli, to whom the postman showed these strange stamps that came from distant worlds, or more simply, from the world, had conceived a high opinion of the "doctor," and had credited him with a knowledge of languages, which is the height of knowledge. Don Antioco accepted his fame in silence, so his fellow townspeople made much of him, as if they themselves knew the language through him. So much so that on one occasion, when one of those Germans with a passion for digging up stones turned up at Orotelli, and went to visit Don Antioco, and talked to him, leaving him quite bewildered, they were furious with the stranger and nearly beat him up, because he didn't make himself understood.

This sort of idolatry was not, as it might appear to be, in conflict with the destructive spirit that set the Nuorese against one another. In the bottom of their hearts they did have some hope in life; it was just that individually and collectively they felt incapable of making it come true. This same hope led them to create phantoms for themselves to cling to, as in the case of Don Antioco and Ludovico; but the real hopeless cases were the very idols whom fantasy or hallucination had brought into being, so that they sought salvation in an artificial solitude. In short, it was a reciprocal metaphysical deception. Except that Ludovico's law office was a reality he had to measure up to, all the more so because in the shadow of Don Sebastiano clients began to flood in; and clients mean action, whether it is a question of a neighbor who crosses a field when he ought not to, or a window made without respecting the legal distances, or a property hemmed in by others: the petty lawsuits of a rural economy in the Sardinia of those days. But the man who had discovered that "everything has its own time," and had made it his rule of life, lost no time in discovering that "there is no such thing as a petty suit." The fear of living provided his eyes, as it were, with two magnifying lenses that enabled him to move with circumspection. Those modest women in costume, who were dotted about on the staircase, would wait to be received for hours and hours, if not days; and then, if they succeeded in getting into the office, they were confronted with a thin face that emerged from a row of books, and a pair of eyes that looked at them as if with their complaints they were the bearers of mysterious messages that it was up to him to decipher. In a husky voice he would expound on the theme of justice, leaving the poor things speechless, since for them justice or injustice was the rainwater that ran off the neighbor's roof into their courtyard. "Servitude of stillicide," Ludovico would thereupon exclaim in Italian, and these difficult foreign words really impressed the women, who went away convinced that they had found their messiah; and they spread his renown in the outside world. But it may be that this episode is not true, and that it was invented as a caricature by Avvocato Meleddu (one of those from the villages), whose office was a table at the Caffè Tettamanzi, where he raked in the vagrant clients by sniffing the odor of the cheeses they carried in their haversacks.

Don Sebastiano, with the optimism that came naturally to him, was overjoyed to see his stairs crowded with people sitting waiting, and things seemed to have gone back to the old days, before Giovanni had dethroned him. But Donna Vincenza suffered agonies, partly because the women who came into the kitchen to unload their country offerings of eggs, or honey, or lambs and kids in season, would beg her to persuade her son to receive them. She had tried once, and been told: "Everything in its own time." It would have been such a simple thing to deal with the clients and make some money. But it was this very simplicity that had no place in the life-scheme of a man who, as a boy, had waited forever to read his first book. Even now it could be said that he was waiting for his first client. And in the meantime he "organized" the office, creating a thoroughgoing bureaucracy and filling it with registers and forms; which was also a way of avoiding action. In the very room where in the course of fifty years Don Sebastiano had accumulated a fortune, with all those morocco-bound notary deeds still lined up behind the glass panes of the bookcases, his son had stopped time, and was waiting for the pendulum that had measured out so many hours over the bent head of Don Sebastiano to start swinging again. His vocation was orderliness, which is the basis of creation. Accordingly, when a letter came he would turn it over in his hands for a long time, gazing at it meditatively; then he would put it away in a file without opening it, because everything had its own time. And so, it seems, he behaved with the people who came to him to talk of their troubles: he succeeded by magic in always putting them off until tomorrow, a tomorrow that never came.

It has to be said that he was aided and abetted in this by the Nuorese themselves, who in him had at last found their perfect lawyer. The most important thing in their lives, and in those of the villagers who gravitated toward Nuoro as the seat of the law courts, was to have a lawsuit going. It was not a question of winning or losing it, and indeed it was vital to do neither, for otherwise the suit would be over and done with. A lawsuit was part of the personality, if not the only visible sign of it, to such an extent that there was often no real animosity between the litigants, because they both needed each other. The Nuorese had immediately felt a profound fellow-feeling for this young lawyer, and they came in hordes, only too eager to sit on the stairs and wait for the sanctuary to open. When it did open, and one of the faithful succeeded in penetrating that paper world, he went back home proud of himself and full of faith in the future. And as

I think I have suggested, this enchantment also worked within the family. Don Sebastiano had to all intents and purposes handed over the reins to this son possessed of such wisdom, his brothers tacitly recognized him as the center of the family, and scattered here and there as they were, they thought of him as the guardian of the deserted house. Only Donna Vincenza, among the shadows crowding before her faded sight, saw this son as far from her as the ones whom the dispersal had dotted around on the Continent, or even farther. Lacerated by loneliness, she shouted out to him ten times a day from her chair under the pergola, and either he would not answer at all or he would be huffy about it.

Ludovico was incapable of responding. He was like a man walking a tightrope over an abyss, and could not distract his attention for one moment without falling. That business of his waiting to read his first book was not a joke, any more than was Don Antioco Mores's subscription to magazines in languages he did not understand. It was a vocation for knowledge without a corresponding ability to learn, and it therefore led to these ridiculous cover-ups. It is, in any case, a relatively common thing in life in the provinces, and I think it is the reason why magnificent libraries may even today be found in towns at the back of beyond. In the end, what is at work is always the dream. The Nuorese were ignorant, but they did not dream. Even when they were getting drunk or sitting at the tables in the Caffè Tettamanzi to while the hours away, they were functioning, not dreaming. Ludovico's trouble was that life would not allow him to dream; it urged him to take part in reality; it exposed him to an exhausting risk, exactly like that of the tightrope walker. He could get away with making no response to Donna Vincenza when she called him, but how could he avoid responding to the demands of others, which are constant, continuous, and inexorable?

The first such demand arrived one April evening from the windows of Don Gabriele Mannu, the house just across the street from that of Don Sebastiano's. The Mannu family, against which, if you remember, Don Ricciotti Bellisai vented his spleen, was certainly the oldest in Nuoro, and indeed in both the people and their belongings there was a touch of archaism, which kept at a distance those who were aware of being fated to a brief, anonymous journey on earth, which is to say all the Nuorese. There were various branches, nearly all of them stemming from women, and therefore with different names; but they were all closely connected. The result was that as the relatives were so numerous at least one died every year, so that the Mannus were always dressed in black mourning. Perhaps this explains the reputation for stinginess that had accompanied them down the centuries. I do not know if they were stingy toward others, but they certainly were toward themselves—unless this is the only true way of being stingy. From the tables of the Caffè Tettamanzi one looked across at the row of balconies on the first floor of their "palace" (the only one in Nuoro remotely worthy of this name, even though the stucco was falling to pieces), with the windows always closed and the shutters nailed fast. These were the windows of the great salon, and they had not been opened for years, because no one except a farm manager ever entered the Mannu front door, and their mourning would not have permitted them to receive guests, even if they had wanted to. Within those walls the Nuorese seated at the caffè saw Don Gabriele's wife and daughters moving around like ghosts, and being either bachelors or unhappy husbands, as they all were,

they talked sneeringly of them, imagining them intent on counting money, and yawning with hunger.

But Don Gabriele's daughters were by no means ghosts. Life,
which knows no barriers, filtered through those walls of stone
and mud, and pierced the patina of pride that covered women
of marriageable age like a breastplate; and if this left the windows giving onto the Corso closed, it opened another which
overlooked Via Asproni, and from which Ludovico could be seen
bent over his registers or stamped official paper. At that window
it was, though standing back a little, as befitted her position, that
the eldest daughter Celestina stood looking out, and so it came
to pass that one day Ludovico raised his head and their eyes met.
This also was a very simple thing, but Ludovico felt himself already lost. The summons was peremptory, for one could not
speak to Donna Celestina Mannu as one spoke to the country
women from Oliena who came to complain about the water drip-
ping from their neighbor's roof. For the first time he felt that life
was getting out of hand, that he was unable to program it, because someone was pushing him violently into the abyss. Closed
in on himself, in the contemplation of his ailments, he had never
thought about love, nor had love ever thought of him. Now everything was crumbling.

He spent sleepless nights questioning his mind and his senses,
but he got no answer. He felt that his true calling was that of a
bachelor, like so many Nuorese who lived and died like mush-
rooms. Getting married meant entering the life of another
person, and having this other person as part of one's own life.
An insane undertaking, or indeed simply an undertaking, which
required a decision, and he could not decide without having the

necessary data in his hands. If it had been a question of the marriage between Zio Priamo and Zia Franceschina, who joined their two lives purely so as not to die alone, it would have been an easy matter. It was a question of living, and this was not easy: it was impossible. Punctually at seven she would appear in the window embrasure, with her slender, elegant figure and the pallor of one who has grown up in shadow. Instinctively he would look up and meet her gaze, which excited and depressed him at the same time.

He decided to make a profound study of the physiology of marriage, and he got hold of the books then in circulation, looking either for some advice or an escape route in science. But in his heart of hearts he felt that the ineluctable was bound to happen. One could not say no to Don Gabriele's daughter; and then, he was secretly flattered at being singled out. When he thought the time was ripe he wrote a letter, which he sent the maid to deliver, based on the style used in concluding a law case, except that it concluded nothing. It was an extremely long message in which he spoke of himself, of his attitudes with regard to life and, since he knew that the women of the Mannu family were intensely religious, of God as well. But he talked about himself even when talking of God. It was one of the theses he had worked on at school, which had gained him the reputation of being learned and a thinker. Celestina interpreted the letter according to her own wishes, and the following day she made a beckoning sign from the window. He stepped nearer, and she asked if he would allow her to talk to her father about the matter. Drawn on by the train of events, he said yes, and so it was that a few days later in the pharmacy Don Gabriele spoke to Don Sebastiano, asking him to make the request official. The days and the times of day on which Ludovico could visit Celestina (Monday, Wednesday, and Saturday from five until seven in the evening) were agreed on. This was the ancient custom. And indeed it was a reasonable custom, since it is not right for an engaged couple to disturb the whole household.

Don Sebastiano was all too glad to make a family connection with the Mannus, who were no more aristocratic than he was, since all the noble families of Nuoro had the same beginnings, but they had enhanced their nobility with long centuries of inertia, being careful not to work, but to keep their lands, collect their rents, and invest them in other properties. This was how they had amassed their sullen wealth.

But Donna Vincenza was not happy. Not, of course, that she could have asked for better. All the same, for fifty years she had lived opposite those people, and not once had they sent across the maid with a shovel to ask for a few embers. Nothing. And then there was Ludovico. His poor mother had no illusions. Her mind was unable to comprehend this son, who had remained close to her but only in appearance, and made no response to her appeals. To her he seemed alien to everything, intent only on hiding from others and from himself. Some obscure feeling warned her that this marriage would never take place, and for this reason, using her health as an excuse, she refused a meeting with the future daughter-in-law. Furthermore, the visit could not take place except in the presence of Sanna, and she would be unable to put up with the idiocies to which her delighted husband would no doubt abandon himself.

Meanwhile Ludovico busied himself with his new role as a fiancé. On the eve of each day fixed for meeting he would prepare a subject for discussion. It might be the family, politics, or philosophy, and since he was very careful not to exceed his limitations the discussion came down to a monologue in which he rehearsed general ideas, accompanying them with a smile and a slight intake of breath, as if to surround them with mystery.

The presence of Donna Sabina, the future mother-in-law, helped to maintain the iron conventionality of these encounters. For Ludovico this was providential, because it enabled him to avoid effusions that in a *tête-à-tête* would have seemed only right. He spoke only in Italian, even when the women tended to reply in Sardinian, because the remote, *recherché* language made things more abstract. When the last ray of sunshine filtered through the firmly closed shutters, he would rise and take his leave. This was the only moment at which their eyes met, but Ludovico lowered his at once, fearful of that arcane communication which so brusquely thrust him into the real world. He went down the steep granite steps without looking back, and crossed the road hurriedly, eager to be alone with himself.

Donna Celestina had the traditional chastity of the Mannus in her veins, and would have felt that love implied a lack of respect. But she had grown up in solitude, which had brought her close to God while at the same time making her long for the outside world. She also had the morose intelligence typical of the Mannus, and this made her diffident. Furthermore, she was educated, because in that desolate house someone had once accumulated some books, and she had read them all, those she understood and those she did not understand. Therefore, after the first period of expectation, she found herself entangled in a net of doubts, and the first doubt concerned the very existence of the person who was to become her husband. What did this man, who was so refined, so handsome, and spoke as if he were quoting from an invisible book, have in common with other men? Those generalizing discourses that he started on as soon as he sat down in the drawing room, still lit by candlelight alone, might deceive Donna Sabina, but not her: she emerged from them exasperated. Had it not been for her upper-class pride she would have offered herself to him, just to see what he ultimately wanted. But she was sure that the result would be to give him a pretext for escape, and she did not want Ludovico to escape her. And so, little by little, she found herself trapped, resigned to going along with the wishes of a man who had no wishes whatsoever.

This was the beginning of an engagement destined to last twelve years. It would be more correct to say a marriage that ended in engagement, because on the day when Celestina asked Ludovico never to show his face again, in those two houses that stood facing each other the doors and the windows closed on their life, but both of them carried their own chastity away with them like an everlasting bereavement. For each of them it would have been impossible to marry, and in fact the rumor went around Nuoro that every Monday, Wednesday, and Saturday a shadow passed through Don Sebastiano's door, arrived in front of Don Gabriele's, lingered a little, and then, sadly, withdrew.

21

After many months I once more take up this tale, which perhaps I should never have begun. I am swiftly growing old, and feel that I am preparing a sad end for myself, because I have chosen not to accept the first condition for a good death, which is forgetfulness. Maybe it was not Don Sebastiano, Donna Vincenza, Gonaria, Pedduzza, Giggia, Baliodda, Dirripezza and all the others, who begged me to set them free from their lives: it is I who have called them up to rid me of mine, without calculating the risk to which I was exposing myself, in making myself eternal. And then today, outside the windows of this remote room where I have taken refuge, it is snowing: a light snow that settles on the streets, and the trees, as time settles upon us. In a little while everything will look the same. In the cemetery of Nuoro one will not be able to tell the old from the new, and "they" will have some fleeting peace beneath the cloak of whiteness. I was a little boy myself once upon a time, and I am assailed by the memory of watching the swirl of the snowflakes with my nose pressed against the windowpane. We were all there then, in the room enlivened by the fire, and we were happy since we did not know ourselves. To know ourselves we must live our lives right to the end, until the moment we sink into the grave. And even then we need someone to gather us up, to revive us, to speak about us both to ourselves and to others, as in a last judgment. This is what I have done myself these last few years, which I wish I had not done yet will continue to do, because by now it is not a question of the destiny of others, but of my own.

[*Salvatore Satta died on 19 April, 1975, without having completed his fresco of Nuoro as he would have wished.*]

Translator's Note

"Nuoro was nothing but a perch for the crows", writes Salvatore Satta of the scene of the events in his book, with its "7,051 inhabitants at the last census". He is writing about the last years of the 19th century and the first quarter of the present one, but then as now, though with a fifth of today's population, Nuoro was the urban centre of the wildest and most isolated part of Sardinia. Good modern roads now writhe their way between villages once "as remote one from another as are the stars", and the shepherds no longer spend night and day with their sheep, coming to town "once every two weeks to change their clothes and lay in a stock of bread". They sleep in the villages and get to their flocks by car. But have a breakdown on one of those roads on a January evening, at 3,000 feet, in a mist, with a milestone reading "Fonni 13" and the first flakes of snow on the sightless windscreen, and you still have every reason to feel lonely. There are limits to what can be done to alter the bleak, awe-inspiring grandeur of that landscape: right below Nuoro the "fearsome valley of Marreri, haunt of footpads", is so steep and deep that you don't notice that in the bottom of it, infinitely distant, there is a motorway.

At the time of which Satta is writing, the roads were rocky tracks negotiable with difficulty even on horseback or by the Sardinian carts designed specifically for them. There was, of course, the little train, like a bus on rails, that wound through the mountains to link Nuoro to "Macomer and the world", but the place remained a fastness. "The people of Nuoro", writes Satta, "are like the garrison of a sinister castle: close and taciturn...intelligent and treacherous". At an advanced age, one of the main characters, Zia Gonaria, though middle-class and a schoolteacher, "had not seen many roads in the course of her life", while Zio Priamo, who had been mayor of the town, left Nuoro and its immediate surroundings only once, on horseback. The 120 kilometers to Sassari and school (Nuoro had no secondary school) was "the equivalent of 12,000 today", while the diocese of Nuoro (which seems to have been the sole reason for the existence of the town) "was the least in Sardinia, and therefore in the world". The whole island, in short, was cut off and antediluvian, but even in Sardinian terms Nuoro was the back of beyond. It was to the world as the world is to the galaxy, a place and a people under siege by outer darkness and, for both body and soul, dreadful in its solitude.

If Satta had cast around for a microcosm of human life, of what is called the "human condition", he could scarcely have chosen a better one for his purpose. But he did not choose it; or rather (to apply a phrase of his own to a different context), it was "the result of a tribal feeling, a choice as free as whether or not to be baptized". He was born there in 1902, and his childhood and youth was Nuoro, nothing but Nuoro, with its streets, its people, its mighty, pagan landscapes, and its skies pellucid or wrathful. The things of Nuoro were what he carried with him into his later life, "and felt himself still bound to them, among people who had never seen those things, and were therefore unable to understand him". At least on one level we feel that he tells us all these things lest they should perish. For his later life he spent on the "Continent", where he had a most distinguished career in law, acknowledged as the great authority on Italian legal procedure.

The author is, in fact, a thinly disguised character in his narrative, but he several times enters it in the first person present tense, notably in Chapter 7 on a visit to the Nuoro cemetery. "I have come here between ferry boats", he says, "to see if I can put a little order in my life, join the two halves together, re-establish the dialogue without which these pages can go no further…". This dialogue takes place not only between his present and his past, but between himself and the dead of Nuoro. Priests and notaries, gamblers and prostitutes, bishops and beggars, peasants and shepherds and rogues of every description, they are all *his* dead, the characters in his book, and all of them ghosts. Some at length, others in a few brief words, he calls them up "as on the day of judgment", and they all act out the meaning of their lives. And each life is a ferocious question about the worth and purpose of it all. This is what gives Satta's book its "metaphysical dimension", and explains why, when published in 1979, four years after his death, it struck the Italian literary world with the impact of myth, or of truth; or rather, as a work in which the two are indivisible.

Moreover, just as this all-pervading "dimension" is not abstraction, but embodied in one life-story after another, so the peculiar, obsessive intensity with which the inquiry is pursued may be traced to concrete facts. Salvatore Satta, with all his long-remembered material to hand, began to write *The Day of Judgment* when he was nearly seventy, knowing that death was almost upon him. It is the work of a man driven to come to terms with his destiny while he still had time. He died before he finished it.

Historical Note

Though technically a kingdom since the 11th century A.D., Sardinia suffered the fate of so many islands, that of being constantly dominated by foreign powers: Carthage and Rome in ancient times, Pisa and Spain in more recent ones. In the early 18th century it came into the possession of the dukes of Savoy, who were forced to accept it in exchange for the far richer prize of Sicily. They thereupon became kings of Sardinia. Satta calls this kingdom "a joke", and indeed, with their capital at Turin, the Piedmontese paid little heed to their backward island, except to exploit it. Clumsy legislation during the 19th century led to the increasing enclosure of land, which in a largely pastoral community led inevitably to privation, discontent and lawlessness. When Victor Emmanuel of Savoy, King of Sardinia, was proclaimed king of united Italy in 1861, the island became part of the new kingdom. Naturally enough Italians ("Continentals") were for a long time thereafter regarded as foreigners, and the laws were considered as "imposed from outside" Sardinia.

About the author

SALVATORE SATTA (1902–1975) was born in Sardinia. During his lifetime he was known as one of Italy's foremost jurists and the man who rewrote the Italian Penal Code after the Second World War to rid it of its Fascist aspects. Among the papers found after his death was the manuscript of *The Day of Judgment*, with evidence showing that he had been working on it for more than thirty years.

About the translator

PATRICK CREAGH (1930–2012) was the award-winning translator of Antonio Tabucchi, Salvatore Satta, Italo Calvino, Flavio Conti, Gesualdo Bufalino and Claudio Magris.

More from Apollo

THE LOST EUROPEANS
Emanuel Litvinoff

Coming back was worse, much worse, than Martin Stone had anticipated.

Martin Stone returns to the city from which his family was driven in 1938. He has concealed his destination from his father, and hopes to win some form of restitution for the depressed old man living in exile in London. *The Lost Europeans* portrays a tense, ruined yet flourishing Berlin where nothing is quite what it seems.

BOSNIAN CHRONICLE
Ivo Andrić

For as long as anyone could remember, the little café known as 'Lutvo's' has stood at the far end of the Travnik bazaar, below the shady, clamorous source of the 'Rushing Brook'.

This is a sweeping saga of life in Bosnia under Napoleonic rule. Set in the remote town of Travnik, the newly appointed French consul soon finds himself intriguing against his Austrian rival, whilst dealing with a colourful cast of locals.

THE MAN WHO LOVED CHILDREN
Christina Stead

> All the June Saturday afternoon Sam Pollit's children were on the lookout for him as they skated round the dirt sidewalks and seamed old asphalt of R Street and Reservoir Road that bounded the deep-grassed acres of Tohoga House, their home.

Sam and Henny Pollit have too many children, too little money and too much loathing for each other. As Sam uses the children's adoration to feed his own voracious ego, Henny becomes a geyser of rage against her improvident husband.

MY SON, MY SON
Howard Spring

> What a place it was, that dark little house that was two rooms up and two down, with just the scullery thrown in! I don't remember to this day where we all slept, though there was a funeral now and then to thin us out.

This is the powerful story of two hard-driven men – one a celebrated English novelist, the other a successful Irish entrepreneur – and of their sons, in whom are invested their fathers' hopes and ambitions. Oliver Essex and Rory O'Riorden grow up as friends, but their fathers' lofty plans have unexpected consequences as the violence of the Irish Revolution sweeps them all into uncharted territory.

DELTA WEDDING
Eudora Welty

> *The nickname of the train was the Yellow Dog. Its real name was the*
> *Yazoo-Delta. It was a mixed train. The day was the 10th of September,*
> *1923 – afternoon. Laura McRaven, who was nine years old, was on her*
> *first journey alone.*

Laura McRaven travels down the Delta to attend her cousin
Dabney's wedding. At the Fairchild plantation her family envelop
her in a tidal wave of warmth, teases and comfort. As the big day
approaches, tensions inevitably rise to the surface.

NOW IN NOVEMBER
Josephine Johnson

> *Now in November I can see our years as a whole. This autumn is like*
> *both an end and a beginning to our lives, and those days which seemed*
> *confused with the blur of all things too near and too familiar are clear*
> *and strange now.*

Forced out of the city by the Depression, Arnold Haldmarne
moves his wife and three daughters to the country and tries to
scratch a living from the land. After years of unrelenting hard
work, the hiring of a young man from a neighbouring farm
upsets the fragile balance of their lives. And in the summer, the
rains fail to come.

THE AUTHENTIC DEATH OF HENDRY JONES
Charles Neider

> *Nowadays, I understand, the tourists come for miles to see Hendry Jones'*
> *grave out on the Punta del Diablo and to debate whether his bones are*
> *there or not...*

A stark and violent depiction of one of America's most alluring folk heroes, the mythical, doomed gunslinger. Set on the majestic coast of southern California, Doc Baker narrates his tale of the Kid's capture, trial, escape and eventual murder. Written in spare and subtle prose, this is one of the great literary treatments of America's obsession with the rule of the gun.